MORE ADVENTURES OF KAKABABU

MORE ADVENTURES OF KAKABABU

VOLUME 2

SUNIL GANGOPADHYAY

TRANSLATED BY RIMI

ILLUSTRATED BY KALYANI GANAPATHY

HarperCollins*Children's Books*

First published in India in 2022 by HarperCollins Children's Books
An imprint of HarperCollins *Publishers*

HarperCollins Publishers India, Cyber City, Building 10-A, Gurugram,
Haryana-122002, India
www.harpercollins.co.in

2 4 6 8 10 9 7 5 3 1

Text © Sunil Gangopadhyay 2022
Translation © Rimi 2022
Illustrations © HarperCollins *Publishers* 2022

P-ISBN: 978-93-5422-841-4
E-ISBN: 978-93-5422-897-1

Cover illustrations and design: Kalyani Ganapathy

Typeset in 12/16.2 Century at
Manipal Technologies Limited, Manipal

Printed and bound at
MicroPrints India, New Delhi

This product is made of FSC®-certified and other controlled material.

HarperCollins Publishers, Macken House, 39/40 Mayor Street
Upper, Dublin 1, D01 C9W8, Ireland

"*I once saw a man limping towards the summit of a very high hill. It didn't look like the limp was slowing him down. I was young then – about the same age Shontu is in this story – and the immense strength of the man's will impressed me profoundly. It was at that moment that I realised that no matter the circumstances, if a person has the confidence and the will to succeed, no trouble was insurmountable. 'Kakababu' is modelled on that man.*"

Sunil Gangopadhyay, 1979

CONTENTS

TERROR ON THE MOUNTAINTOP

ORIGINAL TITLE: *PAHARCHURAY ATONKO*

FIRST PUBLISHED: MARCH 1981

CHAPTER 1

Oh, the cold. The *unbelievable* cold. The wind in this place had teeth! It pounced on the body and sank needle-sharp canines straight into the blood. Despite layers upon layers of warm clothes, Shontu felt chilled to his very bones. And he wasn't new to cold places, either! He had travelled to Kashmir with his uncle when he was only in Class Eight. But the cold in Kashmir was no comparison for this biting, freezing, ice-fanged weather.

Hmm, "ice-fanged weather". Wasn't *that* an interesting idea? Shontu closed his eyes and imagined the freezing wind as an enormous, shapeless monster, tearing into him with hundreds of invisible, needle-sharp teeth. He was wrapped in multiple layers of wool from head to foot, but bits of his cheek and nose were bare. That was where the winter-beast attacked. With every step he took, Shontu could feel the wind swooping in for a sharp nip on his nose. In a few short minutes, his face had become so numb that he had to touch his nose to make sure it was there.

Shontu had just begun to imagine what these "ice-fangs" of the winter-beast might have looked like, when he suddenly pulled himself up short. Why on earth was he standing in the freezing wind thinking about monster-teeth that didn't even exist? His uncle's recent obsession with strange teeth was clearly rubbing off on him.

'No more thinking about teeth!' he admonished himself. 'No, not even a single thought! No matter how *biting* the cold is, wind is just wind, not an invisible monster!'

Then, with a firm shake of his head—as if to dislodge the idea for good—he strode ahead along the mountain path.

This place was called Gorak Shep. Shontu wondered how the name had come to be. What did it mean? He was curious, because personally, he found the place rather hard to describe. It was at the foothills of the Himalayas, but was neither a town nor a proper village. As far as Shontu could see, it barely had enough people to qualify as a hamlet. In fact, the three things that he had seen the most since reaching Gorak Shep were boulders, stones, and ice. Humans didn't even make it to the top-five list.

Take this road, for example. It was completely empty. The only sign that other people had passed this way was the remains of bonfires, and the empty tins. Some of the labels on the tins could still be read: milk powder, peas, cooked pork. Discarded tins were the sure signs of a camp, his uncle had explained. Mountaineers usually set up camp on these short stretches of valleys between peaks, and left behind a trail of refuse. In fact, Shontu was fairly certain that the newer-looking tins were from the UK. When they had reached Gorak Shep a few days ago, they had been informed that a team of British mountaineers had passed by just a week ago. These particular tins were bound to be theirs.

The first big peak after this valley was called Kala Patthar. Shontu had heard people say that it was a relatively small peak. But that "small peak" was still large enough to hide one of the world's towering glories. If one climbed to the top of the Kala Patthar, one could see it right in front of their own eyes: the pristine, the snow-capped, the majestic ... *Everest!*

Yes, *that* Everest! The highest peak in the entire world! That was how far his uncle had brought them this time!

For the last few days, Shontu had seen the Everest every single day. The thrill of waking up in the presence of such splendour was indescribable. Besides, when he went back home he would have a brilliant story to tell. No other boy from his school had ever had such an incredible adventure. In fact, never mind school — Shontu was sure that no other boy from his entire city had seen the Everest the way he was seeing it. This place was completely off the usual Himalayan tourist routes. Families didn't come here on holiday.

No, he was definitely the first boy from Calcutta to be here. And he couldn't *wait* to go back and brag about it!

For this excursion, Shontu had acquired a small camera of his own. He had taken endless pictures of the Everest with it, from different angles and at different times of the day. He was also itching to return to Calcutta to develop that reel. The idea of having actual photos of Mount Everest—ones he had taken himself!—made him balloon with pride. If he could, he would go back to Calcutta this very day and start printing the photos. But he was, as always, at the mercy of his exasperating uncle. Kakababu refused to even discuss returning. In fact, he refused to discuss anything at all about this expedition. Shontu had no idea how long he intended to stay in this land of ice, or how much farther towards the Everest he planned to go. As thrilled as he was to see the majestic peak whenever he liked, the snowstorms and bone-deep chill were beginning to wear on him. Sometimes, when he woke up freezing and miserable in the middle of the drearily cold nights, he would be overwhelmed by the thick silence and impenetrable darkness that surrounded him. The darkness had a weight, and that weight had slowly settled into his chest. Every time he opened his eyes and saw it, he was absolutely sure that something bad would happen to him – that he wouldn't survive to see his home again.

The daylight hours were usually more cheerful. The sun shone with exceptional brightness at these altitudes, and the snowy roads glittered like they were encrusted with gems. The glare was so strong that Shontu had to wear sunglasses throughout the day. His uncle did the same. The men with them, however, walked about bare-eyed. They were all of Nepali origin, as far as Shontu could tell, and the glare didn't seem to bother them at all.

Kakababu had picked seven men to accompany them on this trip. Two of them were Sherpas. Their job, as his uncle explained, was to lead the group through the treacherous mountain paths and keep them safe. The other five men were in charge of their luggage. When they had made camp here, the men had set up their tents right next to each other. They had offered to put up a tent for Shontu and Kakababu as well, but Kakababu had refused. Instead, he had his and Shontu's things set up inside an abandoned old tower.

The tower was a stone building about three storeys high, topped with a dome. The ground floor was just about broad enough for two people to sleep comfortably in their sleeping bags, but it tapered as it went up. The only way in and out was through a pair of heavy iron doors that could be latched from both sides. A spiral staircase along the inner wall led to the top of the tower, opening to a small sitting place in front of a tiny window. This window was the bane of Shontu's nights. It let in a steady stream of bitterly cold mountain air, turning the tower into an ice-box. But it was also their only source of fresh air, so they couldn't close it unless they wanted to suffocate to death.

No one knew who had built the tower, or why they had chosen to build it in such a remote area. The Sherpas said that it was at least a thousand years old. When asked why it was built, they shrugged philosophically. Who could remember such minute details, they asked Kakababu, after a thousand years had passed? Shontu, of course, had been thrilled to know that their camp was going to be in such an ancient building. But after the Sherpas had left, his uncle had explained that given the tower's style and building materials, it could at most be a hundred years old. Kakababu had been an archaeologist at the Archaeological Survey of India, so he knew about these things. He likely even had theories of his own about who the original builders had been, and what they had been doing in this icy desert. But like all scholars, Kakababu refused to "speculate without proof", as he called it. Shontu knew it would be fruitless to ask him what his ideas were. His uncle would only discuss his ideas after he had found evidence to support them, not before.

Shontu, however, had no such compunction. After hearing that the tower was only about a hundred years old, he had decided that it had been built by a mountain-obsessed sahib. The sahib had probably wanted a personal observatory near the Everest. Everyone knew that certain Western folk were prone to taking their hobbies to the extreme. They were also far more obsessed with "conquering nature". So if someone had built a tower in this god-forsaken place in the last hundred years, then it *had* to be a sahib obsessed with the Everest. He probably liked to sit at his little window in the evenings, and watch the last sunlight on the peak. There, simple. He had solved the mystery.

The only problem with his solution was that the tower's window didn't, in fact, have a view of the Everest. Kala Patthar, "small" though it was, was large enough to stand in the way of that view. But Shontu didn't let this fact deter his theory. Kakababu had often spoken to him about the "youth" of the Himalayas, explaining how it made the landscape shift. An earthquake might force plain land to rise in peaks, or make peaks come crashing down. Sometimes the moving land swallowed rivers, his uncle had said, and at other times made new ones spout abruptly from groundwater. So it was entirely possible, wasn't it, that the Kala Patthar had been lower than it was now—or non-existent, even—when the tower had been built? Or perhaps *this* area had been higher, so that one could see Everest over Kala Patthar's shoulder? Yes, that sounded perfectly reasonable.

Shontu's conviction in the theory of shifting landscapes had been further strengthened by a terrifying morning earlier in this expedition. One of the stops along their way to this tower was a place called Kund. It was a fairly well-established village, unlike Gorak Shep. It had shops and schools, even a hospital. They had stopped there for two days to rest and replenish rations. On the second day, Shontu had been startled by a sudden explosion of sound from above. It had sounded like an army of jets roaring across the sky. But when he had looked up, the sky had been bright, sunny, and completely empty. Then he had noticed the local people. Several of them were running about in panic, shouting at each other in their own language.

Kakababu had taken a wooden stool to the edge of the valley earlier that morning, intent on taking in the scenery. People's panic usually left him unperturbed, but once the noise begun that morning he, too, had started calling for Shontu, his voice urgent. Shontu had sprinted over, thinking his uncle was calling for help to get to safety. But when he reached the edge of the valley, Kakababu had simply pointed at a peak five or six miles away. 'Look at that, Shontu. We're very lucky to have been here today! That's not a sight you see every day!'

Shontu had turned obediently to look, but the peak that had been clearly visible just moments ago had all but disappeared behind a curtain of billowing white smoke. After a few seconds of watching the smoke, Shontu had realized that the awful noise was, in fact, coming from that very peak.

'Kakababu, what's happening there?' he had asked, worriedly.

'Don't you see?' his uncle had exclaimed, barely containing his excitement. 'Avalanche! The snow from the mountaintop is rolling downhill!'

'That white smoke is *snow*? Can it reach us?'

'Technically, yes. There's a river further downhill – it is in the avalanche's path. If the river can hold all the ice-melt, then we'll be all right. But if it fills the river and makes it overflow, then ...'

At this, Shontu had become rather alarmed. 'Then? Kakababu, what shall we do then?'

His uncle had turned away from the mountain to look straight into his eyes. 'Then we would die, I imagine,' he had said, in a perfectly calm voice. 'Such things are not unusual in this region. Many small settlements have been flooded in the past because of avalanches a few miles away. It's one of the hazards of living in young mountains. You are at nature's mercy. Thousands of people live with that risk every day.'

And then he had turned back to watch the white clouds – the white clouds of possibly impending death.

His uncle's quiet answer still haunts Shontu.

Before that day, he had had no idea that snow could actually be dangerous. He certainly could not have imagined being so helpless in his own home, a prisoner to the whims of nature! Imagine watching a river's worth of snow advance upon you, knowing that no matter how fast you ran, you could never escape it. It was terrifying. As much as he admired his uncle's bravery, he found Kakababu's lack of fear at the prospect of such a death absurd. Shontu was no coward himself, but he never wanted to feel the helplessness that he had felt that morning.

That morning had disturbed him so deeply that on certain nights, while ensconced within his warm bedding in the freezing tower, Shontu woke up to what he was sure was the echoing sound of a distant avalanche. He had no way of knowing if he was imagining the sound, or if there was an avalanche in the distance. Scared and lonely in the cold, thick darkness, he wondered if a nearby avalanche could roll down into the valley they were in. If it did, could the old stone tower withstand the force of thousands of tonnes of snow? Probably not. And if it came at night, when they were all asleep, the snow would likely roll on top of them like a giant wave, drowning them alive before they even knew it was happening. No one would know where to find them, because the tower itself would probably be buried under pristine, innocent-looking snow.

The horror of it made him break into a sweat, even in the biting cold.

The domed tower was usually kept under lock and key by the Nepal government, but Kakababu had managed to wrangle special permission to have it unlocked and set up as a temporary residence. They had moved in six days ago, and since then time had passed very, very slowly. While there was daylight,

Shontu could still manage to roam a bit, and explore the area a little. However, as soon as the sun went down, there was nothing to do but lock himself in under the dome. It was far too cold to even sit around outside and chat. No amount of sweaters, mufflers, or jackets could keep the chill out. So by seven-thirty in the evening, Shontu was inevitably inside his sleeping bag, which looked for all the world like an overstuffed sausage. The trouble was that while one could go to bed by seven-thirty, one couldn't magically fall asleep. At home, Shontu always dealt with sleeplessness by reading. Here, even reading was a mammoth task. It wasn't the impenetrable darkness that stood in his way. Kakababu had brought a new sort of lamp with him this time — an imported, battery-operated variety that shone brightly with a neon yellow light. Once it was switched on, one could easily prop a book up against something and read it from inside one's sleeping bag. However, one had to take at least one hand out at regular intervals to turn the pages. That little gap in the zip was all the wind needed. Every time he turned a page, it rushed in and chilled his wool-swaddled body down to its very bones. In the end, Shontu had simply given up on reading.

Kakababu, however, seemed oddly untouched by the cold. He spent almost every night up by the small window at the top of the dome, wearing nothing warmer than a thick leather jacket. Sometimes he woke up in the middle of the night, and instead of simply turning over and trying to go back to sleep, he unzipped himself from the sleeping bag and went upstairs to have a look around. Shontu found his uncle's behaviour both incomprehensible and impressive. How on earth could Kakababu leave his bed so casually in this cold? Shontu was years younger, and able-bodied to boot, yet just the idea of leaving his warm sleeping bag in the middle of the night made him shiver!

So, while his uncle sat at the window above, Shontu packed himself tighter inside his sleeping bag and stared into the neon-lit darkness. His hometown would be bursting with life at this hour. The roads would be full of buses and trams and brightly lit shops. The streets would be bustling with people. There would be ... oh, there would be such a *variety* of sights and sounds. Seven-thirty barely felt like the evening back home, much less the night. And here was this place, deathly silent at seven. It was almost as if he had stepped into an alternate universe. He couldn't believe that a place like this could exist in the same world as bustling cities and towns!

Perhaps it was a good thing that Kakababu went to bed late. That way Shontu could have a few more hours of light, thanks to the lamp that stayed on till Kakababu came down. He needed the light to navigate the narrow staircase safely, and do his pre-bedtime pottering about. He turned it off just before going to bed. Honestly, Shontu would have preferred it if the lamp stayed lit all night. The uncanny silence of the valley, combined with the complete blackness of the night, made the hair on the back of his neck tingle. It wasn't fear, exactly. At least, it was not a fear of something concrete. He knew what fear of specific things felt like. When he had gone into Jarawa territory with his uncle, he had looked death in the face multiple times. This fear was not like that, because he knew that he was perfectly safe inside the locked tower. Technically, there was that fear of being buried under an icy landslide, but despite his worries, Shontu knew that the chances of it actually happening were very, very small. No, *this* fear was more a sense of eerie disquiet; a sense that he was stuck in an entirely different world—a world that he knew very little about—and could not find his way back home. The fact that he had no one to talk to probably made matters worse. Kakababu wasn't one for heart-to-hearts.

Speaking of Kakababu's fondness for silence, Shontu still had no idea why they were in this remote place. What mission was being fulfilled by living inside this dome day after day? The Sherpas and luggage-bearers were becoming restless, too. They were an active, hard-working people, and this schedule of cooking, chatting, eating and sleeping wasn't sitting well with them. After the fifth or sixth day of lounging around in the same spot, their leader Mingma had approached Shontu with their concerns. Mingma was in his mid-thirties, and an old hand at mountaineering. He was in such good shape that his body looked like it had been carved out of stone. Right before coming on this trip, he had been part of an expedition that had taken him very close to the peak of the Everest. Reaching that summit was his most cherished goal. Shontu knew this because Mingma had mentioned it more than once. Indeed, Mingma had joined this expedition because he had believed that Kakababu's mission was to climb the Everest. 'What's with Uncle?' he had asked Shontu after the first few days of camping. 'Why has he stopped here? Isn't he going to move towards the Everest?'

Shontu hadn't been able to answer him.

However, though the nights were scary and the days a haze of hopeless lassitude, the last half-week had been relatively pleasant for Shontu. Kakababu had finally allowed him to explore the area without his supervision ... provided he always had one of the Sherpas with him. So Shontu had developed the habit of trekking up to the Kala Patthar, and basking in the glory of an unobstructed view of the Everest. Something about that majestic peak sent shivers down his spine. Could a human being really have scaled that height? Shontu couldn't fully believe it. Despite the closeness, it seemed unconquerably remote. On the other hand, humans had recently landed on the moon! That had been unthinkable just a decade ago. Times were changing — even improbable things were doable these days. It wasn't that the Everest was less awe-inspiring than it looked, but that people had become more capable. Then again, Kakababu wasn't just another average person who was determined to use modern technology to do extraordinary things. He needed crutches to walk. How could someone like that climb the Everest, no matter how resolute?

No, it was an impossible task, even for his uncle.

But why else would he be here?

The night crawled at a painfully slow pace while Shontu tried to puzzle his way through the mystery. Kakababu was still upstairs at the window, looking at the darkness outside. With nothing else to do, Shontu turned to stare at the makeshift table upon which the lamp was kept. It was really just an empty wooden crate, one that had been used to pack their rations. Kakababu had it placed between their two sleeping bags to act as a shared bedside table. Besides the lamp, it held three things: a travelling clock, a battery-powered torch, and a small glass box that resembled a mini jewellery-case.

This box was at the heart of the mystery that surrounded their trip to this lonely, icy desert. It carried a tooth. A single human tooth. At least, Shontu assumed it was human. He avoided looking at the box as much as he could, for seeing a tooth outside a human mouth sent a wave of tingling discomfort down his spine. Kakababu, on the other hand, treated the tooth as if it were a piece of rare treasure. Whilst travelling, he had always kept the box hidden on his person. But now that they had privacy inside the tower, he had given the box pride of place on the table. Shontu had caught him staring intently at the tooth several times, lost to the world around him. But of course, he wouldn't say a word about it.

Shontu hadn't known about the tooth till just a few days ago. Kakababu had brought it back from his most recent visit to Europe and promptly secreted it away. This was typical Kakababu behaviour. Other people brought back fancy presents from their trips abroad, so naturally his contrary uncle brought back a dead man's tooth. The reason he had been abroad so often recently was their last adventure in the Jarawa islands. The Indian media had talked about their excursion widely, and the event had made international headlines. Kakababu had since been invited by several institutes, both within the country and abroad, to speak about their experience. In just the last six months, he had been out of the country twice. First to speak at an anthropological conference in Geneva, then immediately afterwards to England.

Right after the tour of England, however, the visits and lectures had abruptly stopped. Kakababu had returned to Calcutta and taken refuge in his ground-floor room in the family-home. For the next several weeks, he had devoted all his time to reading and research, barely coming out for meals.

Shontu hadn't known of the tooth then, but knowing his uncle as well as he did, he had suspected that a new mystery was on the horizon. And he had been right. A few months into his taciturn phase, Kakababu had suddenly sent for him.

'Fancy a trip to the Everest, Shontu?' he had asked, without preamble. 'I'm planning on going soon, so if you want to come along ...'

Come along? Shontu's heart had practically jumped to his mouth at the word "Everest"! Did his uncle mean the *real* Everest? That ... that would be amazing!

But then several practical problems had flooded his mind. Kakababu had spoken so casually, as if going to the Everest was at par with taking a walk along the road. But it couldn't be that easy, could it? People had died while trying to climb that peak. Had he misunderstood his uncle?

'Er, Kakababu,' he had ventured. 'Are we really going to *the* Everest? The famous Everest?'

'Of course we are,' his uncle had responded, somewhat irritably. 'Why do you ask? Do you think there's another Everest worth going to? Or do you think I'm pulling your leg?'

Shontu had hastily abandoned his questions. His uncle was famously stern-faced and solemn. He seldom joked, and never about serious matters. But what Shontu had wanted to ask, but couldn't find polite words for, was this: how could a person who needed crutches to walk expect to climb the highest peak in the world?

In the end, he had concluded that Kakababu would be travelling with a group of seasoned mountaineers, and that there would be a special kit to help him along. About whether he would go – well, of course he would! If Kakababu was going to go on an adventure, then Shontu would *not* be left behind.

Besides, he had had his own reason for wanting to go to the Everest. Technically, the peak was no longer unconquered. Shontu knew this from books and newspapers. After New Zealand's Edmund Hillary and the subcontinent's own Tenzing Norgay, people from several different countries had reached the summit of that peak. There were Indians amongst them, too. But were there any Bengalis amongst them, especially ones his age? Shontu was willing to bet there weren't. If he succeeded in reaching the peak, he would become the world's first fifteen-year-old to have conquered the Everest, which would be marvellous! And if by a stroke of awful luck another fifteen-year-old had managed to do it before him ... well, Shontu was absolutely sure that *that* fifteen-year-old would not have been Indian. Either way, he would be famous! *His* name would be known all over the world then, just like Kakababu's was now.

Back then, it would never have occurred to Shontu that his uncle might not make it to the top of the peak. He had complete faith in his uncle's determination and immense power of will. To be fair, such faith was justly earned. If Kakababu decided he wanted to do something, then he usually ended up doing exactly that, no matter how hard it was or what barriers stood in his way. Besides, if he succeeded in his Everest adventure, then he would set a world record of his own – the first man on crutches to conquer the world's highest peak! The thought of it had filled Shontu with such excitement that he had wanted to leave for the mountains right away. In an attempt to show his uncle that he, too, knew something about the history of their new adventure, he had asked, 'It was actually a Bengali man who had discovered the Everest, no Kakababu? The British deliberately kept his name out of things because he was Indian ... no?'

His uncle had given him a small, quiet smile. 'I wouldn't say he "discovered" it. The existence of the Everest was not a secret. It had always been known to the people who lived in the area. But yes, a Bengali gentleman had a small part to play in recognizing it as the highest peak in the world.'

'That's what I said! His name was Radhanath Shikdar, wasn't it? The peak should have been called Radhanath after him, not Everest. It's not fair!'

'That's not how things work, Shontu,' Kakababu had explained gently. 'Radhanath Shikdar was merely an employee of the Great Trigonometry Survey office, whereas George Everest had been the Surveyor General of India. Radhanath's work had to go through Everest first, before it could be presented to the rest of the world. Which is why the peak was named in Everest's honour, not Radhanath's.'

'But Kakababu, is it true that Radhanath Shikdar never climbed the Everest? How could he have known the height of the peak is if he hadn't climbed all the way up?'

'There are ways to measure the height of a peak without climbing it,' Kakababu had explained. 'Earlier, people could measure small hillocks by the extent of their shadows. Now there are several sophisticated tools and mathematical formulas. You use the tools to measure the land and get some numbers, then you put those numbers into the formulas to get your answer. But just so you know, Radhanath wasn't a complete novice about hills. He had explored the Himalayas on foot when he lived in Dehradun. But yes, the "discovery", as you call it, was made in Calcutta several years later. They say it happened while Radhanath Shikdar was sitting in his office, working out the height of a series of peaks. At that time, most peaks of the Himalayas were unknown to us – people who studied them simply assigned a number to them. The Everest had been labelled Peak Number Fifteen. Now, while doing his sums, it suddenly struck Radhanath that the height of Peak Fifteen—which was more than 29,000 feet above sea level—was the highest that he had ever calculated. Certainly higher than any other peak that he knew of. Excited, he took his papers to his boss. Well, Everest sahib had retired by then, so he wasn't technically Radhanath's boss. But, as I said, he had far higher prestige and experience, and ... well, and people named the peak after him. It's how these things work.'

This had been a long speech from his usually reserved uncle. To Shontu's delight, Kakababu had gone on to tell him many more stories about the Everest that afternoon. But the very next day, he had retreated into his usual shell and resumed his reticence. After a few days of near-complete silence, Shontu had begun to wonder if Kakababu had forgotten about their conversation. Had his uncle decided he was too young? Had the plans fallen through? He had lived in a state of agitation for several days, unable to ask his stern uncle anything directly. Then, with no prior warning, Kakababu had suddenly declared that he was leaving for Darjeeling. Wild hope had flared in Shontu's heart. Was this it? This must be it! Darjeeling was in the Himalayas – obviously, that was where they were meant to start their trek!

But his uncle had neither taken him along to Darjeeling, nor spoken to him about what happened there when he returned just a few days later. Instead, he had left for Germany immediately afterwards, delivering talks at the German government's invitation. It had been a month and a half before he had returned.

And then, that utterly unbelievable thing had happened. The very next day after his return, Tenzing Norgay had come to their house!

Kakababu had clearly meant to keep the visit a secret, but word of it had somehow leaked, and their house had been swamped with people. People had opened their gate and come into the garden, peeking through every window to get a glimpse of the famous mountaineer. The whole family had had to run around locking doors and windows, hiding indoors till the crowd had been chased out of the gate. But they had hung about right outside, and when Tenzing had left their house, they had nearly mobbed him trying to get an autograph.

Kakababu, as usual, had paid the ruckus no heed. While the shouting and cheering went on outside, he and Tenzing had sequestered themselves in Kakababu's ground-floor room, talking. Shontu had fiddled about just outside the room, hoping to hear scraps of their conversation. But both his uncle and the famous mountaineer had kept their voices so low that he had ended up knowing no more about the meeting than the crowd outside. Only when Tenzing was taking his leave did he overhear their final exchange. Shaking Kakababu's hand firmly, Tenzing had said, 'Good luck, Mr Roychoudhuri! I wish you every success. I know you'll solve the mystery. And when you do, people will realize that my warnings were well-founded. Had I not been as old as I am now, I would most certainly have gone with you.'

Though he hadn't spoken to Tenzing himself, that visit had given Shontu a lot of clout at school. Earlier, when he had first told his friends that he would be spending the autumn holidays climbing the Everest, every single one of them had laughed at him. The idea that one of their own could climb *the Everest* had been so unbelievable, so completely absurd, that they had called him a liar to his face. This was the problem with his friends. No matter how many adventures he went on with his uncle, his friends still treated him like a fibber, dismissing his experiences like they were tall tales. But this time, he had been armed with proof. Tenzing Norgay, world-renowned mountaineer and the first to conquer the Everest, had actually come to his house, and the whole neighbourhood had witnessed it!

'Tenzing Norgay had come down to discuss our Everest trip,' he had told his friends casually the very next day, trying to sound like this sort of thing happened to him all the time. 'He spoke to Kakababu for hours, planning our trip. He even wanted to come with us, but I suppose he's not as well as he used to be. He was very upset about being left out.'

And for once, his friends' disbelief had had no leg to stand on. It had been very satisfying.

Then, on the very first day of the autumn holidays, Kakababu had informed Shontu of their date of departure. 'We leave next Monday, Shontu. Pack your things right away.'

Shontu had imagined that they would leave Calcutta with an enormous amount of luggage. After all, they were setting out to climb the world's highest peak! But when he saw that Kakababu had packed only a small suitcase for himself, he followed suit. Between the two of them, they had just two pieces of luggage, plus their own shoulder-bags. That was how they had flown from Calcutta to Kathmandu, the capital of Nepal. For the next six days, Shontu had twiddled his thumbs at the hotel while his uncle scoured the city from morning till early evening. Shontu told himself that the wait was worth it, because his uncle was obviously out buying all the things they needed to survive the Everest. But Kakababu had never returned to the hotel with so much as a single box. At the end of the sixth day, he had simply said, 'Repack the bags, Shontu. We are leaving tomorrow.' And that had been that.

The next day, the taxi had taken them back to the airport. Used to his uncle's whimsical ways, Shontu had assumed that their trip had been deferred, and that they were going back to Calcutta. But he had been wrong. Instead of the big planes they had flown in on, Kakababu had led him to a much smaller plane in the far corner of the airport. There had barely been ten or twelve other people on that flight. Minutes after the plane had taken off, Shontu had been amazed to see high, snowy peaks on every side of their aeroplane. For the rest of the flight, he had been dazzled by their glittering peaks, twinkling like diamonds in the sun's blaze.

After several minutes of flying, their tiny plane had landed on an equally small airstrip in a place called Syangboche. When he had first looked down at the rough airstrip from the sky, Shontu hadn't believed that a place as tiny as that could merit an airstrip of its own. But apparently it was quite a convenient stop for those going to the Base Camp. Upon getting down from the plane, Kakababu had recruited two men to carry their luggage, and then the two of them had set off, finally on their way to the Everest.

But as they progressed on the Everest trail, Shontu had become increasingly sceptical about his uncle's chances. To begin with, they had no tents, no dry food, no mules, and most importantly, no Sherpa to guide them. Shontu had read about these provisions in his tales of adventure and expedition, and as far as he understood, it was impossible—not to mention extremely dangerous—to even try climbing a mountain without these things, and without an experienced Sherpa. Kakababu was above all a practical and reasonable person, so why had he not arranged for any of them? Suspicion began edging into his unwavering faith in his uncle. Was Kakababu even truly going towards the famous peak? Or was the Everest a cover for yet another of his secret missions? How could anyone hope to climb the Everest with just two luggage-handlers?

They had had a lot of company at the beginning of the trek. Many of their fellow-travellers were foreigners, sahibs from the west. Shontu had read that these treks were very popular with sahibs. Some of them climbed mountains as a hobby, while others treated it like a holiday. There were so many sahibs around the Everest, in fact, that the Japanese had built an enormous modern hotel at Syangboche to cater to them. What he *hadn't* read about was the presence of women mountaineers. Between leaving Syangboche and reaching Gorak Shep, he had seen several trekkers who were women. And each woman had been carrying her own large pack on her back, just like the men. Shontu had been very impressed.

What he hadn't liked were the looks. Though usually known for being discreet in public, several of these foreign men and women had stared openly at Kakababu. The surprise and disbelief on their faces were far too easy to read. They had probably never seen a disabled man trek so casually along at such an elevation. Kakababu, however, had taken no notice of them. He had walked steadily on, his crutches making a rhythmic tak-tak sound as they hit the uneven ground. Young though he was, Shontu had had to stop every now and then to catch his breath. But Kakababu had been completely at ease. He had set a pace for himself, and had kept to it.

Shontu had been quietly admiring his uncle's stamina from a few paces behind when he had suddenly realized the awful truth. It had hit him so abruptly and so hard that he had almost stopped breathing for a few seconds. This road—this narrow, hilly road—was exactly the sort of place where Kakababu had had his terrible accident, the one that had crushed his leg beyond repair. Had Shontu gone through such a life-changing ordeal, he would *never* have returned to the mountains. Never. Nothing could have made him put a foot back on even a low hill, never mind plan a trek to the Everest. Yet here was Kakababu, braving the treacherous heights that had already betrayed him once. There was no trace of fear in his bearing, only a quiet determination. Admiration had, once again, filled Shontu's heart, and pushed his suspicions aside.

After passing the small town of Phuntsholing, uncle and nephew had sat down for breakfast on a large roadside rock. It was a simple meal of cold toast, hard-boiled eggs, and fruit, packed when they had last stopped to rest. Shontu had just finished his bread and eggs and was beginning to peel his orange, when he saw a group of local men come running down the hill.

'Run! Run!' the men had screamed, when they had come a little closer. 'Wild bears are roaming the roads above! Run!'

Alarmed, Shontu had nearly dropped his orange. Run? Run where? There was just the one road, with dense woodland on one side and a steep drop on the other! Phuntsholing was too far behind them – they couldn't run all the way back. In fact, he had suddenly realized with cold horror, his uncle could not run at all. For all his fitness and strength, Kakababu could only hobble. If these bears decided to come down the path, then he and Kakababu would be sitting ducks for them!

His uncle, meanwhile, had calmly finished his own orange and lit a pipe. 'Why are you littering the road with your fruit peels?' he had chided Shontu, as if he hadn't just heard a warning about wild bears. 'Pick them up and put them inside a paper bag. One must never desecrate the mountains with one's rubbish.'

Shontu had followed the instructions mechanically, not daring to disobey. But his eyes had kept straying uphill. The place they had chosen for their breakfast suddenly felt eerily quiet. At that point, the mountain road had been bracketed in between a sharp gorge on one side, and dense forest on the other. Several feet below, at the bottom of the gorge, a silvery river twinkled in the sunshine. What if a bear suddenly jumped out of the forest? Would he and his uncle tumble down the slope and fall into that fast-moving stream? He had wanted very badly to ask his uncle to run away, but the placidity on his uncle's face had kept him from admitting his own fears.

A few minutes later, while Kakababu was still smoking his pipe, two foreign tourists had come running down the path. 'Why are you still here?' they had shouted at Kakababu as they ran past. 'A wild bear has been sighted above! Run!'

Kakababu hadn't responded. To Shontu's chagrin, he had continued to leisurely puff his pipe, slowly blowing the smoke out in rings.

After a few minutes, a babble of alarmed voices had exploded further ahead along the path. 'That must be the bear!' Shontu had thought, alarmed. 'It is the bear, and it's chasing people down!'

Moments later, a group of local people had come running down the path, practically falling over their feet as they carried an injured man on their shoulders. The man had been bleeding so freely that their path had been marked by his blood. Kakababu hadn't even needed to ask what happened. The group had volunteered the story as they had jogged past. Apparently, a wild bear had gone on rampage in the forests above, and had slashed open the injured man's stomach. When the group passed them by, Shontu had caught a glimpse of the man's entrails peeking out through his wound. To his horror, he had realised that the man was still conscious. He had whimpered and moaned in pain while bobbling up and down on his friends' shoulders.

Shontu had not seen his blood on the path till the group had already disappeared down the mountain. When he did, a shudder had run down his spine. Even now, in Gorak Shep, he could taste the horror of the moment in his mouth. He had never before seen human blood flow freely enough to stain the ground red!

Kakababu, meanwhile, had taken the gruesome interlude in his stride. 'Mountain bears are vicious creatures,' he had said, calmly. 'More vicious than lions and tigers, some say, for they kill without reason.' Then, taking his revolver out of his coat's pocket, he had looked at Shontu. 'Are you scared?'

Shontu still wondered, to this day, what his uncle had expected him to say. They had just seen a man whose belly had been sliced to ribbons! The creature that had done it could have been barrelling down the path that very moment! Had his uncle really expected him to be relieved at the sight of a revolver? A revolver couldn't do anything to stop a mountain bear! Shontu had seen hunting documentaries on TV. Hunters had to use rifles as large as their own arms to bring such beasts down.

Of course, he had not been able to say any of this to Kakababu. He had simply swallowed a few times, and given his uncle the answer he had wanted to hear. 'No Kakababu, I'm not scared.'

Kakababu had been satisfied. 'Here, hide behind this boulder,' he had instructed. 'We'll have to go up this path, and soon. We can't waste a lot of time dealing with this nonsense.'

'Kakababu, can't we go back down?' Shontu had suggested, timidly. 'We could spend tonight at the village downhill, and come back again tomorrow. Look, even the sahibs are going back down.'

'What do you mean, "even the sahibs"?' his uncle had asked sharply. 'Do you think foreign folk are braver than us?'

'No no! That's not what I meant at all!' Shontu had stuttered hastily, deeply embarrassed. 'It's just that … uh …'

For several uncomfortable seconds, Kakababu had stared sternly at his nephew. Then, in a soft but steely voice, he had said, 'I have never turned back from a mission before. When I set out to do something, I get it done. When you travel with me, you will have to remember that the only way ahead for me is forward.'

Then, before Shontu could respond, he had turned swiftly back towards the path and fired his revolver in the air with a resounding crack.

CHAPTER 3

The sound of the shot had echoed around the valley, bouncing off mountains further and further away. It was as if the peaks were talking amongst themselves, each mimicking the sound of his uncle's shot and then lobbing it back towards them. The very land beneath their feet had seemed to shudder at the intensity of the amplified noise. It had been both scary and disorienting.

When the noise had died away, Kakababu had gently blown on the barrel of the revolver. 'Do you want to learn how to use it?' he had asked Shontu.

Shontu had nodded eagerly.

His uncle had extended the butt of the firearm towards him. 'Hold it here, tightly,' he had instructed. 'You're old enough to learn this now. We're on the trail of a particularly dangerous mystery this time ... there might be dangers hidden at every step. If any of them claim me, then you should know how to defend yourself.'

At first, Shontu had cradled the hand holding the revolver to his chest. He had seen films in which the people had shot their weapons like that. But his uncle had corrected him right away.

'Not like that, not like that! If you hold your gun like that then the only person you'll be injuring is yourself. Hold your arm straight out. Now hold it firmly in place – make sure it doesn't bounce back easily. No, don't bend the elbow! You'll feel a sharp rebound the moment you fire. Your arm should be able to absorb that force. Do you understand?'

Shontu had nodded mutely. Holding a real firearm was thrilling, but it was a scary sort of a thrill. What if he failed? What if he hurt himself? Kakababu didn't know this, but he had secretly taken his uncle's weapon out before, and had examined it. In fact, once in Andaman he had even fired it, though the rebound had knocked him straight off his feet and onto the forest floor. He had been so shocked by the noise that he had no memory of what had actually happened. But now, *now* he could shoot with his uncle's permission! His whole body quivered with anticipation.

'Imagine the bear is running down that path towards you,' his uncle had said from behind him. 'Will you be able to shoot it?'

Shontu had nodded eagerly.

'It's not that easy,' his uncle had said. 'Do you see the top of that pine tree? If that is your target, can you shoot it?'

Shontu had nodded again.

'You think so?' his uncle had challenged. 'Show me.'

Shontu had thought back, once again, to the heroes in films. Then, following their lead, he had closed one eye and taken careful aim through the other. Fixing his glance at the top of the pine tree, he had pulled the trigger. The noise from the other end of the barrel was so explosive that his ears had begun ringing almost instantly. Terrified, he had shut his eyes and whipped his face away from his shooting arm. When he opened them again after several seconds, his uncle had been laughing at him.

'The tree has had a narrow escape,' he had said, in mock-seriousness. 'Your bullet didn't dislodge a single leaf.'

Shocked, Shontu had looked at the pine in disbelief. He had taken such careful aim! The barrel of the revolver was still facing the tree! How could he not have hit *anything*? Had the bullet swerved away? Why?

'Shooting's not that easy,' Kakababu had said with an air of finality, taking the firearm back. 'You will have to practise long and hard before you hit anything.'

Their two luggage-bearers had gone down the steep side of the mountain to the river below. Moments after Kakababu put his revolver away, they had appeared back on the road, clearly alarmed at the sound of two successive gunshots.

'What is it, sa'ab?' they had asked Kakababu in Hindi. 'What's wrong?'

'Nothing much. A wild bear has been sighted above,' Kakababu had responded calmly.

The luggage-bearers had looked even more alarmed. Everyone knew wild bears were vicious creatures — even the Everest-braving mountain folk were wary of them. Just as they had been about to say something, three Japanese tourists had come down the path. They had not been running like the others, but had still been in a hurry to go downhill.

'Have you heard anything further about the bear?' Kakababu had asked them in English.

Unfortunately, the tourists were not particularly fluent in English. It had taken a couple of attempts and a few illustrative gestures for them to understand what Kakababu was asking. Then they had explained, in a similar mix of words and gestures, that the bear had been banished back to the forest. A group of locals had banded together, apparently, and given it chase. 'We unlucky,' one of the tourists had added cheerfully. 'We miss seeing bear.'

'Now that's bravery,' Kakababu had said appreciatively, after the group had taken their leave. 'Form a group and give chase. Excellent initiative on the part of those men, I must say. It's broad daylight outside, so many people are going up and down the path ... what was one bear going to do?'

'But the bear sliced a man to ribbons!' Shontu had exclaimed. 'We saw him, Kakababu!'

'He was probably a stupid man. Went too close. Anyway, let's carry on, then. Even if the bear had been coming downhill through the forest, the sound of gunshots has probably scared it away.'

Then he had turned to the luggage-bearers and said in Hindi, 'The bear has run away. The road is safe. Lift the bags, we're going forward.'

The luggage-bearers, however, made no move towards the luggage. Instead, they looked at each other, and averted their eyes from Kakababu's face.

Before Kakababu could say anything, a rapid clopping had floated up the path from below. Turning around, Shontu had seen two policemen on horseback advancing swiftly towards them. In a matter of seconds, they had reached their little four-men gathering.

'Did any of you hear gunshots a little while ago?' one of them had asked.

'Yes,' Kakababu had replied honestly. 'That was us. I was giving my nephew a bit of a shooting practice.'

At this, the two policemen had jumped down from their saddles, outraged. 'You were *practising shooting*? Are you aware that this is a protected area? We do not allow hunting here!'

'Well, it's a good thing we weren't hunting, then,' Kakababu had responded. 'Out of curiosity, what if a bear had attacked us? Is it against the law to defend oneself against an aggressive animal?'

The policemen hadn't answered. Instead, one of them had advanced upon Shontu and taken him roughly by the wrist. The other had glared at Kakababu.

'You've broken the law,' he had growled. 'Come along, we're taking you to the station.'

'And where is your station?' Kakababu had asked, not moving.

The policeman had pointed downhill, towards Syangboche. This made sense to Shontu. Syangboche had looked small from the sky, but it was the last big town they had left behind. It had hotels and a hospital. It stood to reason that the police station would also be there. Kakababu, however, had been in no mood to comply with the law.

'I have no interest in retracing my steps just to visit your station,' he had snapped. 'Let my nephew go. It cannot be illegal to practise shooting in the open air.'

'We'll chat about legalities in the station. Now move!' the policeman had barked back, clearly furious.

'Don't touch me!' Kakababu had said sharply, stepping back from the man's extended arm. Then, bringing out a piece of official-looking paper from his coat's inner pocket, he had thrust it at the advancing cop.

'Can you read? If you can, then read that! The officer-in-charge at Syangboche knows who I am.'

The policeman had taken the paper with open scepticism, but his eyebrows had risen higher and higher as he read through it. Once he had finished reading, he had showed the paper to his partner. The second policeman's face had registered similar shock. Then, as one, the two officers had clicked their heels, brought themselves to attention, and crisply saluted Kakababu. Kakababu acknowledged it by slightly raising his right hand. By then, however, one of the policemen had been stealing surreptitious glances at Kakababu's leg.

'Sir, we sincerely apologize for this misunderstanding,' the other had said. 'We didn't know.'

'I didn't do anything illegal, is my point,' Kakababu had said, stiffly. 'And yet you were determined to haul me back to the police station.'

The policeman had looked distinctly worried. 'Sir, please, forgive us just this once. Mistakes happen. We had not been informed about you, honestly.'

The other officer—the one who had been stealing glances at Kakababu's leg—had suddenly said, 'Sir, are you *really* planning on climbing the Everest?'

'We'll see how it goes,' had been Kakababu's crisp response.

Sensing a possible misstep, the first policeman had hastily stepped in again.

'Is there anything we can help you with, sir? Anything at all?'

'No, thank you. Just instruct my luggage-carriers to accompany me wherever I go, without making a fuss. That is all I need.'

The policemen had done as Kakababu had asked, though perhaps they needn't have. The luggage-bearers had been incredibly impressed by the sudden change in attitude that a simple piece of paper had brought about in uniformed officers. In remote areas such as these policemen were often next only to god, and to see not one, but *two* policemen salute Kakababu had made the luggage-bearers' opinion of Kakababu shoot through the roof. The moment the policemen saluted Kakababu a final time and rode away, the two luggage-bearers had popped the question Shontu himself had been dying to ask.

'Sa'ab, what was in that paper? How did it make the police let us go?'

Kakababu's Hindi was not very good, but in simple, broken sentences, he had explained that the paper was a letter given to Kakababu by the Prime Minister of Nepal. It proclaimed Kakababu as a guest of the government, and authorized him to carry out investigations into a particular matter that was of great national importance. To this end, the letter instructed all police personnel on the way to the Everest to aid Kakababu in every possible way, and not impede his progress.

If the bearers had been impressed by Kakababu before, now they were in complete awe.

'This is what an education gets you,' one had whispered to the other as Kakababu had resumed their trek. 'If you study far enough, even the Prime Minister writes letters for you! We started work too early – should have stayed in school and studied a bit more.'

'Well, there's a new school in our neighbourhood,' the other had whispered back. 'I've put my youngest brother in it, told him to stay put.'

After that, the group had walked in peaceful silence. Nothing interesting had happened after that day. When they reached Thyangboche, Kakababu had announced a three-day halt. Thyangboche was the last big town on the way to Everest, and it was full of shops selling tents, camping and climbing equipment, and food. Kakababu had bought all their supplies there, and engaged five more luggage-bearers to carry it. Finally, he had recruited two Sherpas to show them the way. Most people in town had been shocked to hear that a middle-aged, disabled man was planning on climbing the Everest. Some had openly laughed at his uncle, whereas others were downright alarmed. A local doctor had come to their rooms to personally convince Kakababu not to go further ahead. But Kakababu was immutable. As Shontu knew all too well, his uncle was an incredibly stubborn man – sometimes stupidly so. Warnings and discouragement only made him more determined to do what he had set out to do.

In general, Shontu had been happy that they had stopped at Thyangboche. Though he kept confusing the name with Syangboche (which was the place with the big Japanese hotel), he had actually preferred this place to the other one. Syangboche had been nice, but Thyangboche was much prettier, much more unspoilt.

There was a monastery close by, and Shontu thought that it lent the area a calm, peaceful air. On their second day in Thyangboche, he had been out early for a walk. The path had eventually taken him towards the monastery. A few minutes after the monastery had come in sight, the mist that spread over the horizon had cleared briefly, and Shontu had seen three majestic snow-covered peaks in the distance. The view had been so breathtaking that he had stopped and simply stared for several seconds. Then the mists had descended again, drawing a curtain over the splendour. It had only occurred to him on his way back that one of those peaks had been the Everest. He had been looking at the Everest! Even before properly setting off, he had had a glorious view of their destination!

At Thyangboche, they had stayed at the state-run guest house. There had been several foreign tourists staying there at that time of the year. Just like the local folk, many of these tourists had been quite startled to hear that Kakababu and Shontu were on their way to the Everest. A few of them had introduced themselves to Shontu, and asked him why his uncle was so determined to risk such a dangerous climb. 'This is madness!' some of them had admonished him.

Shontu had not been able to explain his uncle's motivations to them. Kakababu had, as usual, kept his reasons close to his chest. The only secret Shontu had been allowed to know was that his uncle was carrying something precious inside a glass case, and that he was paranoid about losing it. Ever so often, he reminded Shontu never to let knowledge of the glass case slip. One evening, while at Thyangboche, Shontu had come into the room to see his uncle in a rare state of panic. 'Shontu, where's my tooth?' he had demanded urgently.

Shontu had automatically looked at his uncle's mouth, but of course, his uncle had not been speaking of his own tooth – at least not the ones in his mouth. He had meant the one in the glass case.

'I don't know, Kakababu,' Shontu had answered honestly. It was impossible for him to know the whereabouts of the tooth, because Kakababu always kept the glass case with himself.

When Shontu said he did not know where the tooth was, Kakababu had become frantic. He had almost torn the room apart looking for it. Finally, the box was discovered under Kakababu's own bed. He had hidden it there for extra security, then forgotten about it. Once the case was found, Kakababu's relief had been palpable.

'Thank goodness, oh thank goodness!' he had exclaimed. 'I thought I had lost it for good … Shontu, you are never to leave the room when I am out, is that clear? Always keep an eye on this! Do you know how expensive this was?'

'What is it, Kakababu?' Shontu had asked. 'Whose tooth is it?'

And just like that, his uncle had clammed up. 'You needn't know all that now,' he had said. 'I'll tell you later, when the time is right.'

And then Kakababu had recruited the Sherpas, and they had left Thyangboche. Now they were at Gorak Shep. This was apparently where everyone made their base camp. Kakababu made camp, all right, but he seemed disinclined to take the next step. For several days now, they had been at this abandoned tower in Gorak Shep, languishing in the cold. Shontu was tired of it. He was tired of the snow, he was tired of having nothing to do, he was tired of the long hours of darkness. Every now and then, he would climb the nearby hillock to see Mount Everest, and think about his uncle's motivations. Would he actually have the chance to climb that majestic peak? He honestly didn't know, and Kakababu seemed not to care.

Lately, he had taken to chatting with the lead Sherpa, Mingma. Kakababu allowed him to wander a little during the day if Mingma was with him. Mingma was both strong and agile, and had already been on two successful Everest expeditions. Unfortunately, both times his employers had prevented him from reaching the summit. They had wanted to keep that glory for themselves. This had broken Mingma's heart. This time, he said, he planned to go all the way to the top of the peak himself. Then he would become as famous as Tenzing Norgay, and all the western countries would felicitate him, as they had felicitated Tenzing.

Multiple trips with foreigners meant that Mingma knew several English words. He could speak it after a fashion, too. The jackets and trousers left to him by the sahibs made him look rather spiffy. He cut a fine figure during their walks, and used the time to confide his opinions in Shontu.

'Listen, Shontu sa'ab, your uncle will never be able to climb the Everest with his leg. How can anyone with one leg climb a mountain? Who put such a strange thought into his head?'

'You don't know my uncle very well,' Shontu said, defensively. 'He can do anything he sets his mind to — he has a very strong will.'

'Will! It's not your will that takes you to the summit! You have no idea how much further we still have to go. One needs strength for that, not just will. Look, let's think of a sensible compromise. Convince your uncle to stay here at base, and let you go ahead with a few of us. It will take some effort, but if we take South Col I can take you all the way to the top.'

Shontu sighed. These conversations were pointless. Mingma didn't know it yet, but his uncle was too stubborn to listen to other people. He would do exactly what he wanted to do, and everyone else would follow.

What with Mingma's company and the short walks, the days had become slightly more bearable. But the nights were still awful. Shontu crawled inside his sleeping bag while it was still technically evening, but he could not force himself to fall sleep. So he tossed and turned—a difficult feat inside a sleeping bag—and wondered what his uncle looked for every night from the small window at the top. Inevitably, during the tossing and turning, his eyes would fall on the glass case on the makeshift table. Something that large could not be a real tooth, Shontu told himself. It was probably an unrefined gemstone of some kind that had formed in the shape of a tooth. Still, the idea of a giant tooth in a glass case made him uncomfortable. He had even dreamt of the thing a few times. Once he dreamt that the tooth had grown to the size of a spade and was digging into his body. To keep such nightmares at bay, he tried to keep his eyes averted from the table. But the harder he tried to look away, the more his eyes strayed to it. This tussle of wills went on till Kakababu came down and turned off the light. And so the days went.

'Shontu! Shontu!'

For all his complaints against sleeplessness, Shontu must have fallen asleep during the evening. When a low voice suddenly called his name, he tried to instantly sit up. Sleeping bags had not been designed to allow that, so his first thought was that someone had pinned him down. After fighting against the constraining fabric for a few seconds, Shontu finally remembered where he was. Then he looked around suspiciously. Had he imagined the voice?

'Shontu!' the voice whispered again. 'Shontu! Are you awake?'

Ah! It was Kakababu. He was calling down from the top of the tower.

'What is it, Kakababu?' Shontu whispered back.

'Come up, right now!' his uncle hissed. 'Quickly!'

Sleeping bags had not been designed to facilitate quick getting-up either, Shontu found out. After some struggling, he finally found the bag's chain and pulled. A metallic ripping sound filled the silence of the tower. Immediately, the biting cold engulfed him. Shivering, Shontu slipped an arm into his coat. This was why he always kept his coat right next to his sleeping bag. After buttoning himself up, he went up the narrow staircase.

Upstairs, his uncle was almost trembling with excitement.

'Look outside, quickly!' he whispered, thrusting his binoculars at Shontu. 'There! Do you see something moving? In the darkness over there?'

CHAPTER 4

Baffled, Shontu looked through the binoculars. What did his uncle expect him to see? The place was a snowy wasteland. Still, he dutifully looked at the area his uncle had pointed out. But, just as he had expected, there was nothing to see.

'Did you see it?' his uncle asked eagerly from beside him.

'No, Kakababu.'

'You're looking straight. It wasn't straight, it was a little to the right.'

Shontu dutifully turned his head to the right. Then he looked to the left, then below, and even above. But he couldn't see anything. The darkness here was unbroken by light. Despite the occasional moonlight that came through the cloud-cover, it was difficult to make out anything after sundown. Besides, there wasn't actually anything around to see. There were no people, no houses, no trees, not even birds during the day.

'Anything yet?' his uncle asked.

'No, Kakababu.'

Kakababu took the binoculars back and looked through them himself.

'That's ... that's strange,' he muttered, peering hard into the night. 'I just saw something right there ... was I wrong? Was it an illusion? Maybe I'm straining my eyes too much ...'

'Kakababu, what exactly did you want to show me?' Shontu cut in.

'How can I say what I expected you to see when I can't even be sure I saw it myself?' his uncle responded testily. Then he put the binoculars back on and stared into the darkness again. In the end, however, even he had to give up.

'Well, we'll clearly see nothing more tonight,' he said, with obvious disappointment. 'Let's wrap things up for the night and go to bed.'

Shontu didn't need to be told twice. He came quickly down the stairs, cast off his coat, and jumped back into his cosy sleeping bag. Kakababu followed at a much more sedate pace. Once downstairs, he showed no sign of going to bed. Instead, he pulled out a small black notebook and began flipping through the pages. Didn't his uncle feel the biting cold? Why would anyone want to sit out in just a coat when they could be inside a warm sleeping bag? The few minutes that Shontu had been out of his bag had been enough to make him shiver uncontrollably.

The foreign-made lamp was excessively bright. Shontu could feel its brightness through his closed lids. When it was turned down after several minutes, he knew his uncle was finally done for the night. After a few seconds, his uncle let out a low grunt of relief. It was the sound he made every night, when he finally rested his back after a day's work. Within half an hour of making the noise, he would be fast asleep.

Unfortunately for Shontu, his own sleep had been chased away by the little interlude with the binoculars. He was really, really curious about what his uncle thought he'd seen through the window.

'Kakababu?' he ventured into the semi-darkness.

'Yes?'

'Will we really be going all the way to the Everest?'

'Certainly, if we need to,' was the crisp and unhelpful answer. What possible "need" could there be to climb the Everest? But there was no point in asking Kakababu to explain. His uncle had deliberately chosen to obfuscate. Shontu was sure of it.

'Will we be able to scale the steep sides?' he asked instead.

'Everyone can do everything, if they try hard enough,' was the firm reply.

Shontu gave up on conversation. Personally, he didn't think that trying hard automatically meant

being successful. But of course, he could never say
that to his uncle. Not when his uncle so obviously
believed that discipline, dedication, and the power of
will could help him overcome his physical limitations.
And in truth, his uncle was much more mobile in
these altitudes than Shontu had expected him to be.
He moved around briskly on his crutches, undeterred
by the rise and fall of the land. During the walk
from Syangboche to Gorak Shep, he had not needed
assistance once. Yes, he had slipped and fallen a few
times, but that hadn't stopped him in the least. In
fact, now that Shontu thought about it ... Kakababu
had been very independent during their adventure in
Kashmir, too. Perhaps his uncle was right, after all.

Still, climbing an actual peak was different from
trekking. Shontu had seen videos of mountaineers
making their way up foreign mountains. They had
thick ropes tied around their waists, and had to make
handholds for themselves using a hammer-like tool.
There had been no walking in those videos, only a
lizard-like scaling of steep, jagged peaks. How could
Kakababu manage that with his crutches? It was true
that Kakababu was as strong as he was determined,
and he kept himself fitter than most people decades
younger than him. But at the end of the day, he had
only one leg to support himself!

On the other hand ... Shontu thought back to the
scrap of conversation he had overheard between
Kakababu and Tenzing Norgay. Tenzing had been very
confident of Kakababu's abilities. 'I wish you success,

Mr Roychoudhuri. I know you will do this' – those had been his exact words. If Tenzing Norgay thought Kakababu was capable of going up the Everest, then who was Shontu to cast aspersions?

Then again, did Kakababu's work actually involve going up the Everest? Or was that just a ruse? Were they actually going to the Everest, or were they secretly going somewhere else?

Flustered by all the contradictions and possibilities, Shontu didn't notice when his fitful sleeplessness was replaced by deep, oblivious sleep.

By the time he woke up the next morning, his uncle was already up. Usually, at home, Kakababu spent the first hours of the morning reading. Here, too, he had his black notebook out, and was going intently through its already-full pages. Occasionally, he made notes of his own.

Someone banged hard on the iron door of the tower.

'Ah, Shontu, you're up,' Kakababu said. 'Could you open the door, please?'

Shontu scrambled out of his sleeping bag and into his coat. Mingma was standing outside the door with a flask of tea and cheap plastic glasses. He hurried inside the moment the door was open.

'Shut the door, Shontu sa'ab,' he called over his shoulder.

In the second that it took Shontu to bolt the door again, a gust of freezing wind rushed into the tower. It shook him to his very bones. Shontu hastily slammed the door and retreated to the centre of the room.

Mingma, meanwhile, had poured tea for him and Kakababu. The steaming tea warmed the cheap plastic tumblers and seeped into Shontu's palms. It would have been a nightmare in Calcutta's humid heat, but here the heated glasses felt like heaven.

'Pour yourself a glass too, Mingma,' Kakababu invited. 'How is today looking? How's the wind?'

Mingma looked hopeful. 'Today's great, sa'ab! No wind to speak of, and the sky is absolutely clear. First class weather for travel, sa'ab!'

'That's excellent,' Kakababu said.

'Are we going forward then, sa'ab? Shall I start packing up?'

'Nah, not yet,' Kakababu said. 'We'll have to stay here for a few more days.'

Mingma deflated. His eyes met Shontu's over their respective glasses of tea. 'Why do we have to stay longer?' they seemed to wordlessly complain to each other.

Kakababu, of course, took no notice of their discontent. 'Do we have more tea?' he asked. 'Here, pour me some more.'

Once the sun came up, Shontu bundled himself up and went out of the tower. Outside, the luggage-bearers were already planning the day's menu. With nothing else to do, cooking and eating took up all their time, from sunrise to sunset. Norbu, the other Sherpa, was not as chatty as Mingma. He preferred to keep to himself, occupying the hours by carving small wooden toys with a knife. He had given Shontu a bear from his collection. This morning, he was sitting a little distance away from the luggage-bearers, working on another piece of wood. At first glance Shontu thought he was carving a monkey, but then he looked at it more closely. The creature was a primate, but it was definitely not a monkey. It had an arched back, and arms that practically reached its feet.

'What creature is this, Norbu-bhai?' he asked.

'Tijuti,' said Norbu shortly. He did not like being disturbed while working.

'Tijuti? What's a tijuti?' Shontu asked, baffled. This was not a name he had heard before.

'Arre! A tijuti is a tijuti, what else will it be?' Norbu snapped irritably.

Shontu did not prod further. Instead, he quietly walked ahead to where Mingma was playing his mouth organ. It was what he sometimes did when he had nothing else to do.

'Mingma-bhai, what is a tijuti?' he asked.

Mingma stared at him for a few seconds. 'Why do you ask?' he finally asked.

'Norbu-bhai was carving a new toy. When I asked him what it was, he said it was a tijuti. But he didn't say what a tijuti was.'

Mingma grinned. 'A tijuti is a small child – smaller than you. When they are middle-sized, like at my age, they are called miti. And when they are bigger, much bigger, they are called yeti.'

Yeti?

As in, the mythical creature???

A bulb suddenly went off in Shontu's head. So *that* was why Kakababu was here! To gather evidence of the yetis' existence! Honestly, it should have occurred to him earlier. The pretence of going to the Everest, establishing camp in a place far away from everything and everyone else, staring into the darkness every night ... it seemed so obvious now. And that thing in the glass case – that must be a yeti's tooth! Euphoria coursed through Shontu. He wanted to throw his head back and laugh. He had cracked his uncle's secret! And if Kakababu was successful ... well, this trip would make him even more famous than he had imagined! It was going to be his very own version of *Tintin in Tibet*! (Shontu loved the Tintin comics. He had several of them on his bookshelves in Calcutta.)

But ... Shontu was suddenly brought up short. Tintin had met the yeti in Tibet. Hence the name of the book. Why had Kakababu come to Nepal, then? Shontu closed his eyes and tried to think back to the book's plot. Tintin had landed in Patna, then gone to Nepal, and only then gone to Tibet. So perhaps Nepal was important, after all. Was this tower one of the places that fell along the route from Nepal to Tibet? In his excitement, he grasped one of Mingma's arms.

'Mingma-bhai, have you ever seen a yeti? With your own eyes?'

Mingma shrugged. 'Nobody has, Shontu sa'ab.'

'Nobody?' Shontu felt incredibly let down. 'But if you haven't seen them, how do you know they come in three sizes?'

'It's what everyone says.'

'Well, do you know of anyone else who has seen a yeti? Another Sherpa, perhaps?'

'No, Shontu sa'ab. Some people claim they have seen one, but they lie. No Sherpa has seen a yeti in a long time. My father had an uncle – a very old man. People said that he had seen a yeti once. But he died many years ago.'

'What about Norbu-bhai? How can he make the tijuti-toys if he hasn't seen them?'

At this, Mingma laughed loudly. 'He is only copying toys that other people make, Shontu sa'ab. Many people carve all sorts of things from wood.'

'Well, have *those* people seen a yeti, then? I mean, how can anyone make toys unless they've actually seen the creature in real life? It's not possible, Mingma-bhai!'

'Shontu sa'ab, hundreds of people regularly make statues of Kartik, Ganesh, and Lakshmi maiji. Are you saying they have met these gods and goddesses? Seen them with their own eyes? Ganeshji has an elephant's head! Do you think these people actually saw someone with an elephant's head?'

Shontu pursed his lips. He did in fact think that the gods visited earth fairly often. Not now, perhaps, but they definitely did a few centuries ago. The first craftsmen had obviously seen them in person. How else could they have made idols in their likeness? People nowadays may not have seen them first-hand, but they had those idols to tell them what each god and goddess looked like. But Mingma clearly disagreed with this, so Shontu thought it best not to bring it up. Instead, he asked the other important question.

'Do you know the way to Tibet? Can one get to Tibet from this place?' he asked.

'Of course,' Mingma answered. 'Do you know Namche Bazaar? It's a town-area, lower down on the route you took.'

'Yes, near Syangboche. We passed it on our way here.'

'Well, if you want to go to Tibet, you have to go left at Namche Bazaar. Once you reach the village of Thamichak, you have to keep going straight. It's one high mountain after another along that route. The biggest is called Kangtega. Do you know what that means? It means "white horse". The mountain looks like a white horse, so people say. Once you cross the Nang Pa pass, you'll be in Tibet. Simple!'

Shontu needed no further confirmation. If Tibet was close by then this was definitely a place where yetis could be seen. He could not wait to tell Kakababu that he had discovered the secret! He turned around and ran full-tilt towards the tower. Seconds later, he was on the ground, face buried in the fresh snow.

'How many times have I told you not to run in the snow, Shontu sa'ab?' Mingma scolded him from behind. 'The hidden ice is slippery! Always take small, steady steps!'

After brushing himself off, Shontu heeded Mingma's advice. He walked back to the tower instead of running, but he still went as fast as he could. He could barely hold still from excitement. Kakababu was just getting ready to go out when he ran inside the tower.

'Kakababu! We are here to find yetis, aren't we?'

For a few seconds, his uncle simply stared at him. Then a mischievous smile lit up his normally stern face. 'Ah, so there *are* such things as yetis?' he asked.

Shontu was taken aback. Kakababu didn't know if yetis were real? Did that mean yetis were *not* why they were here, after all? Or was his uncle testing him? Shontu looked around the room, trying to find something to bolster his belief. His eyes fell on the glass case.

'If there are no yetis, then whose tooth is that?' he challenged, pointing at it.

'You're very curious about that, aren't you?' his uncle said, smiling indulgently. 'All right. I have to go out now, but when I come back, I will tell you all about that tooth.'

CHAPTER 5

The snowfall that had begun earlier carried on through the afternoon. Before he had come here, Shontu used to think that snowfall was exactly like rainfall, just in a solidified form. Once it fell on the ground, he had imagined the snow melting into a puddle just like rain-puddles. But over the last few days he had slowly understood that this place was too cold for puddles. Even after it fell, the snow almost never melted. It was either a light snowfall like today, which felt like cotton drifting down from the sky, or it was snowstorms. Those darkened the skies and made being outdoors impossible. Visibility was destroyed to such an extent that one could barely see a foot ahead of themselves.

Shontu ate his lunch and decided to burrow inside his sleeping bag. The single window of the tower allowed very little light to come in, so the bottom stayed dark even during the day. Kakababu had returned, but was sitting next to the battery-operated light and making lengthy notes in his black notebook. The glass case with the tooth inside still lay between them, on top of the packing box that was currently their table. After the revelation about yetis, Shontu had reconsidered his earlier opinion. The tooth was actually a tooth, not a gemstone in the rough. But it was almost two inches tall – six times the size of a normal human tooth! Did this mean a yeti was six times as large as a human? That was genuinely scary. At the prospect of meeting a creature six times Kakababu's size, Shontu swiftly changed his mind about the tooth again. No, it was not real. It was likely a piece of sculpture, like the oversized shoes one saw outside the fancier shoe-shops in Calcutta.

What was disturbing about the tooth (or sculpture) was its colour. Despite his unwillingness to look at it, Shontu had sometimes found himself staring at the tooth. Sometimes it appeared yellow, like a normal ageing tooth. At other times it seemed pearly white. There were even moments when Shontu was certain it had a slight red hue. Did the tooth really change colour? Or were his eyes playing tricks on him inside this dark stone tower?

Just then, Kakababu put his notebook down and lit his pipe. Shontu couldn't hold his curiosity any longer.

'What were you going to tell me about the tooth, Kakababu?'

Kakababu smiled. 'You're terribly curious about the tooth, aren't you? I hadn't planned on telling you about it this early, but ... well, let's begin at the beginning.'

Then he inhaled deeply from his pipe, and released the smoke in a mist. 'Whose tooth do you think this is? A human's?'

'Yes!' said Shontu. It looked exactly like a human tooth, after all. But then he thought of the oversized shoes at shop windows. Exactly like shoes, but not real shoes at all. 'Uh, no,' he quickly amended.

A ghost of a smile appeared briefly on his uncle's face.

'And that is the crux of the problem,' he said. 'Scientists all over the world were involved in a tussle over the provenance of this tooth. Some said it was definitely human, others said that was impossible. This one here has gone through several kinds of laboratory testing. But before we get into that, I should mention Ralph von Koenigswald. He was a palaeontologist interested in early human ancestors. For his research, he travelled to many parts of the world – he had come to India, he had even gone to China. Now, in the Chinese city of Peking ...'

'It's now called Beijing!' Shontu piped up.

Kakababu stopped speaking and simply looked at Shontu. Shontu remembered his uncle's dislike for being interrupted. His joy at remembering a bit of geographical trivia vanished. He quickly looked down at the tower's stone floor.

'Fine, Beijing, then,' his uncle said after a few seconds. 'But back in the 1930s, when this happened, it was still Peking. Now in those days, a group of people used to sell various sorts of animal remains on the streets of Beijing. You can still see sellers of this sort in Kolkata. They spread a thick cloth on the pavement and put their wares on it. Dried animal bones, feathers, bills from hornbills, and so on. It was amongst one such seller's wares that Koenigswald found three enormous teeth. He was astonished. The teeth were too large to belong to a human mouth, yet they were indubitably human. He kept asking the seller where he found them, but the seller didn't know. He kept saying, "From the mountains". Which didn't really mean anything. So Koenigswald decided to buy the teeth. He bought them very cheaply, in fact.'

'Kakababu, may I ask a question?'

'Yes?'

'Why do these people sell pieces of old bone? I mean, who would need such a thing? Medical students?'

'Perhaps. But traditionally, the Chinese believe that humans can become as strong as certain animals if they eat certain parts of their body. For example, they believed that grinding the bones of a powerful animal and eating it would make a human similarly powerful. It's why some still eat the horns of a rhinoceros.'

'Horns of a rhino? Humans eat rhino horns?'

'Yes. It's why poachers kill so many rhinos each year. Do you know what poaching is? It's killing animals on the sly. These days killing animals willy-nilly is illegal, so people sneak into forests to secretly hunt animals. In the case of rhinos, the poachers sell the horns all across the globe, but especially to Arab millionaires. Each horn sells for thirty to forty thousand. People who believe in the powers of the horn apparently eat it raw.'

'But what did Koenisworld do with the teeth?'

'Koenigswald, not Koenisworld. What he did was find out if the teeth he had bought were the only three of their kind in the world. Turned out that they were not. Peking, Hong Kong, Java, Sumatra, Batavia — many places in the region had traditional medicine shops that sold teeth like this. They were mostly not as large as the ones he had, but were still fairly large. People bought them for toothaches and things like that. Grinding the teeth and brushing with the powder supposedly cured whatever ailment they had. Intrigued, Koenigswald began searching further and wider for the origin of the teeth. Upon examining them under a microscope, he found a slight yellow residue around the edges. This turned out to be traces of soil from the caves of a particular mountain area along the Yangtze river. From this, Koenigswald surmised that the creatures with the teeth used to live in that region. However, it didn't tell him what the creatures *were*. To have teeth that big, they must have been at least twenty feet tall. But humans, or human-like creatures, had never been that big. Not even in prehistoric times. Koenigswald decided to name these hypothetical humans. He called them gigantopithecus, meaning "giant-sized ape-like creatures". However, most of his fellow scientists disagreed with his conclusion.'

Kakababu stopped to briefly take a puff from his pipe.

'During the Second World War,' he continued, 'Koenigswald was in Java. He had the misfortune of being imprisoned by the Japanese. He was locked up in the barracks, and all his things were taken away. Life was hard. In a few years his hair turned white, and he became thin and ill. Most people assumed he wouldn't live for much longer. Considering him no longer a threat, the Japanese let him go before the war was formally concluded. At no point did they realize that he had kept his most valuable possessions in a little pouch around his waist – those three teeth.

'After his release, Koenigswald began the long trek back to the west. Months later, he arrived in North America. At Harvard one afternoon, while at lunch with several fellow academics, talk turned to ancient human-like primates. One of the professors gently mocked Koenigswald's pre-War theory about the gigantopithecus. "You gave us quite a shock with that," the professor said. "Imagine a man with two-inch teeth! How large would his mouth have to be?"

'When Koenigswald realized that his peers were dismissing his theory as nonsense, he lost his temper. "Do you think two-inch teeth are a lie? Well, do you?"

he shouted. "Then what are these?" A waitress had just reached the table with the cutlery and china. Koenigswald tossed the teeth angrily on the plate she had just put down. At the sight of the enormous teeth, the waitress screamed and dropped the rest of the plates. They crashed to the ground and shattered, and she fainted right beside them. The professors jumped up from their seats, the club's staff came running, other members screamed – there was absolute chaos. The upshot of it was that the three teeth disappeared under the broken china and stamping feet. After much searching two of the original were found, but no matter how hard everyone looked, the last one couldn't be traced. Heartbroken, the war-battered Koenigswald began weeping for his lost treasure. He died soon after.'

Excitement was beginning to course through Shontu. He pointed at the glass case. 'Is that the third tooth, Kakababu?'

'Clever boy,' Kakababu smiled approvingly. 'Yes, this is that third tooth. The first of the three is in the Museum of Natural History. The second was gifted to Koenigswald's friend Mark Shipton shortly before Koenigswald's death. The third was swiped by a member of the club's staff that afternoon. Several years later, he sold it to a scientist named Sir Arthur Rockbottom. I got it from his son, Lenon. He and I have been friends for several years now.'

Kakababu seemed to think he had adequately explained the history of the tooth to Shontu, but

Shontu was still confused. Were gigantopithecus real? If not, whose tooth was this? And if they had been found in Beijing, why had Kakababu come to Nepal?

'So, is it really a yeti's tooth?' he asked.

'You seem very sure that yetis actually exist,' Kakababu said mildly. 'Tell me, what do you think they are like?'

'Uh ... they are a sort of human species. They live at the very top of the Himalayas. Oh, and they are very aggressive.'

'Has anyone seen them?'

'Well, many people say they have. Of course, none of them have photos of their encounters. But I'm sure there are yetis in this area, Kakababu. Norbu-bhai makes wooden baby-yeti toys.'

'Oh, he does? I must see them sometime. Have you noticed how many toes the toys have?'

'Toes? No. Why?'

'Because one must observe everything carefully. Every footprint of a yeti that has ever been found has four toes. Every other large primate has five. Humans, gorillas, chimpanzees ... they all have five toes. It's beyond reason that the yeti would have four.'

Shontu kept quiet. He had never heard of this little detail.

'Now we come to the yeti's height. Those that claim to have seen a yeti call it tall, but never more than six or seven feet tall. That's not very tall at all. An undiscovered type of mountain bear could easily be that tall. But as I said before, no human-like animal that was only six to seven feet tall could have such large teeth. So no, this is not a yeti's tooth.'

Shontu was even more at sea now. 'Then what *is* it, Kakababu?'

'Do you remember Ghatotkach from the *Mahabharata*? He was so tall that when Karna shot him to his death, he fell on top of hundreds of Kaurava soldiers and killed them. While this might be an exaggeration, it is possible that a species of very tall humans once lived in the forests and mountains of India. These were probably the "rakshasas" of myth. Perhaps some of them still survive amongst us.'

'Still? As in, nowadays?'

'Sir Arthur had carbon-dated this tooth. It proved to be barely two hundred years old. So yes, I would say they still live amongst us now. Arthur, of course, believed that these were humans, just with a hormonal imbalance. Sometimes, when our glands malfunction, it is possible to have such unusually tall people.'

'So … are we here to look for unusually tall people, then?'

'No. I can't tell you why we're actually here. It's classified. However, there is a secondary reason. Have you heard of Kane Shipton?'

'No?'

'He is Michael Shipton's son. Michael, to whom old Koenigswald left his precious tooth. Kane is a semi-famous mountaineer. "Was", I should say. He had set up camp here about two years or ago. Like us, he was on his way to the Everest with a small group. One evening he went for a walk, and within just two hundred yards of the camp, he disappeared. Vanished, just like that. Many newspapers had reported it then as a mysterious disappearance. His team, and many others besides, had searched the area thoroughly. But he was never found. Here, this is a picture of him that I had cut out of the newspapers then.' Kakababu extended his black notebook.

Shontu looked at the picture that had been glued to the page. A man of about thirty-two or thirty-five, he thought. Bearded and moustached, with a necklace of sorts peeking from under his jacket and shirt.

'That's where he carried the tooth,' Kakababu said quietly, pointing at the necklace. 'Michael gave his good luck charm to his son. Kane used to believe in things like charms. He wore the tooth because he thought it would bring him luck on his dangerous adventures. But if you ask me, it was the tooth that took him. Kane Shipton disappeared from this part of the world because he had it around his neck.'

CHAPTER 6

'Has the snowfall stopped?' Kakababu asked.
Shontu opened the iron door and peeked out.
The weather here was strange. One moment it would
be overcast and snowing, the next moment it would be
dazzlingly sunny. Just this afternoon it had started to
snow with such force that Shontu had been certain it
would continue till nightfall. Yet here he was, peeking
out at a bright blue sky, and glittering fresh snow on
the ground.

Kakababu came up behind him to glance outside.
'Good weather,' he said. 'Come, let's go for a stroll.'

This terrain was difficult for a man who walked on
crutches, but Kakababu managed it well. The snow

was not really a problem in itself. The crutch tended to sink into the powdery stuff, but that was all. However, the fluffy snow sometimes hid hard, slippery blocks of ice. Those were dangerous. The crutch slipped off those, taking Kakababu with it.

Mingma was sitting lightly on the ropes of a tent, playing his mouth organ. When he saw Kakababu and Shontu come out, he came up to them. 'Where are you going, sa'ab?' he asked in Hindi.

'The sky's cleared up, so we're going for a stroll,' Kakababu replied. 'Come along, we'll go to Kala Patthar and see if the Everest is visible today.'

'Where are your gloves, Shontu sa'ab?' Mingma chided. 'Go get them. Your fingers will feel the bite the moment the sun goes down.'

Shontu nodded and went back to get his gloves. He kept forgetting about them during the day, despite knowing first-hand how cold the evenings could get. And it wasn't just the discomfort. Slipping and falling could really hurt the hands if there wasn't a glove to cushion them. Besides, his uncle had told him about frostbite. In places as cold as this, the blood in an uncovered hand can almost freeze. If it isn't warmed back up immediately, a doctor might actually have to cut off a few dead fingers from the hand.

By the time Shontu came back with his gloves, Kakababu and Mingma had gone several steps ahead. It was tempting to catch up with them in a quick run, but Shontu had learned his lesson about running in the snow. Instead, he took really big steps, putting one foot as far ahead in front of the last as he dared, till he caught up with the other two. "Crane-footing", he called it.

'Mingma, have you heard of Kane Shipton?' Kakababu asked just as Shontu caught up with them.

'Haan, sa'ab,' Mingma said. 'Everyone around here knows about Shipton sa'ab. Strong young man, he was. Huge beard, thick moustache. Poor man, he died in these snows.'

'Were you with his team, then?'

'No, sa'ab, I was down with fever when he was recruiting. Terrible stomach ache.'

'Did anyone you know come with him? Norbu, perhaps?'

'No, sa'ab, not Norbu. But my friend Tsering had come with that group.'

'Do you know anything about how Shipton died?'

'Yes, sir. Everyone around here does. This is where they had made base, you know. Right in this area. Everyone who met him down below thought that Shipton sahab would make it straight to the top of the Everest — that was how fit he was.'

'Then how could he have died?'

'Bad luck, sa'ab. No one can stop bad luck. He knew how fit and strong he was, so he went out on solitary walks. The mountains have a rule, sa'ab: no one should ever go out on their own. It invites trouble. Go with another person, all will be well. Never go alone. Shipton sahab refused to listen to that. Went alone, and then who knows what reached out of the ice and pulled him in.'

'I read in the papers that his body wasn't recovered.'

'It wasn't. The government looked. They were determined to find him. Then his friends from America came and looked. Nothing, sa'ab. Shipton sahab disappeared into the snow forever.'

'But Mingma, how far can a man go on foot in this cold? If his base camp was here, then he could not have walked far. Even if he fell down a ravine, there would be traces of his body, wouldn't there? There aren't any particularly deep ravines here that I know of. What could have happened to him?'

'Sometimes, sa'ab, a solitary walk is all it takes. We say "the ice pulled him in". You may smile, sa'ab, but sometimes the ice reaches out and pulls people in.'

'Creevas!' Shontu suddenly exclaimed.

Kakababu looked at him, surprised. He had not expected his nephew to know the word. *Shontu really does know a lot more than I give him credit for*, he thought.

Shontu, meanwhile, was explaining the word that he had found in a book of adventure stories.

'A creevas is a narrow crack in the rock. People can put their feet on the snow on top of it without realising they are stepping into a hollow. Once someone slips into a creevas, it's certain death!'

'Quite right,' Kakababu said, encouragingly. 'But the word is not creevas. The original French was "cravace", but the word in English is crevice. You've mixed the two up and made a French-Anglo-Bengali word of your own.'

Mingma apparently knew the word. 'No, sa'ab,' he said quickly. 'There are no crevices here. Crevices are further ahead. But it's true that the ice takes it due, sa'ab.'

'So you're saying other people have died like this, too?'

'Yes. We lose people in every expedition. Sometimes we find the body, sometimes we don't. Sherpas die, the luggage-bearing kulis die, sometimes even the employers die. Just last year I had a narrow escape, myself.'

'Then why do you keep coming back?' Shontu exclaimed. 'This is a dangerous place!'

'We are of the mountain,' Mingma said, straightening his back. 'We do not dream of dying comfortable deaths at home. Only cowards and women die in their own beds. We dream of dying high up in the peaks, or deep in the snow. Think of lying down to rest eternally in the snow, Shontu sa'ab. Such peace, such peace!' He closed his eyes and crossed his arms on his chest, as if he had already been laid to rest in a snowy grave. From the corner of his eye Shontu saw Kakababu nodding appreciatively at Mingma, as one brave man to another.

After a while, Kakababu resumed walking. 'My point is this, Mingma,' he said, 'Shipton was not an amateur. Neither was he foolhardy. He knew one should not go on solitary walks in the higher altitudes, and he certainly knew better than to stay out after nightfall. Given that, how far could he have actually gone? The place he disappeared from has to be quite close. Besides, the people in Shipton's group have said that that evening wasn't the only time he had gone out on a walk. He had gone out thrice, on three successive evenings. He had even said something quite strange to his two best friends, who had come with him on the expedition. Unfortunately, his friends had not believed him. Apparently, it had been in Shipton's nature to prank his friends with tall tales.'

'That's right, Shipton sahab was a very jolly man. My friend Tsering said that Shipton sahab would say such funny things that the crew would clutch their bellies and laugh.'

Kakababu grimaced. He looked past Mingma and at Shontu. 'Shipton had left a diary behind. Would one, no matter how big a prankster, write his made-up tales in his personal diary? I don't think so. Except Shipton did. I would hesitate to call such an obviously good man a liar, but it's impossible to believe what he wrote.'

'What had he written, Kakababu?'

Instead of answering, Kakababu looked at Mingma again. 'How many expeditions have you been on, Mingma?'

'Seven and one-fourth, sa'ab,' Mingma said, his eyes glittering with humour.

'One-fourth? How's that possible?'

'Well, this expedition has not even reached the halfway mark, sa'ab,' Mingma shot back, grinning. 'We've stalled at the quarter-way point.'

'Ah, I see! Good one. But Mingma, given how often you've come here, have you ever seen anything odd? A large bear, perhaps? Something that might look like a yeti?'

'No, sa'ab. Never.'

'Have you heard of anyone who has seen something like that?'

'Not that I have heard of, sa'ab.'

'Have you heard of Tenzing Norgay, Mingma?'

Mingma instantly folded his palms together and brought them to his forehead in reverence. 'Of course! I consider him the guru of all Sherpas.'

'Well, Tenzing Norgay told me that he believes humanoid creatures of some sort live at these altitudes. Yetis, in other words. Colonel Hunt says the same thing in his writing. Only Edmund Hillary refuses to comment on the matter, but he has never explicitly denied the rumours. So, given what these prominent experts say on the matter, tell me: do the local people really not believe in yetis? Or do they just not want to talk about it?'

Mingma did not speak for a few seconds. Kakababu saw that his face had lost some of its colour, and now wore a distinctly nervous look. 'Sa'ab, can I say something to you, truthfully?'

'Yes, of course.'

'Sa'ab, if the people back at camp realize you have come here to look for yetis, they will abandon camp in a heartbeat. Us mountain folks, we believe in the yeti. But more than that, we are terrified of it. Yetis are like a dangerous god to us – we believe they exist, but never talk about them lest we draw their ire.'

'Are you telling me you'll abandon camp too?'

'Not me!' Mingma said, some of his old cheerfulness coming back. 'Mingma is never scared. I fear nothing!'

'Well, that's good to know. Not that it matters. I am not here to mess with dangerous things. As everyone knows, I am here to climb the Everest.'

As if climbing the Everest was a piece of cake! Shontu wanted to roll his eyes at his uncle. But it was clear that Kakababu was being deliberately silly, for he was wearing a rather mischievous smile.

'Kakababu ...' he began.

'I know what you want to know. What had Shipton written in his diary, right? I'll tell you. Shipton had written that one evening, he had seen a human-like creature stand quietly near that smaller mountain, the Kala Patthar. The creature was twice as tall as Shipton, and had enormous, shovel-like teeth. In other words, it was a Ghatotkach-like man.'

'And? What did the creature do?'

'Nothing. That is the surprising part. Shipton said that the creature simply stared at Shipton, as if surprised to see another person there. And then he disappeared.'

'What? Who? Shipton?'

'No, the creature. One minute he was there, and the next minute he was gone.'

'What!'

'Yes. Or at least, so Shipton wrote. One could argue that he was writing a fairytale in his diary, but his story matches a common tale about yetis. People say that yetis eat a certain kind of grass that grows under the snow. This grass gives them the temporary ability to become invisible.'

Mingma, who had been listening closely so far, suddenly burst out laughing. 'Grass! Eating grass makes you invisible!' he bellowed, clutching his belly and laughing.

'Well, loneliness and vast openness has a certain effect on the mind,' Kakababu said. 'Many mountaineers and trekkers have claimed to have seen such enormous, disappearing men. People who go on long solitary expeditions at sea similarly claim to have seen enormous creatures rising out of the water. It's the high-altitude version of a desert's mirage.'

Mingma paid no attention to this scholarly explanation. He was too busy laughing. 'Vanishing grass!' he gasped, before dissolving into laughter again.

His mirth was so infectious that even Kakababu smiled slightly. 'Well, the thing is, Shipton wrote this in his diary, and then he disappeared himself. Can we conclude that he found this special grass? Or did something else happen to him?'

Mingma didn't respond. He was still chortling. But Shontu had just seen something rather strange. About fifteen or twenty yards to the right of Kakababu and Mingma, a small green plant had sprouted in the snow.

It even bore a white flower. Surprised, Shontu looked around. Were there any more plants around? No, that was the only one. How had just one plant survived in this bitter, terrible cold? And how could such a small plant already have blossomed?

Suddenly, Shontu's heart missed a beat. What if this was that magic grass? Could they be looking at the spot where Shipton had seen the yeti?

Forgetting all caution about running on the snow, Shontu took off towards the miracle-flower at full speed. Kakababu and Mingma kept walking ahead, deep in conversation and completely unaware of Shontu's sudden change in direction.

When he had almost reached the plant, Shontu finally slipped on a piece of hidden ice, and once again pitched face-first into the snow. With one hand he blindly grasped at the ground around him, and felt his fingers wrap around the plant. And then something terrifyingly bizarre happened. Instead of lightly falling into a couple of centimetres of fluff, Shontu's face went into the snow … and kept going deeper inside. There was a hole beneath the surface, and he had fallen head-first into it! Unable to shout for help, Shontu tried desperately to break his fall. But his feet found no purchase. Instead, they went up into the air, flailing helplessly.

Kakababu and Mingma saw nothing. They were still deep in their own conversation, now several steps ahead.

CHAPTER 7

This was the end, Shontu thought, as his head kept going down into the snowy crevice. His hands had no purchase and his feet were waving in the air. Kakababu and Mingma were too far ahead to have seen him. There was no hope.

But hope works in mysterious ways. Despite knowing there was no way out, Shontu couldn't give up. He began flailing desperately. And just then, almost as if in answer to his fight, his head hit something harder than fluffy snow. It took Shontu a second to realize that he was no longer falling down a snowy death-trap. There was support beneath his head. He began flailing with renewed vigour. A split second later it occurred to him that he could use his hands to push against whatever it was beneath his head, and try to

find purchase with his feet. After several seconds of
desperate struggling, his feet finally found purchase on
something. Perhaps another piece of rock, but Shontu
didn't waste his time wondering about that. Instead,
he began pushing his legs and arms down harder, and
using that force to bring his head and shoulders above
the snow. By the time his nose cleared the top of the
shallow snow-pit, his insides were burning from lack
of air. His heart was beating so fast that it felt like it
would burst out of his chest. When the cold, clear air
hit his face, Shontu opened his mouth and sucked in
several deep, frantic breaths.

Just as he was beginning to think he was out of
danger, Shontu noticed that his legs were slowly
sinking into the crevice. The heavy pushing of the
last few seconds had probably dislodged the rock that
had supported them. Now it was sinking, and taking
Shontu with it. Alarmed, Shontu began to scramble
desperately for the top. 'Kakababu! Mingma!' he
screamed.

Could they hear him? Is this what sinking into
quicksand felt like?

His uncle and Mingma had walked quite far ahead.
At first, they didn't hear his cries. When they did, both
whipped around. Seeing just the top of his head above
the snow, Kakababu began hobbling back at running
speed. He lost his footing almost immediately, and
crashed into the fresh snow.

'Don't stop! Help Shontu!' he screamed after
Mingma.

But Mingma needed no instructions. He had spent his life saving people in situations like this. Instead of running on the snow like an amateur, he jumped from point to point, getting rapidly closer to Shontu's location. When he came within speaking distance, he dropped his body to the ground and began rolling towards Shontu. Thinking back later, Shontu realized that he had done it to minimize the chances of slipping into a narrow crevice himself. Once he was right above Shontu, Mingma thrust his arms down into the hole.

'Hold my hand!' he barked.

Shontu did not need to be told twice. He grasped Mingma's arms tightly, and let the other man pull him slowly out of the hole. Then he rolled away from the pit of danger, just as he had seen Mingma do. By the time the two of them got back on their feet, Kakababu had picked himself up and made his way over to them.

'There was a crevice there, Kakababu! I slipped into a crevice!'

'You were right behind us!' his uncle snapped. 'What made you wander off like that?'

'I saw a flowering plant in the snow!'

His uncle's brows furrowed. 'A flowering plant? In the snow? How can there be a flowering plant in this weather, Shontu?'

'It was here! I touched it! And then I slipped into the crevice.'

'It happens sometimes,' Mingma interjected. 'Hardy perennials sometimes survive the snow. We see it every now and then.'

'Still, I had no idea there would be quicksand-like snow in the mountains,' Kakababu bit out. 'This is dangerous. Did Kane Shipton fall down something like this?'

'It's not very deep, Kakababu,' Shontu said. 'After going down a little my head hit something solid. Probably a rock. That's how I stopped going further down.'

'Your head hit a rock?' Mingma exclaimed. 'Goodness! It's sheer luck that you came out of that hole alive!'

'Shontu ... where is that plant that you saw?' Kakababu asked, looking around.

Shontu looked around, too. He was still shivering, though he wasn't cold. He was slowly realizing just how close he had come to a terrifying death. He had not let go of Mingma since the man had pulled him out of the crevice. Now he gripped his arm even tighter. 'I must have uprooted it when I fell into ... when I fell.'

'Which means we have lost the marker. That will not do. Can we mark the area ourselves, Mingma? Others need to be protected against that crevice.'

What could they mark the hole with? Shontu looked at the featureless whiteness that surrounded them. Here there were no branches or pebbles or broken bits and bobs – things that were easily procured at lower altitudes. But Mingma was more resourceful than he was. He began swiftly shaping fistfuls of snow into a snowman. Or rather, into a baby snow-gorilla. When he was done, the thing looked a lot like the tijuti-toy that Norbu had been carving. Mingma lifted it in both arms, and carried it carefully over to the edge of the quick-snow area.

'There!' he said, placing a red handkerchief around the snow-yeti's neck with a flourish. 'Norbu is not the only artist in our camp! What he can make with wood, I can make with snow!'

Kakababu was not particularly impressed. 'What about tomorrow? A few hours of strong sunshine might reduce that to a lump.'

'I'll come along before that and plant a large red flag here,' Mingma assured him. 'I'll warn our kulis not to come this way tonight.'

'Then let's postpone our walk to Kala Patthar. Sundown is in an hour, and everyone will have to be warned.'

Shortly after they returned to base, Shontu had a quick meal of coffee and sandwiches, and zipped himself into his sleeping bag. Kakababu, as usual, sat down on his sleeping bag with the notebook, and began making notes.

After a while, Shontu had a dream.

In the dream, he saw that Kakababu had gone to bed, and that he was quietly slipping out of the tower with a spade. He followed himself out of the tower and past the tents. The notes of a mouth organ filled the silence of the mountains. Everyone else was fast asleep, except Mingma. Apparently, he played his music even in bed. The dream-Shontu walked under the pale moonlight till he reached the baby snow-yeti, with the jaunty red cloth around its neck. Then he dropped to the ground as Mingma had done, and rolled past it. Once he was sure he had come close to the crevice, he stopped rolling and began digging. He intended to find the little plant with the white flower. Once he found the plant, he would dig around it. He was now sure that earlier that day, when he had fallen into the hole, his head had hit a sheet of metal. Not a rock.

How could a sheet of metal have found its way into this uninhabited place? One so artfully buried, at that? Shontu did not know, but he intended to dig it up and show it to Kakababu. For once, his uncle would be impressed with what he did.

Clang!

There! There it was! He was right about the metal sheet! Eager to take a look, dream-Shontu leaned into the hole he had dug. The shovel slipped from his hand and fell into the hole. Dream-Shontu reached down to snatch it up. And once again, he found himself falling, falling, falling. Head-first into that dark, airless hole with no way out.

In the tower, Shontu began groaning and grunting in his sleep. But a small part of himself seemed to break away from the dream and speak directly to him.

'This is a dream,' it said. 'I am fine. I am not in danger.'

'No!' countered the rest of his mind. 'My head is going deeper into the snow! There is no way out! I am choking! I am dying!'

'Look at the light!' the other part of his mind snapped.

Light? What light? Shontu turned his face ... and suddenly bright light filled his vision.

Startled, Shontu woke up. He was in his sleeping bag, perfectly safe behind the iron doors of the tower. The neon lamp shone brightly, filling the tower with its light. What a strange dream that was, he thought. Metal buried under snow? Where did his brain get that idea? Whatever would Kakababu say when he heard? Shontu turned to look at his uncle's sleeping bag.

It was empty.

Where was his uncle? Did he leave the tower alone? Surely not! Not after what happened to Shontu today, after what they knew happened to Kane Shipton?

'Kakababu?' he called out, his heart racing.

'What is it?' answered his uncle, from above.

Oh. His uncle was sitting at the window again. Thank goodness. But why was he up so late? Was he planning on staying there all night? He would fall ill if he kept up such a punishing schedule! 'What's the time, Kakababu?' he asked.

'Nine-thirty. Why?'

Nine-thirty? Seriously? Shontu had been sure it was past midnight. That dream alone should have lasted an hour – what with walking from the tower to the crevice and all that digging. Nah, telling time at these altitudes was impossible for him. Nine-thirty in Calcutta was considered evening. It was full of lights and sounds. And here? The only sound was the distant notes of Mingma's mouth organ.

Wait, hadn't he heard exactly those notes in his dream? Did that mean he had actually been half awake while he had that dream? Or was the music a coincidence? Never mind, the bigger question was whether he should tell Kakababu about it. His first instinct was to tell him everything. But then he thought better of it. Kakababu would probably laugh. He might even think that fear and anxiety were making Shontu lose his mind. Metal under snow, indeed! No, it was best to keep the dream to himself.

He fell asleep again a little later. Kakababu remained next to the window.

When he woke up the next day, the sky outside was a clear, bright blue. Kakababu was fast asleep in his sleeping bag. Shontu came out of his sleeping bag and immediately started jumping up and down. This was the best way to stop the shivering that inevitably set in the moment he left the warmth of the bag. The sound of Shontu jumping on the stone floor woke Kakababu up. 'How are you this morning?' he asked.

'Very well, Kakababu.'

'You slept very deeply last night. I called you a few times, but you didn't respond.'

'You were calling me? Why?'

'I saw something very strange last night. I wanted to show it to you, but ...'

Kakababu opened the zip of his sleeping bag and sat up. 'Pass me my crutches,' he said. 'This is important.'

Shontu almost ran to his uncle with the pair of crutches. 'What did you see?' he asked excitedly.

'Two distant spots of light. Quite far from here. Much closer to Kala Patthar, I would say. It wasn't a mistake, either. I checked several times.'

Shontu was puzzled. 'Lights? Where would lights come from? That place is completely uninhabited.'

'That's the question, isn't it? No one from our crew would go that far, definitely not at night. What was more interesting was that the lights didn't lead up to or lead away from the spot. They suddenly appeared, moved about for a few minutes, then disappeared. It was quite abrupt. Even if we concede that yetis or yeti-like creatures exist, no storyteller has ever accused them of walking about in the snow with lamps.'

'Kakababu …' Shontu said thoughtfully. 'Could it have been a mirage?'

His uncle looked equally thoughtful. 'A mirage? In the snow? That's not something I've ever heard of. But even if it was, this matter still bears investigation.'

CHAPTER 8

Later that morning, Kakababu sent for Mingma. 'Let's wrap up here, Mingma,' he said. 'We're going forward today.'

Absolute joy lit up Mingma's face. 'Towards Everest, sa'ab? We can do it! I will pick you up on my back and carry you, sa'ab.'

'That won't be necessary,' Kakababu said. 'I'm sure I'll be able to walk on my own. We'll set up first camp at Kala Patthar.'

Mingma ran outside to inform the rest of the group. After he left, Kakababu opened one of the packed boxes and took out a wireless communication set. It was yet another thing he had brought back from Europe the last time he had been there. Just like the lamp, this ran on battery, not electricity. As soon as he switched it on, a tapping sound filled the tower.

'Step outside for a minute, Shontu,' Kakababu said.

Shontu obediently went outside, but he really wanted to know who Kakababu was speaking to. He had seen the set when Kakababu had packed it in Calcutta, but he had never seen Kakababu use it before. Who was Kakababu contacting? And what secrets were they discussing that he needed Shontu to leave the tower? A little distance away, the luggage carriers and the two Sherpas were busy unhooking the ropes that held the tents in place. With nothing else to do, Shontu started helping them. After a few minutes, Kakababu came outside.

'Shontu,' he called. 'You can go inside and pack your things now. Be quick.'

'Sa'ab, can't we wait till we've eaten?' Mingma asked. 'It will be easier if we get that over with before we set out.'

'No no, the skies are clear. We need to set out as soon as we can. If we keep up a brisk pace, we'll reach Kala Patthar by afternoon. That is where we'll have our meal.'

'Well, then at least have a glass of hot tea,' Mingma said, holding out a steaming glass towards Kakababu.

Shontu had been walking towards the tower. Mingma called him back as well. 'You have a glass too, Shontu sa'ab. It'll do you good.'

Shontu was always happy to drink tea in this cold. Just cupping the hot glass in his palms made him feel better.

'So, uncle sa'ab, how many days are we planning to stay at Kala Patthar?' Mingma asked, after a few sips of tea.

'"Stay"? Why do you think we'll stay at Kala Patthar? We'll start again the very next day. We have a mission to reach Everest, don't we?'

Mingma looked confused. 'But sa'ab ... if you planned to go to Everest all along, then why spend so many days here? We could've covered a lot of ground in these seven days.'

'It was necessary,' Kakababu said. 'My nephew and I are not from the mountains. We needed to acclimatize our bodies to such extreme temperatures. But on to serious matters, Mingma. How long will it take us to reach the Everest from Kala Patthar?'

'If the gods of the sky bless us, then seven, maybe eight days, sa'ab.'

'Only seven days?' Shontu exclaimed. He had thought that Everest was much further away.

'Yes, sa'ab. It shouldn't take more than that. Once we reach the foothills, we'll go up via South Col. You'll stay with me – we'll do it together.'

'If it's a week, then we have sufficient rations,' Kakababu said. 'That was what I was worried about.'

'I still can't believe we're finally going towards the Everest,' Mingma said, but mostly to himself.

Kakababu immediately looked offended. 'What do you mean, "can't believe"?' he asked sharply. 'Did you people think I had lied to you? Of course we'll go up to the Everest. If we manage to reach all the way to the top, then every person in this team will be rewarded. The Government of India, the Government of Nepal — everyone will know our names. *All* of our names!'

Mingma's eyes strayed towards Kakababu's disabled leg. Shontu saw Kakababu see it, but his uncle gave no indication that he had noticed. Instead, he turned to Shontu and said, 'Still here? Go on, run inside and pack your things.'

Shontu didn't want to risk wasting any more time. He walked as quickly as he could to the tower. When he reached the tower, however, he nearly jumped back outside in shock. A stranger was squatting on the floor, his back towards the door, looking at something in front of him.

A second later, he realised it was the other Sherpa, Norbu. He relaxed. It was, after all, perfectly normal for Sherpas to help people pack their things the right way. But then he noticed that Norbu wasn't packing anything. Instead, he was staring intently at Kakababu's glass case.

'What is it, Norbu-bhai?' he asked, startling the man out of his reverie.

'What is this thing, Shontu sa'ab?' Norbu asked, without getting up.

'Tooth. It's a tooth.'

'Whose tooth?'

Shontu almost said that it was a yeti's tooth, but he controlled himself at the last minute. Mingma had said that mountain people tended to be superstitious about yetis. If they thought Kakababu was carrying around a part of a yeti's body, they would probably abandon them in this godforsaken place. In fact, now that Shontu thought about it, Kakababu had never once let anyone from the crew know about the tooth. In an attempt to reassure Norbu, he pretended nonchalance. 'I don't know, Norbu-bhai. It belongs to my uncle.'

Norbu looked at him intently. 'This is too big to be a human tooth. Tell me the truth, sa'ab. Whose tooth is this?'

Shontu was surprised. Norbu seldom spoke to him, or even to the rest of the crew. He was a serious man, and kept himself occupied with his work and wood carving. It was odd to see him press on a conversation. When Shontu didn't answer, Norbu turned back to the glass case, and made as if to open it. Immediately, Shontu started forward. 'No! Don't open that. Don't touch that thing.'

'Why not?' Norbu challenged.

Shontu was a bit irritated now. 'Because Kakababu said so,' he bit out. 'It's his. No one else is allowed to touch it.'

Norbu turned back to the case. 'Well, I'm going to see it,' he declared.

'No!' Shontu shouted. 'What did I just say? Kakababu will be angry if he knows you opened that. Let's finish his packing instead. Norbu-bhai, you can take this big box outside.'

Norbu paid him no attention. Instead, he stood up with the glass case. Being so blatantly ignored made Shontu furious. He could run outside and tell Kakababu that Norbu was messing with his things. But in Thyangboche, Kakababu had made *him* responsible for the safety of the case. Instead of leaving, therefore, he advanced upon Norbu, glaring. 'What are you doing?' he snarled. 'Didn't I already tell you not to touch that thing?'

Norbu looked up. His eyes were unfocused. It was as if he could not see Shontu. Clutching the case, he made straight for the door, shoving Shontu aside when the latter planted himself in his path. Shontu was about to fall, but he caught himself at the last moment. Furious, he aimed a roundhouse kick at Norbu's chin. Norbu was much more muscular than Shontu, but the impact of the kick took him flying back. In seconds, he was on the ground. The glass case flew from his hands.

'Oh no!' Shontu gasped, running to retrieve it. He was terrified that his impulsive action had shattered it. But it hadn't. When it first fell from Norbu's hand and hit the ground, it had bounced once, but that was it. The glass case wasn't made of glass, Shontu realized. It was made of very clear plastic.

On the floor, Norbu's eyes had come back into focus. Now he was glaring at Shontu, as if he couldn't believe that a boy Shontu's age could have kicked him to the ground. The very next second, he jumped up and threw himself at Shontu. This time, Shontu thought it prudent to just slip out from under him. Missing his target, Norbu once again crashed to the floor. He was a strong man, but unlike Shontu—who had been training in martial arts for several years now—Norbu did not know how to fight.

Before Norbu could get up again, Kakababu came inside the tower. He looked startled at the sight of the man on the floor. 'Why are you on the ground?' he asked Norbu.

Norbu did not respond.

Shontu began thinking fast. If he told his uncle about Norbu's absurd behaviour, Kakababu would no doubt be furious. He might very well punish Norbu, probably throw him out of the expedition. It was up to Shontu to avoid drastic things like that.

'Norbu-bhai just slipped and fell, Kakababu,' he said hurriedly.

Kakababu turned towards Shontu. 'And what are you doing with the glass case out in the open?'

'Ah ... I was thinking I will keep it with me, Kakababu.'

'No. That will stay with me,' his uncle said firmly. 'Norbu, go outside and get more people. Pack up and clean this room as quickly as you can.'

Norbu did not answer. Nor did he challenge Shontu's version of events. He simply looked around once and left the tower quietly.

CHAPTER 9

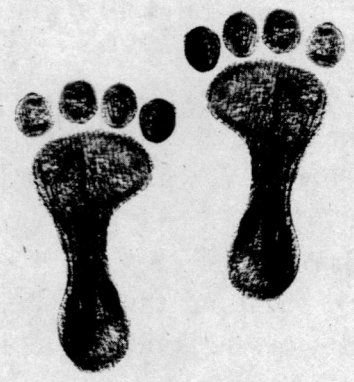

They started out at exactly nine in the morning.

Shontu had gone up Kala Patthar before. If it didn't snow, then he was sure they could make camp there by afternoon.

Mingma and Kakababu led the way. Shontu followed close behind. As was his nature, Mingma was keeping spirits up with funny anecdotes and light-hearted banter. Behind them, Norbu walked in absolute silence. This was his norm, but today his reticence had an overt unfriendliness. Just to be safe, Shontu stole occasional glances at him. But Norbu seemed determined not to look at him.

Progress was slow. It was impossible to walk quickly through the snow, and on top of that everyone was weighed down by luggage. Even Kakababu was carrying a bag on his back. Shontu was waiting for the moment when they could drop everything at the new campsite and he could make his way to the top of Kala Patthar. He couldn't wait to see the Everest again. Would they really be there within a week? With such a small group? And with Kakababu on his crutches? Though he had started in the lead, his uncle had been steadily falling behind all morning. And this was a relatively flat route. Try as he might, Shontu had a hard time believing that he could climb the Everest.

Just then, his uncle's voice rang out.

'Shontu! Come here for a minute.'

Looking back, Shontu saw that his uncle had really fallen behind. Shontu made his way back as quickly as he could.

'My meds, Shontu!' his uncle called again.

Kakababu had to take certain medicines thrice a day. He had trouble extracting them from his pack while walking, so Shontu helped him take them out. But it was not time for his mid-day medicines yet. Was the walk putting more strain on him than usual?

When he reached his uncle, Kakababu nodded towards his right pocket.

'Kept it there for easy access,' he said. Shontu noticed that he was breathing rather heavily.

'Are you feeling ill, Kakababu?' he asked worriedly.

'Not at all. Listen, do you think this place is far enough from the tower to look like it is at the base of the Kala Patthar?'

Shontu looked uncertain. Why would his uncle ask such a strange question?

'I think it is,' his uncle said. 'I'm fairly sure that this was where I saw the two lights last night. Do something. Give me the medicine, then walk ahead till you catch up with the others. Make sure no one comes to fetch me. I want to examine this area on my own.'

'Should I tell Mingma to take the group ahead? Then I can come back and help you.'

'No. I want to do this on my own. You go along with them. Tell Mingma to make camp right at the base of the Kala Patthar. I'll see you soon.'

After Shontu left, Kakababu lowered himself carefully on a rock and lit his pipe. He simply sat there, smoking comfortably, till the others had gone far, far ahead. Then he stood up. First, he turned his head around and did a thorough visual survey of the area. Then he took out his binoculars and surveyed the area through their lens. Something slightly to his right caught his attention. 'Hmm,' he said to himself. Then he began to slowly move towards the area.

After going a few metres to the right, Kakababu came upon the thing he had seen. It was a set of depressions in the snow. Up close, it was obvious that they were footprints. Large footprints. About the size of an elephant's foot, he surmised. But the prints did not look anything like an elephant's. In fact, they looked very much like a human's. An enormous, elephant-sized human, who had four toes.

'Strange,' Kakababu breathed, as he lowered himself to the ground next to the first print. 'Incredible.'

For the next several minutes, he busied himself with recording the footprints in different ways. First, he took out a small camera and took multiple photographs from different angles. Then he took out a tape-measure and noted the measurements of the prints. There were six prints in all, and each print clearly showed four toes. All toes were of the same size. There were no big or little toes. Even at these altitudes, a few hours of sunshine was enough to melt the edges of a footprint. The sun had been shining all morning, but these prints, Kakababu noticed, were crisp. Which meant that they had been made recently. *Very* recently.

Despite gathering such an abundance of evidence, Kakababu did not look pleased. He wore a slightly puzzled frown, as if he could not quite put his finger on what was bothering him. Then suddenly, a distant noise made him look up. A figure was running down the path that the rest of the group had taken. It was running straight at him.

Kakababu did not react. He simply pocketed his instruments and quietly slipped his revolver into his palm. Otherwise, he remained as he was.

After a few seconds, the first figure was joined by multiple other figures. Kakababu peered at them, then relaxed. It was his own crew. But why were they running back? Kakababu pocketed his revolver and stood up, waiting for them to reach him.

Running on ice and snow is dangerous business, but Mingma managed to reach him without any accidents. 'Sir!' he gasped. 'Yeti! This big! Huge!'

Scepticism laced Kakababu's voice. 'Really? Did you see it yourself?'

'Norbu did! We have to move, sa'ab! It isn't safe here!'

Just then, Shontu came to a panting halt next to them.

'Is this true, Shontu?' Kakababu asked. 'Did you see it? With your own eyes?'

Shontu was pale. His eyes were bright with warring astonishment and fear. Like Mingma, he too was panting hard. 'Yes, yes I did.'

'What did it look like?' Kakababu demanded, excitement gripping him. 'Like a man? A gorilla?'

Shontu swallowed. 'I ... I didn't get a good look. I was thinking of something else. I looked up when Norbu-bhai and the luggage-bearers screamed, and saw something large and black quickly slip behind a large boulder.'

'That's it?' Kakababu shouted. 'That's all you saw? Idiot! Why didn't you run forward and try to take a closer look? If I knew you were such a coward I wouldn't have brought you with me!'

Shontu instantly looked ashamed. But Mingma flared up in his defence. 'What are you saying, sa'ab! Shontu sa'ab would have died if he had chased the yeti! Thank god we saw it while we still had time to run away!'

'Sounds to me like the yeti ran away from *you*,' Kakababu remarked, acidly. 'Did any of you actually look back to see if this creature was actually running after you? Or did you just run?'

But by then Mingma had seen the prints of the elephant-man.

'Oh, Ram! Oh, Mahadeo! The yeti had come here, too!'

By this time, Norbu and the luggage-bearers had reached them. Everyone tried to talk together, creating an incomprehensible cacophony. After a few seconds, Kakababu lost his temper.

'Quiet!' he shouted. 'Everybody, quiet! Speak one by one. What happened? What did you see?'

A resentful silence descended on the group. Then Norbu pushed his way forward.

'Turn back, sahib. We're not going forward,' he said. Quite rudely, Shontu thought.

'Look, you have nothing to fear as long as I am here ...' Kakababu began, but his voice was drowned by an instant storm of protests. The crew did not want reassurances. They wanted to head back. Everyone had seen the huge footprints by now, and not a single person believed that Kakababu could hold off such a creature.

Kakababu tried to argue with them for some time. In the end, he said, 'Fine. If you want to go, go. Leave us alone.'

But this was not what the Sherpas and luggage-bearers had in mind. They had been charged by the local police to take good care of Kakababu. If they returned without him, they feared that they would be punished. They wanted Kakababu to return with them.

Kakababu, of course, refused. The bearers begged and pleaded with him; the Sherpas shouted about dire consequences. But Kakababu did not budge. These people had no idea how stubborn his uncle could be, Shontu thought. And if Kakababu remained, then so would he. True, the glimpse of that enormous creature had terrified him. He had thought immediately of King Kong, and the destruction he had wreaked. But there was no question of leaving his uncle behind in this place, no matter how scared he was.

Then Norbu said something to the luggage-bearers in a language Shontu didn't understand. Seconds later, they all jumped on Kakababu and pinned him to the ground. Then a couple of them lifted him up on their shoulders. Another caught Shontu by the scruff of his neck. Norbu called out another instruction, and everyone briskly set off the path they had come. Shontu could have tried fighting his way out, but when he saw the other two were practically making off with his uncle, he gave in and went along.

When they reached the stone tower, Kakababu called out loudly. 'Thank you for the lift! Now please put me down and be on your way. I will stay here.'

'No!' growled Norbu.

'We will go down to Thyangboche tonight, sa'ab,' Mingma said. 'If we can't go all the way, we will at least go down to Fericha Village.'

Kakababu might have lost a leg, but he had extremely powerful arms. When the men refused to put him down, he pushed down on their shoulders with his arms, and vaulted off their backs. The only trouble was that he could not immediately jump back on his feet. He needed a few seconds to scramble up. In that time, the men tried to pick him up again. And found themselves staring down the barrel of Kakababu's revolver.

'I don't want to become a murderer today,' he barked. 'But if you push me, I cannot guarantee that I won't.'

As one, the group took a step back.

'Shontu, hand me my crutches,' Kakababu said, not taking his eyes off the men.

Mingma had been carrying the crutches. He handed them back. Kakababu sneered at him. 'I thought you said you weren't scared of anything? And now the mere rumour of a yeti is chasing you off the mountains?'

'Sa'ab, I don't have a firearm like you do. Give me a firearm and I won't be scared.'

At this, Norbu spat a few words at Mingma. Shontu did not understand their language, but it seemed to him that Norbu was saying human bullets could not harm a yeti. Kakababu cut in.

'Look, if you are that scared, you can go back. I'll pay you right now for the days that you have worked. But don't try to take me with you. I will stay right here.'

'Sa'ab, please, don't do this. Come back with us. I promise we can come back again, once we have guns and pistols and a few sahebs to accompany us.'

Kakababu scoffed. 'Sahebs! You need sahebs to protect you? Why? Do you think sahebs have special yeti-fighting powers? Go on, leave. Leave! I don't need cowards like you on my side.'

To Shontu's disappointment, the group actually did leave. Once the sound of their departure faded away, the silence of the area descended like a heavy cloak around the tower. Till this morning, the area had been quiet, but not this deathly silent. There had been conversations from the tents, and the sound of chores being done. Now there was nothing around the tower but an uninterrupted stretch of snow. He followed his uncle inside the tower and shut the door.

'Are you hungry?' his uncle asked. 'The bags are all packed, but see if you can find biscuits and cheese. That'll do for now.'

Pale-faced, Shontu began opening the packed bags. They could not go back even if they wanted to, he suddenly realized. Not only did the luggage-bearers and Sherpas do all the chores, they were also the only ones who knew the way. Without them, he and his uncle were stranded in the middle of a snowed-in desert.

Kakababu noticed his sudden apprehension.

'Scared?' he asked, putting a biscuit and a bit of cheese in his mouth.

Shontu swallowed. 'N...no,' he managed.

'Did you really see something? Or did you hear Norbu's scream and just ...?'

'I saw. Only for a second, but I saw.'

'Could it have been a tall human?'

Shontu swallowed again. 'No, Kakababu. Much bigger. Completely black, covered in fur ...'

'Did you see its face? Could it have been a mountain bear or something like that?'

'Couldn't see the face, but it wasn't a bear. It was standing straight, like us.'

'A yeti, then. Is that what you think?'

Shontu looked up. 'What else could it be, Kakababu?'

His uncle did not answer that. 'I suppose the movement I had seen last night had also been a yeti's?'

Shontu nodded. 'You saw the footprints yourself,' he said, in a defeated voice.

'Hmm. I suppose you and I are now at the yetis' mercy, then. But do yetis scour the mountainside with torches or lanterns at night? What were the lights that I saw?'

Why was his uncle so resistant to the truth? 'Kakababu,' Shontu ventured. 'They were probably yetis eyes. Animal eyes glow in the dark, you know. I have seen pictures of lions and tigers with glowing eyes.'

'Lions and tigers!' Kakababu sounded impressed. But Shontu had a faint feeling that he was actually being mocked. 'These yetis are turning out to be rather impressive creatures. They walk like humans, have feet the size of elephants, can disappear at will, and now they have glowing eyes like lions and tigers! If we can catch such a creature, or even take a picture, we should be famous the world over. All the more reason to stay back, eh?'

Shontu paled further.

Kakababu smiled at him. 'Much of this is bound to be fiction,' he said, gently. 'Humans have long been spurred by two completely opposite feelings. One, to hunt down every mystery and strip it bare. The other, to mythologize the far reaches of our experiences, and preserve them as such. Neither group takes well to detractors. The yeti debate is something that brings them into open conflict. I know this is scary, but we have nothing to worry about. This tower is strong — not even a yeti can breach it. We'll stay inside. I have already contacted Thyangboche by wireless. Their rescue-team is on its way. That team will reach us by evening, tomorrow.'

A little later, Kakababu dusted off the crumbs and went inside his sleeping bag, but did not zip it up. Instead, he lit his pipe. Shontu tip-toed to the large iron doors and opened them a little. It was cold outside, and dark. Though technically early evening, dark clouds had swallowed the last light of the sun. It looked terrifyingly lonely.

'Best not to go out tonight,' Kakababu called. 'The yeti is unlikely to have chased us this far down, but better safe than sorry. Pull the latch tightly when you're done.'

After a little while of sitting around, Shontu decided to go to bed. This was the other thing about the mountains. Without people around, there was nothing else to do. Soon, he fell asleep.

That sleep was rudely broken in the middle of the night.

Someone was banging on the iron doors of the tower. Hard.

Terrified, Shontu whipped around. His uncle was sitting bolt upright in his sleeping bag. His revolver was pointed straight at the door.

CHAPTER 10

Shontu's heart was pounding in his chest. The sound of it filled his ears, almost drowning out the noise of the door. Kakababu seemed perfectly calm. He had aimed his revolver at the door, but wasn't doing anything else. There was a stillness about him that would make the casual observer think he was meditating. But Shontu could see that his entire being was focused on the door.

The pounding on the door doubled in force.

'Who is it?' his uncle finally shouted. At that, the noise abruptly stopped.

'The door is strong. It will hold,' his uncle whispered. 'Run up to the window and see if you can make out who's outside.'

Shontu had taken his shoes off when he had gone to bed. He struggled to put them on and slip into his bulky overcoat. Then he ran for the stairs. The moment he put his foot on the first step, the pounding began again.

'Who is it? Who are you?' he shouted at the door. Again, there was no response.

A few seconds later he was at the top of the stairs. He eagerly thrust his head out of the window, but he saw nothing but whiteness. Too late, he realized that the window was on the other side of the tower. It didn't offer a view of the door at all. Even if he angled himself along the wall and tried to peer sideways, he couldn't see the doorway.

'Who is it? Show yourself!' he shouted instead.

Whoever it was did not bother to respond.

Kakababu had finally had enough. Making tell-tale wooden noises, he hobbled up to the door. 'Who are you?' he demanded. 'What do you want?'

In response, the banging stopped briefly, then began again.

'Is this Mingma? Norbu? Why are you banging on our door?'

The banging continued.

'I'm opening the door!' Kakababu called out. 'Stop banging and move aside. If you don't, I'll open fire!'

Shontu was horrified. 'Kakababu, no!' he shouted from above. 'Don't open the door!'

His uncle reached up and hit the patch next to the latch with his fist. It made a convincing "thud!". Shontu breathed out in relief. His uncle was only pretending to pull the latch down, thank goodness. But whoever was on the other side must have believed him, because the banging stopped. Shontu ran down the stairs to join his uncle.

'I think it is Mingma or Norbu, trying to scare us into leaving,' his uncle said, irritably. 'Of all the stupid things to do …'

Shontu stared at his uncle in open disbelief. Why was Kakababu still trying to pin this on humans? Norbu and Mingma had been gone for hours. This was clearly the work of a yeti! Shontu had seen its shadow. Everyone had seen its footprints! Besides, what human could pound a door that hard? It was clearly a yeti that was trying to break their door down. Despite not wanting to show weakness, he began shivering so much that he could barely stand.

The pounding started again.

Kakababu kept shouting at the door, switching between English and Hindi. 'Who is it?' 'Kaun hai?' 'What do you want?'

No one answered, but the pounding continued. Then, as abruptly as it had started, it stopped.

For the next several minutes, Kakababu and Shontu stood frozen in front of the door, waiting for the pounding to start again. It didn't.

'Let's open the door and see what they're up to,' Kakababu finally said.

'No!' Shontu yelped in terror. 'Kakababu, this is a trick! They're baiting us. The moment we open the door, they will …'

'Who is this "they"?' Kakababu cut in. 'This is what baffles me. You seem to think that there is a hoard of yetis outside, dying to get in. But why? No one has ever claimed that yetis were in the habit of chasing humans down or breaking into their homes. If anything, yetis are supposed to be shy. They either run away or disappear when spotted by humans. So even if I accept that you saw an actual yeti at Kala Patthar, why on earth would it chase us all the way to this tower?'

Shontu did not answer. He was still shaking. Kakababu seemed to make up his mind.

'I'm going to open the door. You stand behind me. Even a yeti can't escape a shot fired at such close range.'

Then he reached up and pulled the large latch down, and pulled the door's handle.

The door did not open.

Kakababu's brows jumped together in a severe frown. He pulled again, harder.

The door remained where it was.

'Now what?' Kakababu muttered. 'Rusted hinges? Pushed too hard from the other side? Shontu, give me a hand.'

Reluctantly, Shontu joined his uncle in pulling the handle inwards. But even together, they couldn't move it an inch. Frustrated, Shontu kicked the door a few times. After several minutes of fruitless pulling and kicking, they had to concede the obvious: someone had locked them in from the outside.

Now even Kakababu looked worried. *Who could possibly have wanted to lock them in?* he wondered. *And, more importantly, why?*

'They haven't just put a lock on the door,' he suddenly said. 'There is no latch on the outside, just a rounded handle on each door. Remember how it was when we first came? You can put a lock through the handles, but it doesn't fully close the door. There's always a little gap in between. No, what they were doing was boarding this door up. We mistook their hammering for banging. Someone wanted to make sure that we stayed inside the tower tonight.'

Then he smiled briefly at Shontu. 'Well, this should settle the matter for you. It's humans that are after us. Not yetis.'

Shontu's legs almost gave out from under him. This was so much worse than seeing a yeti. Much, *much* worse. They were boarded inside a tower in the middle of nowhere, with limited rations and just a small window for ventilation. Who on earth would want to imprison them that badly? Would they come to let them out? What did they plan to do with them? Scared and frustrated, he kicked the door a few more times.

'There's no point in that,' Kakababu said, reasonably. Then he turned around and went back to his sleeping bag. Lowering himself to the ground, he lit his pipe again. Then, suddenly lifting his head, he said, 'Put the latch back up, Shontu. If they come back to take the boards off, we should make sure that they still can't open the door.'

Shontu tightened the latch, then walked slowly back to his uncle. His legs barely carried him. The prospect of a yeti outside was scary, but the prospect of being locked inside this tower was absolutely terrifying. Shontu had been on a couple of adventures with his uncle before, but he had never felt this helpless. What baffled him was that this time they had no enemy that he knew of. If anyone had been following them, then it would have been very obvious in this snowy, empty place without trees or buildings to obscure one's view. No one had. So who were these door-boarders, and how did they get to this place? Were they tracking Kakababu? How did they know about his expedition?

After a few minutes, he realized his uncle was speaking, but almost to himself. 'We will never be able to break that door down. Unless someone comes and opens it from the outside, we are stuck. I have messaged the base, but it would take two or three days for them to walk all the way up ...'

'Two to three days!' exclaimed Shontu. 'Kakababu, we will suffocate by then!'

'"Suffocation" might be going too far. We'll keep the window open. It'll make this place cold, but we'll have fresh air. It will be hard, very hard, but we'll make it. On the other hand, if they try to break the door down again ...'

'Who's "they", Kakababu?'

'That's exactly my question. Who are these people? Why do they walk about at night with lamps? Are those really yeti footprints? Do me a favour, Shontu, take the wireless set out from the box.'

A few minutes later, Kakababu put the headphones on and began sending a message. For the first few seconds, the machine only emitted a whirring noise. Then, Kakababu started speaking.

'Hello! Hello! Peak number 114 calling base. Peak number 114 calling base … S.O.S. from Roychoudhuri. Do you read me? S.O.S. from Roychoudhuri. Your code, please. Over.'

Something must have come through from the other side into Kakababu's headphones, because Kakababu held them closer to his ears and listened intently. Then he started responding. Shontu didn't understand anything of his response. Kakababu's words were in English, but the message was incomprehensible. There were lots of numbers that he kept calling out. Shontu had no idea what any of them meant. He gave up and stared at the door instead, wondering again who could've imprisoned him and his uncle.

Kakababu spoke on the wireless for several minutes. Towards the end, he seemed to be getting increasingly angry and worked up. Finally, he bit out a terse 'Over and out' and pulled the headphones off angrily. Then he jammed his pipe back into his mouth and cast about for his lighter. When he didn't immediately find it, he let out an exasperated snarl.

Kakababu's overcoat had about ten pockets. He stuffed them with various things, then forgot where he had kept what. The lighter turned out to have been

in the fourth pocket he searched. Looking marginally
mollified, he lit his pipe and took a deep puff. After
a few more puffs, his temper seemed to cool a little.
'They have left base,' he informed Shontu. 'But that's
not good enough. Base is all the way down at Namche
Bazaar. It'll be too late for us if they come on foot. The
only way they can reach us in time is if they get a
helicopter. But these people apparently don't have a
helicopter. They'll have to request one and hope that
the request is quickly granted. In the meanwhile, we'll
have to do the best we can.'

Shontu had never seen his uncle worried before, and
they had been in some unusually dangerous situations.
While trying to unearth Emperor Kanishka's lost
head in Kashmir, Kakababu had rolled several feet
down the side of a steep mountain. In Andaman, he
had swum through shark-infested waters to get to a
forbidden island. None of those had affected him as
much as being cooped up inside this tower. He watched
in silence as his uncle puffed angrily on his pipe.

'I don't understand. I don't understand,' his uncle
burst out after a while. 'Who locked us in? Why? And
you saw a yeti, on top of everything! Are you still sure
that is what it was?'

'Yes, Kakababu.'

'Why didn't I see it? Why? I was the one who needed
to see it!'

Shontu did not know what to say to that. It was
not as if he had wanted to see the yeti. He would have

been perfectly happy to never have seen that enormous black creature.

His uncle checked his watch. 'It's almost six. Probably already dark outside. There'll be no sleep tonight, Shontu. We'll have to keep watch. I'll stay here. You take the binoculars and go sit at the window. Keep an eye out for lights near Kala Patthar. And if the helicopter arrives, perhaps you can signal them too.'

Shontu went upstairs with the binoculars. It was bitterly cold by the window, but he sat next to it for hours, nonetheless. Being rescued was more important than being warm. He came down once to eat a few biscuits and a little cheese, then went back up again. Kakababu sat on his sleeping bag, reading a book. His revolver rested on his thigh.

Shontu's eyes grew tired of looking into the darkness. This was not the darkness of cities. It was a heavy, oppressive darkness that made one forget that light existed. Every time he looked through the binoculars, it felt like the darkness was sitting heavily on his eyes. He kept closing his eyes to relieve the imaginary weight. At some point he simply did not open them again, and fell fast asleep.

Sharp pain woke him up several hours later. Someone was piercing his face with hundreds of very sharp needles. Shontu cried out in agony. The binoculars dropped from his numb hands and began rolling down the stone steps.

'Shontu? What is it?' his uncle called out.

Shontu could not answer. His jaw was frozen in place, and he was shivering uncontrollably. A snowstorm had started while he had been asleep, and the lashing winds had turned his body to ice. Gusts of ice-cold winds blew fistfuls of sleet into the tower. In another few minutes, it would freeze him and his uncle to death! Moving his limbs with difficulty, Shontu tried to shut the window. But the freezing gale had no intention of being kept out. It whipped the shutters back and forth, making it impossible for him to drive the latch home. Finally, after several minutes of struggle, Shontu managed to shove them shut. Then he came down the stairs, barely able to put one foot in front of the other.

'Ka...k...b'bu. Shhhnow...shhtr'm,' he managed, through barely-moving jaws.

Even his unflappable uncle was alarmed. 'Come here, come here quickly!' he urged. Then he began to vigorously massage Shontu's cheeks and jaw with his palms. After several minutes of this, Shontu began to feel his face thaw a little.

'Inside your sleeping bag. Now!' his uncle ordered. Shontu dragged himself over to his bag, and crawled inside. He zipped himself in, keeping only his nose outside.

'One catastrophe on top of another!' his uncle snapped, sounding oddly angry with himself. 'First a yeti, then a lock-in, and now a blizzard. Who knows how long it'll last! Even if they get the helicopter, how will it land in this weather?'

CHAPTER 11

The blizzard raged through the night. The inside of the tower had become increasingly misty with the icy winds seeping in. Despite Shontu's best efforts, there had been a gap between the shutters of the window above. And that was not a bad thing, he thought, though it did turn the tower into an icebox. Had he been able to shut the window completely, Kakababu and he would have suffocated to death.

The minutes dragged along. The night began to feel like an unending nightmare. Shontu had been caught in a blizzard before, but that had only lasted a couple of hours. This one seemed determined to seal them in an icy grave for all eternity. His uncle's voice broke through his dark thoughts.

'Shontu, there's no point keeping yourself awake. Go to bed. I'll stay up and keep watch for the next few hours.'

'Aren't you sleepy?'

'Nah. Besides, I'll need to stay awake for the helicopter. If it comes, that is. And if someone tries to break in ... well, one of us is enough to alert the other. You sleep, now.'

Shontu closed his eyes obediently, but sleep was the last thing on his mind. Knowing he couldn't leave the tower made him desperate to go out. Would the helicopter actually come? Shontu remembered Kakababu saying that the other people—whoever they were—had said they would request a helicopter only if Kakababu asked for one. As far as Shontu could tell, Kakababu had not been able to send the message confirming that he did indeed need one. Even if he had, how could the helicopter have flown in this weather? No, there was no hope of rescue. He and Kakababu were stuck in this freezing tower.

When he woke up, the pale light of early morning had diluted the darkness of the night, even at the bottom of the tower. Kakababu was sitting in the same position as last night. Shontu stretched contentedly. The night's sleep had left him refreshed. He had temporarily forgotten all the horrors of the previous day.

'What's the time, Kakababu?' he asked.

'Eight thirty,' his uncle responded, worriedly. 'You'd better get up. The storm stopped about an hour ago, but the helicopter is still not here. I wonder what's wrong ...'

And just like that, the awfulness of their situation crashed back down upon Shontu. They had literally been left to die. Still, he thought, it would not do to show fear. Instead, he climbed to his feet and tested the door a few times. It was just as immovable as it had been.

'I've made us a flask of tea,' his uncle said. Shontu thought he sounded rather tired. 'Drink some of that with a few biscuits. Then go up and keep watch by the window. I'll try and get some sleep. We have nothing to do now, but wait.'

Shontu ran upstairs to look out of the window even before he had drunk his tea. Everything was calm now, after the blizzard. Fresh snow covered the ground as far as the eye could see. There were no birds here to announce the morning. Instead, weak sunlight fell on the snow and made it glitter. Odd scraps of ice caught the light and shone brightly. In a word, it was beautiful. Who knew such beauty could also be so dangerous?

Shontu came slowly down the stairs. He ate four or five biscuits with his tea, but his body wanted more. Even with him and Kakababu barely eating anything, rations were running out. If the rescuers didn't come by nightfall ...

'I'm keeping the revolver here.' His uncle indicated the side of his sleeping bag after zipping himself in. 'If someone barges in, you can shoot at them, can't you?'

Shontu nodded.

'Good,' his uncle said, then turned in.

Shontu sat staring at the door. It had not even been a full day since they had been locked in, yet it felt like weeks. Is this how prisoners felt in jail? How did they not go mad? To be cooped up all the time, knowing there was no escape ... it was torture! Still, he supposed prisoners had other prisoners to talk to. Here, the blanket of silence made time slow down to a crawl.

In the end, Shontu started writing a letter to his mother. He had last written to her from Syangboche. That was several days ago. After that there had been no postal offices to drop letters into. Still, it was comforting to write to her, though he knew that his mother may never receive the letter. Perhaps another group of mountaineers would come here in the future, and take his last letter back down with them and post it. One could hope, after all. Swallowing his fear, he prepared to put down his final thoughts to his mother.

The letter had barely reached the halfway mark when there was a sudden single blow on the door. Shontu's heart jumped to his throat. The pen dropped to the floor and rolled away.

The blow boomed again. And again.

Shontu looked at Kakababu. He was still sleeping. He must have been utterly exhausted to be able to sleep through this. Shontu did not wake him. Instead, he quietly picked up the revolver.

Suddenly, a perfectly normal human voice shouted, 'Is there anyone inside this tower?'

Shontu almost collapsed in relief. This must be the rescue team.

'Yes, we are here!' he bellowed back, body weak with relief.

'What's your code?' the voice outside wanted to know.

'Wait, please give us a moment!' Shontu begged. He didn't know of any codes. 'My uncle will know, please let me wake him up!'

Kakababu was already sitting up in his sleeping bag. 'What is it?' he asked, groggily.

'People outside, Kakababu! Just arrived. They're asking for a code.'

Kakababu hobbled right up to the door. He had taken his revolver back from Shontu. Pointing it at the door, he called, 'Who is it?'

'Is that Mr Roychoudhuri?' the voice called back.

'Yes. Peak 114. Is that base? Please open this door.'

Loud booms began on the other side. Kakababu swiftly caught Shontu by the collar of his coat and pulled him back. 'They're shooting the planks off!' he exclaimed. 'Stand back, stand back!' After a few seconds he said, almost to himself, 'I wonder how they came here. Didn't hear a helicopter ...'

Neither had he, Shontu realized. He had been so engrossed in writing a final goodbye to his mother that he had not even noticed the loud noise of a descending copter.

In a few seconds, the shooting stopped. People were now pushing the door from the other side, trying to open it. Shontu remembered that he had latched the door from the inside. He ran and pulled the latch down. Immediately, two men in uniform pushed it open and ran inside. One of them was clearly in the service of the Indian government. The other most likely served the government of Nepal. They were both carrying impressive-looking firearms. The man wearing the Nepalese uniform spoke first.

'What happened here, Mr Roychoudhuri?'

'We were boarded into this tower,' Kakababu responded in English. 'Someone clearly wanted us dead.'

Shontu didn't wait to hear the rest of the conversation. He ran out into the snow outside. Free, free, free! He was free! He rolled about in the snow a few times, then began dancing in sheer exhilaration. The helicopter had landed a short distance away from the tower. Shontu could just about make out a Nepalese gentleman at the controls.

Meanwhile, inside, the officers were introducing themselves to Kakababu. The Nepalese officer was Jung Bahadur Rana, and the Indian officer was Gurudutt Varma. Both of them shook Kakababu warmly by the hand.

'We are glad we made it before serious harm could come to you, Mr Roychoudhuri,' Rana said. 'Now, if you could tell us what happened ...'

'It's a long story. You've arrived at the very nick of time. Let's sit down first.'

'Who's the man outside?' Varma interjected.

'Outside?'

'Oh, didn't you know? ... Was he one of the people sent to board the door up, then? Poor chap, to have collapsed right outside ...'

'Just a minute! Who is this man? No, wait. Let's go outside ... I need to see this for myself.'

Outside the tower, between its now-open door and the wall behind it, lay the corpse of a man. He looked to be in his mid-thirties, and was likely Chinese. And he was very, very dead. Kakababu gently turned the man over. There were no wounds on either side of the body, and no blood. How had the man died?

Rana was looking at the man in sympathy. 'Poor man. He had probably come to seek shelter at the tower. Mr Roychoudhuri, the beating on the door was probably him trying to get in.'

'Then who hammered these boards on the door?' Varma asked, sceptically.

Rana looked conflicted. 'Perhaps this man had come to board the door up, but was unable to return in the blizzard?'

'That makes no sense. Why would a Chinese man come to board up the tower? What would he get out of it?'

As the two argued, Kakababu knelt by the man, trying to bend his knees and elbows. Neither could be moved. The man was as stiff as a board. A look of surprise settled on Kakababu's normally unreadable face.

'This is strange. Very strange,' he muttered.

Rana and Varma heard him. 'What is strange?' they asked in unison.

'We went inside the tower yesterday afternoon. The door was boarded a little later. It's morning now – not even 24 hours later. But this man has been dead for much longer than that. In fact, unless my grasp of forensics is completely wrong, I would say that he has been dead for longer than 48 hours.'

'48 hours! Then you didn't see him alive at all?'

'Not just me. Till last afternoon the luggage-bearers and Sherpas were with us. None of us saw anyone who wasn't part of our group. Look at this place – plain ground as far as the eye can see. If there was someone else around, we would have seen them. The nooks and crannies are not big enough to hide a man.'

'This is very strange, Mr Roychoudhuri. Is there any chance you might be wrong?'

Kakababu shrugged. 'It's possible. I won't pretend to know how this man came here, or why. But I am not wrong about the time of death. This man died at least two days ago. Could be earlier than that, but definitely not sooner.'

Further ahead, Shontu had been admiring the helicopter. It was their way out of this horrible, scary, lonely place! He turned around, hoping to ask either Rana or Varma if he could take a closer look, but what he saw brought him up short. His uncle and the two officers were outside the tower's door, crouching down to look at something right outside the walls. Curious, he walked up to them. There, in between the three men, lay a fourth. He was dead. And his dead eyes looked straight at Shontu.

'Kakababu, who is this?' he asked in a dry, frightened voice.

'That's what we're trying to work out, too,' his uncle answered, puzzled.

CHAPTER 12

Having a corpse thrust unexpectedly at his face made Shontu feel physically ill. He turned away from the dead man's eyes and stared resolutely at the glittering snow. But the face was now burned into his brain. As much as Shontu did not want to look at him, he wanted to know how a dead man had suddenly appeared outside the tower while he and Kakababu had been locked inside. He decided to eavesdrop on the adult conversation, while still looking firmly away.

'I am curious about this man,' his uncle was saying. 'But we have a lot of work to do. We can't stand around trying to solve the mystery of his death.'

'Let's bury him here,' Varma proposed. 'The Chinese bury their dead, they don't cremate.'

'Then let's try to quickly dig a grave. Shontu, get the spade.'

'Wait,' Rana said. 'This man is probably a Chinese national. Look at the coat he's wearing. We don't get coats like this in Nepal. The government is bound to investigate the death of a foreign national on its soil. We will have to send the corpse for a post-mortem.'

'You mean we have to ferry this man to Kathmandu?' Varma asked.

'Yes.'

'Do you have records of a Chinese trekking or mountaineering team passing this area recently?' Kakababu asked.

'Not that I know of,' Varma said.

'The last Chinese Everest expedition was two-and-a-half, maybe three years ago,' Rana said. 'We have no reports of anyone being lost. I do know they lost two of their members, but that was an accident near Camp Four. But Camp Four is very far from here. Much further ahead.'

'Even if we assume that one of those two survived the accident, and that this is him, how on earth did he stay alive at these altitudes for three years? No, that does not make sense.'

'It's possible that he died back then, but was buried under the snow. Bodies are preserved extremely well at these altitudes, especially if buried.'

'And then a yeti dug him up, carried him from Camp Four to here, and chucked him at our door for a laugh!' Kakababu mocked. 'Yes, that sounds plausible. Tell me another one!'

Varma looked mildly affronted. 'Mr Roychoudhuri, you seem to think yetis are a joke. But if you're such an unbeliever, why are you carrying one of their teeth around with you?'

Kakababu did not respond. Instead, he stood up and moved away from the body. 'Do whatever you need to do,' he said. 'We've lost enough time as it is.'

Rana and Varma carried the man's corpse to the helicopter. Shontu helped them as much as he could. Kakababu followed behind.

'It's a pity we have to send the helicopter away,' he said. 'It would have been useful to have a helicopter at hand.'

'Just a couple of hours, and it will be back,' Rana assured him. 'We're sending this man to Syangboche, not Kathmandu. The office at Syangboche will arrange for further transport.'

'Are you carrying rations, by any chance? If you are, then let's unload them before the copter leaves. We have been surviving on biscuits since last afternoon. Look at my nephew, poor boy's ravenous.'

'Oh yes, we're carrying a lot of supplies,' Rana reassured him. 'But let me propose something, Mr Roychoudhuri. This helicopter is big enough to safely carry all of us back to the base of operations. Why don't we all pack up and go back together?'

'You must be mad, Mr Rana!' Kakababu sounded appalled.

'Why is that, Mr Roychoudhuri?'

'"Why"? Because we have an enormous mystery to solve here, that is why! How could you think of abandoning a mission at the first sight of danger? If anything, it is proof that we are moving in the right direction. Why bother studying for years, why bother

getting a job, why bother mounting an expedition —
if we abandon it all at the first sign of trouble? Why
be human at all! No, Mr Rana, you two can leave if
you like. I am staying here till I have the answers
I need.'

As much as Shontu wanted to leave the cursed
tower, his uncle's anger made his heart swell with
pride. Kakababu was not a coward. No sir, he was not!
Even when armed government officers balked, his
uncle stood firm!

'Rana, you clearly don't know Mr Roychoudhuri,'
Varma said. 'He is famous for being unbelievably
stubborn in the face of overwhelming danger. Would
you believe it if I told you that he went to the Jarawa
islands alone? It's protected territory — the government
does not allow anyone to even go near it. But Mr
Roychoudhuri went all the way to their village. You
won't convince him to abandon a mission.'

'But what *is* his mission? I have not been briefed on
that at all!'

'I'm happy to tell you all about it,' Kakababu cut in.
'But first, the food.'

There was a sheet of tarpaulin at the back of the
helicopter. Kakababu made them spread it out on the
snow and put the food on it, like a mountaintop picnic.
He was loath to go back inside the tower after being
locked in it for almost a day. Rana and Varma had
brought a lot of food with them. Much to his delight,
Shontu noticed that none of it was standard rations.
There were cooked sausages, cooked burger-patties,
thick-cut sandwiches, and flasks of hot coffee.

Sitting out in the snow was surprisingly pleasant. There was no trace of last night's blizzard in the morning sky. The sun was up in all its glory, raising the temperature considerably. Rana gave a few instructions to the other man in the helicopter. The man nodded and slid into the pilot's seat. After a few minutes, the helicopter took off with the corpse of the Chinese man. Rana came back and joined the group on the tarpaulin.

'Let us say that yetis are real,' he began placatingly. 'In that case, isn't it wiser to go back now and return with reinforcements? I mean, if we intend to confront them, then what chance do the three of us stand against an enormous mythical creature?'

At the word "three", Shontu frowned at the officer.

'I apologize, I apologize!' Rana said cheerfully. 'I meant "the four of us", of course. This young man is both brave and resourceful! We're proud to have him with us. But really, Mr Roychoudhuri, four is not a hopeful number. Not in these circumstances.'

'First let's talk about the yetis,' Kakababu said. 'We have seen the footprints. My nephew says he has seen an actual yeti. The luggage-bearers and Sherpas said the same. That was why they ran away, in fact. So, if we ...'

'Just a minute, Mr Roychoudhuri,' Varma interjected. 'Could the kulis and Sherpas not have come back to lock you in the tower?'

Shontu frowned again. Why did everyone want to pin this on Mingma and his people? 'That's not possible,' he said shortly.

'I don't think so,' Kakababu agreed. 'The team had left long before the hammering began.'

'But they could have come back.'

'I suppose, but why? How would freezing us to death benefit them in any way?'

'Oh, it would benefit them greatly! The Nepal government has charged them with following your every command. If you returned and disclosed their desertion, they would get into a lot of trouble. Much easier to kill you, and spread the word that the expedition had to be abandoned because of your unfortunate death. No?'

'Mingma really liked us. We had become friends,' Shontu interrupted. 'He would never do that. Never.'

Rana nodded. 'Sherpas are known for their steadfastness and integrity. They would never do something like that, nor allow the others to do it.'

'Besides,' Kakababu said, 'if the Sherpas and bearers locked us in, then who was the Chinese man? How does he fit into that explanation?'

'Well …' Rana dithered. Then he turned towards Shontu. 'Did you really see the yeti?'

'Yes.'

As one, Rana and Varma turned towards the Kala Patthar. It was far, but from the officers' expression, not far enough.

'To go back to what I was saying,' Kakababu said a little loudly, 'even if the yeti exists, look at how prepared we already are. Both of you are carrying light machine guns and ammunition. I have my revolver.

What does the yeti have? Teeth and claws. We have nothing to be afraid of. Four people are enough for this mission. Now, if you posit that yetis are smarter than humans, then it's a different matter. I'd actually be very interested in seeing if that's true. They have, after all, successfully evaded capture for decades. There aren't even reliable pictures of them. But my point is, even if yetis are clever, we are adequately prepared. The mission can safely continue without reinforcements.'

'The yeti is your mission, then? You want to see if they're real?'

'Yes ... and no. You're forgetting Kane Shipton's disappearance. He, too, had seen a yeti. At least that's what he wrote in his diary. Then he disappeared. If yetis are indeed intelligent creatures, then one might argue that they have kidnapped him. But *how* did they do it? How did he disappear so abruptly? Why was no trace of him ever found? Did the yetis eat him, bones and all?'

'Well ... we don't know what happened to him, but it is true that he disappeared from this area. We had spent a lot of resources looking for him.'

'Right. I want to see if there's a connection between his disappearance, and the myth of the yeti.'

'Is that why you're carrying that tooth?' Varma asked suddenly. 'But what if that makes you disappear, too?'

For the first time in two days, Shontu saw his uncle smile. 'That would be just fine, Mr Varma. Becoming invisible is a skill I've always wanted to learn.'

'Let's discuss this seriously,' Rana cut in sharply. 'What do you plan to do now?'

'Why don't all four of us walk towards Kala Patthar?'

'Isn't it better to wait for the helicopter to return?'

'What's the point? The helicopter won't be useful in a ground survey. We'll only have use of it later. If you don't want to go all the way, then let us at least walk up to the place where Shontu saw the yeti. We have several hours of daylight left.'

'All right then,' Varma said, getting up. 'If we must go, then let's start now.'

'Yes, let's,' Kakababu said, slowly getting to his feet. 'Incidentally, did you know that no other group since Shipton's has passed this base yet? A Japanese group attempted the climb recently, but nearly all of them fell mysteriously ill as soon as they arrived here. Interesting, don't you think?'

This was directed at Rana, but Rana was looking at the remains of their snowy picnic. 'Mr Roychoudhuri, shall we leave the food and coffee out in the open? Or should we take it inside?'

'Leave it out,' Kakababu said dismissively. 'It's not like there are thieves or scavengers here. Unless yetis are partial to coffee and sandwiches, eh?'

A sudden movement caught the corner of Shontu's eye. 'Kakababu! Look!' he shouted.

All three men instantly turned around. There, along the far road that led down to Thyangboche, a figure in blue was running towards them. Rana and

Varma's firearms swung up, pointed straight at the figure. Kakababu whipped out his revolver, too.

'No!' Shontu shouted in panic. How could they not see? 'It's a friend! Don't shoot!'

The man in blue raised his arms above his head as he sped towards them. He was not running, exactly, but jumping from point to point to avoid falling into loose snow. Despite Shontu's pleas, Rana and Varma kept their guns pointed at him.

The man came closer. Now people could make out his face. Kakababu's eyebrows went up. 'Arre! It's one of our Sherpas, Mingma!'

'I recognized him right away,' Shontu said. 'That's why I asked you not to shoot.'

Mingma went down on his knees in front of the group. He brought his palms together and raised them to his chest. 'Sa'ab!'

'What is it?' Kakababu asked sternly. 'You were determined to abandon us. Why are you back? Had an accident on the way down?'

'No, sa'ab. I came to apologize. I was scared when we left, I wanted to get away from here. But then I kept thinking of you two. We left you after I gave you my word that I would always stay with you ... my shame brought me back, sa'ab! I have always been taught that we do not go back on our word, yet there I was, breaking my promise! Shame on me, shame on me!'

'Tell us the truth!' Rana snapped at the man in his own language. 'If there's a hidden reason behind your return ...'

'I don't have time for this drama,' Kakababu interrupted shortly. 'Are you here to stay with us, or do you intend to go back again? You can do whichever you like – it makes no difference to me.'

'I won't move from your side, sa'ab,' Mingma swore resolutely. 'When I left, my heart was screaming at me, "You worthless man! How could you abandon your charges? An old Bengali with a limp could stay back, and you ran away? Is this what a Sherpa does? Coward!" Then I told myself ...'

'Never mind what you told yourself,' Kakababu cut in irritably. 'Daylight is precious. Let's not waste any more hours of it than we have to. Let's start, gentlemen.'

Despite his protests, Mingma took Kakababu's haversack from him.

'Uncle sa'ab, if you have trouble walking, I can take you on my back too,' he offered.

'You're talking too much again, Mingma,' Kakababu snapped. 'Now lead the way.'

Shontu was thrilled to have Mingma back. The cheerful, chatty, and very capable Sherpa made trekking through this treacherous terrain look easy. When Mingma had left with the others last afternoon, Shontu had been certain that he would be back by nightfall. His friend was too brave and honourable to abandon them. Mingma had returned a few hours later than he had expected, but Shontu was still happy to have been proven right.

'How far down did you go last night, Mingma-bhai?' he asked.

'Let's not talk about that, Shontu sa'ab. I'm so ashamed. Were you all right during the night?'

'You wouldn't believe what happened, Mingma-bhai! Someone came and locked us into the tower!'

'What? Lock you in? But ... how?'

'They used beaten sheets of iron to board the doors,' Rana said from behind them. 'Are you sure your men did not return to do that?'

'My men?' Mingma asked in genuine astonishment. 'Why on earth would we come back to yeti-territory to board someone in?'

'Would have been convenient to have your employers dead, wouldn't it?' Rana said blandly, watching Mingma closely for his reaction. 'After all, dead employers do not report dereliction of duty.'

Horror at the idea radiated from Mingma's features. 'I swear upon Pashupatinath ji, sa'ab! Sherpas are not traitors — not like *that*! Besides, we were very, very far away last night.'

'Did you really see a yeti?' Varma asked, quickly changing the subject.

'I was sure I did, but now ... who knows? But we definitely did see *something*. A large animal, covered in black fur. That much I am sure of.'

'Can you show us where you saw it? Now?'

'Of course.'

'Then let's head to the spot. What do you say, Mr Roychoudhuri?'

Once again, Kakababu had dropped a little behind the group.

'Yes, good idea,' he called back. 'You go on, I'll follow at my own pace.'

'We'll stop at intervals for you,' Varma offered.

'No, there's no need. You go ahead at your own speed. I'll catch up with you eventually. You know what they say about the slow and steady, Mr Varma. I'll win the race, haha.'

'All right then. We'll see you at the spot.'

The group went ahead. Kakababu let out a breath and slowed down further. The fluffy snow from the blizzard had settled all over the land. It made his crutch sink far deeper than he was comfortable with. At each step, he had to work much harder to pull the crutch out of its snowy hole. Still, he refused to ask for help. That was not how he dealt with problems.

The glare of the sun had melted little bits of snow here and there, creating mushy puddles. Rana slipped and fell once. Varma fell almost immediately after. But Kakababu did not fall – not once. Being disabled had taught him to be extra cautious, and never take his safety for granted. He tested the snow in front of him for hidden puddles or ice before very carefully placing his crutch in it.

Shontu was a lot less careful. But he was also younger and lighter, and faster on his feet than the older men. He almost flew ahead of them, easily keeping pace with Mingma. The blizzard of the night before had cleared the skies completely, and the air was warm and crisp. If they managed to reach there before the weather changed, he would see the Everest again! Before he came to the mountains, Shontu had not understood the thrill of seeing the same sight over and over again. But now he did. Though he had seen the Everest twice already—even taken pictures of it with his camera—his whole body shook in anticipation of seeing it again.

Suddenly, Mingma grasped his shoulder from behind.

'Shontu sa'ab,' he whispered. 'Don't run ahead like that! Let those officer sahibs go first.'

'Why?'

'Well, what if the yeti is waiting for us? Let them face it first!'

Shontu felt laughter bubbling up from his belly at the idea, but then he remembered the enormous creature that he had seen. The laughter died in his throat. After last night's troubles, he had forgotten how terrifying the yeti had been. But every bit of that terror came rushing back now.

'We have two machine guns,' he forced himself to say. 'What can the yeti do against machine guns?'

'Yetis can make us disappear,' Mingma whispered, pulling him back further.

'That's nonsense!' Shontu said. But his voice wobbled.

'I didn't believe it either, Shontu sa'ab, but we both saw it yesterday, didn't we? Huge furry creature, in front of our eyes one second and gone the next! Right?'

Shontu nodded. This was, in fact, what had happened. He had turned his face away in terror for a few seconds, and when he had turned back, the creature had disappeared. Where could it have gone in a few seconds? Mingma must be right. But how could a living creature just *vanish*?

Seeing Shontu waver, Mingma tightened his grip on his shoulder. Rana and Varma were several paces behind them. Heavier than Shontu and a lot less experienced than Mingma, they had become extra cautious after falling hard on hidden ice. Besides, their firearms were "light" only in name; in actual fact they weighed quite a bit. So Mingma held on to Shontu till both Varma and Rana caught up with them.

'Is this where you saw the yeti?' Varma asked, looking around.

'No, that's much further ahead,' Shontu replied. His voice, he was happy to see, was steady again.

'Then why did you stop? Come on, let's go. The moment we see the yeti, I'm going to shoot at it, no questions asked! If we manage to catch an injured or even a dead yeti —can you imagine the uproar? We'll be on every newspaper across the world! Let's go!'

Mingma relaxed his hold on Shontu. He and Shontu began walking again, taking care to stay a few steps behind the two officers.

'I am beginning to believe in the yeti,' Rana said conversationally. 'Shontu is a bright lad. If he says he saw the creature ... I mean, the Sherpas and the bearers might be a superstitious lot, but ...'

'Unless he saw a bear or something like it,' Varma said.

'There are no bears here,' Rana said, firmly. 'Hundreds of mountaineers have gone past this point, no one has ever seen a bear before.'

'Well, no one has ever seen a yeti before either.'

'Kane Shipton has. He wrote about it in his diary. Isn't that what Mr Roychoudhuri said? Personally, I think an unknown large animal from around Tibet has somehow made its way here. That's what everyone saw.'

'Kakababu saw footprints, too,' Shontu chimed in. 'They were exactly like human feet. Only they had four toes.'

'Well, there is that,' Varma conceded.

'Mr Varma, sir, how do you speak such good Bengali?' Shontu asked. 'I heard you talking to Kakababu ...'

Varma grinned. 'I went to school and college in Calcutta. Stayed at the Hardinge Boy's Hostel after my family moved. You live in Bhawanipur, don't you? I know that area well, too.'

'I know some Bengali, too,' Rana said, smiling. 'I went to North Point School in Darjeeling. We had several Bengali boys in our year. I've stayed with them on holidays, too.'

'Sahib, look!' Mingma suddenly exclaimed.

All three jumped. Mingma had gone a little ahead, and was pointing at the snow. They scrambled to reach him.

There, a few feet in front of Mingma, was a giant footprint.

Varma and Rana hurried up to it and knelt into the snow. Both of them began examining it closely. Shontu turned around to call Kakababu, but Kakababu had fallen back quite a bit.

'Just one print? This must have happened this morning,' Varma said. 'If it happened before the blizzard then the new snow would have covered it up.'

'Let's wait here for Mr Roychoudhuri to catch up. He will want to examine this,' Rana said. 'How far back is he?'

All of them turned back to look.

'Arre! Where is Mr Roychoudhuri? How far back did he fall?' Rana asked, surprised.

'Perhaps he's resting somewhere,' Varma supplied, turning back to examine the print.

'Rest where?' Shontu demanded. 'There are no rocks or stones to sit on. Besides, it's been only a short while since we last saw Kakababu – he should still be visible, even at a distance.'

'Are you saying he fell? Good lord, what if he has hurt himself? Rana, we must go back and look.'

Rana was not really listening. 'Why is there only one footprint?' he asked, almost to himself. Shontu saw that he was clutching his firearm hard, and looking suspiciously about.

Mingma had also been looking around. Now he cupped his mouth and shouted, 'Uncle sa'ab! Uncle sa'ab!'

There was no answer.

'I'll run back and look for him, you can stay here,' Shontu offered.

'Don't go alone,' Varma said. 'Take Mingma with you. We will stay here, next to the print. Call us if you need help.'

Shontu began retracing his steps. He was worried. Unlike Rana and Varma, he had been keeping an eye on his uncle. Kakababu had kept a stable distance of about two hundred yards between them, and was progressing steadily. How had he suddenly disappeared?

After walking back a few metres, his blood suddenly froze. 'Mingma!' he called. It was almost a wail.

Alarmed, Mingma ran up to him. 'What is it, Shontu sa'ab?'

Shontu could not speak. He simply pointed at the ground. There, on the fresh white snow, lay one of Kakababu's crutches. And a patch of fresh blood.

CHAPTER 14

Varma's face was the picture of fearful astonishment. 'This ... I mean, how ... where did Mr Roychoudhuri *go*?' he whispered.

'This is strange. Very strange!' Rana agreed. 'He was right behind us. I had looked back once or twice to check. Could he have gone back to the tower?'

'How's that possible?' Varma asked sharply. 'Do you think he had suddenly developed the ability to run? Besides, why would he leave without speaking to us?' Then he stared intently at the lone crutch, as if willing it to speak.

'It's true, he can't walk without both crutches,' Rana conceded. 'But then *where* ... and also, whose blood is that? His? This is very baffling.'

Shontu was also staring at the crutch and patch of blood. He was in shock. Dimly, he realized that his whole body was shaking, and that he couldn't get words out of his mouth.

Mingma broke the spell. Cupping his hands around his mouth again, he screamed, 'Uncle sa'ab! Uncle sa'ab!'

Kakababu did not answer. But the shout shattered the oppressive silence of the frozen mountaintop. Mingma's alarmed cry began bouncing off the surrounding mountains and coming back to them. 'Uncle sa'ab!' echoed the nearest mountain. 'Uncle sa'ab!' answered the peak on the other side. And on and on it echoed, getting fainter as it moved away. Shontu shivered harder. But Mingma was undeterred. He kept shouting for Kakababu, each call more desperate than the last.

In the end, Rana put an end to it. 'That's enough. Mr Roychoudhuri didn't come here to play hide and seek. Either he cannot hear us, or he cannot respond.'

'Look,' Varma began, uncomfortably. 'The truth is, I've also heard rumours about yetis and their ability to vanish with lone humans. I'm not saying that's what happened, but … I mean, if it was a yeti who did this …'

Rana stared at Varma in disbelief. 'Yeti? Now *you* believe in yetis, too?'

'What other explanation can you think of for this?' Varma pointed at the crutch. 'This is why I had told Mr Roychoudhuri to leave now and come back with a larger group. Being alone in the mountains ... Wait! What is that man doing?'

Tired of conversation, Mingma had gone down to the ground on his belly. When Varma noticed him, he had been crawling slowly towards the crutch and the patch of blood.

'He's checking to see if there is a crevice in the ground,' Rana replied, watching Mingma closely. 'If there is even a shallow one, Mr Roychoudhuri could have slipped into it.'

Varma shuddered and almost jumped back in response. Then he visibly shook himself. 'There aren't any crevices here,' he said. 'We've followed the same path. We would have fallen in first.'

'Sometimes there are small crevices. Easy to overstep, but if one foot goes in ... Mingma is right to lie down. The full body won't go in, but he'll find it if it is there.'

'Blood!' Shontu gasped. He had managed to finally wrest control of his voice from his shivering body. 'Why will there be blood? Falling on snow doesn't cut you open!'

'Good point! Why is there blood?' Varma demanded.

Mingma, meanwhile, had reached the crutch. He picked it up gingerly, then much more firmly. Then he began to tap on the ground close by. A little later, he moved forward to the bloodstain and tested the ground around it. After a minute or so, he stood up, disappointed. 'No kirvaas here, sa'ab,' he said in Hindi.

'Then where did he *go*?' Rana demanded, once again looking around.

'Look, Rana, I think we should head back to the tower,' Varma said. 'I'm just as rational as the next man, but something about this place is bothering me.'

'And leave Mr Roychoudhuri behind?' Rana asked. 'My department has been specially requested by the Government of India to provide protection to him at all times.'

'How do you propose to find him in this?' Varma demanded, waving his hand at the vast expanse of snow. 'There's nothing here that could shelter him. And it's not like he could have run away from us — not with one crutch lying on the ground. If we can't even work out what happened to him, how can we be of assistance?'

'If we sit and think for a while, I'm sure we will come up with something. As you said, he could not have run away. Which means that he is here somewhere, close by. The only question is, where?'

'Look, Rana, let me be honest with you. You know that line from Shakespeare: "There are more things in heaven and earth, Horatio, than are dreamt of in your philosophy"? There is something mysterious about this place. Don't you feel it? Whatever may have happened to Mr Roychoudhuri, I don't think we can hope to understand it by just sitting here.'

'You really believe the local mumbo-jumbo, don't you?' Rana asked, half in surprise and half in disappointment.

'Well, when you're surrounded by the footprints of enormous beasts and disappearing men, you have to adjust your worldview!' Varma snapped back. Then he dropped to his knees in the snow, brought his joined palms to his chest, closed his eyes, and began muttering what sounded like prayers. Half a minute later, he climbed back to his feet.

'I'm terribly cold,' he said, in a voice that brooked no argument. 'I cannot physically stay out any longer. We are going back to the tower.'

Rana seemed taken aback by his sudden change in behaviour. 'But ... that would mean abandoning our charge ...' he tried.

'We might find him on our way back. Perhaps he had left something at the tower and had gone back to get it. Now let's move!' Varma urged, looking around and suppressing a shudder.

'That's ridiculous! I kept looking back to keep an eye on him. He hadn't turned around.'

'Can we agree that none of us saw him walk past us? Good. Then it follows that he must be somewhere behind us. So why can't we go back instead of standing here in the cold? My legs are beginning to freeze. If I don't get back to the tower I might actually die, and then you will have *two* corpses on your hands!'

'Sir, can I say something?' Shontu interjected, looking at Rana.

'Yes?'

'Let's go back to the tower. We can all talk once we're warm,' Varma insisted.

'I had fallen into a crevice somewhere here. Mingma had pulled me out.'

'That's right, sa'ab,' Mingma nodded eagerly.

'I had gone quite deep into the snow. And then something odd had happened. My feet had landed on something hard. Back then I had assumed it was rock, but now that I think about it, I'm fairly certain it was a sheet of iron.

'What?' Varma and Rana exclaimed in unison.

'An iron sheet, sir. I am sure of it.'

'A sheet of iron beneath the snow?' Varma looked at Shontu like he had lost his mind.

'How could you tell?' Rana asked. 'It was rocks, obviously, but what made you think it could be metal?'

'It felt different, sir. Metal and rocks feel different. This was definitely metal.'

'Did the metal make a noise?' Varma asked. 'A heavy body falling on metal should make a noise.'

'No, it didn't,' Shontu conceded.

'Where was this crevice?' Rana asked.

'Only a little further. Mingma had tied a red handkerchief next to it as a warning.'

Varma breathed out in exasperation. 'Look, even if we concede that someone once left a sheet of metal here, what does it prove? Why are we wasting time talking about it when Mr Roychoudhuri could well be injured somewhere along the way back?'

Shontu took a deep breath. 'Kakababu told me that Kane Shipton had disappeared from here. Almost this exact area. And now Kakababu is gone. I think the two might be connected. We shouldn't go back, we should look here.'

Varma threw his hands up. 'Now we're just clutching at straws! Shipton was a foreign national who disappeared in Nepal. The Government of India has no jurisdiction over his disappearance. Mr Roychoudhuri is here to research the myth of the yeti. He clearly said so in his application to the government. I personally have a theory about Shipton. I'll tell you on the way back.'

Rana, however, was focused on the younger man. 'What are you actually trying to say, Shontu?'

'I am saying that we should dig around the patch of blood. There is no way Kakababu could have made his way back with one crutch.'

'But why?' Varma demanded. 'I understand your urge to do whatever it takes, but Mingma just examined that spot. The ice there is solid, there are no crevices. Why are we so keen to freeze to death when we know there's nothing to find?'

'If you're that bothered by the cold, then you can head back,' Rana finally snapped. 'I think Shontu has a point. We'll dig at the spot.'

'Have you seen the sky?' Varma asked, nodding upwards.

Everybody looked up. During their debate, the morning's bright sunlight had ebbed. Black clouds had gathered at the edge of the sky, and were steadily advancing upon them.

'It's going to start snowing soon,' Varma pointed out. 'We need to seek shelter as soon as we can.'

'I'll be quick about it, sa'ab,' Mingma assured him. Then, without waiting for further permission, he began shovelling the snow at the patch of blood. Despite his worries, Shontu marvelled at his skill. Mingma was lithe and strong, and very adept. Within minutes, he had dug quite deep into the snow.

Rana and Varma had inched closer as Mingma had dug deeper. Suddenly, the shovel bounced back with a clang. Shontu's heart jumped in his chest. Renewed, Mingma went back to work at double the pace. Even in the freezing cold, sweat glistened on his face. His breathing became laboured. After five or six more scoops of the shovel, he abruptly stopped. He looked up, wiping sweat from his forehead with his left hand. Disappointment was written all over his face.

'Stone, Shontu sa'ab. Stone. Not iron.'

Then he held up a piece of rock he had just broken off.

'Like I said: a waste of time,' Varma said, turning away. 'Now let's go. We've lost several precious minutes. I only hope we can outwalk the storm.'

'So do I,' Rana sighed. He followed Varma.

Mingma climbed out of the hole. He was the only one who felt the depth of Shontu's disappointment. 'Come on, Shontu sa'ab,' he said, taking Shontu's arm. 'We have to go back.'

Shontu bit his lip. He could not cry in front of these strangers, but walking away felt like abandoning a helpless Kakababu in this very dangerous terrain. On the other hand, Varma was right. They should not be in this open, shelterless land when the storm broke.

The sky became progressively darker as they walked.

'The other trouble with the storm is that it will not let the helicopter fly,' Varma said conversationally. 'Do you realize what that means? Spending the night in that godforsaken tower! Can you imagine staying there after everything that has happened? That's why I was hurrying everyone along.'

No one responded. Shontu could barely put one foot in front of the other. Finally, after forty minutes of trudging through the snow, they reached the tower. Mingma ran ahead to look inside.

'No sa'ab, uncle sa'ab is not here!' he called out.

Rana's face fell. 'That's our last hope gone.'

Just then, a rhythmic rat-a-tat filled the air. The helicopter was coming back. Varma brightened.

'Thank goodness! This means we can outfly the storm. Let's pack up and go.'

'And leave Kakababu behind?' Shontu asked sharply.

'I can see you think I'm a coward, but young man, think of the situation,' Varma said. 'The Government of India has to be informed of Mr Roychoudhuri's disappearance immediately. We can't do that from here. Something's happening here that is not quite human. I know how to fight a visible enemy, but not one that can make a man disappear into thin air. We need to return right away, so that we can come back quickly with a bigger task force.'

'You're not wrong,' Rana said thoughtfully. 'Yes, we need to leave. The storm will be here soon. Let's pack the essentials and go.'

'No!'

Both Rana and Varma looked at Shontu, surprised at the abrupt outburst.

'Do you mean you don't want to go?' Varma asked.

'I mean I won't,' Shontu confirmed, mulishly. He stepped swiftly away from the officers' reach, lest they try to pull him along.

Rana and Varma both reasoned and pled with him for several minutes. But Shontu stuck to his guns. He would stay alone in the tower. He wasn't putting anyone in danger, so what was Rana and Varma's problem? They did say a task force would be coming soon. Why could Shontu not wait here for them? Where was the harm?

'He's lost his mind!' Varma finally said in exasperation. 'Staying alone at these altitudes! After everything that has happened!'

'I'll stay with Shontu sa'ab,' Mingma finally offered.

And just like that, Rana and Varma agreed. It was almost like they were looking for an excuse to leave. Leaving behind rations for Shontu and Mingma, they boarded the helicopter. Rana reminded them several times to stay inside, and keep the door latched from within. He promised to return the next morning. Then, with a deafening roar, the copter took off into the darkened sky. Shontu and Mingma stood outside the large iron doors, watching their sole chance at safety flying away.

CHAPTER 15

Kakababu opened his eyes to a translucent darkness.

At first, he thought that it was night, and that he was outside on the snow. Then he felt around. Against all probability, he was lying on a raised stone slab. Which meant, for one, that he was indoors. But where? Had someone brought him here after he had lost consciousness? Who? And where was Shontu? Or Rana and Varma, for that matter?

Then, like a flash, he remembered how he had lost consciousness. It had not been an accident. Someone had quietly come up behind him and struck him on the back of his head. On reflex, he reached for the spot and felt it. It was sticky with blood. He had a thumping headache, too.

After a few seconds' hesitation, Kakababu sat up. His captors, whoever they were, had not thought to tie him up. Then he felt inside his pockets, and nearly whistled in surprise. They had also left his revolver with him! Who *were* these people? Then he shook himself. It was best not to look a gift horse in the mouth. He should explore his surroundings while he still could. Where were his crutches? He reached out and felt the stone slab around him once again.

No crutches.

That was odd. Why would these people take his crutches away, but leave his revolver with him? Did they not have time to check his pockets? Or did they know how helpless he'd be without his crutches? It was certainly much more than he would be without his revolver. Slightly stymied, Kakababu waited till his eyes adjusted to the darkness. Then he looked around more closely. There were no stars visible anywhere. Which meant that the building had no windows ... or that the building was, in fact, a cave. There was a strange sort of incandescence in the distance, but everything around him was in darkness.

Then he heard voices. Faint, but definitely human voices. They sounded tinny and unnatural, as if they were coming from a machine or a transmitter. Kakababu shook his head, as if to dismiss the idea. Why would there be transmitters in a cave in the middle of nowhere? Wait a minute — could all of this be a dream? Had he actually passed-out on the snow, and was merely dreaming of being inside a cave? Concerned, Kakababu shook his head again to wake himself up. Immediately, blinding pain stabbed behind his eyes. All right, so he was not asleep. But it was probably best to pretend he was, and stay absolutely still till the pain subsided.

For the next several minutes, Kakababu stayed as he was, and tried to relax his muscles. After the pain ebbed a little, he once again cast about inside the pockets of his overcoat. His medicine should be in one of them. After a minute, he found it in the top right pocket and extracted a tablet. It was hard to swallow large tablets without water, so Kakababu sucked it like it was a lozenge. The tablet was deadly bitter, but bitterness was better than pain. After it was all gone he sat up gingerly, and tied a bandage around his head with his scarf. It was a good thing that the cave was warm, he thought absently.

Then the meaning of that thought truly hit him.

Hurriedly, he took his gloves off. His fingers felt fine. There was no biting cold. The tip of his nose felt normal, too. And he could breathe easily. Which could only mean one thing: this *was* an underground cave, only it had been extensively modified to be comfortable. Who could have taken so much trouble in a remote place like this?

Just then, something landed with a snarl on Kakababu's back. Startled, Kakababu whipped around and shoved it off. The thing crashed to the floor, but instantly jumped back to its feet and began barking furiously at Kakababu. Even in the darkness, Kakababu could make out a small white dog.

The dog launched itself at Kakababu's leg. Luckily, it tried to bite the disabled leg. Kakababu used his functioning leg to kick the dog off it. The dog landed on the ground once again, but rebounded just as quickly. It raced at Kakababu, this time trying to bite his other leg. Kakababu kicked it off again. His thick woollen trousers kept the dog's teeth from sinking in.

After being kicked off twice, the dog chose to stay outside Kakababu's range. But it bared its teeth and growled. Kakababu touched his revolver. He could silence the dog with just one bullet. Even in the darkness, the dog was too close to miss. But he couldn't bring himself to do that. First, the dog was small. It looked like a German Spitz. A few of this breed could be rather bad-tempered, but they were hardly lethal. And second, Kakababu liked dogs. He did not want to harm one, no matter how aggressive it was being at the moment.

Taking a different tack, he began whistling quietly at the dog. The dog paid no attention to this friendly overture. Instead, it suddenly launched itself at him from a different angle. Unfortunately for it, Kakababu had anticipated its move. He was once again able to kick it off, this time rather hard. The dog shook the defeat off easily, but three kicks made it even warier. Now it began circling Kakababu, barking loudly, looking for a weak spot to attack.

Kakababu sighed. This dog was going to be a problem. But he couldn't bring himself to harm it too much. Would distraction work? Taking one of his gloves from his pocket, he threw it at the dog. The dog snatched it smartly out of the air, then began snapping at it and tearing it. Then it took it in its mouth and ran away into the darkness. It was back in a few seconds, but without the glove.

Kakababu groaned. In a moment's frivolity, he had lost one of his gloves. He would not survive the snow without it. Still, what good was one glove without the other? He took the other one and tossed it at the dog as well. The dog snapped this one up, too. After a few seconds of playing with it, it once again picked the glove up and ran into the darkness. This time, it did not return.

Kakababu waited for it for a few seconds. Then he began to think. What was a pet dog doing in an underground cave? It had to be a pet, for how else would a German Spitz find its way into these mountains? No, he had rested enough – he needed to explore this place and find out what it actually was.

Sliding carefully off the slab, Kakababu aligned himself against the rough stone wall. Walking without crutches was extremely difficult for him, but not impossible. Then, carefully balancing himself on one leg, he moved slowly in the direction that the dog had disappeared. The darkness persisted for a few metres, but then gave way to the strange misty light he had seen. He had only gone a few paces when the tinny transmitter suddenly came to life again. This time, when he strained his ears, Kakababu could make out a few words. Well, not words, exactly. What he heard was a voice calling out a string of letters and numbers:

'NCO 3295 ... RGT 45000 ... TO1H88000 ...'

Then the voice stopped, and a loud clang filled the line. Then everything went dead.

Frowning fiercely, Kakababu tried to work out what the message could have been. What did the numbers and letters refer to? In his distraction, he didn't notice when his foot first touched something large in his way. A second later he tripped on it and tumbled to the ground, hard.

For a few seconds, Kakababu saw actual stars behind his eyes. Pain exploded behind his eyes and spread to the rest of his head. Alarmed, he shook himself mentally. He could not afford to lose consciousness again! Not when he had the chance to escape this mysterious prison.

After a few minutes of sitting quietly on the floor, the pounding in his head went down a little. Kakababu reached out carefully, and felt the object in his way. It was an iron strongbox. Almost instinctively, he tried to lift the lid. But the box was locked. Baffled, Kakababu pulled himself to sit on the box, and began wondering once again what sort of a place he was in.

He did not have long to think. The pesky little dog was back from wherever it had been. Kakababu could see it in the distance, barking and jumping at something in the misty light. He wished it would go away. In any other circumstances, he would have liked to have made friends and scratched its head, but having the dog announce his presence could only lead to danger.

But the dog showed no interest in coming for him again. Instead, it kept barking and running around in the light, trying to play with someone he could not see. Then, after a few minutes, it disappeared into the darkness again. Relieved, Kakababu began planning how to best move towards the light whilst avoiding detection. There was clearly something important near the light. Perhaps even his captors. It seemed to be the source of both the light and the transmitter-chatter.

Just as he had taken a step past the strongbox, the dog appeared again. But this time it was not alone. An enormous shadow-like creature appeared beside it.

Kakababu's heart missed a beat. The shadow-creature was two-legged.

Before Kakababu could take a good look, the shadow disappeared. Then it appeared again, only to move out of sight a second later. This happened three or four times. Kakababu held his breath, holding his revolver close. This had to be the creature Shontu had seen. It was a primate – there was no doubt about that. It leaned slightly forward while walking, as many large primates did. But why did it keep slipping in and out of sight? Did it have a tail? Kakababu couldn't see.

The creature came back into view. The dog yipped joyfully around it. The creature did not disappear this time. Instead, it bent forward and picked the dog up with both arms.

'It'll break the poor dog's neck!' Kakababu thought. He unlatched the safety on his revolver and cocked it at the creature.

But the creature didn't harm the dog. Instead, it threw it gently back on the floor, as if they were playing. This time, the dog turned and ran towards Kakababu, barking loudly. Kakababu hastily took shelter behind the strongbox. He could not kick while standing on his good leg. He would have to defend himself with his arms.

But yet again, the dog did not attack. Instead, it barked a few times at Kakababu, then ran back towards the light. Then it ran back towards Kakababu, barking again. This time, the enormous creature took note. It turned, and began following the dog. It had a strange rolling gait that unnerved Kakababu. The dog ran all the way up to Kakababu, and began barking enthusiastically at him. Kakababu paid it no attention. His entire being was focused on the large creature now coming straight at him. There was no time to hide. So Kakababu simply stood against the wall and watched the creature approach. It came within five or six feet of it, then abruptly stopped.

Kakababu lifted his arm and took aim. The creature was tall – very tall. But no matter how big, a close shot from a revolver would still give it pause. The creature looked at his extended arm. Neither moved for a few seconds. Then the creature let out a gurgling roar.

Kakababu had the distinct impression that it was a mocking laugh. The creature was mocking his puny weapon. Kakababu glared at the creature. Then he noticed that the creature had oddly rounded eyes, and distinct eyebrows. Its arms were very long, and its coat was made of exceptionally long hair.

The creature abruptly stopped laughing. Then, raising its arms over its head, it let out a blood-curdling scream of pure malevolence. Still screaming, it began advancing on Kakababu. Its face was a terrifying picture of bared teeth and flared nostrils.

Kakababu thought quickly. He could not bring himself to shoot the creature. If it was indeed a yeti, then it needed to be studied, not killed. But it was clearly intent on killing *him*, so he had to protect himself. In a split second, he decided to shoot, but at its leg. That should stop the creature, and the wound would be easily healable. Taking aim, he fired.

There was an empty click.

Alarmed, Kakababu rapidly fired several more times. Ominously harmless clicking sounds filled the cave. Kakababu froze. His revolver was empty. For the first time in years, a chill of pure fear ran down his back.

CHAPTER 16

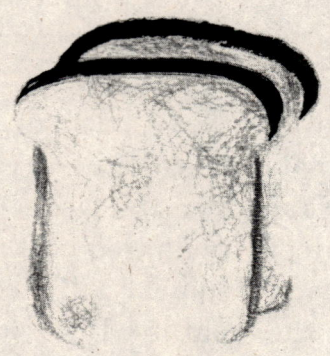

As the creature advanced upon him, Kakababu thought swiftly. He distinctly remembered loading his revolver the previous afternoon. Someone must have emptied it after he had blacked out. But why? And why had they put it back in his pocket?

The gorilla-like creature had come very close. There was no time to solve the mystery of his empty revolver. With no other weapon at hand, Kakababu hurled his empty firearm at the creature's head. To his astonishment, the creature snatched it out of the air. Then it stopped and stared at it for a few seconds. Just when Kakababu was wondering if he could use this chance to scramble away, the creature began to laugh. There was no other word for the sound he was making. Tossing the revolver aside like a toy, it began gurgling derisively.

Suddenly, a light bulb went off in Kakababu's head. After watching the creature closely for a few minutes, he, too, began laughing.

The creature was taken aback. Its malicious laughter was drowned out by Kakababu's laughter of genuine amusement. For a few seconds, it stopped laughing and simply stared at Kakababu. Then it let out another blood-curdling shriek and began advancing upon him again, turning its claws out to grasp Kakababu's neck.

Kakababu calmly waited for the creature to come within arm's reach. Then he swiftly reached out and pulled it sharply by the extended arm. The creature lost its footing and almost tumbled down on Kakababu. Kakababu tried to take that opportunity to grasp it by the waist and toss it away, but the creature proved stronger and smarter than that. It quickly regained its footing and jumped away. Then it stared at Kakababu in silence.

Most people saw Kakababu's limp and assumed that he was, at least physically, a weak man. They had no idea that he was, in fact, exceptionally powerful.

After blinking for a few seconds, the creature once again began to howl and roar at Kakababu. It was a terrifying noise, but Kakababu simply grinned back at it.

'Mr Kane Shipton, I presume?' he asked, quite cheerfully.

The creature stopped abruptly mid-growl. Then, after clearing its throat, it said in perfect English, 'You presume wrongly, Mr Roychoudhuri.'

Kakababu ignored this. 'Please remove your mask and this ridiculous disguise,' he said instead. 'It'll be easier to talk to your real face.'

The man reached behind his neck and pulled off the terrifying gorilla-like mask. However, beneath it he wore a yellow face-cap of a stretchy, shiny material. Probably a breathable form of polythene, Kakababu guessed. When the gorilla-suit came off, Kakababu saw that the man's entire body was covered in a tight-fitting yellow suit of the same material. His eyes were covered from scrutiny by mirror-like sunglasses. Once out of the suit, his height decreased considerably. There were probably raised platforms built into the feet of the suit.

'What is the meaning of this charade?' Kakababu asked irritably.

The yellow-encased person did not answer.

'Is this a circus for your amusement?' Kakababu snapped. 'Stomping about in fur-suits ... did you think I'd run terrified, like a child? It must have been you who took the bullets out from my revolver. Why did you do that? Did you bring me down here just to play these childish pranks?'

The man continued to watch Kakababu in silence, his hands on his hips.

'I need answers!' Kakababu thundered. 'Why am I here? Who are you?'

The man's mask stretched in a thin smile. 'Mr Roychoudhuri ... it feels like *I'm* your captive, not you ours. Do you think it wise to shout at your captor?'

'You assault and kidnap me, and then expect me not to ask why?' Kakababu asked incredulously. 'Are you people insane? How do you know my name?'

'You're a famous man, Mr Roychoudhuri,' said the man in yellow. 'Many people know your name.'

Kakababu was about to respond, but the man took out a shiny silver revolver from his yellow suit's pocket. He played with it for a few seconds, then pointed it straight at Kakababu's head.

'This revolver has bullets, Mr Roychoudhuri. And I assure you, at this distance, I will only need to use one.'

This time, it was Kakababu who did not respond. Instead, he stared straight into the man's eyes. The man spoke again.

'A bullet is not a joke. Things could take a drastic turn in less than a second. For example, if I pull the trigger in three ... two ... one ...'

'Stop this absurd drama!' Kakababu snapped. 'Are you seriously trying to threaten me with death? Use your head! What man with only one working leg would set off for the Everest if he cared about his life?'

The man pocketed the revolver. 'You're right,' he said. 'This would not scare you. Besides, being scared is bad for health ... and it leaves a print on the corpse's face. We will kill you slowly. Over many, many days. Your death will be excruciating, not this easy.'

'So you've set your heart on murder, have you?' Kakababu asked sarcastically.

'You left us with no choice, Mr Roychoudhuri. Had you not poked your nose where it didn't belong, we would not have hurt a hair on your head. But you did. Really, you have no one to blame but yourself.'

Kakababu scoffed. 'Many have threatened me with death before. None have succeeded. If you'd been serious about it, you would have killed me already, not played stupid pranks.'

'You say "pranks". But do you know how easy it is to trigger heart failure with fear? Had you died from shock, it would have been a great convenience. To us, that is.'

This time, Kakababu laughed outright. 'If your scheme was to kill people with a fright, then you've picked the worst possible candidate for it.'

The man laughed as well. It was not a nice laugh. 'You have rather a high opinion of yourself, don't you, Mr Roychoudhuri? We haven't killed you yet because it doesn't serve our purpose. Corpses talk. Say we shot you, or poisoned you. What do you think would happen?'

'I'm sure that will be a fascinating conversation, but can I sit down for it? As I'm sure you know, I have considerable difficulty standing for a long time without my crutches.'

Without waiting for the man's response, Kakababu sat down on the iron lockbox. He fished his pipe out of his pockets and put it in his mouth. Then he reached for his tobacco. But his tobacco-pouch was nowhere to be found.

'We've thrown it away,' the yellow-man explained helpfully. 'Your tobacco pouch, I mean. As I'm sure you've worked out, this place is built underground. We cannot allow smoking here.'

Kakababu bit into his pipe to control his temper. When he spoke, his voice was perfectly calm. 'Very well. There will be no smoking while I am your guest. What were you saying?'

'We were talking about your corpse, Mr Roychoudhuri. We cannot store it here – the smell would make it quite difficult for us. We would have to throw it outside. But the outside is covered in snow for much of the year. This is along the route to the Everest, so someone would find it, eventually. Perhaps even within a month or two. And then you would talk, Mr Roychoudhuri. You would talk to them with your dead lips.'

'I assume you mean that they would perform a post-mortem,' Kakababu said dryly. 'And the post-mortem would reveal that I had either been shot to death or poisoned. Or bludgeoned.'

'Quite right. And then the government would be compelled to investigate. A lot of unnecessary sniffing around that we could do without. Which is why we prefer to kill by natural causes. That way, even if one found your starved and shrivelled body, they would assume that you had lost your way in the snow, and couldn't find your way back. A neat and simple solution.'

'So it is. But the problem, my friend, is that I have no intention of dying at your convenience. I fully intend to live for another thirty or forty years.'

'Hah! Don't we all! And you could have. Had you stayed in Calcutta, or gone on a safe little trip to Darjeeling, you would have been perfectly fine. Who asked you to come here? Who asked you to set up camp in the tower? Who asked you to look into the night with your binoculars? If you wanted to live a long and healthy life, then you should have made very different choices.'

'Ah, so you've been watching me,' Kakababu said, thoughtfully. 'Either you had a spy in my group, or you intercepted my wireless messages. Whatever it was, I'm not about to oblige you by dying.'

The man's face stretched in a smile again.

'But you will, Mr Roychoudhuri. Do you know what kills most people in your country? In India?'

Kakababu breathed out. 'Ah. You want me to starve to death.'

'Not actual starvation. Most people in your country live on one meal a day. We'll be giving you the same. Two pieces of toast. If a child of five was given two pieces of toast a day, he would not survive three months. For an adult of your stature ... well, we're hoping it won't go beyond a month, maybe six weeks.'

'That Chinese man!' Kakababu said suddenly. 'That was you. You starved him to death, then left him at our doorstep to scare us away.'

'That man was extraordinary,' the masked man said with reluctant admiration. 'Do you know how long he held on, on two pieces of bread? Two-and-a-half years! He was a good prisoner, really. Quiet, kept to himself, no ambitions of escape. We quite liked him. But duty before preference, Mr Roychoudhuri. We could not let him out after what he had seen.'

'Astonishing!'

'Yes, isn't it? Thirty months on bread alone!'

'That too, but I'm astonished that you've been here for two-and-a-half years.'

Mirth coloured the man's voice. 'Would you like to guess how long we've been here?'

Kakababu gritted his teeth. The man was mocking him. He sorely missed his tobacco-pouch. In situations like this, having a smoke helped him calm down and think. Which is probably why these people had taken it away. They did not want him to be able to think calmly. In a moment of futile rage, Kakababu took the useless pipe out of his mouth and smashed it on the stone floor.

'*I quit!*' he silently promised himself. '*I'll get over this dependency! If I manage to go back to Calcutta, I'll give away all my pipes.*'

At the sound of the clattering pipe, the little white dog came forward and began sniffing at his trousers again. It made no violent moves this time. Kakababu reached out and patted it on the head. The dog happily accepted his overture of friendship.

'We're doing you the courtesy of not locking you up because you're disabled,' the yellow man said finally. 'I'll give you a bed, too. You can pass the rest of your life in comfort.'

'Very thoughtful of you,' said Kakababu, with forced calm. 'I usually need two pillows.'

'We'll send them with the bedding. Sturdy rubber air-pillows — you can blow them up to as high as you like. Anything else?'

'This dog of yours has stolen my gloves.'

'I'll send them back. And, before I leave ... do you take your toast soft, or well-browned?'

In a split second, Kakababu picked up the dog and threw it at the man. Hard. Then he bent down, grasped the man's legs, and pulled them out from under him.

The man did not even have time to shout. He hit the floor hard, and lost consciousness.

CHAPTER 17

Shontu could not sleep. He tossed and turned in his sleeping bag, wondering how Kakababu could have disappeared. The only explanation was a crevice, but though he himself had fallen into a crevice, there were none where Kakababu had disappeared.

Every now and then sleep would sneak up on him, but the moment he dozed a little he would be assailed by the feeling of falling helplessly down a snowy hole till his head hit a sheet of metal. The feel of metal was so unmistakable that after dreaming the same dream three or four times, he woke up absolutely convinced that it *had* been metal at the bottom of that hole, not stone. But what could it mean? Why was his brain so determined to convince him of this?

It was barely dawn when he woke Mingma up. Mingma slept like a log, but the slightest shake woke

him up completely. Seeing Shontu beside his sleeping
bag, Mingma began rubbing the remaining sleep out
of his eyes.

'What is it, Shontu sa'ab? Didn't you sleep?'

'Mingma, when you dug beneath Kakababu's crutch,
are you absolutely sure you found no metal?'

'Absolutely, sa'ab. Only stones. No metal.'

'It can't be! It just can't be!' Shontu exploded.
'Listen, can you pick out the spot where I sank under
the snow?'

'I had put a red handkerchief there. But after the
blizzard … I don't know. It could have been blown off.
Or buried under the snow.'

'Then we have to find it again!'

'But why, Shontu sa'ab? The place where uncle sa'ab
disappeared is a fair bit further than that crevice.'

'Doesn't matter! We have to find that place.'

'I honestly don't understand why you're so focused
on this. What difference does it make if there's indeed
a bit of metal under the snow?'

Shontu sat down next to Mingma. 'Because stone
occurs naturally. Metal sheets don't. If there is a sheet
of metal underground, then that's an aberration that
we *really* need to look into. Come on, let's take the pick
and shovel and go!'

'We should wait for the helicopter,' Mingma pointed
out sensibly. 'Rana sir and Varma sir will be coming
back. They should know where we have gone.'

'What if they're late? No no, never mind them! We
should leave as soon as we can.'

'Let us at least have some tea before? Our bones won't warm up without a few cups of hot tea.'

'Fine,' Shontu said, giving in to temptation. 'But let's make it quick.'

The stove and rations had been packed into the tower the previous evening. Mingma lit the spirit-stove and put the water to boil. Shontu began running and jumping on the spot to warm himself up. After a few minutes, he thought it might be a good idea to go outside and run laps around the tower. He was almost at the door when Mingma called out.

'Wait, Shontu sa'ab! Don't go out alone. Let me finish, then we'll go out together.'

'Don't worry, I'll be right outside,' Shontu answered. Then he very carefully opened the door a crack, and peered outside.

Everything was quiet. The sky was lit in the colours of dawn, casting a mellow light on the snow beneath. The top of the Kala Patthar had just begun to turn red with the first rays of the sun. But there was an uneasiness in the surrounding beauty. The silence was oppressive, not peaceful. Shontu felt like everything around him was holding its breath, waiting for something to happen.

Then he looked right, and found what it was.

Several severed hen and chicken heads were strewn on the snow just outside the tower. Blood and feathers marred the pristine snow.

For a few seconds, Shontu stood transfixed. Then he stepped back inside the tower and pushed the heavy

door shut. When he tried to walk back to Mingma, he
realized his legs were shaking. Who could have done
this? He had heard no noise whatsoever the previous
night. Was this ... was the yeti truly supernatural?

Mingma noticed his white face right away. 'What is
it?' he asked urgently.

'Feathers,' Shontu mumbled through cold lips. It
was all he could say.

'Feathers? You were frightened by feathers?'

After a few seconds, Shontu managed to calm down
a little and tell Mingma about the gory view outside.
Mingma looked more resigned than scared.

'At least the tea is hot,' he said, pushing a mug
towards Shontu. 'Drink up. We can worry about what
happened later.'

Shontu could barely grasp the mug. The sight of the
severed heads danced in front of his eyes. He dimly
realised that his hands had started to shake again.

Mingma, on the other hand, decided it was best
to fortify himself against the unknown danger. He
downed his tea with ten biscuits. Then he lit a locally-
made bidi that was almost the size of a cigar, and
exhaled deeply.

'Good. Now let's go see what feathers and chickens
you were speaking of.'

Shontu stepped outside with some reluctance. The
wind had blown the feathers far and wide, but the
heads were very close to the door. Their cloudy eyes
goggled. Shontu realised with a shock of revulsion

that someone had choked them before breaking their necks.

Beside him, Mingma let out a low whistle. 'Who would bring live chickens here?' he asked, softly. 'These have been freshly killed.'

Then, at the same chilling moment, their eyes fell on footprints in the snow. Fresh, enormous footprints. With four toes on each foot.

Neither needed to say anything. After the first moment of terror, they simply looked at each other. Then they turned around as one, and raced back to the tower. Once inside, Mingma shut the door with a loud bang and shot the latch home. Then he practically collapsed on the floor. 'Yeti!' he gasped. 'Yeti, yeti! Yeti!'

'And we're not armed!' Shontu wheezed. 'The revolver is with Kakababu. We're alone!'

Mingma pushed back against the door and simply repeated himself. 'Yeti! Yeti! Yeti!'

After a few seconds, they both calmed down a little.

'Do yetis eat chicken, Mingma?' Shontu asked. 'Where did it get fresh chicken from?'

'Look, we're not going out till the helicopter comes,' Mingma said. He had zero interest in the yeti's food supply.

'Is the yeti still outside? Was it watching us? Mingma, is it true that yetis can disappear?'

Mingma turned his palms upwards in helplessness. He didn't know.

For the next ninety minutes both of them remained piled up next to the tiny window, willing the helicopter

to appear. Their eyes began to water from staring at
the sky and the snow, but neither yeti nor helicopter
appeared. Was the yeti hiding outside, biding its time?

After a few more minutes, exasperation began
to overcome Shontu's fear. How long could one stay
cooped up, waiting for something that didn't appear?
Besides, the idea of a hostile yeti was beginning to
puzzle him. He had read lots of stories about the yeti.
None of them had suggested that they were aggressive.
In fact, most made yetis seem shy. Yet here was one
following humans to their camp, only to quietly eat
chickens outside. It didn't make sense! Shaking off his
remaining fear, he stood up.

'Mingma, we've waited enough. Let's go.'

'Right now? Aren't we waiting for the helicopter?'

Shontu did not answer. He ran down the stairs and
threw open the door.

Worried, Mingma ran down after him. 'Shontu
sa'ab! What are you doing?'

Shontu stepped outside. The carcasses were still
there, but this time he was not scared. He ran a quick
lap around the tower. There was nothing on the other
side. When he returned to the front, he had had enough
of waiting.

'There's nothing here. Let's go find that place,
Mingma.'

'Which place?'

'The place where you had left the red handkerchief.'

'Let's wait a little more. If the helicopter comes ...'

'No. I don't want to wait any more. If you don't want to come, I'll go alone.'

Then he ran back inside and came out with a snow-axe. Seeing that he was determined to go, Mingma reluctantly went inside and came out with his tools.

Shontu led the way. Sometimes, in his determination to go fast, he went astray. Mingma called out directions from behind to keep him on the path. Over the next few hours, they moved slowly, examining every bit of the route. But no matter how hard they looked, the red handkerchief could not be found. Both Mingma and Shontu kept looking back for signs of being followed by large four-toed footprints. The sun was bright and the sky a clear blue, but the fear still lingered in the air. Shontu had pinned his hopes on suddenly running across a sleeping or unconscious Kakababu, half-hidden by the snow. After all, a man cannot *actually* vanish into thin air. But there was no trace of him.

The search was growing desultory when Mingma suddenly stopped in his tracks. Shontu was about to wander ahead, but Mingma's hand shot forward and clasped his forearm. 'No! Don't!' he whispered urgently.

Then he lay belly-down on the ice and inched slowly forward. After a point he stopped, extended his arm, and brought down his pickaxe hard on the snow. Instantly, a small radius of loose snow caved in, revealing a hole.

Shontu was astonished. How did Mingma know? Could he smell the danger in the air?

Mingma hit out at several points around the hole to figure out how far the mouth of the crevice extended. Then he stood up and began shovelling the snow away from one edge. Shontu joined him. Physical labour was difficult for him at this altitude. In just a few minutes, the rarefied air seemed to suck all the oxygen out from his lungs. His arms and legs grew heavy. Mingma, on the other hand, carried on as if nothing had happened. After several minutes, he managed to dig a sizeable hole in the packed snow. Then he jumped inside the hole and kept digging. After a further few minutes, he looked up at Shontu.

'You were right, Shontu sa'ab. There is iron beneath the snow!'

Excited, Shontu jumped right in. Mingma was indeed standing on a piece of solid iron. Over the next few minutes, the two of them cleared out as much snow as they could to see how far the sheet of metal went. But the more snow they cleared, the more the sheet became visible.

'We must find how far it goes,' Shontu insisted. 'This is already too big for a group of trekkers or climbers to have carried it here with them. So, what is it?'

Mingma wiped sweat off his forehead with the back of his arm. The labour so far had been hard, and he didn't relish the prospect of digging more. On the other hand, he was just as intrigued by the unexpected metal-sheet under this very familiar route. If he dug further, perhaps he would discover how it got here.

A tingle of anticipation ran down his spine. With renewed enthusiasm, he began digging again.

After many more minutes, it became clear to both Shontu and Mingma that they would not be able to dig to the edges of the metal. The more they dug, the wider the metal-sheet became. In the end, Mingma simply stopped and looked at Shontu.

'Tell me what you want us to do, Shontu sa'ab?'

Shontu looked around in indecision. On the one hand, they could not keep digging. On the other, this was an astounding discovery, and they could not leave it to be swallowed back up by the snow. Just as he was weighing his options, the sound of a helicopter's blades filled the sky.

'They're back!' shouted Mingma, jumping up and down to catch the pilot's attention. Shontu, too, looked up in relief. Neither of them noticed a hairline crack appear across the length of the iron beneath them.

A second later, the floor gave way under Shontu's feet. He fell into the darkness below, too fast to even let out a scream. Mingma nearly fell in too, but his reflexes were much better. Reaching up on instinct, he grasped the edge of the hole he had dug. But before he could pull himself out, the two halves of the metal began to close again. Half his body was still inside when the two sheets ground to a death-grip around his waist. Mingma let out an ear-piercing scream.

But there was no one around to hear him.

CHAPTER 18

After picking up the man's revolver, Kakababu hobbled back to the wall as swiftly as he could. Then he turned around and cocked the little thing straight at the fallen man.

The man made no move to get up. In fact, he did not move at all. He remained where he was, face-down on the stone floor. Did he hit his head and lose consciousness? Kakababu dismissed that thought. No, he hadn't fallen anywhere close to hard enough for that. Then why wasn't he getting up? Was the man trying to fool him?

'Get up! Get up and answer my questions!' he called out angrily. 'Any more of your juvenile tricks and I'll blow your brains out – I have excellent aim!'

The man did not respond.

Kakababu realized that the man was waiting for him to step closer. The moment he did, the man would try to pull his legs out from under him. Tit for tat. The dog, meanwhile, had returned, but was keeping cautiously away from both men. Kakababu paid no attention to its mewling in the background. He was focused completely on his assailant.

'I'll count from one to five. If you don't sit up by five, I'll shoot at you. One ... two ...'

As if on cue, the beam of a powerful searchlight flooded the tunnel. It was so bright that Kakababu's eyes squeezed shut against the assault. He lifted his free hand to shade them.

The man now sat up, slowly.

'Turn your back to the light!' Kakababu barked sharply at him. 'And don't you dare stand up!'

An amplified voice filled the narrow tunnel. 'Your attention please, Mr Roychoudhuri. Can you hear me? Please drop the revolver you're holding.'

Kakababu looked around. Was the tunnel fitted with a loudspeaker? Where was it? He could barely make out anything in the painfully bright light.

The voice behind the microphone repeated its message.

'Who are you?' Kakababu shouted back. 'Whoever you are, come talk to me face-to-face. I won't disarm myself till I see you.'

The microphone went silent. The abrupt silence seemed to almost physically add to the tension in the room. The masked man on the floor continued to stare blandly at Kakababu.

'Where have you people come from? Which country?' Kakababu demanded.

The man just smiled.

'If I don't get answers I'll start shooting!' Kakababu threatened.

The man shrugged.

Kakababu was about to say something, when the sound of loud footsteps filled the tunnel. Seconds later, three men came into view, marching purposely towards him. They were dressed and masked in exactly the same way as the man on the floor, but instead of a revolver they carried long, thin, deadly-looking firearms.

'Don't come closer!' Kakababu shouted at them. 'Stay where you are, or I'll shoot this man.'

The masked men didn't even slow down. 'Feel free,' one of them called back cheerfully.

Setting his jaw, Kakababu raised the revolver and took aim. But he did not shoot. Within seconds, the three men were at his side.

'I thought you were going to shoot him?' the one that had already spoken asked. Kakababu could tell that he was amused.

'I'm not a professional killer, unlike some,' he bit out. 'I would never attack a disarmed man with a weapon.'

'Mr Roychoudhuri, let's not make a ruckus,' another of the masked men said, much more seriously. 'We don't want to harm you, but ...'

'Who *are* you?' Kakababu asked.

'No questions, Mr Roychoudhuri. That's the rule here. If there are questions to be asked, they will be asked by us. Now, before we move you, we'd like to cover your eyes.'

'No.'

The man sighed. 'Mr Roychoudhuri, we really don't want to have to force you.'

'I'm grateful for that immense kindness,' Kakababu said caustically. Then he raised the revolver once again and pointed it at the man on the floor. 'Listen, I don't kill people, but I can disable them in self-defence. If you lay so much as a finger on me, I shall shoot him in the leg. He'll be disabled for life.'

'Sounds good!' the jovial man laughed. 'Please go ahead. After the way he's mucked up this operation, he deserves to be shot.'

'Nooo! Don't tempt Mr Roychoudhuri!' the man on the floor moaned, feigning fear. 'He's kicked me so hard that I'm still seeing stars!'

While the jovial man laughed, the two other members of the team stepped up and put a hand each on Kakababu's shoulders. Immediately, Kakababu raised the revolver at a wall and fired. He had meant to scare them, but to his shock, the mouth of the revolver simply flashed and emitted a rat-a-tat noise. There were no bullets.

All four men burst out laughing.

'It's a toy,' the cheerful man pointed out helpfully.

Disgusted, Kakababu threw the toy across the cave. 'Why on earth would you send this clown with a toy pistol and a yeti-suit? Did you seriously think these things could frighten me?'

'Let's just call it a harmless prank,' the cheerful man said, smiling. 'Our life here is rather boring – a little distraction now and then is good for us. But before you get any ideas, I should tell you that the guns we're carrying are not toys. Just in case you don't believe us ...'

He lifted his strange-looking gun and fired at the far wall of the cave. In a split second, stones chipped off from the wall and sprayed the tunnel. A few of them hit Kakababu.

'Tie a cloth firmly around Mr Roychoudhuri's eyes, No. 7,' the man instructed briskly. His light-hearted tone had disappeared.

'But why?' Kakababu asked.

'For shame, Mr Roychoudhuri. For such a smart man, you have a very poor memory indeed. What did we just say about asking questions?'

The two sombre men on either side of Kakababu pulled him away from the wall. Kakababu's jaws tightened. 'Fine,' he said. 'You are four and I am one – you can do what you like. But I want my eyes to remain open. And I would prefer to get my crutches back.'

The man grinned. 'You would like your eyes to remain open? Very well, we won't force you. If you can keep them open, you can have them open.'

All four men whipped out slightly odd-looking dark glasses and put them on. Then one of them raised his voice and said, 'Lights!'

The already dazzling light became brighter. Kakababu was once again forced to snap his eyes shut. Mocking laughter filled his ears. 'So, not a success at keeping your eyes open, then,' the jovial man mocked.

Kakababu freed himself from the two men beside him and turned his back on the light. 'I can keep them open now,' he said mulishly.

'They won't be of much use to you if you stand here facing the wall, now will it?'

'Where do you plan on taking me? Why do my eyes need to be closed?' Kakababu asked.

'No questions, Mr Roychoudhuri!' the man chided playfully.

One of the other men slipped a black rubber cover over his head. It was bunched behind his head and tied like a ponytail.

'And now I suppose you'll tie my hands?' Kakababu asked mockingly.

'Oh, we won't need to go that far,' the spokesman of the group replied.

'But what if I reach up and undo my mask?'

The leader laughed again. 'That is a Persian knot at the back of your head. Alexander himself couldn't undo them.'

'Ah, so you're a group of *educated* goons!' Kakababu exclaimed, now openly contemptuous. 'You speak of

Alexander and history, yet you stomp about in masks with guns, attacking people. A fine use of an education!'

'Haven't you read the Phantom comics?' the man laughed. 'He's a man in a mask stomping about with a gun and attacking people, too. Would you call him a goon, too?!'

'Don't be ridiculous!' Kakababu snapped. 'You don't want to have a serious conversation with me? Fine! Take me wherever you want to take me. But let me tell you, within three days you will all be behind bars!'

'Is that right, Mr Roychoudhuri? Are you threatening us?'

'I am, and they are not empty threats. You were stupid to go out in a fur-suit and put fake footprints on the snow. People are going to see through such gimmicks, and soon.'

'And you give "people" three days to do so? Who are these people, then?'

'The military police, for one. You might have a big group here, but not big enough to fight the military.'

'And how do you think the military police will find us?'

'Because I told them. When I heard about yetis appearing and disappearing in seconds, I told them that they likely had an underground lair.'

'That is a fairly obvious guess. But how will the military police know exactly where to dig? Even with their resources, they cannot afford to dig through the entire Himalayas!'

Kakababu pursed his lips.

'Ah, so you don't want us to know their plans,' the man said. 'But let me tell you, all searches will be in vain. We're impossible to find.'

'Nothing is impossible,' Kakababu countered. 'Let's say I have a secret power. I can send telepathic signals. I will inform my friends of my whereabouts, and they will direct the armed forces here.'

All four men laughed loudly at that.

'Oh, we know about your secret powers,' the leader cheerfully informed him. 'We've taken steps to curb it. Now let's go.'

The men began to march him forward. After a few seconds one of them said, 'We should have remembered the crutches. This is harder for Mr Roychoudhuri than I imagined.'

'Let's lift him up,' another suggested.

Before Kakababu could protest, the two men swung him up over their heads. He sighed and let himself be carried. There was no point in protesting.

After only a short while, he felt the group slowing down. A few minutes later, the men carrying him stopped and swung him down on the floor.

'Put him on that chair,' a new voice instructed. 'And remove his mask.'

He was lifted once again and settled on a chair. Then one of the men cut the knot behind his head with a knife. Kakababu noticed they went straight to cutting, without even trying to undo the knot. Perhaps they were right about it being a Persian knot.

When the bag was removed from his head, he opened his eyes to look at the owner of the new voice. What he saw instead made his blood go cold.

'What have you done!' he screamed, all composure lost.

CHAPTER 19

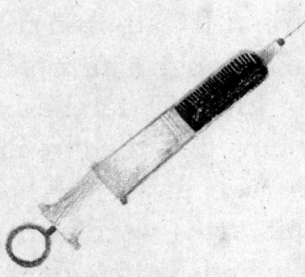

The terror of those first few moments were the worst Kakababu had ever felt. There was a rough-hewn table of stone in front of him, and a boy was lying on top of it, perfectly motionless. Shontu!

Kakababu tried to bound out of the chair and run to the table, but his captors held his forearms in iron-strong grips. Despite his immense strength, Kakababu could not free himself.

'What have you done to the boy?' he asked, on the brink of tears. 'How did he come here? What have you *done*?'

The masked group did not respond. Instead, a voice from his right said, 'Hello, Mr Roychoudhuri. Do you recognize me?'

Kakababu turned slowly towards the voice. There was a throne-like chair at the far end of the table. A tall man sat on it, dressed in black from head to toe. The man was obviously foreign-born, with fair skin and a head full of red hair. A locket hung from a thick gold chain around his neck. It was a human tooth, only several times larger. It had been framed in gold.

Kakababu saw it all through a haze of helpless tears. Few people had seen him cry, for he hated showing weakness no matter how dire the circumstances. But now the tears flowed freely down his cheeks. He could not wipe them, for his arms were still pinned to his sides. He always knew he loved his nephew, of course, but he had not realized how much. Now that he saw him lying on the cold stone slab, bitter regret filled his heart.

'Why won't I recognize a scum like you?' he snarled. 'You're Kane Shipton. You've murdered my nephew. You vile, *vile* creature. I am your enemy, not the boy. Why did you hurt him? Coward!'

Shipton burst out laughing.

'I knew your father,' Kakababu carried on. 'He was a good, upstanding man. He told me that you were a bad seed. That you were obsessed with making money. He told me about your history of being a mercenary in the Congo. It broke his heart. The moment I heard about your yeti-sighting and disappearance, I knew you were up to your old tricks. Spying on us for a foreign power! But did you have to stoop so low? My nephew knew nothing about you! What would your father say if he saw you now?'

'That's enough drama, Roychoudhuri. Now shut up,' Shipton said brusquely. 'This nephew of yours is a real terror. He's done what no one else had been able to do so far – not even you. He found our opening into the world above. We could not let him live, not after that.'

Kakababu sagged. The fight seemed to go out of him. 'At least he died a hero,' he murmured in defeat. 'If he found the way in, he must have left some sign around it. The armed forces will know how to find you now. I am proud of my nephew. He died serving the nation.'

Shipton smiled, showing several teeth. 'Don't be too optimistic, Roychoudhuri. We have sealed our doors again. It's impossible to find our entryway unless we open it ourselves. And no, your little toy won't help you, either.'

Then, turning to his men, he snapped. 'Undress him!'

The two men pinning Kakababu to his chair now pulled him to his feet. They held him in place while the others began pulling the layers off him. There was no point in fighting these many men, so Kakababu stood quietly and let it happen. After his overcoat, sweater and shirt came off, a small box became visible on his woollen vest. One of the men tore it out of the vest and handed it to Shipton.

'Cute,' Shipton said, examining it from all sides. 'But pointless. You see, Roychoudhuri, we have been intercepting the messages you've been sending from that stone tower of yours. We know exactly what this is. This little thing sends signals at intervals to the receiving centre at Syangboche. That's how your friends know where you are. Well, we have news for you: ever since you've been caught, we've jammed all wavelengths this is capable of sending. As far as your friends can tell, you're lost and out of range. You can say goodbye to your hopes of a dramatic rescue. Everything that happens to you now will be at our say-so. Clear?'

Kakababu ignored the implicit threat. Instead, he simply said, 'Can I have my clothes back? I'm cold.'

This was not exactly true. The temperature of the cave was quite well-regulated. There was an occasional burst of cold air from somewhere, but that was not why Kakababu wanted to be dressed again. At Shipton's signal, the masked men moved a few steps away, allowing Kakababu to dress. Kakababu put his shirt and coat back on. Then, taking advantage of the men's distance, he swiftly hobbled over to the stone slab and threw his arms around Shontu's corpse.

The masked men immediately scrambled to stop him, but Kakababu stepped away from the slab before they could even reach him. The anguish on his face had been replaced by a small, deeply satisfied smile.

Shontu's body was warm.

Shipton noticed the change in his attitude. 'Yes, the boy is alive,' he confirmed. 'We pushed tranquilizers into his vein to keep him from seeing this place.'

'Thank you for not hurting him,' Kakababu said. He meant it. 'But why arrange him like a corpse? He looks like he has been readied for a post-mortem.'

'Because he could be dead soon,' Shipton said blandly. 'It all depends on you. We can either kill him, or leave him outside. Which will it be?'

Kakababu thought quickly. He would not let these people kill Shontu. But could he keep them from harming him? Even if they did take him outside, where would they leave him? Certainly not at a safe location. They would probably just leave him on the snow. Where were Mingma, Varma, Rana? Why had they let Shontu wander out alone? If they were out looking for Shontu right now, then there was a chance that his nephew might be found and saved. But if they were not, or if these people chose to take him outside in the dead of the night, then Shontu would freeze even before the tranquilizers wore off. Come to think of it, what time was it now? Was it day or was it night? It was impossible to tell from inside the cave.

'What do you mean, it all depends on me?' he asked instead. 'What do you want from me?'

'Simple,' Shipton said, nodding at a fenced-off area. 'Our work here is nearly done. The systems have been installed and the machines will soon be automated. We will then leave.'

Kakababu followed his nod and saw that the fenced-off area sloped sharply into a fairly large and deep hole. A bluish mist rose from its depths and hung lightly over the nearby cave and tunnels. That must be the machine-room.

'What machines are those?' Kakababu asked. 'Things to spy with? You're spies, aren't you? Which group are you working for these days?'

Shipton acted as if Kakababu had not spoken. 'As I said, the system will become automatic in two months, and then we will all leave. This place will need just one person to stay behind, and make sure that it keeps running smoothly.' He grinned nastily. 'That person will be you, Roychoudhuri.'

'Me?'

'Yes, you. We cannot let you escape after everything you've seen here. Our choice is between starving you to death, or actually getting some use out of you. Given that, working for us is in your best interests. You'll want for nothing. Our people will come every three or four months and stock the pantry for you. They'll bring you anything else you might need, too.'

'You're being remarkably obtuse, Shipton,' Kakababu said calmly. 'The moment you leave, I will begin tearing your base down. Do you genuinely think I will help foreign spies? For what, money? Hah! If I cannot leave this cave, what use is money to me?'

Shipton smiled. 'Destroying this place is beyond you. There are things here that will kill you if you touch them the wrong way.'

'Nuclear devices?'

'I thought you were smart. Hadn't you worked that out already?'

'I suspected ... I didn't know for certain. I had told the governments of both India and Nepal that a network of spies was involved in something major in this area. They didn't take me seriously.'

'Is that why you brought that prehistoric tooth with you? To make your charade about hunting yetis more believable?'

'You're wearing a tooth too. What's your reason?'

'Mine brings good luck. Since putting it on, I have failed at nothing.'

'That's stupid superstition. Amazing that a so-called Western, civilized person believes in rot like that. But no, my search is not a charade. I genuinely believe that remote enclaves of prehistoric people exist in these areas. Perhaps at a higher altitude, in remote and uncharted regions.'

'Should have stuck to looking for them, Roychoudhuri. Had you not gone out of your way to poke your nose in our affairs, you and your nephew wouldn't be in trouble. Look, the offer to keep you here is an offer of generosity. It's my way of sparing your life. We don't actually need anyone to oversee the machines – they work perfectly well on their own. So, if you're not keen on watching this place for us ...'

'Don't threaten me, Kane Shipton,' Kakababu said calmly. 'My life has been at least ten times as dangerous as that of an average person. By that metric, I have already lived ten lifetimes. If you kill me right at this moment, I would die a contented man. But let me tell you: now that I know what you're up to, I will try till my dying breath to expose you to the governments. You can threaten and torture me all you like, I will not betray my country. But ...'

'You do tend to go on, don't you, Roychoudhuri?' Shipton interrupted. 'Normally we wouldn't have time for your dramatic speeches — we have far too much to do during the day. But today we're celebrating the completion of our work here, so we'll indulge you. Go on. "But" what?'

Kakababu swallowed the insult. 'But ... I want my nephew to survive. He's young. Very young. Not that I wouldn't be proud if he martyred himself to protect the nation, but he doesn't need to. Let him go, Shipton. You can do what you like with me.'

'You should have thought of your nephew before you attacked my men. Bit stupid of you, wasn't it, trying to strangle people and kick them with your useless leg? If we see that sort of behaviour again, we'll toss you in a corner in chains and forget about you.'

'I'm fine with that. But how can you toss an innocent boy out in the cold? If it snows in the night, then he'll be buried alive before the tranquilizer wears off'

'That's not our problem. He'll live if he's lucky, die if he's not. We'll put a few yeti footprints around him just in case. If he's rescued and starts talking about a cave, people will assume he means a yeti's cave.'

Hopelessly, Kakababu glanced at Shontu. But then a shock went through him. Shontu's eyelids were fluttering. The hand that had flopped to his side was moved lazily and came to rest on his chest.

Shipton had seen the movement as well.

'Quick! Sedate him!' he shouted. 'The kid must not see his uncle here!'

Two more of the yellow-clothed men ran into the room seconds later with a full syringe. Shontu turned on the table, groaning. His eyes remained shut. Shipton turned to Kakababu's captors.

'Take Roychoudhuri away! Quickly!'

The men clamped down on Kakababu's arms. Unable to fight back, Kakababu began shouting. 'Don't sedate him! Don't inject my nephew! Let him go!'

CHAPTER 20

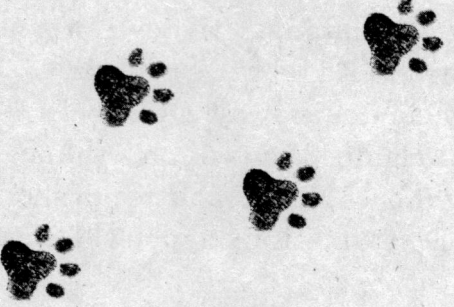

When the iron plates closed in on either side of him, Mingma felt like he was being slowly cut into two. He began screaming at the top of his voice in pain. The helicopter was bobbing up and down in the air almost exactly above him, but they appeared not to have noticed him frantically waving his arms.

People can sometimes perform near-miraculous acts when caught in the jaws of certain death. As the iron plates began biting deeper into his flesh, Mingma braced his arms on them, and gave his lower body a desperate final push. To his own amazement, his legs swung upwards with force, lifting his waist out of the way of the plates. In a split second, the plates snapped shut beneath him. He was free!

But the injury that the plates had inflicted was deep. After pulling himself to his feet, Mingma tried to walk back to the tower, but barely managed five steps before collapsing heavily on the snow. After that, he knew no more.

The helicopter circled the lower skies a few more times before landing at a distance. Three people emerged from it: Varma, Rana, and Thomas Tribhuvan. The latter was a Nepali gentleman of Christian faith, and a local by virtue of living in Syangboche. He had spent his life being the local manager for foreign trekkers and climbers, and knew the area like the back of his hand. He had finally retired when all his hair had turned white, but refused to leave the area. Hence his retirement-home in Syangboche.

All three were surprised to find the tower empty.

'Arre! Where's the boy and the Sherpa?' Varma asked, looking around.

'We asked them to stay inside and keep the doors locked,' Rana said worriedly. 'Did something happen while we were away?'

'Roychoudhuri is insane,' Varma grumbled. 'Doesn't give a damn about his own life. Fine, I suppose. It's his life. But can you imagine bringing such a young boy to a place like this?'

Thomas Tribhuvan had been looking around outside. 'Rana!' he called. 'Come see this. There's a cluster of hen feathers here.'

'Looks like the boy and the Sherpa have had a picnic here,' Varma said caustically.

Rana seemed to take this comment seriously. 'But where would they get live hens from?' he asked. 'And ... look at this! Footprints! Such enormous footprints!'

Varma's cynicism disappeared. He stumbled back from the footprint, rummaging his pockets for his revolver. 'A yeti!' he gasped. 'A yeti had come for them!'

Tribhuvan had sat down on the snow next to the prints. He appeared to not notice Varma's fear. 'I've seen these before,' he murmured, examining them closely. 'These, and other things beside. There's something in these mountains ... a mystery that hides itself well.'

Rana, too, seemed more intrigued than scared. He ran back into the tower for one of Kakababu's cameras, and began taking pictures from various angles.

'The last time I was here, I saw the pawprints of a dog alongside these large prints. Now, I don't know anything about yetis, but I *do* know that it's impossible for a small dog to survive alone in these altitudes. I had also seen an iron plate on the ground hereabouts. I intended to mark the area, but heavy snowfall that night had hidden it completely from view the next day.'

The conversation had helped Varma regain his composure. Now he snorted. 'An iron plate? That's even more amazing than yeti footprints! Why on earth would trekkers carry iron plates with them? And why would they leave them here?'

'That boy, Shontu – he had mentioned iron plates too,' Rana added thoughtfully.

'And we proved that he was speaking rubbish!' Rana retorted. 'We dug for several minutes, didn't we? And what did we find? Nothing! These places of permanent snow often throw up illusions like that.'

'May I say something?' Tribhuvan asked. When the other two looked at him, he gestured at the wide expanse of snow around them. 'I have travelled through this place many, many times. I know it well. I distinctly remember there being a crevice close by, and near it an underground cave. They were within a few hundred yards of this tower. Then suddenly, they disappeared. It was as if someone had razed the topography to make it look like a plain. But this area has not seen an earthquake strong enough to do that. So where did the caves go?'

'So not just a crevice, but an actual cave has been filled in?' Varma asked. 'Is that what you're saying?' Then he looked at Rana and winked, tapping the side of his head to show that he thought Tribhuvan had lost his marbles.

But Tribhuvan was confident. 'Oh yes, it has. In fact, if you have a piece of paper, I can draw you a rough map of where it used to be. Since its disappearance, I have been noticing a pattern of people disappearing from this area, too. Those two must be connected. There is no other explanation for it.'

'Well, the search team from Kathmandu should be here by tomorrow,' Rana said. 'Let's pack ourselves in for the night in the tower and wait for them. That way if the yeti returns, we will be able to see it.'

'What? Absolutely not!' snapped Varma. 'We are definitely not spending the night here. The way people are disappearing, it'll be us next! And anyway, no search team will be coming tomorrow.'

'What do you mean?' Rana asked, alarmed.

'I mean I checked the weather forecasts before we left. The weather in Kathmandu will be very bad for the next few days. No planes will be taking off in the next two or three days at the very least. Do you really want to risk staying here for that long?'

Tribhuvan had been looking around while Varma and Rana argued. Now he said, 'There's a man coming this way.'

Rana and Varma whipped around. Rana lifted his binoculars to his eye. 'It's the Sherpa – I've forgotten his name.'

Mingma was limping. Badly. Both sides of his waist were bleeding freely. His face was twisted in acute pain. When he reached them, he began speaking in painful gasps.

'Sa'ab! Have to go! Big iron door ... Shontu sa'ab fell inside! Nearly bit me in half.'

'Seems to have lost his mind,' Varma said, irritably. 'Hey, you! Focus! Where is Shontu? Tell us the truth!'

'Inside ... the iron doors,' Mingma gasped. 'Very big ... doors!'

'Lost it, like I said,' Varma said, giving up.

'Why did the two of you leave the tower?' Rana asked Mingma in Nepalese. 'And where did the feathers come from?'

Mingma took a deep breath before answering. But when he opened his mouth, whatever little energy he had deserted him. He keeled forward into the snow.

Rana immediately sat down and began examining him. 'He's unconscious! What ... what is this? He is covered in blood!'

'Blood? From where? Did he kill Shontu?' Varma asked, alarmed.

Rana looked up from beside the bleeding Mingma. 'It sounds to me like it's you who has lost his mind, Varma. Why would he kill Shontu? What possible motive could he have? Remember, he came back for Mr Roychoudhuri and Shontu after the group left them!'

'That's what makes me suspicious,' Varma pointed out. 'Why come back alone through the snow and sleet unless he had good reason to?'

'Let's get him inside and get some hot milk or tea into him. That might revive him, and we can ask him to explain what happened. He mentioned an iron door too, as you heard.'

'Iron door, iron door, iron door!' Varma snapped. 'Good lord! If we stay here for longer I think we shall all go mad!'

Tribhuvan looked at Rana. 'Do you have provisions to make tea inside the tower?'

'Yes, yes we do. Mr Roychoudhuri has a medical kit as well. You're an old hand at these things —see if you can find something useful. We must wake this man up. He has vital information that we need right away.'

'Look, let's be sensible about this,' Varma interjected. 'This man needs to be in a hospital. Instead of messing about with first aid here, let's take him back to Syangboche.'

'What, right now?' Rana asked, astonished. 'Won't we look for Shontu?'

'We will, once we come back. But right now, this man needs intensive, hospital-based care. If he dies, we'll never know what he meant. Have you noticed where he's bleeding from?'

Rana looked at Mingma closely. 'From his waist!' he exclaimed. 'That's astonishing.'

'Astonishing indeed,' Varma said, looking grim. 'Everything about this place is odd. One could understand an injury on the hands and feet, perhaps even on the chest or the back. But on the waist? Unless a bear or a yeti tried to bite him ...'

'But Varma, he clearly said that Shontu had fallen into something. We need to revive him to know what that is. If we leave now, we won't be able to come back in time to rescue the boy.'

Just then, Tribhuvan came out of the tower holding something in his hands.

'Here, give him this medicine,' he said to Rana. 'I've put the kettle on for tea. Something warm will do him good.'

'Let's take him inside first,' Rana said. 'I'll carry him. Then we can clean and bandage his wounds.'

Just as Rana bent forward to pick Mingma up, Varma whipped out his revolver.

'There's no need for that,' he said in an oddly calm voice. 'Tribhuvan, throw the medicine down.'

Rana straightened, looking astonished. 'What? What's the meaning of this?' he asked.

Varma pointed his revolver at the two men. 'Inside the tower, both of you!' he instructed. 'Try anything and I'll shoot.'

'Have you actually lost your mind?' Rana snapped. 'What do you think you are doing?'

Varma advanced threateningly. 'Inside, Rana. Now! I gave you enough chances to get on that helicopter and go away, but you were too stubborn to listen. Well, now you die. You've already learnt too much. We can't let you know any more. So shut up and get inside the tower.'

Reluctantly, Rana and Tribhuvan trudged back inside the building.

'I knew he was up to something,' Tribhuvan muttered. 'Kept going on about yetis and stopped us from exploring ... I wonder what he's *really* up to.'

As soon as the two were inside the tower, Varma shut the iron door and bolted it. 'Stay imprisoned for as long as you can live!' he called out. 'I've disabled the wireless – you can't message headquarters, either!'

Then he turned back and began trudging away from the building. When he reached Mingma, he stopped for a second. The man was bleeding out on the snow. Should he kill him, or let him die on his own? It was tempting to just walk away, but a neater ending was probably better. Varma aimed his revolver at Mingma's head.

And that was when Mingma performed his second miraculous act. He was still barely conscious, but in the last few minutes he had recovered enough of his senses to grasp that something was dangerously amiss. When he saw the man in front of him calmly raise a gun to his face, Mingma gathered his dwindling strength, and kicked Varma hard in the stomach.

Varma had not expected Mingma to move, much less attack. He collapsed in a heap on the snow. Enraged, Mingma dragged himself on top of Varma, and began pummelling his face. Despite the utter weakness of his punches, Varma's nose began to bleed. Soon after that, he, too, lost consciousness.

CHAPTER 21

Mingma had, in fact, landed exactly four blows on Varma. After the fourth, he toppled beside Varma. The fight had sapped what little energy had returned to him. Horrific pain from both sides of the waist was pushing him, once again, towards blacking out.

Realizing that he did not have many more conscious minutes, Mingma looked around for Varma's revolver. When he had kicked Varma, the revolver had fallen from his hand and landed a few feet away. With enormous effort, Mingma struggled to his feet. Then he began to wobble slowly towards the revolver. After only a few feet, however, his body gave out. He collapsed.

A few feet away from a locked tower, two men and a revolver lay on the pristine snow, perfectly still.

Inside the tower, Rana and Tribhuvan were still in a state of shock. Rana, in particular, was so stunned by the sudden turn of events that he kept staring blankly at the door that Varma had locked minutes earlier.

'Who is that man, exactly?' Tribhuvan asked in a low voice.

'He ... he is a representative of the Indian government. They sent him specifically to help Mr Roychoudhuri. I don't understand how he ... I mean, he has worked with us for so many years!'

'Did you personally check his ID and papers?'

'No, not personally. But he must have submitted his papers to our head office at Kathmandu!'

'Those could have been faked. Always check documents yourself. Anyway, remember what he said? "You've already learnt too much". What does he think we have learnt?'

'Perhaps about the doorway in the ground. He kept interrupting Mingma when Mingma was trying to tell us about it.'

Tribhuvan shook his head and sat down on a wooden packing box. 'Let's first protect ourselves,' he said. 'Could you lock the door from the inside? Varma might come back, and if he does, he should not be able to walk in on us.'

Rana immediately went to the door and locked it. Then he put his ear on the thick metal to see if he could hear anything from the other side. He could not. Defeated, he walked back to Tribhuvan.

'They have several packets of biscuits, butter, jam,' Tribhuvan observed, looking at the replenished supplies. 'We won't starve. At least not immediately. How long are we expecting to stay here?'

'The rescue team from Kathmandu was supposed to reach today. But I don't know. Varma said the weather was too bad to fly ...'

'I wouldn't automatically trust the things he said. Perhaps he was lying. Or perhaps *he* sent word that rescue was no longer necessary, and that's why the flight is delayed. But let's not go down that road just yet. First, I'll make some tea. A hot cuppa should calm us down. We both need to stay as calm as we can.'

He turned to the little spirit-stove and put on a kettle. Outwardly, he seemed perfectly in control of himself. Rana, however, could not sit still. While the ice-cold water began to slowly gather heat, he clutched and unclutched his hair several times, and walked anxiously about in circles.

'To be locked in this little place! If only we could call for help, Mr Tribhuvan. But he has ruined the wireless set, the devil!'

'Well ... I am fairly familiar with simple electronics. Let's drink our tea. Then I'll tinker around a little with it and see what happens. Have you noticed something, though? The helicopter hasn't taken off yet. Which means Varma is still in the area. I wonder why.'

'He's not going to leave the area. Oh, I've been so stupid! When Mr Roychoudhuri disappeared so abruptly, I should have immediately understood that there was something underground ... somewhere a person can just slip into and vanish. How else can we account for all these lost people? They didn't sprout wings and fly away into the sky!'

'And they're pretty well settled, too,' Tribhuvan added thoughtfully. 'A dog's paw-prints, fresh chicken feathers ... they have quite the colony here. I had seen those paw-prints last time, too. This is not a transient group. These people live here. I wonder who they are.'

'Spies, obviously!'

'But what are they spying on? Our land is a land of ice and nothingness. What do spies hope to see here, especially if they live underground?'

'It's not about "seeing things" these days. They're here to install machinery underground ... I'm sure of it. Think of where we are, Tribhuvan. The borders of so many large nations meet here: India, Russia, and China via Tibet.'

'A delicate spot, yes,' Tribhuvan agreed thoughtfully. 'And then there is Varma. A government insider hand-in-glove with the spies ...'

Just then, the kettle began to whistle. Tribhuvan turned away to make tea. Unlike the agitated Rana, he was quite calm, focusing on tasks at hand instead of pacing about their small prison. He took his time to brew the tea and drink it. Finally, after draining his cup, he looked ready to start work.

'There's a small sitting place above, next to the window. We can keep an eye on things from there if we have binoculars. Could you look around for a pair? Meanwhile, I'll look at the wireless set.'

Rana immediately began searching every corner for binoculars. Tribhuvan began to sedately examine the communication device.

'He's physically broken the set,' he observed after a little while. 'When did he have the time to do this?'

'I have no idea,' Rana said bitterly. 'Can't believe I dragged you into this mess, Tribhuvan. You were not even supposed to be here, but I made you come with us.'

'I have been in situations like this thrice in my life so far, and have, as you can see, survived them all. So please don't worry on my account. Look at the positive side instead: Varma could have shot us. We were sitting ducks. He didn't. Which gives me hope that we might survive this, too.'

Rana looked ready to bite his own hand off in frustration. 'Why didn't I think to come armed? Dammit, I left it in the helicopter! So close, but ...'

'It wouldn't have helped,' Tribhuvan pointed out calmly. 'A firearm can only help if you're aware of the danger. But we were not aware of Varma's betrayal. Had you been aware, you would have tried to stop him much earlier. And had you tried to stop him, he would have shot you. Trusting him has, in fact, saved our lives. Did you find the binoculars?'

'No. Now that I think about it, Mr Roychoudhuri had worn his binoculars around his neck. They have probably disappeared with him ... wait! Why am I looking for Mr Roychoudhuri's binoculars? I have my own! Here, they are in the inside pocket of my snow-jacket. How on earth did it slip my mind? You asked me to look for binoculars, and I immediately started looking for them inside the tower, without even thinking of the ones inside my own pocket!'

Despite the danger, Tribhuvan chortled.

'Check your other pockets, Rana,' he invited. 'Perhaps there's an emergency firearm stashed in one. Then our troubles will truly be at an end.'

Just to be sure, Rana gave his pockets a perfunctory pat. 'Nah, nothing,' he said dejectedly. 'Anyway, I only have that one work-issued LMG. I don't carry personal weapons like Mr Roychoudhuri does.'

'In which case, let us go up and see if that window can help.'

The two of them went carefully up the old stone staircase. The window was too small for both men to look out of at once, so Rana and Tribhuvan took turns. People with binoculars tend to focus on distant things. Tribhuvan and Rana, too, scanned the distant mountains for signs of life. They missed Mingma, who was lying in a heap practically at their own doorstep.

Daylight had begun to die along the horizon. Impenetrable darkness would be upon them soon. The small helicopter was still visible from the tower. Because of the people they had intended to take back with them, Rana had flown the craft himself instead of bringing a pilot. Of course, Varma knew how to fly the helicopter, too. Had he wanted to escape, he would have left by now. Why hadn't he?

It was Tribhuvan's turn to scan the vast snowy stretches when the binoculars suddenly slipped from his hand and bumped down the narrow stone staircase.

'I'll get, I'll get them!' Rana called hurriedly, racing after the instrument. Unable to examine the distant peaks without his visual aid, Tribhuvan casually glanced out of the tower at the ground below.

That was when he saw Varma and Mingma. His heart skipped an enormous beat.

'Rana! Rana! Come upstairs, see this!' he whispered urgently.

'What is it?' Rana called back, alarmed at Tribhuvan's tone. Then he raced back up the stairs with the binoculars. Tribhuvan moved swiftly aside to let Rana look out of the window.

'My god!' Rana exclaimed, all discretion forgotten. 'Are they both dead?'

'No ... how can that be? Who could have killed Varma? Mingma was already unconscious when Varma had locked us in.'

'But he wasn't there. He had collapsed much further to the left. Much further. He must have regained his senses briefly and tried to come to us. But why is Varma down? Did you hear a gunshot?'

'No. He doesn't look dead, either. I think they've both lost consciousness.'

'Tribhuvan, look! Varma's revolver! It's lying right there on the snow!'

'Good lord! If that scoundrel Varma wakes up first, he's going to kill Mingma.'

'We need to wake Mingma up first. He can open the door, and then we'd be three against one.'

'But how? We can shout for him, but ...'

'No, you're right. Shouting might wake Varma up instead.'

'But we must do *something*. Throw water on him, perhaps? Mingma is a lot closer to us than Varma.'

'What are you going to use to throw the water out?'

The back-and-forth would have continued for several more minutes, but a movement in the distance brought both men to an abrupt halt. The skies had dimmed even further, and in the evening's first darkness, two figures were approaching the tower. Two enormous, bipedal, human-like figures.

Both men froze in terror and awe.

'Yeti! Yeti!' Rana whispered, clutching Tribhuvan's sleeve.

Tribhuvan peered into the darkness. 'So it would appear,' he whispered back.

The two approaching figures walked loosely, their whole bodies moving back and forth with every step. They were covered in dark fur, just like mountain bears. They stopped every few steps to peer into the darkness around, but made no noise.

The fearful thrill of the moment was almost suffocating. As the creatures approached, the chill of the stone tower seemed to seep into Rana and Tribhuvan's very bones. After a few seconds, Rana whispered. 'S-s-s-o are we fa-fa-fa-finally seeing a ye-ye-ye-ti?'

'Shhh! They'll hear us!' Tribhuvan admonished. 'Damn this darkness – we can't take pictures!'

The yetis stopped next to Mingma and Varma. They seemed to have zero interest in the tower. They stared at the two men on the ground for a few seconds, then abruptly picked Mingma up. Then began a horrifyingly cruel game. The two enormous creatures began tossing Mingma between them as if he was a ball.

'They're going to kill him,' Rana said with dreadful certainty. 'Look at them, tossing him about. He'll die. Damn it, why didn't I bring my arms! I could have shot them down where they stand! The world doesn't believe in yetis? I'd give them two yeti corpses to believe in!'

'Shhh!' hissed the ever-careful Tribhuvan. 'Look, they're putting him down! What are they going to do next? Play toss with Varma?'

But the yetis did not play toss with Varma. Instead, they picked him up gently, and disappeared into the fast-descending darkness.

CHAPTER 22

Shontu felt like he was floating in a sea of darkness. He opened his eyes once, but saw nothing except the dark. He closed them again. He couldn't work out where he was. Anyway, thinking was exhausting. His body cried out for more sleep.

He was about to sink back into oblivion when he heard a confusion of voices. People were shouting at each other. One of those voices sounded like his uncle. A jolt of lightning shot through Shontu. Had he found Kakababu? He turned towards the noise as quickly as his lethargic body would allow.

At first, he thought he was looking at a bright cluster of aliens or ghosts. Ghosts who were trying to wrestle his uncle away from him. Then he realized that they were not ghosts, or aliens for that matter. They were people in an absurd full-body mask. And one of them was approaching him with a syringe.

Before he could wrap his head around the strangeness of the situation, he heard his uncle shout, 'Run, Shontu! Don't let them inject you!'

Instinctively, Shontu kicked at the man with the syringe. It connected with his stomach. Hard. The man doubled over in pain with a choked cry. The syringe fell to the ground and shattered.

'Clumsy fool!' Kane Shipton growled. 'Get another one!'

Before anyone could rush to get a second syringe, Shontu rolled off the stone table and onto the rough floor. Then he scrambled to his feet and ran. He had no idea where he was going – his only aim was to get away from the men in yellow. Behind him he heard his uncle exclaim, 'Yes, Shontu! Run!' But his voice was abruptly cut off, as if someone had slapped a hand on his mouth.

Shontu ran blindly forward, terrified of being caught. The alley he was in opened into a drop-off, guarded by a railing. With no time to look left or right, he vaulted over the railing and hung from it, surveying the area below. At about a floor's drop, there was an array of strange-looking machines. Apart from the machines, it looked empty. In a bid to escape the masked men, Shontu let go of the railing and dropped in front of the machines.

Meanwhile, enraged at Shontu's escape, Shipton dragged Kakababu to the stone table. Pushing him down on the cold stone, he pointed a deadly-looking firearm at him.

'Call your nephew back, Roychoudhuri,' he ordered.

'No!' Kakababu exclaimed, still panting from the shouting and struggle. 'Shontu, if you can hear me — don't come back!'

'I'll count to ten,' Shipton growled. 'Get your nephew back in this room, or I'll shoot. One, two ...'

'Shontu! Don't come back! Run!'

'Three, four ...'

'You think I'm scared of dying? Then you don't know me, Kane Shipton. You can kill me. But if you do, I promise you that you won't escape from this place either.'

'Five, six ...'

'My nephew won't come back!' Kakababu shouted. 'Finish your countdown! My nephew won't come back to be your captive!'

Shontu had planned to land on his feet, but he couldn't. He stumbled onto the semi-dark floor, and his head hit something invisible. Surprised, he reached out and realised he was touching glass. The machines that he had seen from above were behind a thick glass wall, emitting a soft blue light. Four tunnels led away from this circular central area. They were long, dark tunnels ... Shontu craned his neck but could not see an end to any of them.

The sound of running footsteps brought his attention back to the central area. The men in yellow were coming rapidly down a spiral staircase. Panicking, Shontu nearly ran into one of the tunnels, but then he heard Shipton's raised voice and his threats to kill Kakababu. Above him, Shipton was reaching the end of his countdown. Despite his uncle's exhortations, Shontu could not stay away.

'Don't hurt my uncle!' he called. 'I'm coming up!'

Then he raised his arms in surrender and turned to the two masked men on the stairs. 'I am coming with you!' he shouted, for emphasis. 'Don't hurt him!'

'Shontu, don't!' Kakababu shouted frantically from above. 'They'll kill us both! Run, run away!'

Shontu ignored him. There was no way he could leave his uncle to die. 'I'm coming up!' he called out again, before slowly walking towards the men on the staircase. He could hear his heart beating. Would these people really kill his uncle? Suddenly, off to one side of the room, he saw what looked like a set of electrical metre-boxes. They were mounted on the wall of the cave, at a height of about a head above his. A long lever jutted out of one end. To reach the men, he would have to pass beneath the lever.

Like a bolt of lightning, a plan flashed through his mind. He waited till he was almost under the lever, then jumped up and pulled it down with all his might.

Instantly, the cave was plunged into darkness.

Confusion broke out above. An enraged Shipton began barking orders. Several feet began running about in a hurry. Shontu heard the two men on the stairs run towards him in the darkness, using their familiarity with the cave to get to him. But Shontu had expected that. Which is why he had not let go of the lever after turning the lights out. When he heard the men come close enough, he swung his body from the iron lever, and caught the first man square in the chest with a powerful double-footed kick. The man reeled back and crashed into the man behind him. Shontu immediately let go of the lever, and swiftly moved away from it. Seconds later, a bullet cracked through the silence and shattered the lever. The easy way to bring the lights back on was lost.

'You useless lot!' Shipton bellowed from above. 'You couldn't keep up with a boy? Get the electricity back, or we'll all choke to death in this blasted cave!'

Multiple feet came hesitantly down the spiral staircase at the end of the floor. People began whispering around the switchboard, but the lights did not come back. Shontu briefly considered taking advantage of the confusion to go up to his uncle. But that was risky. With even more people coming down to his floor, the chances of being caught were huge. Instead, he slowly began to feel his way along the cave wall and moved away from the noise. After a few minutes, the wall ended abruptly. Shontu realised he was at the mouth of one of the deep tunnels. Relieved, he took off inside it in a run. Almost instantly he stumbled on the rough stone floor and fell, but the noise did not reach the group of men arguing at the switchboard.

Shipton, meanwhile, had joined his men at the switchboard. 'A boy, a *schoolboy*, got the better of you!' he was snarling. 'Worthless, worthless! Where's the torch? Hold it up, let me see the board.'

As it turned out, none of his men had a torch with them. One of them helpfully lit a cigarette lighter. In its weak flame, the group saw that the switchboard was smoking.

Upstairs, Kakababu slowly let himself down from the stone slab. No men had been left to guard him, as far as he could tell. Perhaps they thought him incapable of flight. Which was partly true. He couldn't run away, especially in this darkness. But he could move, though with difficulty. Feeling things around him, Kakababu slowly made his way to the wall. Then he let the wall guide him towards Kane Shipton's chair. He had noticed a thick iron door behind that chair. What was Shipton hiding behind it?

Well. Now was the time to find out.

The door was unlocked. Kakababu pushed it open and slipped inside. Then he swiftly shut the door and felt about for a latch. Happily, there was a fairly sturdy latch on his side. Relieved, Kakababu secured it.

But his relief did not last. As soon as he turned around, he saw a large glowing, malevolent eye— about the size of an old one-rupee coin—staring straight at him.

It took him a second to realize that the eye was an alarm-light on a set of complex machinery. Had the room not been dark, he would have seen the machines, too. But wait! If the room was still in darkness, then how was the light on the machine glowing? Did these machines have a separate electric line? Intrigued, Kakababu began hobbling towards the light to examine it. Up close, one could hear a low buzz coming from around the red light.

Suddenly, Shipton's words came back to him. He had boasted that some of his machines could kill on contact. What if these machines were like that?

Slowly, Kakababu backed off. Now was not the time to take unnecessary risks. Standing on one leg was becoming increasingly painful, so he slowly lowered himself on the rough stone floor to sit. But as he sat, a warm, furry something brushed against his legs. Alarmed, Kakababu's arm shot out to feel the fur.

It was the dog! It had been sleeping on the floor!

The moment Kakababu touched him, he woke up and began barking. Then, before Kakababu could move away, it snapped at him twice.

Kakababu thought quickly. He needed the dog to calm down. But given that he had already kicked it twice, it was unlikely to stop barking around him. Under normal circumstances, Kakababu was sure the two of them could have been friends. The dog was a beautiful creature, and quite friendly with the other men. But right now, it was both furious at and scared of him. How could he get it to trust him, at least a little? Kakababu let the dog get a few nips in, hoping it would calm it down. But that didn't work. The only way it would stop making a racket, Kakababu realised, was if it was reassured that he was not a threat. The next time the little dog lunged at him, Kakababu caught it expertly and closed its mouth with one strong palm. Then, cradling it against his body, he began stroking the dog soothingly.

Below him, Shontu was still blindly running in the dark tunnel when he crashed into a wall and ricocheted onto the floor. When he managed to get up, he realized that he had reached the end of the tunnel. There was nowhere else to go. He could hear voices in the distance.

At that very moment, his hiding-place was flooded with light. Kane Shipton had managed to repair the fault.

Shontu pressed himself against the far wall of the cave. The tunnel was fairly straight, so if the men in yellow stood at the mouth of the tunnel and looked in, they would almost certainly spot him. Just as he had the thought, two of the yellow men walked past the tunnel-entrance. Shontu looked around, desperate for another hiding spot. He spotted the opening of another tunnel a little ahead of him, on the opposite tunnel-wall. He could sprint to that tunnel in a few seconds. But if the men now guarding the mouth of the main tunnel turned around, they would see him making the run. Shontu decided to take the risk. Pursing his lips in concentration, he shot a final look at the guards and ran straight into the smaller tunnel. Within seconds, he had been engulfed in the smaller tunnel's reassuring semi-darkness.

CHAPTER 23

The moment the lights came back on, Kakababu did a quick survey of the array of machines. The dog, meanwhile, was scrambling to get out of his grip. No amount of cuddling and petting had convinced it that Kakababu was a friend worth having. The more Kakababu petted and cuddled it, the harder it fought to be free.

Holding on to the squirming dog, Kakababu looked around the room. There were several large packing boxes in front of the machines. Gingerly opening a few closest to him, Kakababu saw that they were filled with machine parts. Hmm. Kakababu did not know much about machines – even less about modern devices. He stared thoughtfully at the red-topped machine while he tried to work out what it could be. Some sort of a computer? But why would a group of spies dig several metres into frozen ground to install such sophisticated machinery, especially in such a remote, frozen desert?

Abruptly, a thought occurred to him. The dog had been in this room alone before him. Surely, being a dog, it wouldn't know that the red light was a warning, and had probably touched the machines. Yet here it was, full of vigour. Kakababu walked towards the machines with a new confidence.

When he was almost at the machine with the red light, the peace around him erupted in noise. Someone was banging on the thick iron door behind him. Kakababu glanced at the latch. It was secure. As long as it held, he would be safe in this room.

'Don't be a fool, Roychoudhuri! Open this door!' Shipton shouted from the other side.

'I can't at the moment, sorry,' Kakababu called back.

'What? Open it right now!' Shipton demanded.

'Busy at the moment, Shipton. Come back later,' Kakababu responded. He was enjoying annoying his captor.

'If you don't open the door, I swear I'll blast it to the ground!' Shipton threatened.

'It's your door,' Kakababu responded with infuriating calm. 'If you want to blast it to the ground. I'm not going to stop you.'

Then he went up to the machines and began examining them. In addition to the big red light on top, they also had rows upon rows of smaller, colourful buttons. He pressed a button. Immediately, the machine blared, 'Two two nine. KY seven seven. Alpha omega ...'

Kakababu took a sharp step back. He had not expected the machine to suddenly scream in his face. Was that a recording? What did the code mean?

'Don't touch the buttons, Roychoudhuri, you'll die!' Shipton urged from outside the door. Kakababu noted the panic in his voice. 'Open the door. We need to urgently discuss your nephew.'

These were both such obvious lies that Kakababu smiled. Die indeed! Had the buttons been truly dangerous, he would have been dead already. And had Shipton really wanted to discuss Shontu, he would have talked about that right away, not waited for Kakababu to start pressing buttons.

'I'm busy with something a bit more urgent than that, so you will have to wait,' he called back. Then he pressed another button. A panel on the machine snapped open with a loud metallic clang. Inside, there were several tiny clock-like things in a protective glass cover. Kakababu took a cautious step back, but nonetheless pressed the next button. The clocks began to beep in unison.

Outside the door, Shipton abandoned all pretence of patience. He began screaming almost incoherently at Kakababu to open the door and let him in.

Kakababu ignored him. He had just realised why Shipton was so frantic to get him away from the machines. These machines were receivers and transmitters — they sent and received messages to and from whoever had sent Shipton here. If he pressed the buttons at random, then the machines would send a cluster of garbled messages out, warning Shipton's employers that something had gone very wrong. They were likely very dangerous people, and Shipton did not want them to know that he had failed at keeping the cave safe.

'Look, Roychoudhuri,' he finally shouted. 'I want to give you an opportunity. If you open the door and come out, then I will let you go. No one will harm a hair on your head. You'll be free.'

'Really? Why the sudden generosity, Shipton?'

'It's for our own sake. If you touch the wrong buttons on that machine, the entire cave will explode.'

'You expect me to believe that fairytale, do you?'

'I'm telling the truth!'

'Well, since I cannot escape from this cave, I might as well die quickly and take all of you with me.'

'What? I just told you I'll let you go! I'll let your nephew go, too. Now come out.'

'Where's my nephew, Shipton?'

'He's right here! Come out and you can see him.'

'Ask him to say something. I want to hear his voice.'

Shipton abruptly fell silent.

Inside the room, Kakababu grinned. He had caught Shipton in his lie. These men, with all their weapons, had not been able to catch Shontu. His nephew must be darting through the maze of tunnels and sub-tunnels that filled this place, eluding and frustrating the Yellow Suits. Despite the danger, his heart swelled with pride for the boy.

A few seconds later, he heard Shipton's voice again. He was further away from the door, and was shouting at his own men. Kakababu heard snatches of it through the door. 'Can't even catch a boy ... worthless lumps ... get him here!'

Using the brief respite it gave him, Kakababu tried to assess how much of Shipton's warnings could be true. The only reason he could not entirely dismiss the claim of the buttons causing an explosion was that he knew that spies often built such protection into their lairs. They would much rather die than be caught. But there was no one here to "catch" Shipton if he did push a wrong button. They could easily escape and rebuild elsewhere. So why were he and his men not trying to do just that?

'Kane Shipton!' he bellowed. 'I will give you and your men a few seconds to escape. Run! Run for your lives! I will start pressing every button on this panel, in every combination I can think of! Save yourselves!'

'Bloody fool!' Shipton growled. 'You'll kill yourself with this madness! Listen, no one has to die. Come closer to the door. Let's discuss a safe passage for you.'

Just then, Kakababu heard a low hissing noise. He stared at the machines, wondering if he had indeed triggered an automated destruction. But no, the noise was coming from somewhere else. Kakababu turned slowly around. There! It was coming from the door! It took him a second to work out what it was. Shipton had no interest in letting him go – of course not! He was trying to distract Kakababu from noticing that his men were trying to melt a hole in the solid iron door. Once they had even a tiny hole, they could shoot Kakababu through it. This was why Shipton was trying to lure him closer to the door! The closer he was, the greater their chances of injuring him.

Kakababu hobbled back to the machines as fast as he could. His precious freedom would end as soon as a small slot appeared on the door. If Shipton's men caught him again, they would make sure that the rest of his life would be spent in this lonely, blizzard-ridden land.

But what if there was indeed an explosion button, and he *did* end up blowing up the cave? As much as he told himself that Shipton was a liar, Kakababu couldn't get the niggling worry out of his head. Had it only been him, he would not have hesitated for a second before pressing every single button on the panel, and consequences be damned! But he had Shontu to worry about. What if his recklessness killed Shontu?

On the other hand, if these people caught Shontu, then he would die anyway, and rather more unpleasantly.

Kakababu looked down at the panel. Fourteen more buttons remained untested. He would have to take the chance, Kakababu decided. After some hesitation, he steeled himself and pressed a large yellow button.

What happened next filled him with such unbridled joy that his usual stern demeanour gave way to open delight. The button began a low whirring, and within seconds he saw the roof of the room begin to move. It took him a second to note that the roof was not made of rocks, but two iron plates made to look like them. These plates now receded into their frames, and the cold brightness of the blue sky rushed in to chase away the cave's darkness. The freezing air filled Kakababu's lungs with a crisp freshness. After hours of being underground, the needle-sharp air felt like the most beautiful thing he had ever experienced. He closed his eyes, turned his face towards the blue sky, and took several deep breaths.

Though the escape route was now open, the walls of the cave were too steep for Kakababu to scale. So he did the only thing he could do to advertise the cave's presence to the outside world. He lifted the dog he had been cradling, and tossed it upwards – right out of the cave.

The dog landed softly on the snow-covered ground above, and immediately began barking with all its might.

CHAPTER 24

Shontu had been running along the smaller tunnel for so long that he had lost track of time. All he knew was that he must stay ahead of the men in yellow. The tunnel had fewer lights than the bigger tunnels, so for most of the time he was running in semi-darkness. Unlike the main tunnel, this one seemed to be endless. How far inside the mountain did it go? Was he far enough inside to be safe? Almost out of breath, Shontu stopped and looked back at the mouth of the main tunnel. On the one hand, he was not as far away from it as he had hoped. On the other, there were no men in yellow after him. At least, not yet.

While running down this smaller tunnel, Shontu had noticed little caves along the tunnel wall, fashioned into rooms. Now that he had the time to catch his breath, he decided to peek inside one to see what it was like. There were a pair of them just a little ahead of him, deeper into the tunnel. Looking about him cautiously, Shontu slipped into the first one.

It took a little while for his eyes to adjust to the darkness. And then he let out a piercing scream. There were four yetis in the room, staring straight at him! Each of them was about one and a half times the height of a tall human, and they were all sitting with their backs against the far wall. He wanted to run flat out of the room and the tunnel, but he could not bring himself to turn his back on the yetis. His heart was beating a mile a minute. Disoriented and terrified, he took a few stumbling steps back. Then the uneven floor tripped him, and he crumpled into a heap on it.

Scrambling back to his feet, Shontu blindly found his way out of the room. Almost immediately, he heard voices in the tunnel. His shout had given him away. The men in yellow were finally coming after him. They were one dark turn away from seeing him.

And like a bolt of lightning, two things flashed across Shontu's mind. One, he had to go back into the dark room to save himself, no matter how scared he was. And two, those yetis were not real.

As soon as he had the second thought, Shontu ran back inside the room. There was only a little space between the yetis and the wall. He dove into that space, hiding himself behind a yeti's enormous body.

Seconds later, three men in yellow masks lit up the doorway of the room. They each carried a powerful torch and a firearm.

'Where's that boy?' one of them asked. 'I thought he had come this way.'

'Yes, fairly certain the scream came from one of these rooms,' the second replied.

'I don't know ... I thought the scream came from upstairs,' the third man interjected.

The men scanned the room with their torches again. The second man came a few feet inside to take a closer look around.

'Well, he's not here now. Wonder where he went,' he said after a few seconds.

'Let's go upstairs,' the third man insisted. 'Something's happening there ... there's been a lot of noise.'

There was a brief hesitation, then the men walked back towards the larger tunnel. Their boots stomped and echoed on the stone floor.

For as long as the men were in the room, Shontu had held his breath. He was sure that the thumping of his heart would have given him away. When he was sure that they had left, he exhaled deeply. His arms and legs became wobbly with relief, and he slowly slid to the floor. The floor was covered in hay, making it scratchy but warm. The yeti-suits were also filled with hay. That's why they had looked so real from a distance. Shontu stroked them carefully. He was not scared at all now. Had the room had enough light, he would have seen straight away that the "yetis" were not real. To begin with, their "eyes" were not even there. In their place were eye-shaped cut-outs, so that the person inside the suit could see.

Shontu toyed with the idea of slipping inside one of the suits himself. The men would never find him then! But after trying one, Shontu found that he was too small for them. They had been made for the tall men in yellow, not a boy his size. Besides, if he hid inside those suits, then he would have to remain in this room. That wouldn't do. His uncle was alone upstairs, at the mercy of these horrible men. Who knew what they had done to him? Kakababu couldn't even run away, like he had done. Had the men beaten him up? Killed him? No! Shontu would have to go upstairs as soon as he could!

He stepped very carefully out of the room. There was no one in the smaller tunnel. The men were probably already upstairs. After walking along the tunnel-wall in semi-darkness for a few minutes, Shontu realised that he was lost. When he had run into the smaller tunnel from the bigger one, he had thought that it was a simple system of one tunnel leading into another. Now he saw that the tunnels were a branching system, with multiple big and small ones leading off from one another. Half of them were well-lit, the other half were in semi-darkness. He ran backwards and forwards a few times, but could not identify the tunnel he had come from.

Then he found a room. This room had no doors, which told him he had not been in that tunnel before.

A strange cheeping noise came from it. Carefully, Shontu peeked into the room. To his astonishment, he saw a big cage of live hens. Two large refrigerators were next to it, next to them a pile of potatoes and onions. So this was the Yellow People's storeroom and pantry! Suddenly, Shontu realised that this is where those hens must have come from – the ones that had been so mercilessly killed outside the tower! He was tempted to explore the pantry further, but he really had to find a way upstairs, and soon. Reluctantly, he pulled himself away and headed for the next brightly-lit tunnel. Light was now his only way of choosing a path.

As soon as Shontu stepped into the new tunnel, he heard voices. Invisible people were speaking to each other in low murmurs. Someone else was breathing so loudly that it could be heard outside the room.

Shontu froze. This room appeared to have no door either. If he walked past the room, the people inside would see him straight away. What should he do? Should he turn around? No. This was the only tunnel he had found that led towards brighter light, instead of branching off into semi-darkness. Surely that meant that this one led to the stairs? No, he could not abandon this path. If only he knew what the men inside were doing! Steeling himself to run past if the men saw him, Shontu stepped closer to the doorway and tried to listen.

What had sounded like loud breathing moments ago now sounded like laboured, painful gasps. And the "voices" was really one man muttering to himself.

Was this the Yellow Masks' hospital room? Were the men inside ill? Good! Then they wouldn't be able to run after him! Bolstered by this belief, Shontu peeked into the room.

He nearly screamed again.

Who were these people? They looked like walking skeletons! Only two of them were upright. Both were in their underwear, their skin filthy and baggy over their incredibly thin frames. One glance told Shontu that they were very, very sick – likely deprived of food for several months. One of the men looked like he was from China. He could not make out the other's face, because it was covered in matted hair and an unkempt beard. The laboured breathing was coming from both of them. Their eyes were unseeing, utterly lifeless. They stared straight at Shontu, but Shontu had an unsettling feeling that they didn't really see him.

'Who are you?' he asked them.

Neither man responded. They continued to stare at him.

Shontu's heart broke. This was not a hospital room. This was a prison. The two men looked like husks of human beings. They were so thin that Shontu could see their chest rise and fall with each heartbeat. Suddenly, he remembered the man whose corpse had been abandoned near their tower. That man must have been a prisoner here, too! He had been just as emaciated. Oh, these awful, awful people! They locked people up in this maze of tunnels without food or clothes! How cruel could they be?

'Who are you people?' he asked again, taking a few steps into the room. 'Can you come with me?'

The dead eyes stared through him.

Had Shontu been present when Shipton was threatening his uncle, he would have known that these men were, in fact, being systematically starved to death. Once they passed, their bodies would be tossed on the snow outside. If they were ever found, the police would chalk their deaths up to exposure. As it was, Shontu was forced to give up on rescuing the men. He felt dreadful about leaving them behind, but his uncle came first. He had to make his way upstairs and help him.

Forcing himself to look away from the men, Shontu backed out of the room and began walking towards the brighter lights. But the sound of laboured breathing echoed in his ears. He shook his head and began to run, but the sound persisted. Desperate, Shontu clapped his hands on his ears and ran blindly towards the light. Which is why he missed the first sounds of raised voices coming from the other end of the tunnel.

Luckily for him, he took one palm off his ear just before the tunnel merged with a big tunnel. Noise from above exploded around him. Someone was bringing the roof down on someone else, calling them worthless. Shontu shuddered. The man sounded dangerous. On the other hand, if he could hear voices, then he was on the right track. He stopped running and began approaching the bigger tunnel more cautiously. After a few minutes, he saw a familiar blue glow in the distance. That could only come from the downstairs room with the machines. Good! He was on the right path.

The bigger tunnel turned out to be empty as well. The men hunting him must really have gone upstairs. This made Shontu quite happy at first. Without anyone downstairs to guard the area, he could easily slip into the blue-lit room, and take the spiral staircase up. But then he realised that once upstairs, he would have to face the full army of the Yellow Mask.

Just as he was about to step into the machine-room, he heard the voice from earlier shout, 'We have your nephew! If you don't open the door, we will kill him!'

Shontu stopped. The man was obviously talking about him. Had Kakababu barricaded himself into a room? Is that why they were threatening him with Shontu's death? Shontu's first instinct was to shout and tell his uncle not to open the door, that the man was lying about having him. But he immediately understood how stupid that would be. The men had no idea where he was now, but as soon as he shouted, they would run down and capture him. Then Kakababu would *have* to open the door. No, it was best that he kept quiet.

The angry man began shouting again. From what Shontu could hear, he was telling off the others for failing to do something. Then he began shouting at Kakababu to stop pressing buttons. What buttons were these? Was Kakababu near a dangerous machine? Curious, Shontu took several steps into the blue-lit room. He was so focused on hearing what the man above was saying that he did not notice when four men in yellow appeared at the top of the spiral staircase. By the time they began thundering down the steps, it was already too late. They had spotted him.

The moment Shontu saw a revolver aimed at him, he hurled himself at the stone floor. Travelling with Kakababu on his adventures had taught him that people on the ground were harder to hit.

'Don't shoot!' one of the men cried out. 'We have to take him alive!'

Oh, they were not allowed to shoot him? Shontu shot back to his feet. If they were not allowed to shoot him, then he had nothing to fear. He was much faster than these masked lumps! Let them catch him – if they could!

Shontu ran right back into the bright tunnel. The men were several metres behind him, but the trouble was that they could see him. He needed a darker tunnel to disappear into. How far in did the smaller tunnels begin to appear?

Almost immediately, a small tunnel opened up to his right. Shontu dove into it. This tunnel was almost completely dark. Whatever little light it had was filtered in from the brighter tunnels at both its ends. The men chasing him must have missed the tunnel. There was a brief pause in their boot-stomping, but then they carried on down the bigger tunnel. Shontu decided to wait a few minutes, then make his way back to the main tunnel and slip upstairs.

To his complete shock, however, a powerful beam of light hit him straight in the face only moments later. The men had not actually missed the tunnel! They had simply gone further along, and slipped in from the other end! Alarmed, Shontu began running for the entrance he had come in through. He was almost there when he saw two men in yellow blocking the way. Shontu felt his blood run cold. The men in yellow were smarter than he had thought. They had cornered him in the tunnel! Shontu felt like a mouse at the mercy of four very large yellow cats. He could not surrender. He *would* not surrender! But what else could he do?

Now terrified, Shontu began running back towards the middle of the tunnel. Maybe this tunnel opened into another one. All he had to do was slip into it and keep running. He first ran along one wall, then turned and ran along the other. Desperate, he ran along the first wall again. The men were coming closer and closer. Their boots echoed in the narrow tunnel. Almost out of his mind with fear, Shontu began feeling the walls for another tunnel-mouth. The rational part of his mind was telling him that there were no tunnels attached to this one, but he could not make himself stop trying.

And then the cave exploded.

At least, that is what it felt like. A deafening whirring filled the air, and the floor beneath his feet shook violently. A few jutting edges broke off from the tunnel-wall and crashed to the stone floor, one missing him by barely an inch. Despite the danger, Shontu froze. Was the cave collapsing? Would he be buried alive?

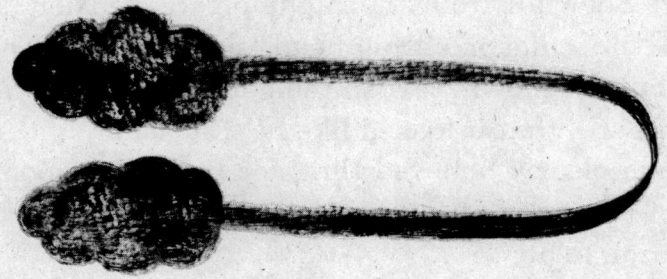

CHAPTER 25

After an hour of keeping vigil by the small window at the tower, Rana had fallen asleep next to it. Thomas Tribhuvan had come downstairs to sleep on the ground floor. When dawn's first light filtered down to his bed, Tribhuvan woke up. Rana was still fast asleep. Tribhuvan lit the spirit-lamp to make tea, then went up with it to rouse Rana.

Rana took a few minutes to wake up. As he stretched and rubbed warmth into his limbs, his eyes fell on the snow outside. Amazed, he whispered, 'Look, Thomas! Look!'

Tribhuvan quickly leaned forward to see. His jaw dropped open as well.

The previous night, after the yetis had played toss with Mingma and then discarded him on the snow, both Rana and Tribhuvan had assumed that Mingma had passed away. It was the only sensible conclusion. No man could survive the brutality of the yetis' game, especially if they had already been horribly injured before. Yet there was Mingma, sitting upright on the snow! Snowfall from the night before had left little fluffy white heaps on his head, shoulders, and back. He made no move to brush them off. In fact, he was so utterly still that it looked like he was dead.

Rana clearly believed that, for he made a noise of regret and sympathy. 'Poor fellow! To sit up and then be frozen to death ...'

'You think he's dead?' Tribhuvan asked, peering at Mingma. 'I'm not sure that's the case.'

'How could anyone be alive after being out in the snow all night?'

'You haven't known Sherpas as well as I have. They are astonishingly resilient. It's almost like they live to defy death.'

Then he cupped his palms around his mouth and bellowed, 'Mingma! MINGMA! M-I-I-I-N-G-M-A-A-A!!!'

Mingma did not even twitch. Undeterred, Tribhuvan kept shouting his name into the freezing air. Rana joined him. But despite their synchronized shouts, Mingma's body showed no signs of life.

'If we only had your firearm!' Tribhuvan said, frustrated. 'A shot would definitely wake him up.'

'Thomas, give up,' Rana advised, disheartened. 'He's not with us anymore. No one would sleep through the racket we made – especially not with such a ramrod straight back. He's been frozen in place, poor chap.'

Tribhuvan did not argue with him. Instead, he went down the narrow stone stairs, and came back up a few minutes later with several things: tins of cheese, a few metal tools and kitchen equipment.

'Mingma is our last hope of getting out of this tower,' he explained. 'We cannot give up till we've tried absolutely everything. Now, I'm an old man, and my throwing arm is not what it used to be. Could you take these things one at a time, and throw them at him through the window? If something heavy hits him, I'm sure he'll wake up.'

Sighing, Rana picked up a small hammer from Tribhuvan's pile. He had considerable doubts about Tribhuvan's idea. Besides, the small window was grilled with iron rods set so close to each other that slipping even a human palm through was hard. Still, Rana managed to push his hand through, and threw a succession of objects at Mingma. Every last one flew over Mingma's head and landed several metres beyond.

'Perhaps you are a bit too strong,' Tribhuvan said dryly. 'Here, let me try.'

He picked up a kitchen tong, and after several seconds of careful aim, hit Mingma squarely on the back with it.

Mingma still did not move.

'We need something heavier,' Tribhuvan declared. Landing the tongs had bolstered his hopes. After three unsuccessful tries, the fourth missile—a tin of cheese—hit Mingma on his back. Mingma finally showed a reaction. He toppled to the side like a felled piece of wood.

'Mingma!' Rana shouted in alarm, just as Tribhuvan hopefully called, 'Mingma?'

Very, very slowly, Mingma turned his head towards the tower. Tribhuvan clasped Rana's hand in excitement. 'Told you! Didn't I tell you? Sherpas are hardy. A little snow can't kill them!'

'Can you hear us, Mingma?' Rana shouted through the window. 'Mingma! Can you hear us? Please unlatch the door. We've been locked in!'

Mingma struggled to sit up again. It was immediately obvious that he was incredibly weak. After a few seconds, Mingma raised his arm and said something. But his voice was so weak that the wind swallowed it.

'Please, my brother, try!' Tribhuvan pleaded. 'I know it's painful, but there's no one else here to let us out.'

Mingma tried to struggle to his feet, but collapsed.

'Mingma, there is a fire inside the tower,' Rana shouted. 'We have hot tea, brandy, medicines. You just have to reach us.'

After a few seconds, Mingma tried again. Instead of standing, he turned on his belly, then pushed his upper body up on his elbows. Then he began crawling towards the tower. Rana and Tribhuvan watched his progress anxiously. After about four feet, however, Mingma's elbows gave way. He fell back on the frozen ground.

'He's fainted again,' Rana groaned.

'No, he's resting,' Tribhuvan corrected. 'Wait and watch.'

True to his prediction, Mingma raised his head after a few minutes. Raising himself on his elbows, he crawled forward for another few feet, before letting go again. This happened a few more times. Despite the near-insurmountable odds, Mingma managed to come within a few feet of the door. But then he went down, and did not come back up. Five minutes passed. Then ten, then fifteen. Rana and Tribhuvan could barely contain their bubbling anxiety. Rana bit his lower lip so often that it was at the point of bleeding.

'What's wrong, Mingma?' he finally shouted. 'Please, you just have a few more feet!'

Mingma raised his head with effort. 'Can't, sa'ab,' he gasped. 'Too ... tired. Can't ... move.'

'Try again!' Rana exhorted. The worry in his voice was beginning to sound like desperation. 'A simple unlatch, Mingma. Then we can save you, and you can save us.'

Mingma tried to move again. But it was, finally, too much for his heavily-injured body. His head lolled to one side, and it was clear to anyone watching that he had lost consciousness once again.

'Even a Sherpa's endurance has limits,' Tribhuvan sighed. 'Still, look at how far he has come. A heroic act.'

'We'll wait till he wakes up,' Rana said. He seemed to deflate with resignation.

For the next several minutes, the two of them watched Mingma almost without blinking. But Mingma remained perfectly still, tantalizingly close to the latched door.

'All right, we need a break,' Tribhuvan finally exclaimed. 'Honestly, we'll give ourselves headaches if we keep staring at Mingma. I'll go down to make us a cuppa. You can wait here if you like.'

The moment Tribhuvan turned away from the window, though, Rana's arm shot out and grasped his.

'Wait! Listen!' he whispered.

'Listen to what?' Tribhuvan asked, surprised.

Rana was peering out of the window again. 'The noise. Can't you hear the noise?'

'Rana ... you should sit back and relax for a while. We have a long wait ahead of us. Don't let the worry get to you. There is no noise.'

'Listen carefully!' Rana insisted, now scanning the sky.

Tribhuvan listened. There was, in fact, a distant mechanical sound, growing louder. It sounded like an engine in full throttle. Soon, the noise of whirring blades filled the sky. Two large helicopters came into view. They were descending rapidly, obviously aiming for the tower. In sheer joy, Rana and Tribhuvan threw themselves into each other's arms.

Within minutes, the copters landed. Eleven commandos jumped out of the first, snapped into a defensive formation, and began running towards the tower. Almost beside himself with joy, Rana pushed his palm out through the narrow grill again, and begun frantically waving his handkerchief at them. The commandos reached the tower in a few seconds. They unlatched the door and swarmed every corner of the small tower.

Rana and Tribhuvan ran past them to Mingma. He was still out cold. Between the two of them, they lifted Mingma and ran back to the warmth of the tower. Rana held him upright while Tribhuvan carefully poured a measure of brandy down his throat. Then they heated water in the small saucepan and began making hot-water bottles for him. Two of the commandos began a complicated process of pressing his chest and blowing into his mouth to get him to start breathing normally.

After the initial melee subsided a little, a commando approached Rana and introduced himself. 'I am Veerendra. I have ten men with me trained in hand-to-hand and ops on these terrains. We need to plan the rescue right now. Our instructions are to move fast.'

'This terrain has been changed,' Tribhuvan cut in. 'Till a few years ago, there used to be several underground caves here, just off the route most trekkers or hikers still take. Their roofs were slightly above ground, which is how we could see them as we came and went. Then, just before I retired, the caves disappeared. None of the new people even know that they used to be here. I have long suspected that agents of foreign powers razed the top to hide them from view, so that they could build a pad for their agents inside. If Mr Roychoudhuri has been kidnapped, then

I am ready to bet that that is where he has been taken. Veerendraji, are you carrying dynamite?'

Veerendra smiled slightly. 'It's a rescue mission in the hills. We are carrying what we need to.'

'Good. I am pretty sure the iron sheet Mingma spoke of is the gateway. We will have to blast our way in.'

'But for that Mingma will have to show us the way,' Rana said. 'Mingma? Are you up for it?'

Mingma nodded. Then, abruptly, he began sobbing. 'I couldn't keep them safe, sa'ab,' he cried. 'Uncle sa'ab and young Shontu sa'ab — I let them be taken! Please sa'ab, bring them back. I'm worthless now. I can't even stand! I'll never use my legs again!'

'That's nonsense,' Rana said firmly. 'A few days' rest and proper medicine, that's all you need. You'll be back on your feet in no time. Now, show us the place so that we can wrap this up. We'll carry you.'

At a slight signal from Veerendra, two commandos picked Mingma up. Once again, the team fell into formation, and everyone set out.

Despite being in immense pain, Mingma identified the spot at once. The commandos began digging with snow shovels. Within ten minutes, the iron sheet began to peek out from beneath the snow.

At Veerendra's order, Mingma was taken far away from the spot and put down on the snow. He needed to be out of harm's way when the battle began in earnest. The men then cleared the rest of the snow, and snapped four sticks of explosives to four corners of the iron sheet. Then they, too, moved out in a very wide circle. Every last person needed to be outside the radius of explosion, so that flying pieces of the exploded iron door did not land on their heads. After everyone was in position, Veerendra readied his team to begin the explosions.

Rana and Tribhuvan had been sent further out than the rest of the team, so that they did not get in the way. As they prepared to cover their ears in anticipation of the blast, a dog began barking behind them. As one, the two men whipped around. How on earth could there be a dog here? It would die of the cold in a day!

'Did you hear that? The dog?' Tribhuvan asked.

'Yes! And if there is a dog, there will be humans. Thomas, we're at the right place!'

Just then, the ground beneath their feet shook, and the iron sheet exploded into a hundred pieces.

———

The door that Kakababu had barricaded himself behind suddenly swung open. Shipton had had his men melt the part of the door that supported the latch. Shipton came into the room jubilant with victory, but as soon as he saw the open roof, his face reddened with fury. He screamed out a long string of expletives. And then he heard his dog bark. Shipton nearly lost his mind with rage. 'That damned man!' he bellowed. 'He's escaped with my dog!'

One of his men in yellow had followed him into the room with the oxy-acetylene cylinder. Shipton whirled to face him. 'Call Four, Seven, and Nine. Fast! We're

going after him right now! We can't let him tell the
world what he's seen.'

The masked man ran out of the room. Shipton
looked at the open roof again. His dog was barking
incessantly now. He tried to call it back into the cave.

'Come here, boy! Come here! Hey, come back!'

The dog paid him no attention. In fact, it began
moving away from the roof-mouth. *Was it following
that crippled fool?* Shipton gritted his teeth. The roof
was not too high, and he was fit and strong. He could
climb up to the roof quite easily. But should he go after
Roychoudhuri alone? *Well*, thought Shipton, *why not?*
Roychoudhuri was disabled and without his crutches.
Shipton was armed. Besides, his men would be right
behind him, whereas Roychoudhuri was alone. Feeling
confident, Shipton tucked his revolver between his
teeth, and prepared to launch himself at the cave-wall.

Just then, two arms came around from behind him,
and tightened like a vice around his neck.

The attack took Shipton by such surprise that for
several seconds he could not even respond. Then he
began shaking his head with all his might, trying
to loosen the grip. But precious time had been lost
in between, and Shipton could feel himself choking.
His jaws slackened, and the revolver fell with a loud
clatter on the stone below. Too late, Shipton realised
that he had been outsmarted.

The truth was that Kakababu hadn't even planned
on tricking Shipton. He was a direct sort of a person,
and not much for underhanded measures. The reason

he was in the semi-dark alcove in one corner of the room was because that was where the panels of buttons were. He had not thought of hiding at all. His plan was to throw himself on the entire panel the moment Shipton breached the door, and reduce the whole cave to rubble. If he could not defeat the spies, then he would destroy them ... and himself with them!

However, Shipton's hasty assumption about his escape had given him pause. And then the overconfident Shipton had become even more careless, and had all but placed his own neck into Kakababu's arms. Trouble was, Shipton was just as strong as Kakababu. If Kakababu allowed their grappling to become a full-fledged fight, then he very well might lose to the man. No, he would have to disorient Shipton for a few seconds. That would give him enough time to commandeer Shipton's weapon. And once he had the weapon, he could win this battle.

Just as Shipton was about to wrench himself away from Kakababu, the floor beneath their feet shuddered violently. Both men collapsed on the floor and rolled away in different directions. Then the cave exploded. Chunks of the wall sprayed across the room, hitting both men indiscriminately on the head, back, and legs. Acrid smoke filled the space. Before losing consciousness, Kakababu had a brief moment of clarity. He felt like he was drowning in a sea of sharp-edged pebbles.

The commandos fired a precautionary round into the cave before swarming in. The attack was so abrupt and swift that the men in yellow were taken completely by surprise. Quite a few of them had been hurt by the explosion. Some of the others put up a fight, but they were both outnumbered and outmanoeuvred by the commandos. Soon, the commandos took over that floor.

Shontu and his captors had been on the floor below. They understood the gravity of the situation only when they came upstairs into the central area. The first two men had been sent ahead to find out what had caused the sudden explosion. These two were smart. They surrendered the moment they faced the uniformed men. But the two holding Shontu refused to surrender. When they discovered that they had been surrounded, one of them raised his revolver to Shontu's temple.

'Keep moving forward,' he whispered. 'Try anything smart, and I'll shoot you.'

Shontu obeyed. He was not particularly scared of the revolver at his temple, but he felt bad at having been caught. Would these men use him to bargain their way out? That would be dreadful! And who were the people who had caused the explosion? Were they the police? The military? Or more bad people?

The commandos saw them coming as they approached another short staircase.

'Don't try to stop us,' the man with the revolver warned them. 'We'll shoot this boy if you try anything.'

The commandos were taken aback. Then, after a rapid whispered consultation, they fell back.

Shontu's group began to climb the stairs. While climbing, Shontu briefly glanced up. To his amazement, he saw Rana behind the row of uniformed men. Immediately, he knew that the uniformed men were there to rescue him and his uncle. They were the good folks, not another group of criminals.

Rana, meanwhile, was whispering with Veerendra. Veerendra proposed something. Rana nodded. Then Veerendra moved discreetly away from him.

When Shontu and his captors reached the top of the stairs, they saw that their way to the exit was lined with men in military uniform. The exit itself had been blown to smithereens, and was now a gaping hole that anyone could simply stroll out of.

'We will be leaving with this boy,' the man holding his revolver to Shontu's temple said. 'If we are stopped, this boy dies.'

'Where is Mr Roychoudhuri?' Veerendra asked.

Before the men could respond, Shontu said, 'My uncle was in the rooms on the left.'

'Shontu,' Rana suddenly said in excellent Bengali, 'after you take the next seven steps, drop to the ground.'

Shontu could not make head or tail of this absurd instruction, but he decided to follow it. Exactly seven steps later, he dropped to the floor and rolled away. Before his captors could react, several submachine guns roared to life. Soon Shontu's captors, too, were on the floor. But unlike him, they no longer had the ability to roll away. Not that Shontu spared them a glance. The moment the shooting stopped, he picked himself up and ran to Rana. Both Rana and Veerendra swiftly patted him down for injuries. When they found that he was unhurt, both men exhaled in relief.

'Where is that traitor Varma?' Rana asked. 'He must be here somewhere!'

But Shontu had no interest in Varma. He wanted to find his uncle. To the left of the stairs was that room with the stone table, the one in which Shipton had been threatening Kakababu. Shontu pushed his way into the room. Rana and Veerendra followed on his heels. The room was empty, but there was a half-melted open door that led into another room. All three of them stepped gingerly into that room.

This room was amazing. It had apparently had a retractable roof, and that roof was currently open. Daylight flooded the room, chasing the cave's darkness into the far corners. It was in such a corner that Shontu spotted his uncle. Kakababu was lying next to a large machine that had been placed against the cave's far wall. He looked unconscious. Stone dust from the exploded cave wall coated his clothes. Alarmed, Shontu ran up to his uncle. 'Kakababu! Wake up!' he demanded urgently, gently shaking the man.

Kakababu sat up after three or four calls. 'Where's he? Where's Kane Shipton?' he demanded.

Rana looked baffled. 'Who is Kane Shipton?'

'That lost man. The top brass. The big boss. Whatever you'd like to call him. He runs this little operation. He must have escaped through the roof during the explosion. Can't hear his dog, either. Must have covered some ground already. You cannot let him escape, Rana. He's dangerous. Call whoever's with you – go after him!'

At Veerendra's instruction, two of his commandos climbed up to the roof in almost the blink of an eye.

'Footsteps on snow, sir!' they called back. 'Leading away.'

'After them!' Veerendra called back. Then he turned to Kakababu. 'Would you like to come with us, Mr Roychoudhuri? You have earned the right to capture this man yourself.'

Kakababu let out a deep sigh. 'Not me. I've had enough,' he said. 'Let your team go ahead.'

'We did hear a small dog, yapping,' Rana said. 'Right in the middle of nowhere. It was damned odd. I even told Tribhuvan that if there was a dog, there must be a man! Anyway, Shipton won't get far. He doesn't have the resources. We'll catch him soon.'

'Well, that's up to you,' Kakababu said. 'My job was to find his lair. I've found it. My work here is done. What you do with him and this place is your business. I want nothing to do with it.'

Then his eyes fell on Shontu. Dragging himself forward, he clutched Shontu's extended hands and stood up.

'Did you hurt yourself? No? Excellent, excellent. You still have an errand left, though. You have to find my crutches. They ought to be somewhere quite close. The corridor outside, perhaps.'

As soon as Shontu left, Rana said, 'Did you see that Varma amongst these people? He's a traitor! A double agent! He ...'

Kakababu held up a hand. 'Never mind that now. There will be plenty of time to talk about these things later. For now, can you get me a cup of tea? It feels like ages since I've had a good cuppa. Who knows if these uncouth spies even drink tea.'

Rana could not help himself. He grinned. 'You're sitting in the middle of an exploded cave and asking for tea, Mr Roychoudhuri?'

'I can't help how I feel, Mr Rana. Right now, I feel like a cup of tea. If these heathens don't have good tea, then let's go back to the tower. I always carry excellent tea with me. I'll make you a cup, too, if you like. Then I'll sleep. For *hours*. These last few days have been dreadfully taxing. My body needs all the rest it can get. Let me tell you, Rana, there's nothing as restorative as good, solid sleep. At heart, I'm a lazy man. I enjoy my sleep.'

This time, Rana could not hold back his laughter. 'Lazy indeed! Mr Roychoudhuri, you've hiked to the Everest base camp, chased yetis, caught a nest of spies ... if this is laziness, why, you've probably set a world record in it!'

'There's a saying in my language. "Even the disabled can cross a mountain if they put their mind to it". You speak Bengali very well – I'm sure you've heard it before. I am a lazy man, Rana, except when I put my mind to things.'

Just then, Veerendra came back into the room. 'I've sent a detail after Shipton. He'll be caught soon. Now, sir, just to get a few things down: how many people did you see here? How many ways in and out, as far as you know? Did these people torture you for information?'

'None of that, none of that!' Kakababu interrupted, waving Veerendra impatiently away. 'I don't want to talk about any of this now. I just want my tea, and then I want to sleep.'

At that very moment, Shontu came back to the room with his crutches.

'There he is!' Kakababu exclaimed in genuine delight. 'All right, Rana, let's go. We'll get out of this dreadful hole and return to the land above. Let's go, Shontu. You've done brilliantly this time! Now we'll walk under the open sky, and cleanse our lungs with fresh air. Life is beautiful.'

Then he reached over, and affectionately tousled his grinning nephew's hair.

THE MYSTERY OF THE EMPTY BOAT

ORIGINAL TITLE: *KHALI JAHAJER ROHOSHYO*

FIRST PUBLISHED: 1984

CHAPTER 1

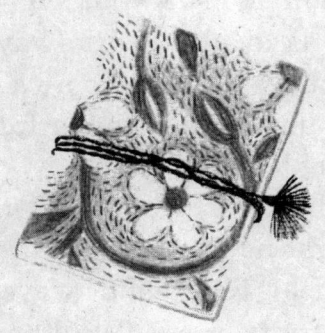

'What do you say to a little excursion, Shontu?' Kakababu asked, putting the morning papers down.

Shontu brightened immediately. An excursion with his uncle was bound to be an adventure. They had been on three holidays together so far, and all of them had been spectacular: the first in the hidden valleys of Kashmir; the second in the Jarawa islands of Andaman; and the third chasing yetis in the Everest! Where was his uncle planning on taking him this time? Abroad, perhaps? Kakababu had recently brought up South America in conversation a few times, talking about its many historical mysteries. That must be it! They were going to South America!

'I'd love to, Kakababu! Where are we going?'

Thanks to his early-morning walks, Kakababu was already in his shoes and outdoor clothes. Now he reached for the crutches that rested on either side of his chair. 'Who knows?' he said vaguely. 'Let's head to the railway station and see what suggests itself.'

Shontu was taken aback. Railway station? Well, that certainly ruled South America out. Still, any travel with his uncle was wonderful, and he quite enjoyed travelling by train, too.

'When does the train leave?' he asked. 'Should I pack my bags right now?'

To his surprise, Kakababu waved dismissively. 'No, no, nothing that serious. We'll hop on whatever's leaving first, and see where it takes us. Just fetch my handbag from upstairs. And tell your mother not to expect us till dinnertime.'

Shontu ran up the stairs and swiftly changed into his outdoor clothes. He wished he had known about this outing earlier. It was a school holiday, so he could easily have invited his friend Jojo along. Jojo was great company, and would be a lot of fun on a long train journey. But there was no time for that now.

When his uncle saw him racing down the stairs, ready to leave, he heaved himself out of his chair. Closing the house-door behind them, he said, 'Run ahead, Shontu. See if you can get a cab.'

The cabs in this neighbourhood could usually be found around a small local park. The park wasn't far, but it was a few lanes away from their street. As Shontu made his way to the park, he tried to work out what his uncle's plan was. Kakababu often went out of town for a day or two, but he had never invited Shontu along on those. His uncle was notoriously independent and prickly about accepting help, so he refused all company unless it was a long expedition to a far-off, dangerous place. Why had he suddenly asked Shontu along on what was apparently going to be just a day in the city? After all, if they were going to be back by dinnertime, they couldn't be going far. And speaking of being back by dinnertime ... what was all this about boarding the first train and going wherever it took them? His uncle abhorred that sort of whimsy! He was quite the opposite, in fact – a deeply methodical man. So what was *really* behind his uncle's spontaneous little excursion?

Given the hour, there was just one cab at the taxi-stand. Shontu began walking hastily towards it. But just before he reached it, a large man swooped in on the passenger-side door and hastily squeezed himself in next to the cabbie. He was rapidly followed by his wife and five young children, who filled the back seat. Seconds later, the cab roared to life and sped off in the opposite direction. Shontu stared gloomily after it. He had been so close! Getting another cab at this hour was going to be very difficult.

Just then, a white car pulled up right next to him. Biman, his neighbour from down the street, leaned out to grin at him.

'Shontu! Where are you off to this early? Get in, get in. I'll take you as far as I can.'

Shontu grinned back, his mood immediately lifting. Biman was good company. He was also famous in the neighbourhood for being incredibly light-skinned. Indeed, his complexion was so unusually rosy that as a baby he had been nicknamed "shaheb" – a fair-skinned foreigner. But as far as Shontu was concerned, what was truly cool about Biman was his job. He was a pilot for Air India. The coincidence amazed Shontu every time he thought about it. Honestly, what were the odds that a child named Biman—which meant "aeroplane" in Bengali—would grow up to actually become a pilot?

'I'm not going anywhere, Bimanda,' he now said. 'Just waiting for a cab.'

'If you're looking for a cab, you're definitely going somewhere!' Biman retorted cheerfully. 'Hop in. It's my day off, I'll drive you. It's too early for most cabs to be up and running. Now, where are we going?'

Shontu hesitated. How could he possibly tell Biman where he was going, when he didn't know that himself? Kakababu hadn't so much as hinted at a place. But that was Kakababu for you, always keeping secrets. Well, his uncle *had* mentioned trains. Perhaps he could just mention the city's biggest railway station?

'It's not just me, Bimanda. Kakababu wanted a cab to take us to Howrah. We have a train to catch, so ...'

'So I'll pick him up as well! What's the problem? Now get in.'

Shontu hesitated again. Kakababu was very picky about the company he kept, and even pickier about the favours he accepted. Still, he could hardly tell

Biman that without also implying that his uncle found Biman's company off-putting. So, he swallowed his worry and slid into the front passenger seat. The moment the car stopped outside his house, however, he jumped out and ran up to his uncle.

'There were no taxis, Kakababu!' he blurted out apologetically. 'That's why I'm with Bimanda. He said he'd take us to the station.'

To his surprise, Kakababu seemed perfectly happy with this plan. 'That's good of you, Biman,' he said, moving towards the car. 'But do you have the time to take us all the way to Sealdah?'

'Certainly! But I thought Shontu said you were going to Howrah?'

'No, Howrah's off-route. We're going to Sealdah to catch a train to Canning.'

This caught Biman completely off-guard. 'Canning?' he repeated blankly. 'But ... why? What on earth is worth seeing in Canning?'

Shontu was equally surprised. As far as he knew, Canning was just a rural railway junction an hour or so from Calcutta. What could Kakababu possibly want in a place like that? But he kept his thoughts to himself. Unlike Biman, Shontu knew better than to question his taciturn uncle. 'Time will reveal Kakababu's plans,' he often told himself. He didn't need to know them in advance.

Kakababu, meanwhile, was smiling slightly at Biman. 'You make Canning sound like the back of beyond. But it isn't, you know. It's quite the bustling little town. Sees a fair bit of tourism, too. Besides, it's the gateway to the Sundarbans. That's where I was planning on taking Shontu today.'

Biman's baffled frown deepened. 'But ... aren't the Sundarbans really dangerous? How many days are you going for? Is that handbag enough? I don't see any luggage or special equipment with you ...'

'We're just going for the day,' Kakababu said calmly.

'For the day!' Biman exclaimed. 'But the Sundarbans are so remote! I mean, aren't they? I always understood that they were very far away, in a secluded sort of a place – probably several hours by train. You know, since it's a jungle full of tigers and bears and whatnot ...'

Kakababu allowed himself a small sigh.

'Biman,' he gently admonished, 'how can you fly across international borders every day, yet know so little about your own hometown? The Sundarbans are only about seventy to eighty miles away from Calcutta.'

Biman visibly started. 'Eighty miles? But that's nothing! A car could make it in a couple of hours. Hang on, Kakababu ... if it's that close, then why on earth do we grow up thinking it's so far away? I don't know of a single person who has actually been there! In fact, everyone says it's a very difficult place to get to.'

'I said it's close, Biman, not that it is accessible. You certainly couldn't get there in a car. The roads are still mostly rural, and many are not motorable. There are two rivers on the way, and neither of them have bridges. Most tourists don't bother with cars. They take the train to Canning or Naamkhana, then take launch-boats through the waterways. These are public boats, mind you, like public buses. They take the long route, stopping at all the islands. So yes, it takes a lot longer to get there than it does to drive eighty miles on a straight road.'

Biman looked thoughtful. Then his eyes widened in sudden alarm. 'But the wildlife – *they* don't need public transport, do they? If the jungles are this close, then couldn't the bears and tigers just come into the city one day? Eighty miles should be nothing to a tiger. Or a bear!'

'First, there are no bears in the Sundarbans,' Kakababu said, firmly. 'As for tigers ... yes, they do sometimes hunt in the villages at the edge of the jungle. But no wild animal voluntarily seeks out the city. Certainly not tigers.'

Biman remained quiet for several seconds. He seemed to be taking the new information in. Then he said, 'Kakababu, can I come along with you two? I honestly don't think I'll end up seeing the Sundarbans if I have to arrange an excursion on my own.'

'If that's what you want,' Kakababu conceded, to Shontu's surprise. 'But what will you do with your car? Parking it at Sealdah for the day is not the best idea.'

'Why go to Sealdah at all? We'll drive straight to Canning from here. I'll park at Canning, we can take the launch-boats, and then I can drive us back in the evening. Do you know the way to Canning?'

Kakababu nodded. 'Head towards Garia,' he instructed, settling himself comfortably in the backseat of the car. 'Then take the turning towards Narendrapur, and keep going.'

The car took off. Shontu was thrilled to have Biman accompany them. Biman was exactly the sort of cheerful company that he would have picked for a big day out. As upset as he had been to lose the cab to the large man so narrowly, he now realised that had he got to it first, he wouldn't be sitting in Biman's much more comfortable car now, letting the breeze blow through his hair.

After crossing the university campus at Jadavpur, the traffic dropped sharply. The houses along the road began to thin out too, taken over by fields. As Biman picked up speed, Kakababu said, 'I take it you aren't scheduled for duty later tonight, Biman?'

'No, I have today and tomorrow off,' Biman explained. 'I'm flying to New York the day after. But you're right, Kakababu. We travel the world for work, but know next to nothing about our own hometowns. It's a shame. By the way, do we need firearms? Since we are going to the jungle?'

His uncle sighed again. 'We're not going there to hunt, Biman. Tigers are an endangered species, hunting them is a crime.'

'But what if a tiger lands right in front us?' Biman argued. 'Is self-protection a crime too?'

'Tigers are stealth-hunters. If one decides to attack you, you'll never see it coming. Don't worry, most people who visit the Sundarbans end up never seeing a tiger. I've no interest in seeing one, myself. I'm going there to look at a motorboat.'

Shontu saw Biman's brows furrow. 'As in, at a boat-builder's? Were you planning on buying a boat, Kakababu?'

'Nah, nothing like that. I live in the city, what would I do with a boat? I meant the one in the news. Haven't you been reading the papers?'

Ah, so *that's* what this was about! The newspapers had been abuzz with "The Mysterious Motorboat". Shontu had been following the news quite eagerly himself. About a week ago, a motorboat of foreign origin had been found adrift in the Sundarbans. It was a very well-appointed vessel, obviously meant for living in. There was a bedroom and a fully-equipped kitchen. But, and here was the mystery: it was completely empty. There was no trace of a crew, no documents indicating ownership or place of origin. The people who stumbled upon it had found uneaten breakfast on a little table in the kitchen – two sausages, a slice of cheese, a piece of toast, and a cup of half-drunk coffee. The radio had been on, though the newspapers hadn't said which station had been playing. Clearly, someone had just sat down to a leisurely breakfast ... and then abandoned ship in a tearing hurry.

Speculations about the boat had been rife in the media. Some insisted that such a plush boat could only have belonged to the smuggling elite. They had probably come to supervise local operations, and then been ambushed by a rival gang. The rival gang had tossed the boat's passengers into the sea, and made off with all the documents and valuables on board. Others speculated that the boat was a spy-ship. It was empty because the spies had sneaked into the jungles that surrounded Sundarban's waterways, and were probably well on their way to infiltrating the mainland. These were not the only two theories Shontu had read, just the two most popular. Multiple people had multiple other theories about the mysterious boat, and no one was shy about printing them.

One of the day's English dailies was rolled up on Biman's dashboard. Biman picked it up and handed it to Shontu.

'The local page has a picture of the boat,' he said helpfully, as Shontu unfolded the paper. 'I've been following the news, of course. Personally, I think these smuggler and spy theories are ridiculous. Why would modern spies spend months at sea when they could fly into the country in a few hours?'

Shontu nodded absently. He was looking at the picture. The mysterious motorboat was a white vessel, anchored in what looked like fairly deep waters. At least, Shontu didn't see any trees or land around it. A few local boys were on a smaller row-boat close by, grinning at the camera. The newspaper said that the police had taken custody of the boat, but Shontu didn't see any policemen in the picture.

'I think this is just a big fishing boat that was caught in a storm,' Biman continued. 'That happens, doesn't it,

Kakababu? They go too far and then they can't return to shore? The crew was probably thrown overboard by the wind. Then the empty boat was carried along by the currents, and now it's ended up here.'

'If the crew were thrown off mid-sea, then why was there freshly-made breakfast on the table?' Kakababu countered. 'And why didn't the document-drawers have either a fishing licence, or a boat registration card, or the owner's passport? No, Biman, this is not a simple accident. Besides, fishing boats look very different.'

'Well, all right, perhaps it was smugglers,' Biman conceded. 'The waterways are actually very popular for smuggling, much more than the air. Having dense forests as cover can only ...'

'What are you doing!!!' Kakababu suddenly shouted, 'Biman – do you think you're flying an aeroplane?'

Biman had sped up as soon as they had left the crowded city roads behind. But in the last few minutes he had been going so fast that Shontu had half expected the car to sprout wings and jump into the sky. Now, looking sheepish, he dialled the speedometer down to a reasonable number.

'Driving can be a bit frustrating,' he confessed. 'Speed becomes such a habit, you know. Just the other day I was stuck in a god-awful traffic jam at Chowringhee, and all I could think of was finding an empty stretch so that I could take off like a plane, and fly over the sea of idling cars!'

Kakababu burst out laughing.

'They should invent a car that can fly *and* float on water,' Shontu said wistfully. He had really enjoyed their brief burst of speed.

Biman laughed. 'I'm sure they will! Have you seen how fast technology advances these days? Pretty soon we'll have amphibious flying cars in the market, don't you worry!'

Thinking of the abandoned ship, Shontu suddenly said, 'Bimanda, has your plane ever been hijacked?'

'Not mine, no. We've been lucky. But I did witness a hijacking once.'

'What, really? What happened?'

Kakababu, too, seemed interested. 'Yes, Biman, what happened?'

'I'll tell you. But first, Kakababu: may I have your permission to smoke in the car?'

To his astonishment, Shontu saw his uncle's moustache lift in a tiny mischievous smile. 'No, you may not. No one is allowed to smoke in my presence.'

Stunned silence reigned for a few seconds. Everyone knew that a man with a job, even if he was years younger than the elders present, was always graciously granted permission to smoke if he asked politely. "Would you mind if I smoked, uncle?" was met with, "Not at all, not at all!", or "Please, feel free!", or even "Here, try one of mine". It was incredibly rude to refuse. Yet here was Kakababu, telling Biman "no" to his face!

At their consternation, Kakababu's smile broadened. 'Listen, I used to be a heavy smoker till very recently.

I always had a pipe in my mouth, or at least a cheroot. Then we went to the Himalayas—you've probably read about it in the papers—and I realised how dependent I had become on smoking. So, I gave it up. But when I smell tobacco, my fingers still itch to light up a cheroot. It's a hard temptation to resist. Which is why I ask people not to smoke in front of me. If you really need a smoke, we can stop for a few minutes. I can go for a walk, or you can have a smoke outside.'

Biman looked abashed. 'No no, Kakababu, it's not as important as that. I'm just a social smoker – a few odd cigarettes here and there when I'm with friends. I've been thinking of giving it up, too. It's a risky habit to have.'

'But what happened to the hijacking?' Shontu cut in, impatiently.

'Ah yes. I was on a Pan-Am flight from Denver in the USA to Edmonton in Canada, where I had a friend. The commander was a friend of mine, so I had been invited to the cockpit for a chat. Suddenly, the door to the cockpit burst open and three people shoved themselves in. Two young men and one young woman. About twenty or twenty-two, no older. All armed, two with firearms and one with a grenade. I'm no expert, but they looked Mexican to me. Anyway, the girl looked like the leader. In broken English, she ordered Teddy—that was the commander, Ted Smith—to turn the plane towards Havana. Then she looked at me and said, "Who are you? Get back to your seat right now!" Then …'

Here the story came to a rather abrupt halt, for Biman had to suddenly brake. A bullock cart and a lorry had formed an inadvertent barricade on the road. A handful of cars and another cart had queued up on either side of it, blocking the road.

'Looks like an accident,' Biman said, as he immediately manoeuvred his car off the road and onto the fields.

'What are you doing?' Kakababu exclaimed, aghast.

'Just bypassing the mess,' Biman answered, surprised. 'This will take some time to clear up, Kakababu.'

'No, no, pull over,' Kakababu insisted. 'One must never walk away from an accident. The people might need our help.'

Unable to argue, Biman parked in the field. The three of them climbed back onto the road on foot.

It was a mess, all right. A jeep had apparently hit the back of a bullock cart, sending it careening off the road. The carter had jumped off and avoided serious injury, but his bullocks had been yoked to the cart, and thus incapable of running away. The heavy cart had twisted the poor animals' necks. They were lying in a heap next to the cart, still alive but howling in pain. It was a dreadful sound. Shontu had never heard anything so horrific and heartbreaking in his life. The jeep hadn't done much better, either. It had rolled off the road as well, and was lying abandoned a few feet away from the animals.

The only person still on the road was a man. The locals had formed a circle around him. He, apparently, had been in the jeep when it hit the cart. The driver had jumped out and saved himself, but this man had been thrown out of the passenger-window, hitting the side of the road hard. From between the crowd's legs, Shontu caught sight of the unconscious man. His face and hair were covered in fresh blood. Between the bullocks and the man, Shontu didn't know where to look. Kakababu, of course, hurried up to the man. Squatting with some difficulty, he checked the man's pulse. 'Very weak, but there,' he declared, almost to himself.

The circle of people was watching him intently, but no one moved to offer help. Shontu could almost see his uncle's temper catch fire.

'What do you think is happening here, a street-show?' he snapped at the crowd, meeting as many eyes as he could. 'Why haven't any of you sent word to the police? Why haven't any of you called for a car to take this man to a hospital? He is still alive! With medical care, he may live. What is wrong with all of you?'

'The village health centre is pretty far ...' one of the onlookers began.

'The police station is far too,' added another.

'And?' Kakababu challenged. 'At least some of you have cycles, I presume? Is it too much to cycle that distance, if it means saving a person's life? If you're human, you have to help out! An accident is not a free show that we can just stand around and watch! Biman, this man needs help immediately. Can you hold him up? We'll get him to the car and take him to the hospital.'

Just then, a man broke through the crowds and stepped up to Kakababu. Shontu had noticed him hovering at the periphery. From his ripped clothes and messy hair, it was clear that he had been roughed up in the last few minutes. Very likely by the same crowd that was now watching. 'Sir, I'm the jeep's driver. Take me with you, please,' he begged. 'My car won't start, and I have no other way of getting out of here.'

In the end, Biman and the driver carried the injured man as gently as they could to the backseat of the car, where they laid him down. The driver climbed in, making room for himself by taking the man's head on his lap. Kakababu squashed himself in the front seat with Shontu. They climbed their way back on the road.

'So, what made you hit the bullock cart?' Biman asked the driver after a few minutes. 'Too slow for your tastes, eh?'

'Sir, it was not like that, sir,' the driver pleaded. 'I was in the middle lane, about to overtake. Those animals had been trundling down that side of the road for ages. But just as I was about to overtake, they sauntered into the middle. That's the trouble with animals, sir – they're not machines. They don't listen to people. I pressed down on the brake as hard as I could. I swear sir, I did! But it didn't take. The car wouldn't stop. Sir, you're a driver yourself. What else could I have done? So I jumped out.'

'Sounds like your machine doesn't listen to people either,' Kakababu said dryly. 'Where were you two coming from?'

'From Canning, sir. Sir, believe me, I'm a good driver. I didn't want to come at all. My car has not been serviced in a while, it's not in good condition. But this man insisted. He said he'd give me two hundred rupees if I could get him to Baruipur in an hour. That's a lot of money for a short drive, sir.'

Shontu turned around to look at the unconscious man. He was wearing a shirt of rough cotton, and a cheap, thin cotton dhoti. He didn't look like the type that could just whip out two hundred rupees on a whim. It must have been an emergency. Why else would a man like this hire a car to go to a neighbouring town, when trains ran throughout the day? Poor man, in his rush to go to Baruipur he may very well end up going to heaven.

Five or six kilometres ahead, they found a public health centre that was just off the main road. Biman helped the driver unload the injured man there. Before they left, Kakababu extended his small notebook to the driver. 'Could you write your names and addresses here? I'd like to know how he fares.'

The driver didn't have a pen, but he spotted one in the injured man's shirt. 'My name is Surenchandra Sanpui, sir,' he said, as he began writing. 'But I can't tell you anything about this man. I don't even know his name. He said he was coming from Jahajghata in Basanti, and needed to go to Baruipur. That's all I know.'

'That's all right, just your own address will do,' Kakababu said soothingly.

Then he took out a small travelling-camera from his handbag, and took several pictures of the injured man's face. He also took one of the driver. Then they took his leave and climbed back into the car.

'Kakababu, why did you take their pictures?' Biman asked, when they were back on the main road.

'Sometimes, in cases of accidents like this, witnesses might be called upon to testify. Or at least to present their accounts. You know the pace at which case files move. I'll probably forget their faces by the time it comes up in court. The pictures will remind me of the details. Biman, did you notice anything interesting about the injured man?'

'How do you mean, "interesting"?'

'He looked like your average villager from these parts. Yet he had enough spare cash to hire a car just to get to Baruipur in an hour. Do you know how much a train-ticket from Canning to Baruipur costs? Two rupees. Three, at the most. This man spent two hundred. Doesn't that seem odd?'

'Well, maybe it was a medical emergency. Perhaps he had just missed a train and didn't want to wait for another. Or maybe he was in a hurry because he was going to see someone who was critically ill?'

'True, true. All of that could well be true. But Biman, I saw his left wrist up close when I checked his pulse. He was wearing a Swiss watch. A very expensive Swiss watch. Do you think it's common for a villager from the Sundarbans to wear such a watch?'

'Smuggler!' Shontu immediately piped up.

'One mustn't assume,' Biman admonished him. 'Some of these village-people may look unassuming, but they can actually be quite rich, you know. We sometimes have passengers who cannot speak a word of English, cannot understand directions, refuse to follow flight protocols, but have bundles of cash bursting from their pockets.'

Kakababu looked thoughtful. 'Hmm. Well, either way, we have to report the matter at Canning police station. Let's go there first.'

Shontu didn't want to go to the police and rehash the horrific accident. He wanted to forget the distressing scene as soon as he could. In an effort to distract himself, he turned to Biman. 'Bimanda, what happened to your hijacked plane?'

But a story, once interrupted, loses its magic.

'Yes, the plane,' Biman resumed, somewhat mechanically. 'They let me remain in the cockpit. One of the boys held a revolver to Teddy's head all the way to Havana. I wanted to smash my fist into his face, but the girl had a grenade, remember? She could blow us to smithereens in the air.'

'Didn't something like that happen in Arizona a few years back?' Kakababu asked. 'Every person on board was killed.'

'Yes. Anyway, so we landed in Havana. The Cuban government was smart. They gave in to every demand after token negotiations. After six hours in the plane, the hijackers finally let us out. As soon as we were out, Cuban special forces swept in and arrested all three of them. The Cuban government hosted us overnight, fed and watered us, then put us back on a flight the next day.'

Shontu couldn't hide his disappointment. That's it? That was the hijacking story? He had expected planes chasing each other, firefights, or a fist fight at the very least. Well, so much for that.

Meanwhile, houses and shops had begun to crowd the sides of the road again. They were either approaching Canning, or already in it.

'It *does* look like quite a bustling place,' Biman admitted. 'Is this a big town, Kakababu?'

'Not big, per se, but it's certainly important. Canning used to be a busy sea-port once. Merchant ships used to dock here. Now the ships go elsewhere, but the waterways still support a large network of passenger-boats. Besides, as I said earlier, it is the gateway to the Sundarbans.'

'Why is it called Canning, though?' Shontu asked. 'Do they have food-canning factories here? Or do they manufacture tins?'

'It's not a reference to that sort of canning,' Kakababu said, shaking his head slightly. 'This place was named after Lord Canning, one of the British Governor-Generals. You've read about him in history, haven't you? Ledikini, the brown roshogolla-like sweet, was named after his wife, Lady Canning.'

'Kakababu,' Biman interrupted. 'I've been thinking about this the entire drive. This empty ship is a police matter, isn't it? I mean, it could be smugglers or it could be spies, but it's not really a big historical mystery. So what is your interest in this? I know you're not interested in catching criminals.'

Kakababu sat back in his seat. He was silent for a few seconds. 'You're right,' he finally said. 'I'm not interested in catching smugglers or spies. I have a different theory about the boat. I'm here to see if I'm right.'

Biman looked sharply at Kakababu in the rearview mirror. 'What's that theory, Kakababu?'

Kakababu looked out of the window into the bustling street. 'Let's see the boat first. Then I'll tell you.'

CHAPTER 2

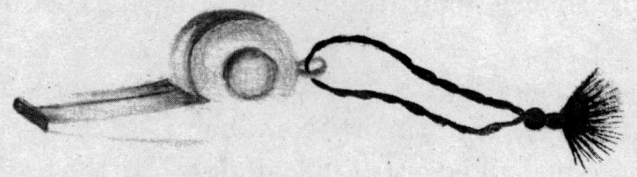

After hearing that it was named after a former Governor-General, Shontu had expected Canning to be a neat, picturesque little town. Like a seaside retreat for the British, perhaps. But Canning turned out to be just another overcrowded commercial town. Its broken, muddy roads thronged with traffic and people, and every narrow street was lined with countless shops. The smell of fish and seawater was overwhelming.

They parked the car in the far corner of a petrol pump for the day (this was apparently common practice), and set out on foot. Immediately, Shontu realized that this town would be a trial for his uncle. The street they were on had no paved footpath, and with every step, Kakababu's crutches sank into the soft, muddy ground.

'I had come to Canning only a handful of years ago,' his uncle said after a few steps. 'I must say, it has deteriorated much faster than I had expected. But you'll like it when we're on the launches, out on the water. Let's find the police station first and get that over with.'

With directions from locals, they reached the police station fairly quickly. The inspector in charge, it turned out, had already been informed of the accident over telephone, and had despatched his assistant inspector to the scene.

'Still, it's best to have as many witnesses as one can,' he told Kakababu. 'Just put your names and addresses down in this log-book. Might help us later. It was good of you to have taken the wounded man to the health centre.'

After filling in their names and addresses, Kakababu said, 'There's another matter we'd appreciate your help with. This foreign vessel that has been making the headlines ... where is it now?'

The inspector's affable demeanour changed. He frowned at Kakababu, raking suspicious eyes from his head to his feet.

'What business is that of yours?' he asked. Quite rudely, Shontu thought.

'Well, we'd like to see it.'

'Are you one of these newspaper people?'

'Not at all. We're just curious.'

'Curious enough to have come all the way from ...' the inspector glanced at the log-book, '... Calcutta?'

'Yes.'

'What about this boat warrants such curiosity?' the inspector demanded aggressively.

'A mysteriously-empty foreign vessel was found suddenly adrift on Indian waters. I'd say it would be odd to *not* be curious. Is there a legal restriction on seeing the boat? From what I understood, it has already become quite the local attraction. Every newspaper has carried pictures of it this morning. Its existence is hardly a secret.'

The officer peered once more at the log-book, and then at Kakababu. 'Your name ... did you say it was Raja Roychoudhuri? Are you the same Raja Roychoudhuri who was on the Jarawa island?'

'Yes!' Shontu exclaimed, jumping in before his uncle's modesty got in the way. 'That's him, that's my Kakababu.'

It had the effect he wanted. The inspector's demeanour changed completely. Smiling broadly, he stood up from his chair and extended his hand to Kakababu. 'I thought as much! Sir, I appreciate you pursuing this visit through proper channels. Otherwise, a man of your connections could have just gone above our heads and ... anyway, what will you have, sir? Tea? Coconut water?'

'Nothing, thank you,' Kakababu said briskly. 'We must be on our way quickly — we're supposed to be back in Calcutta by evening. If you could just tell us where the boat is anchored ...'

'Sir, please, have a seat. Let me at least give you a cup of tea. Do you know the Sundarbans well? Routes can be tricky here if you don't. No? All right, let me get the map first …'

With a flourish, he unrolled a large local map and spread it out on his desk. Then he began tracing their route on it with the back of a pencil.

'You're here now, sir: Canning. You will have to go this way – first to Basanti, then to Gosaba. Gosaba is where the Sundarban properly begins. This broad inlet here is called the Duttar Gaang. It flows along the jungle to meet the Harinbhanga river here. Notice how both banks here are heavily forested? You're well into the jungle at this point. Then here, the Harinbhanga begins to broaden. Here, it becomes very broad, and just a little further ahead, here, it meets the Bay of Bengal. On this bank is the Baghmara Reserve Forest. And this spot is where we found the boat, sir. Very close to the confluence.'

'Is that where you've anchored it?'

'No sir. We have been instructed to bring it to Gosaba. Communications here can be a bit unreliable, unfortunately, so we haven't yet received word from Gosaba that they've brought the boat in. Actually, sir, that gives me an idea. A police boat is going to Gosaba this very morning. Two senior officers have come down from Calcutta to assess the situation – Mr Bhattacharya and Mr Khan. They'll be taking our Superintendent's boat. Once they know it's you, they'll definitely take you along.'

'Bhattacharya, Bhattacharya ... do you mean the Additional Inspector General?'

'Yes sir, him.'

'Hmm. I know him well. It would certainly be convenient to travel with the bosses.'

'Exactly my point, sir. But you must leave for the jetty right away. The Super's boat is supposed to leave early. I would have taken you there myself, sir ... in fact, I was supposed to be on that boat myself, escort the top brass and so on ... but I think I might be coming down with cholera. Can't be away from a toilet for more than ten minutes. Had to excuse myself from the visit, sir.'

Outside the station, Kakababu quickly directed Shontu and Biman towards the jetty. 'You two run ahead and stop the police boat. I can't walk quickly enough on these broken roads to make it in time.'

Once they had permission to move faster, Biman and Shontu actually started running. The narrow streets branched off frequently, and they had to stop often to ask for directions. Shontu had never run on such wet, slippery roads before. They seemed to have risen right out of the water! After several minutes, they finally found the embankment that led to the seafront. By the time they finally skidded onto the jetty, they realised that they had no way of telling the police boat from all the others that had been tethered to the shore. Frustrated, Biman turned on his heel and ran back to the little ticket booth they had passed on their way down.

'When does the police launch leave?' he demanded, panting.

The man looked insulted. 'Why should I know anything about the police launch? The *Daughter of the Forest* leaves in five minutes. I can give you a ticket for that if you want.'

Biman waved his hands impatiently. 'No no, no tickets! I just need to know when the police launch leaves. My friends and I have to be on it. Just tell me when it leaves.'

'Do I look like a criminal to you?' the man growled, now actually offended. 'Why should I know about the comings and goings of the police? What am I, a thief? A robber?'

Shontu, meanwhile, had had a better idea. He had left the paved jetty and had waded into the muddy shallows of the shore. A boy his age was ferrying luggage from the jetty to one of the boats, a big suitcase balanced carefully on his head.

'Brother!' Shontu called. 'Brother, can you show me the police boat?'

The boy stopped and looked up and down the row of anchored boats. 'It's not here, babu,' he finally said, in the local dialect. Then he suddenly jabbed his finger at a boat that had just launched into the water. 'There! There it goes. That's the police boat, the *Heart of the Wind*!'

By then, Biman had given up on the ticket-man and joined Shontu in the shallows. 'It's leaving?' he exclaimed. 'Oh no, no – brother, is there a way to stop it?'

'Of course,' said the boy cheerfully. 'Just ask the sareng of the *Daughter of the Forest* to blow his whistle at it. It'll stop.'

'But where's the sareng? We don't even know who he is!'

'That's him,' said the boy, helpfully. 'That man on deck, in the checked lungi.'

A broad wooden plank had been placed between the jetty and the deck for passengers to walk on. A boat-hand stood at the base, keeping it steady as passengers and luggage-carriers went up and down. The sareng stood at the other end, almost as if he was welcoming passengers on board. But in fact he was caressing his moustache with his eyes closed, indulging in a minute's peace before the boat began its rounds again.

Biman skidded to a halt at the foot of the plank and waved enthusiastically to catch the sareng's eye. 'Sareng saheb, sareng saheb! Could you sound the whistle to stop the police launch?'

The sareng's eyes snapped open. 'Do what?' he bellowed down the plank.

'Your siren, not whistle,' Biman amended hastily. 'Could you sound your siren at the police launch to make it stop?'

The sareng stared at Biman as if Biman had lost his mind. Then, slowly, his lips twisted in a sneer. 'Ah, I see. You want me to stop the police launch because you're just a good citizen trying to report a dreadful robbery — am I right? Or have the dacoits landed in Canning harbour?'

'Sareng saheb, this is not a practical joke. I swear!' Biman said earnestly. 'We genuinely need to be on that boat. Please, just sound your siren and make them stop!'

'No, *you* make them stop,' the sareng retorted. 'Go on, shout at them from the banks. Don't involve me and my boat in your mess with the police! "Stop the police launch," indeed. Ridiculous!'

With that, he turned and went down to the cabin, disappearing from view.

Disheartened, Shontu looked back at the water. The *Heart of the Wind* was already mid-river. They had lost their chance to catch it. The two of them trudged morosely back to the ticket booth.

'That man has quite the personality,' Biman remarked, with reluctant admiration. 'Did you see how he dismissed me? I fly planes and he pilots a passenger-launch, but he just bowled me clean over!'

'Did you notice his moustache?' Shontu asked. 'It was exactly like Kakababu's.' He loyally kept the rest of the comparison to himself.

The young man at the ticket booth frowned when he saw them return. 'Do you want tickets to the *Daughter of the Forest* or not? If not, stand clear of my window!'

Biman glared. 'Is everyone on this jetty trying to put us in our place, Shontu?' he asked archly, in an exaggerated stage-whisper.

Shontu ignored him. 'When's the next passenger launch?' he asked politely.

'Two and a half hours later. If you don't want tickets, then we're going to close this window right now. We'll open again after two hours.'

Biman and Shontu looked at the launch. It was indeed getting ready to leave. A bell went twice from within. The boat-hand began lifting the wooden plank off the jetty.

'Bimanda, Kakababu's not here yet,' Shontu said worriedly. 'What should we do?'

Just then, a man appeared on the embankment, moving forward with obvious effort. His crutches sank into the wet mud at every step.

'There he is!' Shontu shouted.

Biman whipped around to the ticket booth. 'Please, stop the *Daughter of the Forest*. That man has to be on the boat!'

The man at the window scoffed. 'You want me to delay a passenger-launch because *one* man couldn't be on time? Does the world "schedule" mean anything to you?'

'Three! Three passengers! Can you hold off just a little for three passengers?'

The ticket-man appeared to consider this. 'Well,' he said at last, 'I suppose we can wait five minutes for three extra passengers.'

He leaned out of the back of the booth and blew on a shrill, loud whistle. The *Daughter* had just begun moving. At the sound, it pulled back towards the shore, and dropped anchor with a big splash.

They waited for Kakababu to come up to the booth, then quickly filled him in. Kakababu didn't look particularly perturbed at having missed the police launch. 'Very well. Let's take this launch to Gosaba, then we'll get in touch with the police,' he said, handing Shontu money for their tickets.

The launch had backed up to the jetty for them. The boat-hand lowered the plank again. Biman and Shontu ran up it in seconds. Kakababu, however, stopped short. The plank was narrow and rather wobbly. There simply wasn't room on it for his crutches. Even if he tried to squeeze them in, there was a fair chance that he would topple over, straight into the muddy shallows beneath.

As he stood and considered his options, a crowd gathered on the deck to watch him, but no one offered to help. 'They're treating his troubles as if it were a show!' Shontu thought angrily. But he knew better than to go back down and offer assistance to his uncle.

After a further few seconds, Kakababu suddenly looked up. 'Shontu, catch!' he called, and tossed his crutches at him, one after another. Shontu caught them neatly. Then, Kakababu limped gingerly onto the plank ... and speed-jumped all the way to the deck, without stopping once. It was unbelievable. The deck exploded in applause, as if his uncle was a performer with a particularly impressive skill. Shontu's temper flared again. He wanted to tell these people off, but what could he say, really? 'How dare you applaud my uncle's dexterity?' If they didn't realise why treating his uncle this way was wrong, then he didn't think telling them off would make a difference.

The launch was very crowded. There was barely enough room to stand, much less an empty seat. In the end they had to give up trying to even seek shade, and stood on deck under the full glare of the sun. After a few minutes, Biman said he would go to the sareng's cabin and see if he could warm the man up. Shontu suspected that he mostly wanted to have a smoke behind Kakababu's back, but he kept that thought to himself.

'What's this river, Kakababu?' he asked instead.

'This is the Matla. It used to be much wider, much fiercer. Now it's so sluggish that there are silt bars right down its middle. But that's happened to every river in this area.'

Then he pointed to an enormous old house on the shore. 'See that house? That's a former zamindar's mansion. Hamilton saheb, that was his name. He had done a lot for the Sundarbans. You'll see more of his handiwork in Gosaba.'

Biman came back much sooner than Shontu had anticipated. 'The sareng's name is Hasan Mirza,' he declared sourly. 'Tough nut to crack. I told him, "I'm a pilot. I fly planes. Can you teach me how to pilot this boat?" I was serious, too. But he laughed at me! Told me, "Stop drinking so much tea, it clearly gives you indigestion. Soak kulottho overnight and eat its sprouts instead." What's kulottho, Kakababu?'

Kakababu burst out laughing. Shontu grinned, too.

'Sareng saheb thinks you're either mad, or lying to impress him, Bimanda,' he explained. 'I doubt he gets many genuine pilots on his boat.'

'Why? Can't pilots come on holidays in the jungles? And what's so odd about wanting to learn how to pilot a passenger-launch?' Then he quickly scanned the shores. 'Where's the jungle, Kakababu? I don't see any jungle.'

'The jungle is still far away. Starts from Gosaba, remember. But you will see clusters of woodland every now and then.'

Biman rubbed his hands together happily, the sareng's insults apparently forgotten. 'Jolly good morning, all considered,' he said. 'Can't remember when I've last been on the water … ah yes, in college. But that was in the city, boating on the Ganga. Not in the jungle. I'm glad I came, Kakababu.'

'You must lead quite the life,' Shontu said, wistfully. 'Sundarbans today, Calcutta tomorrow, New York the day after.'

'It's not that great, honestly,' Biman said seriously. 'With all the flying, there's very little time to actually see the places. I've been to New York at least a hundred times, but I barely know the city. I much prefer travelling like this. It's not even afternoon, and I've already seen more of my home state than I ever have before.'

'Shontu, do something for me,' Kakababu interrupted. 'Instead of all three of us clustering here, why don't you stroll casually around the deck and lower levels? No one will notice a boy in this crowd. Keep an ear out for any talk about the mystery boat. Then come back and tell me what's being said.'

Shontu nodded and left. He had barely disappeared from view when a man in a saffron dhoti and kurta came up to Kakababu, his folded palms raised in greeting. Much of his face was covered in a salt and pepper beard.

'Namaskar, Roychoudhuri moshai. Whereabouts are you headed to?'

Kakababu looked genuinely surprised by this familiarity. 'I don't believe we've met ... How do you know my name? Who are you?'

The man smiled enigmatically. 'My name is Chhoto Shadhu. That's it, no surnames. My father was Boro Shadhu – Sadhu the Elder. So people called me Chhoto Shadhu – Sadhu the Younger.'

'And we've met? I'm sorry, but I don't remember you at all.'

'Well, perhaps you've forgotten me, sir. But I remember you well. Hard to forget a lame man, after all.'

Biman looked at the man with some irritation. What sort of a sadhu was this? Aren't ascetics supposed to be kind? Why was he rubbing Kakababu's disability in his face?

But Kakababu didn't seem to mind. He smiled at the man, looking straight into his eyes.

'I'm certainly memorable,' he conceded. 'But Shadhubabu, my own memory isn't too bad, either. Indeed, it's said of me that I never forget a face. So, remind me: where exactly have we met before?'

Chhoto Shadhu looked swiftly around. Many of the other passengers had been watching Kakababu discreetly. Amongst the crowds of regular local commuters, the three of them very obviously stood out as city people. Not wanting to be overheard, he leaned forward and whispered in Kakababu's ear.

'Jail. We met at jail. But let's not say any more about that now. You're here to meet Masterbabu at Rangabela, aren't you? If so, then stop by at my place afterwards. I have a small ashram in Rangabela.'

Just then, a young boy wormed his way through the crowds and pulled at Biman's shirt. 'Dada, sareng saheb said he wants to speak to you.'

Glancing once at Kakababu and the sadhu whispering in his ear, Biman followed the boy into the crowd.

Chhoto Shadhu leaned back and asked in a much more normal voice, 'Why are you in a passenger launch with us common folk, Roychoudhuri saheb? You're such an important man. The government should have sent you in a special boat. This crowd, the sun ... it must be very uncomfortable for you.'

'It's perfectly comfortable, though a seat would have been nice. How much longer till Gosaba?'

'Gosaba? That's a good three, three-and-a-half hours. Is that where you're planning on staying?'

'No. We're going back to Calcutta tonight.'

'I don't think that's going to happen, Roychoudhuri saheb.'

Kakababu pursed his lips. 'I'm certain it will. There's nothing to keep me here.'

Chhoto Shadhu smiled slightly. 'You modern city-people don't trust the words of us sadhus and saints. But mark my words: you will not be able to return tonight. I don't know why, and I don't know how, but you'll spend the night deep within our delta.'

'Is that right? Well, just so you know, I'm not going to your ashram in Rangabela. We'll turn right back from Gosaba and return straight to Calcutta.'

Chhoto Shadhu smiled enigmatically. 'We'll see how that goes.'

Just then, Biman came hurrying back. 'Kakababu! You won't believe our luck! The police launch has stalled mid-river. The sareng said that he can range this boat next to theirs, but only if we guarantee that the police know us, and it will not get him in trouble. Will the police recognize you, Kakababu?'

'Well, the inspector said the Additional I.G. is on board. Tell the sareng that I know him well.'

Within a few minutes, the passenger-launch had dropped anchor next to the police boat. In stark contrast to the *Daughter of the Forest*, the deck of the police boat was completely empty, save for the sareng and a police officer.

'Excuse me!' Kakababu shouted at the policeman. 'Please tell Ranabir Bhattacharya that Raja Roychoudhuri wants to speak to him. It's urgent!'

The policeman waved dismissively. 'Newspaper reporter, eh? Meet sir in Gosaba. He's resting now.'

Kakababu's temper, sensitive to insults at the best of times, flared. 'Do as you're told,' he bit out, icily. 'Your sir has no business "resting" at eleven in the morning. He's a public servant!'

Several of the passengers laughed. The police officer's face tightened in response, but before he could retort, a tall man appeared on the stairs leading to the deck. He was unusually dressed for an officer on duty — blue trousers and a plain white shirt. The bright mid-morning glare made him peer narrowly at the other boat.

'What's the ruckus?' he demanded. Then he recognized Kakababu, and his demeanour changed completely. 'Arre, is that Kakababu? What a surprise! Come on over, come on over. We can have a chat once you're here.'

It took a few minutes, but all three of them made their way over to the other launch. At the very last moment, Kakababu grasped Chhoto Shadhu's arm.

'Why don't you come with us?' he offered genially, but his hold was firm.

Chhoto Shadhu, who had been keenly watching developments so far, suddenly looked frightened. 'What? No no! Why me?'

'What do you mean, why you? You're going to Gosaba, we're going to Gosaba. As an old friend, I'm offering you a lift. That launch is much faster than this one. And on the way you can tell us all about this area.'

'I ... I'm not going to Gosaba,' Chhoto Shadhu stammered. 'I'm actually going to Basanti. I have to run several errands there.'

'I'm sure it'll be no trouble at all,' Kakababu said, steadily pulling him towards the other boat.

'I prefer to go by this launch,' Shadhu insisted, trying to work his arm out of Kakababu's grasp. 'I'm a regular. These people know me. I'd much rather be here and catch up with friends ...'

Kakababu's grip on his shoulder became iron-strong. 'Do it as a favour to me,' he said, still pleasantly. 'I'd love to catch up with you too, you know. About the good old times.'

Shadhu gave in, though with very obvious reluctance. He couldn't shake off Kakababu's generous offer without it looking suspicious, and the police were watching.

Once they were all on the deck of the *Heart of the Wind* and the passenger launch had sped off, Ranabir Bhattacharya grinned broadly at Kakababu.

'So what great mystery is it this time? Has a meteor crashed in the heart of the jungle? Has the lost head of Emperor Kanishka made its way to the delta? Can't imagine what else would bring you to this mundane town, a man like you ...'

'I've simply brought these young men out for a day in the Sundarbans,' Kakababu said blandly, gesturing at his companions. 'Shontu, you already know. This is Biman, our neighbour. And this is an ascetic gentleman that we've just met.'

'Let's take this inside,' Ranabir interrupted. 'It's blistering on the deck.'

As they made their way down the stairs, Biman suddenly asked, 'Why has your launch stalled? Is it a fault, or ...?'

'No no, nothing like that,' Ranabir laughed. 'We saw a boat going by with the early morning catch. Fresh parshe-fish, still alive! I told the crew to stop them and buy at least two or three kilos. You never get fish this fresh in Calcutta. Certainly not for this price!'

Biman laughed. 'Well, I'm just glad that you stopped. We'd never have caught up with you otherwise.'

The cabin downstairs had a table and several chairs, only two of which were currently occupied. A pack of cards was scattered on the table. Shontu narrowed his eyes. There had been three men in the cabin before they arrived, but the cards had been dealt for four.

'We were playing cut-throat bridge,' Bhattacharya said by way of explanation. 'This is Akbar Khan, Superintendent of Police for this district. And this is our Deputy Super for the region, Prashanta Dutta. Gentlemen, this is Raja Roychoudhuri. I'm sure you don't need an introduction to him, eh? Though he's more popular as Shontu's "Kakababu" lately, haha! I was in Delhi last month, and the Home Secretary asked me, "How's Roychoudhuri doing these days, our 'Kakababu'? Give him my regards". Even he knows, haha!'

Of the three men, only Khan looked a little like a storybook police-officer. He was tall, fair-skinned, imposing, and had an impressive moustache. Bhattacharya, though tall himself, honestly looked like an affable college professor, lanky and unassuming. Prashanta Dutta was probably only a few years older than Biman. He was lean and athletic, like the amateur cricketers Shontu saw at the neighbourhood park.

'Where did you find this man?' Dutta now asked, nodding at Shadhu.

Kakababu smiled thinly. 'Ah, there's the mystery. I have no memory of him, but he says he's met me before. In jail, no less. Your ascetic highness, I think it's time for you to spill your story. Which jail was this? Why was I there? And why were you?'

Chhoto Shadhu shifted uncomfortably. 'It was seven or eight years ago. I was not a sadhu then, I was ... er, I was pursuing other interests. All right, fine, I suppose there's no shame in admitting it now: I was a small-time conman and thief. Fell into bad company as a youth, sir, it ruined me. Then I was caught, and sentenced to six months. Those six months were hell. I came out swearing never to go back in. That's when I took an interest in spirituality. Fulfilling my duties in life, doing good deeds – that's how I live now. Look sir, you may mock me, but Rishi Valmiki was once a dacoit too ... wasn't he?'

Ranabir Bhattacharya burst out laughing. 'Oh my, straight to Valmiki! Are you also writing an epic of your own?'

'No sir, I've not had much schooling,' Shadhu said seriously. 'But I do have a gift. I discovered a miracle medicine in my dreams. Given to me by the gods, it was. Works on all kinds of stomach ailments. Lots of people hereabouts come to me for treatment. You can ask around, sir.'

'Which jail were you in?' Kakababu interrupted. 'Do you remember why I had visited? And how had we met?'

'Central Jail, sir. At Alipur. There was a convicted murderer with us, Shobhanlal. He had been sentenced to death, and the day before his hanging he demanded to see you. We saw you going to his cell. Shobhanlal fell at your feet and cried. That really struck me, sir. Shobhanlal was a scary man, we all avoided him. Yet he fell at your feet and cried. I couldn't believe my eyes. I've never forgotten your face since.'

'Ah, *that* Shobhanlal,' Bhattacharya said significantly. 'Didn't he make an attempt on your life too, Kakababu?'

Kakababu didn't answer. He was staring intently at Shadhu. 'And afterwards? You left your life of crime?'

'Immediately afterwards, sir. The moment I was released. In all these years I haven't so much as put a toe in that direction. Besides, sir, my father passed away. Someone had to take charge of his ashram ...'

'A good story, but we have rather a different report on you, sadhubaba,' Dutta interjected brusquely. 'Our local stations report that known smugglers visit your ashram late at night, several times a month. Now, why is that?'

'I've had similar reports as well,' Khan added, frowning at Shadhu.

'They come for my medicine, sir,' Shadhu replied promptly. 'People come at all hours in their need, and I give my medicine to whoever asks. I don't ask if they're smugglers or fishermen, sir.'

'You visit Calcutta at least thrice a week, don't you?' Dutta pressed. 'Why does a devout man, with the weight of an ashram on his shoulders, go so often to the city?'

'Ingredients for my medicine, sir. It's a complex Ayurvedic compound, takes several kinds of roots and barks. It's impossible to get them locally.'

'Still, thrice a week? In fact, this is you on your way back from Calcutta yet again, isn't it?'

'Don't harass the man, Prashanta,' Ranabir Bhattacharya cut in jovially, smiling reassuringly at the man. 'Sadhubaba, I suffer from chronic stomach upsets myself. Could you give me your medicine?' He extended his hand. 'A sample would do, but I want it now.'

Shadhu looked anxiously around. 'I, er, I'm not carrying my medicine-satchel, sir.'

'Well, then let's have a look at these roots and barks. I'm an Ayurveda enthusiast myself. Let's see what you've bought from Calcutta.'

Shadhu licked his lips nervously. 'I ... I'm not ... I just placed the order today, sir. Small old shop in Bagbazar, they take time to put together large orders. I'll pick it up next week when I ... '

'Take off your shirt,' Bhattacharya said, still smiling affably.

Shadhu looked completely lost. 'Sir ... what? Take off my shirt? Why?'

'Let's say we want to see how healthy the miracle-curer himself is,' Bhattacharya said, still smiling. 'Do you know, Prashanta, that saints and ascetics often enjoy excellent health? It's all the milk and ghee they have. We're about to see an example of it ourselves. Why's the shirt still on, friend? Take it off, take it off!'

Shadhu tried to rally his defence. 'Sir, I didn't want to encroach on your boat. Roychoudhuri saheb forced me to come. Now you're trying to humiliate me by making me take my clothes off? That's not right, sir. That's injustice!'

'No one here wants to humiliate you, friend. We just want to measure your chest and see if you're adequately healthy. Are you objecting to our concern?'

'Yes sir, I am,' Shadhu tried to say firmly, but his voice shook. 'Basanti is just up ahead. Please let me off here, I'll make my own way.'

Quick as a flash, Khan bent down and lifted a small dark case on the table. Then he flicked it open and withdrew his service revolver from it. His face was the picture of intimidating calm.

'It takes just one bullet to kill a man,' he said, his voice icy and without inflection. 'If a corpse tumbles into the river now, the tide will sweep it straight out to sea. No witness, no acknowledgement that anything happened. Just another unknown man lost in these dangerous waters. Still reluctant to take that shirt off, sadhubaba?'

Bhattacharya smiled his big, friendly smile again. 'There's no need for that, Akbar,' he said genially. 'Sadhubaba knows what's good for him. He'll take the shirt off willingly. Won't you, friend?'

Suddenly, Kakababu barked out an abrupt laugh. 'Regretting talking to me on the launch, aren't you? Had you not taunted me, you wouldn't have ended up in this mess. Isn't that something to think about?'

Chhoto Shadhu's eyes darted around the cabin, but all exits were blocked. Closing his eyes, he slowly took off his kurta. Underneath, his entire torso was covered in bandages. Shontu was horrified to see such extensive injuries. But Dutta simply leaned forward and sharply pulled at a piece of it. To Shontu's shock, a flurry of hundred-rupee notes fluttered out from Shadhu's body.

'Looks like thirty thousand, give or take,' Bhattacharya said dismissively. 'Small fry. Count it and lock it away, Prashanta. This is how fences operate here, Kakababu. They take smuggled goods to the city and bring back the money. Dressing as holy men is a great way to evade suspicion. But, like I said, this chap's just a small cog in the wheel.'

Biman was still gaping at Shadhu. 'My god!' he whispered. 'I didn't suspect him at all. Not once!'

Just then, there was a loud pounding of feet on the stairs outside. The policeman posted on deck came running into the room.

'There's a corpse floating past us, sir,' he panted. 'What should I do? Stop the launch again?'

CHAPTER 3

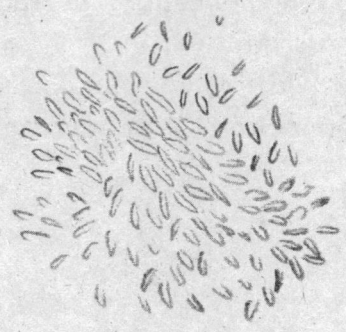

It took them an hour to sort the matter out. The launch's crew had pulled the corpse next to the vessel with a long, hook-ended rod. Kakababu and the officers had gone upstairs to take a look.

'Shontu, you don't need to see this. Stay in the cabin,' Kakababu had instructed before leaving the cabin.

Shontu had stayed, but had tried to peer out of the cabin's window to see what was happening outside. He had already seen several truly horrible things that morning. What harm could just one more thing do?

Luckily, as soon as they were on the deck, Bhattacharya had spotted an empty launch of the Department of Irrigation going in the opposite direction. He had had his crew flag it down and bring it alongside the *Heart of the Wind*. After some negotiation, the Irrigation crew had been charged with ferrying the corpse safely to the closest police station. Dutta had remained on deck to sort out details and give necessary instructions, while Bhattacharya and Kakababu had returned downstairs immediately afterwards.

'This is why travelling with local officers is such a hassle,' Shontu had heard Bhattacharya mutter as the two of them came down the stairs. 'Bodies in the water are not that unusual here, you know? Snakebite deaths are very high in the delta, and none of those corpses are cremated. People just push the bodies into the river. That was probably just another unfortunate chap. Had it been me, I would simply have carried on. But Prashanta is the deputy super, it's his job to make sure that every abandoned corpse has its cause of death determined. So now we're stuck here for however long it takes, while our actual operation languishes.'

A few minutes later, Dutta joined them below. 'Not a snakebite, sir. Murder. Knifed in the back. Thank god for the Irrigation launch, otherwise I would have had to turn this one around. I will send the corpse ahead to Canning with one of my men. They'll start the post-mortem right away.'

'Anyone you knew?'

'No, sir. The crew didn't recognize him, either.'

'Why don't we let our guest take a look? He's more local than either you or me. He might know.'

Shadhu had been sitting on the floor of the cabin all this while, curled into a corner. No one had bothered to cuff him or tie his hands together. Now he quickly sat up and tried to move further away.

'No no, I don't want to see a corpse! Don't involve me in this!'

Dutta glared at him. Then he stomped over and loomed above him, glaring down. 'Up!' he barked.

To Shontu's surprise, Shadhu—who had been loudly protesting till that very moment—immediately stood up. Then, without further fuss, he followed Dutta out of the cabin. Shontu and Biman exchanged a look, then ran after them before Kakababu could forbid it.

Upstairs, Dutta had already guided Shadhu to the side of the deck that was right next to the other launch. The corpse had been laid out on its deck, easily visible from this one. Shontu saw Shadhu take a quick look, and immediately rear back.

'You do know him!' Dutta said triumphantly. 'Who is it?'

But Shadhu was in the throes of genuine disbelief and terror. 'Who? Who would do this?' he wailed, 'Why is this happening to us?'

'Hey!' Dutta cut in sharply. 'Give me a name. Who is this?'

'My cousin, Haru Dafadar. He was like my own little brother. How ... who would do this? He was perfectly fine the last time I saw him. It was just the day before!'

Then he broke down into heartfelt sobs. After a few minutes, Dutta waved his hand at the Irrigation launch, and it began to move away. Then he escorted Shadhu below the stairs. Shadhu was still sniffling.

'It's his cousin, Haru Dafadar. Was alive two days ago,' Dutta summarized for the others.

Bhattacharya grinned. 'You have quite the family, sadhubaba. First, you're caught with black money bandaged to your torso, then your cousin is found murdered in the water. Any link between the two? What did your cousin do for a living?'

Before Chhoto Shadhu could open his mouth, Khan said, 'And think well before you answer. Honest, everyday people who work in the fields or on fishing boats don't get knifed in the back.'

'Haru went to the jungles to collect honey,' sniffled Shadhu.

'Honest honey-collectors may face a hungry tiger, but *they* don't end up knifed to death either,' Khan said drily.

'"Haru Dafadar" sounds very familiar,' Dutta mused. 'Ah yes … he was wanted last week in a case of armed robbery.' He glanced at Bhattacharya. 'Sir, there has been a recent surge in violence in these areas. Known smugglers versus known dacoits. Something new has set them off.'

'Could it be linked to the mystery boat?' Kakababu asked.

Bhattacharya looked thoughtful. 'Why not? We didn't recover a single item of value from that vessel. Where did they go? One of these groups probably found the boat before we did, and stripped it of all its valuables. Now they're fighting amongst themselves for their cuts.' He turned towards Chhoto Shadhu. 'Did your mates send you anything from that boat?'

Shadhu had used the minutes in between to rapidly pull himself back together. 'Stuff from a boat, sir?' he asked, innocently. 'Do you mean passenger luggage? I haven't heard of a launch that has lost its luggage, sir.'

'Do you want us to believe that you know nothing about the foreign motorboat that has been making headlines all over the state? This area has been buzzing with it for a week!'

'I stay away from gossip, sir,' Shadhu said virtuously. 'Sir, you're doing me a great injustice. That cash I was carrying was a favour to a businessman in Calcutta. He wanted me to take it to his fish-farm. I hid it under the bandages to keep it safe from pickpockets. I was just trying to be helpful, sir, I don't know why you think I'm a smuggler.'

Bhattacharya laughed uproariously. 'Of course, of course! We've misunderstood you completely! Well, never mind you, now. Kakababu, you couldn't possibly have come here for this man. He is the smallest of fries — the dregs of the police's fishing net. Yet you brought him on board, and we discovered his cousin's corpse right after. Come now, tell us: why are you actually here?'

'I have no interest in petty criminals, you're right about that,' Kakababu conceded. 'But I am genuinely interested in the boat. And it's not impossible that these people have a connection to it. Who found it first? Was it one of you?'

Bhattacharya nodded towards Khan. 'Akbar can tell you. This stuff is his department.'

Khan sat forward. 'It wasn't us. We first received word from the Department of Forestry. One of the rangers of the Dutta Reserve Forest had been out on his rounds. He met a fisherman on the Horinbhanga river who reported an abandoned motorboat near the confluence. Sukhen—that's the ranger's name, Sukhendu Dutta—went to investigate. The boat was already empty. At first, he thought he heard voices from within, but then he realised it was the radio. It was a foreign channel.'

'Which language was it in? Did the ranger-babu ...?'

'No. Sukhen couldn't identify the language.'

'Interesting. So, everything of value was stolen from the boat, but not the radio?'

'Hmm ... we hadn't considered that. A foreign-made radio is probably fairly expensive.'

'Never mind. What did the ranger do after that?'

'He was smart. He saw that the boat was in reasonably shallow waters, so he didn't try to move it. He sent word to Gosaba. Gosaba contacted us. Prashanta and I have already been by to see it, and ordered it to be brought inland. Gosaba PS is supposed to have it in custody this morning.'

'Well, then we'll see it soon enough,' Bhattacharya said, moving towards the table. 'Prashanta, get your people to lock our sadhubaba in a cabin. Let's spend the remaining time in a quick game of cards.'

'Not me,' Kakababu said, picking up his crutches. 'I'm going back on deck. I haven't seen this area in years. It's time I take in the sights and sounds again.'

Biman and Shontu followed him up the stairs.

———m———

The inspector at Gosaba PS was very apologetic. They had first sent two men to bring the foreign boat over, but the men hadn't been able to start the engine. Parts had probably been stolen from it. Then they had sent a police launch to tug the boat inland. The launch had unfortunately run into a hidden sandbar, and was now stuck just off the banks of the river. If the incoming tide didn't wash it free, then a second rescue-launch would have to be sent.

'Unbelievable!' Dutta exclaimed. 'We thought *we* were running late, but you haven't even been able to move the boat? Why is everyone here so useless? Sir has come from Calcutta to inspect the boat, and you ...'

'Prashanta,' Bhattacharya called from the deck, his voice calm. 'Come back to the boat. Let's have lunch while they sort the matter out. Bad news is better on a full stomach.'

Lunch turned out to be excellent. The crew had cooked the fresh parshe-fish in a very simple broth, fragrant and delicious. They served it with steaming rice, spicy mashed potatoes, and fried slices of local

brinjal. Shontu had heard rapturous stories about
Bengal's "on-board meals"—simple food cooked on
launches, steamers, and boats by all-male crews—but
the food surpassed even those expectations.

'I've never had a broth this tasty,' Biman said,
reverently. 'Nor fish this fresh. This place is heaven!'

Bhattacharya, who was chewing a paan after his
meal, smiled contentedly. 'The question is, what shall
we do now? Prashanta, doesn't the Tiger Project office
have a speedboat in Gosaba? See if we can borrow it.
Who knows when these people will be able to bring
that boat in. I can't spend the next week here, waiting
for it.'

The Gosaba police confirmed that the speedboat
was available, and could be borrowed.

'Great,' Bhattacharya said, rousing himself. 'Tell
you what, Prashanta. Since we have Kakababu with
us, the two of us will take the boat. You and Akbar
stay here and direct operations. We need to round up
as many of the known smugglers, fences, and dacoits
as we can. Some stuff from the boat is still in this area.
They couldn't have moved everything out this quickly.
We need to get back at least a few, or we'll never be
able to trace the boat's owner or its country of origin.
Put some pressure on that sadhubaba there. He knows
much more than he's letting on.'

Bhattacharya had probably not anticipated
Shontu and Biman accompanying Kakababu on their
inspection. The speedboat had certainly not been built
to accommodate five people. Still, they managed to

squeeze themselves in. The only people who couldn't fit in were Bhattacharya's two plain-clothed armed guards.

'That's all right,' Bhattacharya said, after some consideration. 'We're not going anywhere dangerous, after all. It'll be a quick inspection and back, not more than three, three-and-a-half hours. I can look after myself for that long. Let's go.'

The boat started gently enough, but within seconds it took off like a rocket.

'Hold on tight, boys!' Bhattacharya shouted above the roar. 'If you topple into these waters, nothing can save you!'

The very next minute, he nearly lost his own balance and almost tumbled off the boat. Kakababu's hand shot out and grasped him by the shoulders.

'I mean, I'm a very good swimmer,' Bhattacharya amended hurriedly. 'It wouldn't matter if *I* fell in. But Shontu is still in school. Shontu, have you learnt swimming yet?'

Shontu sniffed haughtily. 'Yes. I'm a very good swimmer, too.'

Kakababu grinned. 'Both these boys are good swimmers, you don't have to worry about them. I'm the weak link here. After my accident I learnt how to walk again, but I could never teach myself how to swim. I can hobble along a mountain pass, but put me in water and I'm dead weight.'

'Sir, it really doesn't matter how well one swims,' the pilot of the boat said in the local dialect. 'These saline waters are crawling with kamoth. They'll quietly nip your leg off. All neat, like. And then that's it for you.'

'What's a kamoth?' Biman asked. 'They sound terrifying.'

'It's a species of small shark. They're vicious hunters,' Kakababu said distractedly. He was watching the shores.

'There's no need for anyone to topple over,' Bhattacharya said firmly. 'Everyone, sit tight. And you, brother – take things a bit easy. Safety before speed. We have the rest of the day to get there and back.'

Shontu followed his uncle's eyes. He was watching small groups of people along the riverbanks. The people were in the water, clearly looking for something. Some of them had small fishing nets in a bright shade of blue.

'What are they doing?' he asked, pointing.

'Catching baby tiger-prawns,' the pilot replied. 'It's their season now.'

'But ... aren't they worried about the kamoth? They're thigh-deep in water!'

The pilot shrugged. 'Poor people can't be picky. If they don't go in the water, they don't eat. It helps to be in groups. Kamoths don't come close if several bodies are splashing about. Every now and then someone loses a leg, but catching prawns is their living.'

Shontu had nothing to say to that.

After several minutes of silence, Kakababu suddenly said, 'Chhoto Shadhu had told me in that passenger launch that I wouldn't be able to return to Calcutta tonight. He'd had a vision, apparently. I wonder if he had a vision about his own arrest.'

Biman snorted. 'A conman, that's what he is. Pretends to be a sadhu to fool people. Ranabirbabu, how did your officer know that the money was hidden under the bandages? What gave him away? It wouldn't have occurred to me to use wound-dressing as a hiding place.'

'You pick these things up on the job,' Bhattacharya said. 'There was a barely-suppressed cockiness about the man, like he was secretly rubbing it in our faces that he was getting away with something. Do you know the phrase "taka-r gawrom"? Arrogance that comes from having a lot of cash? That's probably what led him astray. But then he *was* carrying a lot of cash, so perhaps he couldn't help himself, haha!'

'Yes, that was not very bright of him,' Kakababu added. 'He should have kept to himself. Had he not given into the temptation to act mysterious and shake me up a bit, I wouldn't even have looked at him twice.'

'But I'll give him this,' Bhattacharya said. 'He may have been right about you not returning to the city tonight.'

'Why's that?' Biman demanded, before Kakababu could say anything.

'These speedboats aren't reliable. They have engine failures all the time. Look around us: "Water, water everywhere", eh? Haha. It's not like we can swim to the banks for shelter, either. The villages are behind us now, it's all jungles here. If the engine does conk out, our only hope are the fishermen's boats making their way back from the sea. Or an odd miraculous launch that might come by.'

'Why miraculous? I thought the passenger-launches ran all day through these rivers.'

'Yes, but only where they can find passengers. Like I said, we're in the jungles now. No passengers. Arre, brother! Why did you take this narrow canal? The banks are far too close here. Let's stay on the open waterway!'

'This is a shortcut, sir,' the pilot said.

'But have you seen how close the jungle is? You're from the Tiger Project, aren't you? Aren't there tigers on these banks?'

'Yes sir, there are a few on that bank. That's the Shojnekhali Sanctuary.'

Bhattacharya turned to Kakababu. 'See what I mean? Imagine being stuck in the middle of this narrow canal, with tigers roaming freely just a few feet away!'

'Only roaming?' Biman croaked. 'This canal is the size of a large drain! They can jump right onto the boat and carry us off!'

Bhattacharya suddenly grinned. 'Actually, they can jump even further. Tigers are champion long-jumpers – did you know that? But don't worry, they won't be bothering us. Word has spread that the mighty Ranabir Bhattacharya, Additional Inspector General of Police, is swanning through these canals this afternoon. They'll stay away in fear. Hahaha!'

Kakababu sighed. 'They'll stay away because of the sound of our engine. Biman, tigers are a lot like our ancient sages and ascetics. They enjoy their solitude and silence and prefer to stay hidden from outside eyes. You have nothing to worry about.'

Bhattacharya was now openly laughing. 'Sorry about that, boys. I was just trying to scare you a little.'

'I wasn't scared,' Biman insisted. 'But I do have a flight day after. So if the engine stalls ...'

'I didn't think we'd have to come this far,' Kakababu said apologetically. 'I thought we'd go up to Gosaba, spend an hour or so there, then head back home.'

'But I actually really like this little adventure,' Biman reassured him hurriedly. 'I don't think I'd ever come this close to wild tigers before. This feels like a storybook adventure! It's just that I have to report to work in about forty-eight hours ...'

'Don't worry, even if we're stranded tonight, I'll get you to Canning by midday tomorrow,' Bhattacharya said. 'I have to return to the city myself. I have to brief the Chief Minister within the next twenty-four hours.'

Shontu had been scanning the jungle on both sides of the canal. The trees were very, very dense. Sunlight barely made a dent in their darkness. There was no embankment or jetty along these banks, not even a small one. The shores were pure silt, soft and sinister. Shontu was sure he'd sink to his waist in it. Iron rods had been planted at intervals along the shoreline. He wondered why. Every few minutes, he thought he saw a movement in the dark undergrowth. His heart stuttered every time. What if it was a tiger? Would a majestic Bengal tiger leap over the thick bushes, and land with a roar on the silted banks?

Shontu shook his head. He was being fanciful. But honestly, could anyone blame him? It was three in the afternoon now. Even at eight in the morning, when they had already been on their way, he had had no idea that he would be this deep inside an actual tiger sanctuary. This place was so completely different from Calcutta that it was like being on a different planet. And yet it was barely a few hours away! It was marvellous – in that he marvelled at the improbability of it all. Had someone told him just yesterday that a dark, mysterious wilderness lay this close to his home, he would have thought them a very poor liar.

The boat sped along the winding canal, turning sharply ever so often. At every bend, Shontu expected to come upon something dramatic. But there was nothing. Apart from the fact that they were in the heart of the Sundarbans, everything was perfectly normal.

Suddenly, the speedboat began to slow down. In just a few seconds, it came to a complete halt.

Bhattacharya had fallen into a light doze over the last ten minutes. When the boat stopped, he sat up with a jolt. 'What is it? Is it the engine? Has it shorted out?'

The pilot didn't respond. It looked to Shontu like he was listening for something. Shontu tried to listen, too. Till just a second ago, his ears had been full of the roar of the boat's engine. Now, in the sudden silence, he realized that the jungle had a harmony of its own. Ripples made a constant, soothing warble along the banks; water-birds splashed along the shoreline; smaller birds chirped and chirruped from the trees. A few larger birds flew overhead against the bright blue sky, cawing loudly. It was beautiful.

'Don't keep us in suspense, pilot saheb,' Bhattacharya said irritably. 'What is it, are we stranded?'

'No sir. It's the noise.'

'Noise? What noise? All I can hear are the birds.'

'Listen carefully, sir.'

Everyone cocked their ears. At first, Shontu kept hearing just the birds. Then, after several seconds, he heard it. It was the faint sound of human wailing. Someone was crying, but at a distance. No, not someone; there were at least two people, if not three.

'I hear it now,' Bhattacharya said slowly. 'I must say, you have excellent hearing. Can't believe you heard that over the engine.'

'We should have brought your guards, sir,' the pilot replied grimly.

'What? Why?'

'These waters are dangerous. Our people have run into smugglers and dacoits before. We have no arms with us. If they descend on us ... sir, in these jungles they don't just loot. They kill.'

'Is that so? We'll see. Now, where's the crying coming from? The right, isn't it?'

Shontu looked to the right. A few feet ahead, the narrow canal fed back into the broad river, but slightly farther ahead it divided into three canals again. Every canal cut through dense swathes of the jungle, so it was hard to see anything in those canals beyond the entrance. From the corner of his eye, he saw Kakababu quietly fish out a black case from his handbag. Shontu sat up straighter. That was Kakababu's revolver-case.

Bhattacharya shook off his jovial demeanour. 'Let's go into the one on the right,' he instructed. 'Let's see who's crying.'

'It's too narrow, sir,' the pilot demurred. 'We shouldn't go in there.'

'That was an order,' Bhattacharya snapped. 'Into that canal, now. Full speed!' Then, remembering Kakababu's presence on the boat, he turned around and asked more civilly, 'What do you advise, Kakababu?'

'Yes, let's go take a look,' Kakababu agreed.

The boat roared back to life. In a few minutes, they were inside the canal.

The other boat was easy to spot. The crying could now be heard over the engine. But the boat must have spotted them as well, for it disappeared swiftly into the dense, overhanging undergrowth.

Bhattacharya stood up. 'This swathe of the jungle belongs to the Tiger Project. Woodcutting is prohibited here. I bet you those are stealth-cutters. That's why they're trying to hide. They think we're officers of the Project. But why were they crying?'

'Sir, it could be a trap,' the pilot warned. 'We shouldn't approach them unarmed.'

'Range the boat alongside theirs,' Bhattacharya ordered, ignoring him.

The boat was a nouko – a narrow wooden row-boat. It had a woven bamboo awning over the middle for shade and privacy. No one was visible on board. The crying had stopped, too.

'Whose boat is this? Who's inside? Come out!' Bhattacharya shouted, when they had ranged alongside it.

A young man of approximately nineteen or twenty stepped out of the awning. 'Babu, my chacha has been bitten by a snake. His heart is still beating, babu. If you take him to a hospital in your boat, he may survive. Please, babu, have mercy on us!'

'What were you doing in the jungle?'

'Collecting wild honey, babu. It's our only livelihood, we do it to stay alive. But we've never been in such danger before, babu. Please, have mercy on us! Take my chacha to a hospital!'

'When was your chacha bitten? How many hours ago?'

'Just before the sun came up, babu.'

'And he's still conscious?' Bhattacharya asked, glancing back at Kakababu. Kakababu was sitting as still as a statue, the small black case on his lap. Bhattacharya put his hand jauntily inside his own pockets. 'Well, let's take a look at your chacha. Step aside, I'm coming on board.'

And with that, he stepped smartly from the speedboat to the nouko. The young man stepped back inside the awning to let him in. The moment Bhattacharya lowered his head to look inside, a hand holding a stout lathi flashed out, trying to smash his head in. But Bhattacharya had been expecting it. He grasped the lathi and pulled it forward, hauling the man holding it into the open. Losing his footing, the man fell face-first onto the nouko's shallow hull. Bhattacharya's other arm whipped out of his pocket, aiming his service revolver at the man.

'Your chacha is quite young, friend,' he grinned into the darkness of the awning. 'Shall we end his …'

Before he could finish, another man shot out from under the awning. He, too, was holding a lathi. Before Shontu could blink, he smashed it at the back of Bhattacharya's head. Bhattacharya whirled around, then collapsed into the nouko's hull. His revolver skittered out of his hand.

The second lathi-wielder turned aggressively towards their boat. But Kakababu was already pointing his revolver at him, smiling slightly. 'Your skull or your lathi. I'll let you choose which to keep,' he said affably.

The man immediately dived inside the awning. But the first young man stepped out again, this time holding a gun with a long nozzle.

'We'll see who keeps his skull,' he sneered. 'Drop that tiny thing, old man.'

Kakababu kept smiling. 'My dear boy, you'll have six holes in you before you can cock that thing. Use your head.'

Shontu had frozen in his seat. After several adventures together, he knew a little secret about his uncle. Kakababu could never bring himself to shoot someone. In Assam, an opponent of his had worked this out too, and had openly challenged Kakababu to shoot him. Then he had walked straight towards Kakababu's cocked revolver, and plucked it from his hands. What if this man called his uncle's bluff, too? With Bhattacharya out cold, Kakababu was their only hope. Surreptitiously, he turned his head to look at Biman.

Biman was not in his seat.

Alarmed, Shontu had just turned back towards the nouko when Biman erupted behind the gunman, and whipped the nozzle away from the speedboat. They began grappling, and within seconds toppled into the water with an enormous splash. Almost instantly, Kakababu's revolver fired an ear-splitting shot. The man with the lathi had been quietly trying to stand up, and Kakababu had fired at the air above his head. The man threw himself back down on the hull, shaking with terror. His other companion began trembling too.

'Shontu, find Biman,' Kakababu said, keeping his revolver trained on the men. 'He might need help.'

Biman's head burst through the water only a few feet away from their boat. 'Nah, the water's quite shallow here,' he called back. 'I'm fine.'

The water was indeed shallow. With just a few steps, Biman found standing ground. He was holding the younger man by fisting his hand into his hair. The first thing he did after dragging the man onto standing ground was to deliver a resounding slap. 'Bloody scoundrel!' he swore. 'He bit my hand under water. I wanted to choke him to death!'

Their boat's pilot, meanwhile, had leaned over into the nouko. 'Sir,' he pleaded with a prone Bhattacharya. 'Sir! Sir?'

Very slowly, Bhattacharya sat up. 'Ow,' he said, 'He got a good one in, that man. Saw more stars than I see at night. Did I crack my skull?' He felt the back of his head gingerly.

Shontu was impressed. He hadn't expected Bhattacharya to be this cheerful after being coshed on the head.

'Hmm, feels wet,' Bhattacharya broadcasted for the rest of them. 'Is it blood? Or is it water?'

It turned out to be water. Noukos were shallow, narrow affairs, so water often collected at the bottom of their hulls. Bhattacharya's shirt and trousers had been soaked through from falling in that water, as had his hair.

'Well, thank goodness for that,' Bhattacharya said. 'Let's check the rest of the body. Arm? Sore, but not broken. Leg? Still working. Good, good. Though the aches will haunt me for days. We're getting along in years, Kakababu. Too old for scuffling and fisticuffs.'

Then he turned towards the dacoits, who were still lying low in the hull. 'What brought this on?' he asked, still cheerful. 'Why attack a government boat?'

'Sir, they've done it before,' the pilot piped up. 'Wrested a gun from us, sir.'

'What, these people?' Bhattacharya asked. 'You recognize them?'

'I don't know if it was them, specifically, sir. I wasn't there. But they lured one of our boats into a narrow canal and tricked them, then stole our gun. If they don't find anything of value, they strip the passengers bare and escape with their clothes, sir.'

'Which reminds me, where's my revolver? Did it fall into the water?'

The revolver was found in the hull, wet but whole. Bhattacharya shrugged and put it back into his pocket. Then he stepped back into the speedboat.

'What shall we do with these terrors?' he asked. 'Wasted a good bit of our time, and we're already behind ...'

Biman scrambled onto the boat with the young man's gun. 'A country-made shotgun,' he commented, putting it on the floor of their boat.

'You! You're exceptionally brave!' Bhattacharya said warmly. 'I was watching you. You grasped the nozzle with your bare hands and turned it upwards!'

Biman almost blushed. 'Well ... I mean, I didn't really have a choice. Kakababu wasn't shooting, and that man could have shot at any moment. Can't expect an armed dacoit to show mercy, so ...'

'I could have blown his wrist apart in a second,' Kakababu insisted. 'But that would mean disabling a young man for life. But Ranabir, let's not dwell here. If a tiger does show up to examine the racket, my revolver can do very little to protect us.'

'But what do we do with these spectacularly stupid dacoits? We can't let them go, not after we know what they're here to do. We can't take them on this boat, either. Tell you what, let's dump them on the shore and cut their boat loose. We'll let them keep their clothes. We have no use for those rags, anyway.'

'Will they survive the jungle with nothing?' Kakababu asked, concerned.

'Probably not,' Bhattacharya said airily. 'That's the beauty of it. Three murderers dead, with no involvement on our end except cutting the boat's rope.'

They watched the men in silence for a few seconds. Bhattacharya's eyes narrowed.

'Look at them, they're not even scared!' he said to Kakababu. 'Hardened criminals, that's what they are. Anyone else would be crying and begging for mercy. One can hardly be merciful when no mercy is asked for.'

'Ranabir, let's just tie their nouko to our boat and go,' Kakababu said. 'They've cost us too much time already, I don't want to waste more.'

In the end, that is what they did. Thick ropes tied the nouko to the back of their speedboat, and the three men were made to sit in it. Bhattacharya didn't bother with tying them up.

'Go slow,' he instructed the pilot. 'If we go at your usual speed the nouko will capsize.' Then he looked at his watch. 'Goodness! We've lost almost an hour to this mess! Oh, and will you look at that. Clouds in that corner. If it begins to pour, we'll be soaked to our bones.'

'The day just gets better and better,' Kakababu said dryly. 'When I set out to see the boat, I hadn't expected all this excitement. I've heard people say that dacoits have become a bigger menace in the Sundarbans than the tigers, but I hadn't expected things to devolve this far.'

'They weren't afraid to attack government officers, did you notice?' Bhattacharya said, his usual good cheer replaced with anger. 'Desperate, that's what they are. If word reaches local officers that I've been assaulted in their jurisdiction, they'll thrash these scoundrels left and right.'

'Were you actually that badly hurt, or were you pretending?' Biman asked.

Bhattacharya grinned again. 'Well, that first strike missed completely, as you probably saw. But the second one landed. Quite hard, too. But it landed on my shoulder, not my head. Had it landed on my head, my skull would probably have cracked.' He patted his shoulder ruefully. 'Can't remember when I was last beaten up this badly. Certainly not in the last decade.'

Shontu kept glancing back at the three men. They were sitting outside the awning, not even trying to talk to each other. Shontu had always assumed that one could pick a criminal from a crowd by the way they looked and acted. But these men looked perfectly normal. Nothing about them suggested that they were dacoits, or that they could kill people in cold blood. They looked exactly like the villagers he'd met on the way. Yet just minutes ago one of them had tried to kill Bhattacharya, and another had almost shot Kakababu's head off.

When they emerged from the canal, the river had broadened a great deal. It poured into an even broader river up ahead. The jungle on either side had begun to thin out, too. Shontu thought he saw a hut or two. A flock of water-birds had been swooping in and out of the river to their left. At the sound of the motorboat, they took flight. Two roosters were pecking for worms on the nearest bank. They began crowing loudly in alarm and ran deeper inland.

'Roosters!' Shontu shouted, surprised. 'There are roosters here!'

'Those are wild roosters,' Biman said helpfully. 'I'm told they're delicious.'

'They're not wild roosters,' Kakababu corrected. 'This is one of the many points of entry into the jungle that we just came out of. People bring roosters as an offering to Bon Bibi, the spirit of the jungle. This is where they set them free, and enter the jungle.'

'Well, Biman is right in a way,' Bhattacharya offered. 'These roosters may be from the villages, but their chicks will be born here, in the jungle. So technically, we could say that the next generation will be wild roosters. Haha!'

Just before their boat merged into the big river, there were three loud splashes right behind them. Whipping around, Shontu saw that the three dacoits had jumped into the river. Next to him, Biman shot to his feet in excitement. With a jolt, Shontu realized he had done the same. The pilot glanced behind to see what had happened, and immediately began turning the boat around.

'No no, let's not waste any more time on them,' Bhattacharya admonished, gesturing to the pilot to correct their course.

'We won't try to catch them?' Biman asked, outraged. 'It'll be easy!'

The dacoits were very strong swimmers. Their heads bobbed up every now and then, but they mostly stayed under water, making determinedly for the far shore. But Biman was right. They were no match for a speedboat.

Bhattacharya grinned his mischievous grin. 'I was wondering when they'd finally take our leave. Don't you see? We're headed to a stranded boat. There's no police station there, no village nearby. Where would I keep them? They would be a dangerous burden for us to cart around. This is much better.'

'But what if they have to spend the night in the jungle? What if a tiger catches them?' Shontu asked.

'They know these jungles far too well for that. Do you think they jumped off willy-nilly? No, they waited till we'd reached a spot that was safe for them. Essentially, we've given them a lift to their hideout. Don't worry.'

'Or perhaps they were tempted by a chicken dinner,' Kakababu said, pointing. 'Look, one of them has nearly reached the roosters' bank.'

'All right, fine. Let's give them a final scare before we go,' Bhattacharya said, changing his mind. 'Pilot saheb, take us as close as you can to that bank.'

The bank was like the banks of the jungles they had left behind, separated from the water by knee-deep silt. One of the men had just waded his way to the other side, having slipped and fallen into the wet mud several times. At the sound of the approaching boat, he turned alarmed eyes towards them. Bhattacharya immediately assumed an angry, ferocious look. Cocking his wet revolver, he said, 'Tried to brain me, eh? Shall I put this through your skull? Shall I?'

This time, the dacoit crumbled. 'Babu, please babu, please! Let me go. I'll give up this life. I'll scrub my nose on this ground as penance. But please let me go!'

Bhattacharya glared at him for a while longer. 'And how long will that promise last?'

'I mean it, babu! I swear by all the gods. I'll never do this again.'

Just then, the two other men burst to the surface, saw the speedboat, and instantly disappeared beneath the waves again.

Bhattacharya lowered his revolver. 'This is your only chance,' he said grimly. 'Tell your mates that. But you're not getting your things back. If you want to see your nouko and your shotgun again, go to Gosaba police station to claim them. All right, let's go.'

The pilot turned the boat around and headed towards the confluence again. The sky had become significantly overcast in the last half hour. The brown water reflected that darkness, becoming inky. Between the darkening sky and the dark water, Shontu could almost taste a sense of foreboding in the atmosphere. As they neared the bigger river, the waves became bigger and choppier.

'Looks like the tide's coming in,' Kakababu commented.

'How much longer to that foreign boat?' Bhattacharya asked the pilot. 'You've been there once, haven't you?'

'Yes sir, we've gone to take a look. It's fairly close now. Without that nouko we would've reached in fifteen minutes.'

'Well ... see if you can take us there before it starts raining.'

Almost before the words were out of his mouth, large drops of rain began falling around them. Defeated, all five of them sat quietly, letting the cold water drench them. There was little else to do.

'Does anyone want to go to the nouko?' Bhattacharya asked half-heartedly. 'Kakababu? You could sit under the awning.'

Kakababu waved him away. 'I'd rather not move from boat to boat in these waters. But you three can go if you like.'

In the end no one went. They all sat under the dark, stormy sky, dripping cold rainwater from their hair and clothes. The wind had picked up speed in just a handful of minutes. It made the waves splash higher against their boat, and nearly overturn the nouko a few times. They had to slow down to a rowboat's pace to keep the nouko steady. Gradually, as it began to rain harder, a wet mist enveloped the river.

'Can't believe we haven't passed a single launch in the past hour,' Kakababu commented.

'We're practically at sea,' Bhattacharya explained. 'This area is not serviced by passenger-launches. We might have seen a few fishing trawlers or fishermen's noukos, but they've probably returned to shore earlier today, before the storm. People here are very good at reading the weather.'

'Traffic has been sparse the last few days,' the pilot added from the front. 'We've been having these rainstorms almost every day, lately.'

'Oh? But we've not had a drop of rain in Calcutta,' Shontu said, surprised.

'These open areas have a lot more storms and rainfall than the inlands,' the pilot explained. 'We call it the influence of the sea.'

'What's that?' Biman suddenly said, pointing excitedly at a hulking shape in the mist ahead. 'That's the boat, isn't it? We've found the mystery boat!'

CHAPTER 4

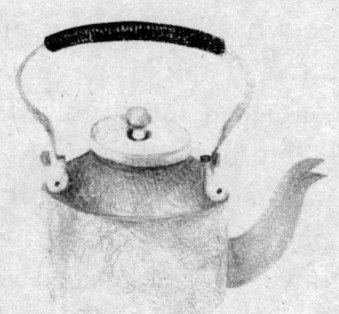

It turned out that they had found two boats, not one. The first was a police launch from Gosaba, the one that had run into a sandbar and become immobile. The actual mystery boat, still pristinely white, was closer to the middle of the river. Floating on inky water against a stormy sky, it reminded Shontu of a graceful swan.

By the time they actually reached the boats, the rain was beginning to taper off. The sound of the speedboat brought a man out on the police launch's deck. He peeked over the railings to take a closer look at the speedboat's passengers. Shontu read the name of the launch off its side: *Honey Bee*. The speedboat aligned itself parallel to the *Honey Bee* before cutting its engine. As soon as they were stable, Bhattacharya stood up. The moment he saw Bhattacharya, the man on deck reared back in fright, and ran back inside the launch.

Bhattacharya started laughing.

'Who's that?' Biman demanded. 'Why did he run off? What's the joke?'

The speedboat's pilot frowned. 'The *Honey Bee*'s sareng is Moidhor. I know him well. That man was not Moidhor. What's happening here?' Then he cupped his mouth and shouted, 'Moidhorda! Moidhorda! Where are you???'

There was no response.

'What sort of a name is Moidhor?' Biman asked Shontu in a low voice. 'The man is called "hold the ladder"? That's so odd!'

'That's just how they're saying it. They mean Mohidhor. It means "the mountain",' Shontu whispered back.

After some more shouting, a rather stout man appeared on deck, still knotting his lungi around his waist. He had very obviously been roused from sleep, and was rather sour about it.

'Is this what the Gosaba police has sent? A speedboat?' he barked irritably. 'What good is a speedboat to me? I had sent word in the morning that we need another launch. Now it's almost evening. My launch has no rations. Do they expect me to starve all day and all night? Who are these people with you, Kashem?'

'He is a senior police officer, Moidhorda,' the speedboat pilot said hurriedly, pointing at Bhattacharya. 'And these babus have come from Calcutta. They want to see that boat.'

'Let them see it, then! What have I got to do with it?' Mohidhor snapped. 'I want to know if I'm supposed to stay here all night without food. Has the Gosaba police sent word at all, or not?'

'You're a strange man, Mohidhor,' Bhattacharya remarked. He was smiling, but Shontu could sense his irritation. 'First you fail to do what you've been sent to do, then you run your own launch into a sandbar, and then you blame the police for your troubles?'

'Look sir, I am not a police employee,' Mohidhor retorted, not at all cowed. 'I rent my vessel to the police on certain conditions. It's not my fault that my launch ran into a sandbar. It happens. But whose fault is it that your people have left me stranded here all day? You tell me that!'

Just then, the man who had run away appeared on deck again. Shontu immediately understood why he had scarpered. Now in uniform, the man was easily identified as a police constable. But when he had first come face-to-face with Bhattacharya, he had just been wearing a vest and a lungi. He obviously hadn't expected to meet a superior officer while posted this far into the jungles. Now, resplendent in his shining belts and boots, he saluted and stood smartly to attention beside the disgruntled Mohidhor.

'Drop the plank,' Bhattacharya ordered. 'We need to dry out a little. Is there tea on board?'

'Only leaves and sugar, sir,' the constable responded apologetically. 'No milk.'

'That'll do. We'll rest a little, have a cuppa, then go inspect the other boat.'

Everyone stood up, except Kakababu. 'Ranabir, tell you what,' he said. 'The rest of you go ahead, but let me go directly to that boat. It's hard enough for me to scramble up and down these planks once. I'd rather not do it twice.'

'That's a much better idea,' Bhattacharya agreed immediately. 'Let's all of us go to the other boat. These people can make a pot of tea and bring it over.'

Everyone sat down again.

'Take us around that boat once, slowly,' Kakababu instructed the pilot. 'I want to take a good look at the outside before going in.'

The speedboat circled the white yacht-like boat from a slight distance. It was as pleasing up close as it was from a distance, but Shontu was surprised to find nothing written on its body. Not its name, not its registration number – nothing. After that, they climbed the ladder on to the deck. Kakababu was helped up by the other three.

From the deck, Kakababu leaned down to speak to the pilot. 'Your name is Kashem, isn't it? Go to the other launch and bring over the tea. And see if they have a towel to spare. We need to at least dry our hair.'

As if on cue, Shontu sneezed loudly. Bhattacharya immediately bore down upon him. 'Take off that shirt, take off that shirt,' he clucked. 'Don't you know wet clothes can give you pneumonia?' As he spoke, he hastily took off his own shirt and wrung it out.

The rain had stopped, and the sky cleared. But there was barely an hour of daylight left. They quickly made their way to the cabins below. The kitchen had the uneaten breakfast and the half-drunk cup of coffee, exactly as reported. But it had absolutely nothing else. Not even cutlery or a tea-kettle. Every bit of appliance, furniture or crockery that hadn't been nailed down had been taken, and not gently. The entire kitchen had a hurricane-torn look.

As a group, they moved slowly through the rest of the boat. Destruction was everywhere. People had taken hammers to the boat's inner walls. In the bedroom, pillows had been sliced to ribbons with a sharp knife. The stuffing was scattered all over the small space. A single slipper had been tossed to a corner. In short, the boat had been ravaged.

'The reason why we suspect spy activity is the complete lack of any identifying documents,' Bhattacharya said. 'Not only have we not recovered the usual official documents, we haven't found even a casual scrap of paper, or anything that might give the boat's origin away. Why would all hints of nationality be erased unless there's espionage involved?'

'But why would a foreign spy come here? What's so secret about the Sundarbans?' Biman asked.

'Arre, who said they were coming to the Sundarbans?' Bhattacharya riposted. 'They were probably coming from Japan or China. Then they either deliberately abandoned ship and let it carry on to throw off suspicion, or someone attacked them and disposed of their body and documents. The empty boat was pulled along by currents and ended up here.'

Shontu glanced at Kakababu. He didn't look like he had heard a word. He was staring at the floor, frowning deeply.

'I think ... yes, I think I know who this boat belongs to,' he finally said.

Bhattacharya's jaw dropped. 'You've worked it out? Already?'

Kakababu looked up with a slight smile. 'Your theory—the police's theory, I mean—is that the owner has either abandoned ship or was murdered, and the boat followed currents and ended up here. Right? But what if the truth is the exact opposite?'

Now it was Bhattacharya's turn to frown. 'How do you mean, opposite?'

'Well, what if the owner had intended to come to our seas all along, but then his engine gave out midway, or he ran out of fuel? That would force him to be adrift, wouldn't it?'

'It's not impossible, but why on earth would a man float about these seas in an obviously expensive vessel, unless he had very specific plans? Unless he's some sort of a circumnavigator, like that other man, what's his name ... Francis Chichester.'

'Chichester sailed on a ketch, not a motorboat,' Kakababu corrected automatically.

'Be that as it may, we haven't seen any headlines about a circumnavigator coming this way.'

'Where's the radio?' Shontu suddenly asked.

Kakababu grinned his approval. 'Good question. Boy has brains, Ranabir. Where *is* the radio? The forestry officer heard it on board. Did he take it with him?'

'No. His report says clearly that he removed nothing from the boat. Everything of value had already been stripped off. Someone must have sneaked in afterwards and made off with the radio.'

'Why leave it behind in the first place? They took everything else, why not the radio?' Biman asked.

'Perhaps it's a larger model that's built into the wall,' Kakababu suggested. 'It might still be here, just not visible because we've been looking for the smaller, portable kind.'

They began looking again, this time for tuners or an on-off switch. Shontu found it first. It was obvious when one knew what to look for. The kitchen wall had three knobs right next to each other. As soon as he turned the first knob, loud music filled the boat.

Kakababu hurried into the kitchen, then listened carefully to the music.

'The robbers had no compunction about destroying the walls,' Biman said, following behind. 'Why didn't they simply break this wall down and wrench the radio out? It's obvious where it is once you find the knobs. It's up there, behind that wire mesh.'

'This boat has been robbed in at least two or three instalments,' Kakababu said thoughtfully. 'The first lot killed the owner and took the most valuable items. The second and third lot simply ransacked the place, taking whatever they could. The first probably had no interest in a radio, and the others didn't know how to find it.'

Biman frowned. 'How do you know there had been different robberies, Kakababu? The same group could have stripped the valuables, and then hammered the walls for hidden goods.'

'No,' Kakababu said firmly. 'The kind of robbers who kill the crew and steal international paperwork and luxurious valuables are not the sort who steal cutlery. Look around, Biman. They've not even left a plate behind. The table is still here because it is built in, but where are the chairs? No assassin would have stopped on his way out to steal a tea-kettle. It's the work of petty thieves who chanced upon the scene.'

Bhattacharya nodded. 'I agree. The first lot were the real criminals, whoever they were. The rest were just people who came upon an empty boat, decided to risk a look, then made off with whatever they could.'

'But still, isn't it interesting that they didn't take the radio?' Biman insisted. 'The ranger said the radio was on, so it must have been easy to spot.'

'Not necessarily. I think what happened was that between that first group leaving and the ranger arriving, the channel had stopped broadcasting. This happens quite often. People fall asleep at night without turning their radios off, and the radios fall silent when the channel stops broadcasting for the night. But the moment broadcasts begin again, the radios come back to life. If the petty looters had come between broadcasting times, they might not actually have known that there was an expensive radio on board.'

'Kakababu, now that we know where the radio is, shall I turn it off?' Shontu offered.

'No,' said Kakababu shortly.

Almost immediately, the recorded music stopped and a man's voice began speaking. Shontu didn't understand a word, but it sounded like announcements. Kakababu smiled.

'You've been flying around the world for years, Biman. Do you know what language this is?'

Biman frowned. 'Not really, no. Some of it sounds like German.'

'Not German.'

'Is it Swedish?' Bhattacharya volunteered. 'I was in Stockholm for work for a few weeks. I don't understand it, but it sounds familiar.'

'Correct! Specifically, this is a broadcast from the Gothenburg area. I'm in no further doubt. The owner of this boat is—*was*—Ingmar Smelt.'

Bhattacharya's brows drew together. 'Who's that?'

Just then, they heard the speedboat draw up outside.

'That's the tea,' Kakababu said, getting his crutches. 'Let's go up and drink it while it's hot. Then we can come down again.'

'If they don't see us on deck, they'll bring it down,' Bhattacharya interrupted. 'Stay here and tell us about this Ingmar Smelt. Did you know him?'

Kakababu breathed out a slow, regretful sigh. 'No, we've never met. Honestly, Ranabir, I cannot believe a man like Smelt met with such a horrific end. Slaughtered by dacoits in our country! To have lost one of the greatest minds of our generation to such petty, stupid greed!'

'One of the greatest minds of our generation? I've never even heard of this man!' Bhattacharya exclaimed. 'Who was he? Was he from Sweden?'

'He was born and raised in Sweden, but he was half-American. He spent several years as a scientist in the USA, too. His name was proposed for the Nobel Prize the year that the Vietnam War properly began, but he petitioned to withdraw his name. He insisted that science was meant for the benefit of mankind, not its destruction. He despised weapons research. He called upon all scientists to stop letting their research aid war and suffering.'

'Ah yes, this made the headlines a few years ago – a scientist asking every other scientist to boycott war. I remember him, I'd just forgotten his name.'

'Yes, that was Smelt,' Kakababu nodded. 'As you can probably imagine, he was isolated and alienated as an eccentric, a loose cannon, an impractical do-gooder. His colleagues argued that they had no control over how their research was used, that military action wasn't their fault. The final fallout of his call was that Smelt was pushed to the margins of scientific society, and deliberately forgotten. Bitter and disillusioned, he disappeared soon after.'

There were footsteps on the stairs. The formerly lungi-clad constable and Kashem came carefully down the stairs, carrying a kettle of tea and four glasses. They handed out the glasses and poured bitter black tea into them.

'Sir, when will you leave?' Kashem asked. 'There'll be trouble if it's after dark. The sky's not looking good, we'll be in the middle of another storm if we don't set out soon. The dacoits will be more daring, too.'

'Wait outside for a few minutes, I'll let you know what we decide,' Bhattacharya said. 'What news of the *Honey Bee*? Has the tide moved it yet?'

'No, sir. It'll need another launch to tug it out of the sandbar.'

'So we'll need two launches just to get this small private boat to Gosaba? Ridiculous! Anyway, wait outside for now. We're discussing matters of great import.'

The moment the constable and Kashem's footsteps faded, he turned to Kakababu. 'And then?' he asked eagerly, like a little boy listening to a riveting story. 'Tell us how you worked out that this was Ingmar saheb's boat. It could have belonged to any Swedish person, right? In fact, it could have belonged to anyone!

I could listen to a Swedish channel if I tuned my radio enough. Lots of people do it for a hobby.'

'I have an unfair advantage,' Kakababu confessed. 'Six years ago, the *National Geographic* had published an article on Smelt. His call to boycott the "misuse of science" had just fallen flat. According to the article, he had been so disappointed by the lack of support—not just in the USA, but from every other country—that he had decided not to be a citizen of any of them. Instead, he had bought and kitted out a boat, and had declared that he would only live on international waters. This was that boat. The *National Geographic* had a picture of it.'

'That's a very strange solution,' Biman said. 'Imagine quitting the entire world because your colleagues wouldn't agree with you.'

'The world is still worth living in because there are people like Smelt in it,' Kakababu said sharply. 'Smelt may have been ridiculed for being naive or too idealistic, but those were his principles and he refused to give them up. When not a single person was brave enough to stand up with him, *he* was brave enough to strike out on his own!'

'But what of food? Wouldn't he eventually run out of food?' Shontu asked.

'Of course. More than food, he would run out of drinking water. In his years on the seas, he made regular stops at various port-towns to replenish his rations. He was an old man of sparse habits. I doubt he needed much.'

'Did you say you read the article six years ago?'
Bhattacharya asked. 'Wow. It's a miracle he hadn't
been robbed several times already. Imagine living in
a boat on international waters for six years! Anyway,
thank you for your breakthrough, Kakababu. We'll
have to send word to Sweden and untangle the legal
knots before handing over the boat to them. Who
knows how long that'll take. But we should head back
now. It's almost dark.'

'Yes, you should head back now,' Kakababu agreed.
'But I shall stay here tonight.'

'Here? You mean on this boat? But why?'

'Well, since I've come this far, I want to explore this
mystery a little more. For example: why was Ingmar
Smelt's corpse not found?'

'How could it be found? It was tossed to the sea.
Who knows where the currents have taken him by
now. And if they've weighed him down with bricks and
stones, he'll probably never surface.'

'All right, fine. But what happened to his books?
Smelt was, above all, a scholar. He would not have
survived a week without his books, much less six years.
So where are those books? Where are his notebooks?
They're just paper – dacoits and looters wouldn't be
interested in them. Shouldn't we look for the work
that a leading scientist has done in the last six years
of his life? Should we just let it go?'

'It's certainly a loss, Kakababu, but we've just
searched every inch of this boat. There's not even a
shred of paper left. The people who robbed this boat

are mostly uneducated, you know? They probably just destroyed his papers while looking for things to sell.'

Kakababu shook his head. 'I can't leave without trying, Ranabir. Smelt was a pacifist, a scholar, a man of exceptional integrity and moral purity. I can't accept that his final works shall be buried at sea. I *can't*.'

Shontu noticed the catch in Kakababu's voice. Suddenly, he had a vision of an innocent, harmless scholar beset by violent, greedy hordes. All Smelt wanted was to use science for the good of mankind, and to live in peace on his boat. These greedy monsters killed him for a few pieces of furniture! Shontu felt his own eyes begin to water.

Bhattacharya stayed quiet for a few seconds. Then, in a softer, cajoling voice, he said, 'I understand your pain, I really do. Now that we know who the victim was, the murderers will be soon apprehended. If they've stolen his research, we'll recover it. I will personally lead a search party tomorrow to scour every inch of this region. But we must go back tonight, Kakababu. It's a quarter past six now. If we leave right away, we can be in Canning by ten.'

'Then please start,' Kakababu said, with a stubborn twist to his mouth. 'You have your briefing, Biman has his flight, Shontu has his homework. I have nothing, and I'm happy to be here alone.'

'But what more could you do on this boat, Kakababu?'

'Nothing, perhaps. But I'm still going to spend the night here. Just send the speedboat back for me in the morning. I want to poke around along the riverbanks a little before going back.'

'Kakababu, you can't spend the night here,' Bhattacharya said, now firmly. 'First of all, there are no rations on the boat. Secondly, this boat is now a target. Thieves, dacoits, murderers ... who knows who else might come by at night?'

'Don't worry about me,' Kakababu said dismissively. 'I've survived so many close shaves in life that I've come to believe that I genuinely cannot be harmed by criminals. Ask Shontu, he knows about some of these incidents. What can your little dacoits do, really? And as for rations, I can easily go a couple of days without food. This is just one night.'

Bhattacharya sighed. 'Kakababu, you know we cannot leave you here to spend the night alone. Please, come back with us. We can return tomorrow.'

Kakababu looked Bhattacharya straight in the eye. 'Listen, Ranabir, I know quite well that if I leave tonight, I won't be able to come this far out tomorrow. I feel like I owe it to the memory of Smelt to at least make an effort. If I go back tonight, just for the sake of convenience, then I'll never forgive myself.'

Bhattacharya gave up. 'Very well then, I'll stay with you. Shontu, Bimanbabu, be careful on your way back.'

'No!' Shontu and Biman protested together. 'We'll stay back too,' Biman added.

'Don't you have a plane to fly day after?' Kakababu asked.

'I do, but reporting's not till two in the afternoon. If I reach Dum Dum airport by one-thirty, I'll be fine. I'm not abandoning the two of you in the middle of nowhere.'

'Are we all staying the night, then?' Bhattacharya asked, rubbing his chin. 'That's not a bad idea, except that we have no rations or water, and I have a very busy day tomorrow. Kakababu, I didn't know bringing you along would be this much trouble.'

'I told you to go!' Kakababu snapped, stung. 'I can stay alone. None of you have to stay!'

'That's absurd, and obviously out of the question,' Bhattacharya said, dismissing Kakababu's outrage. 'Well then, if we're staying then let's settle in for the night. I suppose this is a sort of an adventure, too. Let me tell that boat chap.'

Kashem was waiting near the top of the stairs.

'Do you reckon we can make it safely back if we start now?' Bhattacharya asked him. 'It's already dark, and I'm concerned about dacoits who might be lying in wait for late-night travellers along the way.'

'If we pull through at top speed then they won't be able to catch us, sir. But they might shoot at us.'

'Shoot at us?' Bhattacharya pretended to be shocked. 'These people shoot at boats from the shores? At night? No no, pilot saheb, that's too big a risk! I think it's best that we spend the night here. What do you say?'

Kashem clearly thought it was a bad idea. 'Whatever you think best, sir,' he replied, sourly.

'Then I say we stay. What shall we do about dinner, though? Just tea? Does the *Honey Bee* have enough leaves and sugar to keep us supplied through the night?'

'We have tea and sugar, sir,' the constable assured him.

'Good, good. Anything else? Rice? Potatoes?'

The constable hesitated. 'We have some rice and salt, sir. No potatoes.'

'No potatoes? That's a shame! A steaming plate of rice congee and boiled potatoes, with a dollop of butter on top – ahh, heaven! Still, we'll make do with just rice for tonight. I can't survive on tea alone. Listen, tell your sareng that if he cooks me a plate of plain congee tonight, I'll buy him a bowl of chicken and rice tomorrow! All right?'

'Yes, sir!'

'And see if you have one of those thick sitting-carpets. It's impossible to sit in the mess here.'

'Yes, sir!'

After the speedboat left, Bhattacharya looked at the darkening evening sky and laughed aloud at the absurdity of the situation. 'Gosaba might well lose their minds and send a *third* vessel to look for me! Well, let them come. The more the merrier! Haha!'

CHAPTER 5

Kakababu's decision to spend the night on the boat turned out to be the right one.

There were no sitting-carpets on the *Honey Bee*, but the constable and Kashem had brought them two large woven mats. They were ancient and worn, but clean enough to sit on. They spread the mats on the deck and sat around in a circle under the cloudy, moonless sky. The only sound was of the waves cresting against the boat, and the occasional call of a night bird. Though the river was enormously wide this close to the sea, the boat had been moored close to the thickly-wooded bank. Shontu shuddered when he looked at the dark outline of the trees. They were far too close to the jungle for his comfort. Kashem had assured them that there were no tigers on that shore – apparently it

was just a narrow neck of land between this river and
the next, and the jungle there was too thin to support
large wildlife. But Shontu was sure that the jungle on
the *other* side of the next river was absolutely crawling
with tigers. It was literally called Baghmara, or the
Place for Hunting Tigers. What more proof did one
need?

Biman was similarly afraid of a tiger-attack. 'Is it
true that tigers are strong swimmers?' he asked. 'Can
they swim to us from, say, the jungle on the other side
of that river?'

'I suppose they can, sir,' Kashem replied, hesitantly.
'But sir, we're practically at the mouth of the sea. The
currents are very strong here, and the river quite deep.
Tigers like deeper, denser jungles. They wouldn't come
this far into the open.'

'Hah! There's nothing that a Sundarban tiger
wouldn't do!' Bhattacharya scoffed. 'I don't trust your
local beasts at all. Let me tell you, Bimanbabu: I've
never met a creature more ferocious or more cunning
than the Royal Bengal tiger. If they want to come here,
they will. And all of them are man-eaters. All of them!'

'Did you ever see a tiger?' Biman asked, eagerly.

'Thank goodness, no,' Bhattacharya laughed,
dismissing the possibility with a wave. 'I used to come
here quite often when I was the District Superintendent
for this area. But I always did my best to stay away
from the wildlife, especially tigers.'

'Sir, I had come face-to-face with a tiger once,'
Kashem offered timidly.

Immediately, all heads turned towards him. 'Where?' Bhattacharya asked, on everyone's behalf.

Kashem raised his arm and indicated a direction in the darkness. 'Over there, sir, on the banks of the Raimangal river. There's a small village there called Chhoto Mollakhali. That's my village, sir. Two years ago, we had a stray tiger come into the village ...'

And thus, a chain of tiger tales began.

Only Kakababu refused to join them. He remained downstairs, tapping his crutch on the walls of the boat. They could hear the rhythmic sound from the deck. Bhattacharya had tried to make him join them a few times, but every time he shouted an invitation down the stairs, Kakababu responded with, 'You carry on, Ranabir. I'll join you when I'm done.' Finally, Bhattacharya had rolled his eyes—as if to say, 'Well, what can you do with a stubborn madman?'—and given up.

After Kashem recounted three or four thrilling tales of tigers visiting nearby villages, Bhattacharya interrupted him with a huge yawn.

'It's barely a quarter to eight, but it feels like the middle of the night. I want to curl up and go to bed right here. Kashem, why don't you go over to the *Honey Bee* and see if they'll make us another kettle?'

Kashem left. Bhattacharya stretched himself out on the mats and stared at the overcast night sky. 'As impromptu ideas go, this isn't bad,' he mused. 'As long as a tiger doesn't swim up to see what we're doing, we'll be fine. But let me tell you right now, boys: if we're attacked again, I'm not lifting a finger. Can't fight dacoits twice the same day – not at my age.'

'We have two launches here, and enough people on board,' Biman said confidently. 'The dacoits wouldn't dare.'

Bhattacharya lifted his head slightly to look at Biman, then dropped it back on the mat. 'You don't know these dacoits, Bimanbabu. If they carry just one small machine-gun, we'll all be dust. Heads powdered like sattu in a minute. After the Bangladesh War, many light-grade military arms have made their way into the black market across the border. Dacoits are not what they used to be.'

The darkness and the steady sound of the waves was getting to Shontu. 'Can we go downstairs and turn the radio on?' he asked. 'We could catch a local station.'

'Sure,' Bhattacharya said, not moving. 'Feel free to turn the knobs to your heart's content. And if you hear a missing person's announcement about us, come up here and let us know. Haha!'

Smiling slightly, Shontu made for the stairs. To his surprise, his uncle was standing at the bottom of those stairs, holding a torch in one hand and trying to dislodge one of the steps with the other.

'Kakababu? Are you looking for something there?'

'I am indeed, and I think I'm very close to finding it. Could you call for Ranabir?'

Shontu ran back to the top and shouted for Bhattacharya. In seconds, both Bhattacharya and Biman were at the bottom of the stairs.

'I need your help,' Kakababu said quickly, before either of them could ask him anything.

'What with, Kakababu? Is there something wrong with the stairs?' Biman asked, concerned.

'No. But none of you considered the hammer-marks. Clearly, the dacoits had tried to break the walls of this boat down. But why? They had already stripped the boat of everything. Why go after the walls? I spent the last hour re-checking the walls, comparing the outer and inner size of the machine-room and cabins. And I've realized that a large square space has been neatly hidden away somewhere here. I'm fairly sure that the dacoits had worked it out, too. That's why they had been hammering the walls. Not to break them, but to listen for hollowness. I'm certain they didn't find it, but we must.'

'But how shall we break the iron walls?' Bhattacharya asked reasonably. 'The dacoits at least had hammers. We have nothing.'

'We won't break them, Ranabir, we'll look for the way in. If there's a secret room, there has to be an easy way to open and close it. Easy, but hidden. I've already checked every inch of the walls. There's nothing there. The staircase is our only hope. Let's see if it can be moved.'

For the next few minutes, they pushed and pulled at the frame of the staircase. It didn't yield an inch.

'Just this once, I think your deduction has failed, Kakababu,' Bhattacharya said, panting slightly. 'There's nothing under these stairs.'

'I'm sure there is,' Kakababu said with conviction. 'If we can't move the staircase, then we need to check for detachable parts on each stair.'

This time, they found it. Shontu pulled the top stair, and both that stair and the one below it wobbled. With a little effort, Shontu was able to pull the frame of those stairs away from the supporting wall. A small rectangle of pitch darkness appeared where the two stairs had been. Kakababu hurried up from the bottom of the staircase and shone his torch into it. A bright rectangle had been painted into the inside of the stair-frame, highlighting a button. Biman reached up from the side of the staircase and pressed it. Nothing happened for a few seconds. Then the side of the staircase swung open suddenly, revealing a small, square gateway.

'There's another staircase going down,' Biman whispered.

For the first few minutes, everyone simply stared at the hidden staircase. Then Bhattacharya turned to Kakababu. 'Kakababu, let me touch your feet. I mean it. You're beyond compare. This wouldn't have occurred to me in a hundred years. How on earth did you suspect that there could be something like this?'

Kakababu tossed Biman his torch. 'What's inside, Biman?' he asked, his voice taut with anticipation.

Biman shone the torch into the darkness. 'Kakababu, there's a whole room down these stairs! Bed, bookshelves, stacks of notebooks!'

Shontu could feel the tension leave his uncle's body. When he spoke, he sounded oddly at peace. 'I knew it. I knew Smelt's ideas would be safe. He would have protected them from petty thieves and greedy murderers.'

Ranabir Bhattacharya had recovered from his bout of hero-worship. 'The local police have gone to the dogs,' he said gloomily. 'A whole team had come to take stock and do preliminary enquiries, and none of them found this. It should have occurred to at least one of them to look for hidden spaces.'

'Wait, I'll go in and take a proper look,' Biman called, and disappeared into the darkness. They heard his footsteps going down.

Barely five minutes later he called back up at the group above. 'This place is *stuffed* with books. There are books on the floor. There's a built-in safe, a built-in cupboard ... wait, why is the cupboard open ... AAAHHH!'

'What? What is it, Biman?' Kakababu shouted back.

'A man! My god, they've tied up a man and stuffed him inside the cupboard!'

Kakababu's veneer of calm deserted him completely. 'A man? Ranabir, we've found Smelt! We have found Ingmar Smelt! Is he alive? Biman, is Smelt breathing? Biman!'

'He's alive. But, Kakababu ... this can't be Smelt. This man looks local. Yes, definitely local, Kakababu.'

Bhattacharya's brows jerked together. 'Local? Hang on, Biman, don't touch anything. Let me come down first.'

In his hurry, Bhattacharya lost his footing on the very first stair and slid down the rest of the way. But the moment he stopped rolling, he jumped back to his feet and hurriedly brushed himself off.

'I'm fine!' he called back up the stairs. 'Haven't hurt myself at all, no need to worry! Now where's this man? Where is he?'

Shontu was surreptitiously watching his uncle. The moment Biman had shouted that the man was local, Kakababu had collapsed like a punctured balloon.

'I'm not going to risk those narrow stairs,' he now said, exhaustion and disappointment in every syllable. 'Bring him up, whoever he is.'

Then he went slowly up the main staircase, the one that led to the deck. Shontu heard him drop heavily on the mat, and take in deep, calming breaths.

Bhattacharya and Biman carried a limp body up the dark stairs. Shontu lent them a hand in bringing the man up to the deck. The man looked about thirty. He was wearing a cheap blue shirt and khaki trousers. His hands and legs were tightly bound, and he had been gagged. Even in the faint light of the overcast evening sky, Shontu could make out dried blood all over the shoulder and back of his shirt.

Before they could discuss the next steps, the speedboat dropped anchor next to their boat and Kashem and the constable came aboard. Kashem nearly dropped the kettle when he saw the addition to their group.

'Someone you know?' Bhattacharya asked, narrowing his eyes.

'No sir. But he's ... where did you find him, sir?'

'Your Chhoto Shadhu probably knows him quite well,' Kakababu said to Bhattacharya. 'Cut those ropes. See if we can save him.'

Biman stepped forward before Bhattacharya could. 'Kakababu, allow me. We're trained in first-aid.'

He undid the man's bindings and cleaned as much of his wound as he could with old, thin towels. Then, when he turned the man over gently to dress the wound, he saw that it was both bigger and deeper than he had assumed. There was a deep gash at the back of the man's head, matted with hair and dried blood. Someone had tried to slice his head open. Biman did the best he could, then laid the man back on the deck.

'That's a vicious cut,' Bhattacharya said from the side. 'Fellow must have lost a great deal of blood when the wound was fresh. But he's a fighter, this one. Who knows how long he's been in that room? And he's still holding on! If we can save his life, Kakababu, it will be all thanks to you. Without your persistence, he would have been left to rot.'

'Hmm, the dacoits here are not as stupid as I had expected them to be,' Kakababu mused. 'They had found the secret room. I wonder what else they had found. If this man recovers, he'll be able to fill in a lot of gaps for us.'

'I saw the safe Biman mentioned,' Bhattacharya said. 'It was unlocked and empty. Whatever it had once held—money, gold, scientific research—is not there anymore. The room was a mess, too. I bet the dacoits had fought over dividing whatever was in the safe. And this was the unlucky loser.'

Biman paid no attention to the conversation. He was trying to wrangle some sustenance into the man. 'Add a few more teaspoons of sugar to the tea,' he instructed Kashem. 'That'll have to do for glucose.' Then he lifted the man's head at an angle and very carefully poured tiny amounts of the liquid into his slack mouth. After a few slow minutes of this, the man grunted weakly a few times. But he didn't wake up.

'That's enough, I think,' Kakababu said. 'Let's not shock his system. If he doesn't throw up in the next few minutes, then the little sugar that's gone in will help.'

'You're a real asset, Bimanbabu,' Bhattacharya said, looking appreciatively at the younger man. 'Your help today has been exemplary. But I suggest you tie him back up again.'

Astonished, Shontu stared at Bhattacharya.

'I'm not saying it to be cruel,' Bhattacharya defended himself. 'But you have to admit that he has a talent for survival. What if he revives while we're all asleep, and jumps into the sea? He may very well drown! And then we'll lose our only source of information. Safety first, Shontu.'

'That's sensible,' Kakababu conceded. 'Let's tie him back up, Biman. But perhaps more gently than he had been tied before.'

A bird flew overhead just then, letting out a loud honking noise. It was followed by a distant siren.

'Was that the bird, or was that the siren of an actual launch?' Bhattacharya asked. 'Dare I hope that Gosaba has sent a vessel after me?'

Bhattacharya, Kashem, Shontu and Biman looked hopefully at the direction the sound had come from. They saw nothing but empty darkness. They continued to stare, willing a launch's headlight to appear. But for the next several minutes, nothing moved on the river.

'It was probably one of the ships anchored at sea, sir,' Kashem offered apologetically. 'At night you can hear noises from quite far into the sea.'

'Oh, to hell with it!' Bhattacharya said with a laugh. 'I'd been hoping a launch would turn up before dinner, bearing a decent meal. Well, that's obviously not going to happen. Go on then, pilot saheb. Request our gracious sareng to send over his starch-rice and salt. Let's at least go to bed on a full stomach.'

After putting down the still-full kettle of tea, Kashem left. Dinner arrived about half an hour later. Astonishingly, the plain rice and salt turned out to be rather good. None of those present had ever had just rice for a meal before, but in the face of gnawing hunger and worry, the steaming bowls felt like manna from heaven. When the alternative was going to bed hungry, hot rice felt like the best food on the planet.

After dinner, Kakababu said, 'I'd like to examine Smelt's books and notes. Could some of you help me down those narrow stairs?'

It was hard guiding Kakababu down the hidden staircase, but Shontu finally managed it. Unfortunately, there was no light. The boat had had adequate electrical wiring and lights once, but the thieves and dacoits had taken the dynamo, the batteries, and every last bulb. So Kakababu had to depend on his torch to do his reading. As Shontu turned to leave, he saw his uncle reach for the handwritten notebooks. After barely ten minutes, Kakababu's triumphant bellow erupted from the hole.

'These notebooks are Smelt's diaries! All of you can go back up to the deck. I'm going to stay here all night and read them!'

CHAPTER 6

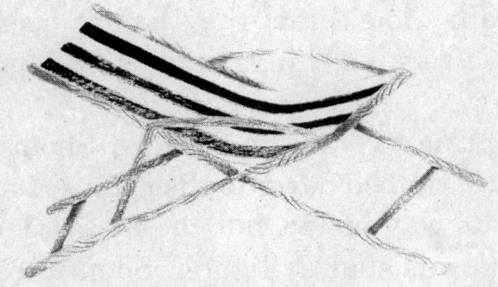

Everyone had imagined spending a long, sleepless night tossing and turning on the deck, but as it happened, they fell asleep fairly quickly. The last thing Shontu remembered was a debate between Biman and Bhattacharya, but sleep had crept upon him long before that conversation had ended. Which is probably why he was the first to wake when the dawn's crisp light washed upon the deck. At first, he tried to scramble to his feet, wildly alarmed by the strange setting. Then his memory gathered itself. Biman and Bhattacharya were still asleep on the mat. The man from the room was still out cold, or at least fast asleep. The constable, who Shontu supposed was there to guard them, was dozing beside the deck-rails.

After taking stock of them all, Shontu realized that none of the things that he had been absolutely sure would happen that night had actually happened. One, they hadn't been attacked by dacoits. Two, it hadn't rained again. And three, they hadn't been attacked by tigers. It was, all things considered, a pretty good morning.

Not wanting to wake the others, Shontu stood up and gingerly tiptoed down to the cabins. Daylight had not made its way inside, but the darkness inside the secret room was slightly lighter. Shontu leaned down from the top of the secret staircase to see what his uncle was doing.

There was no one in the room.

The peace of the morning slid right off him. With his heart thumping desperately against his ribs, Shontu ran down the narrow staircase to the room below. At first, all he saw was the mess. Then he saw his uncle, sitting in a corner with a notebook in his lap. His head was resting on his chest, and his face and arms were covered in droplets of sweat.

Kakababu was sleeping.

Very quietly, Shontu made his way back up the stairs. He couldn't bear to disturb his uncle's rest.

A beautiful morning was unfolding on the river. The pale light of dawn had begun to turn golden as the sun approached the horizon. It tinged the tops of the trees and the water with colour. Shontu leaned on the railing and watched the morning unfold. The other launch was closer than he had imagined last night, one side leaning dramatically on the invisible sandbar. There were no signs of life on its deck or cabins. The crew had likely not left their beds yet. At a distance, he saw a handful of fishing noukos making their way towards the sea, their sails curved with the morning breeze. Just a few hours ago, this place had felt like a slice of a nightmare – full of whispering noises and unvoiced fears. With the slowly-spreading light, the same silence was now blissful.

After about ten minutes, he heard Kakababu call, 'Shontu! Shontu!'

Shontu ran downstairs again.

'These stairs are difficult for me,' his uncle admitted. 'Could you take my crutches first? Now take my hand. I'll need some help getting out.'

Shontu held on as Kakababu hopped up the narrow, unrailed staircase one step at a time. 'How's everything upstairs?' he asked. 'Has that man woken up yet?'

'No, still sleeping. But he's alive. I saw his chest move in and out.'

'And everyone else?'

'Also asleep.'

The two of them came quietly upstairs. Kakababu headed straight for the man and put his palm below his nose. Then he took the man's wrist in his fingers and counted the pulse by his watch.

'Everything's normal,' he said when he went back to Shontu. 'I don't think he's in danger anymore. But he must be weak. We'll let him sleep for now, poor soul.'

'Is it dawn yet?' Bhattacharya's sleepy voice mumbled from their other side. 'Is this daylight I see, or a very bright moon?'

Shontu chuckled. Bhattacharya grinned back, then sat up. 'Can you believe it's morning already? I hadn't slept at all, you know. Just barely closed my eyes for a moment. And already the sun's racing towards midday! Well, where's our morning tea? Constable!'

The dozing constable tried to jump to attention while still sitting, and ended up sprawled on the deck. Embarrassed, he clambered to his feet and ripped off a smart salute.

'Tell them to send over a pot of tea. Quickly! I can't function without a cuppa in the mornings.'

Without the speedboat at his service, the constable cupped his mouth and shouted towards the launch. 'Ae Kashem! Ae Moidhor! Sir wants tea!'

'No water,' came Mohidhor's laconic reply.

'Sir, Moidhor says he's out of fresh water,' the constable elaborated, twisting his fingers apprehensively.

'But how can we start our day without tea?' Bhattacharya asked, appalled. 'What good is all this water around us if we can't make a simple pot of tea?'

'This is sea water, sir,' the constable explained guiltily, as if it was his own fault. 'We can't bear to taste it, it's so salty, sir.'

'Oh, the torture!' Bhattacharya exclaimed. 'We have tea, we have sugar, we have water ... but we can't make tea because of the salt in it? Kakababu, have you ever heard of anything more tragic?'

'"Water, water everywhere, not a drop to drink",' Shontu recited, smiling.

Bhattacharya eyed him with faux disfavour. 'I see you know your English poetry. Do you know the Bengali equivalent?'

Shontu was certain he knew what Bhattacharya meant, but he shook his head, suppressing a grin.

'Hmph! Well, I'll tell you. "Jawl shudhu jawl; dekhe mor chitto hoyeche bikawl". "Water, water everywhere; My soul malfunctions at the sight". There, now you know. But what shall we do about the tea? Oh, to hell with it – Constable, ask them to make tea with sea water!'

The constable stared. He looked like he couldn't believe his ears.

'Oh, don't look so shocked,' Bhattacharya said airily. 'Do they have lebu? Lemons? Tell them to squeeze one in. It'll balance out the salt.'

The *Honey Bee* didn't have lemons. The sea-water tea, when it came, was so indescribably atrocious that even Kakababu, famously stoic in matters of food, took one brief sip before setting his glass aside. Biman and Shontu refused to touch it. But Bhattacharya finished his glass in a single swallow.

'Well, it smells like tea,' he offered by way of explanation when he saw Shontu staring. 'Anyway, how was everyone's night? Kakababu, how was the secret cabin? Did you find anything useful?'

'Very useful. I've only been able to read the last few entries in Smelt's diary because my torch ran out of battery, but what he says there changes everything. To begin with, Smelt had not been murdered by the first group of dacoits.'

'How's that possible?'

'Well, Smelt was perhaps naive in the ways of the world, but he wasn't a fool. He'd had his little room built with considerable engineering expertise. It's hard to detect unless specifically looked for. Smelt kept all his books, paperwork and valuables there. A month and a half ago, Smelt replenished his rations in Japan. Then he resumed his usual life at sea, but his engine broke down. Usually under such circumstances, the crew sends out SOS messages over the wireless to nearby vessels. But as I explained yesterday, Smelt was determined not to seek any help from the world. He didn't even have a wireless set on board, lest he be tempted.'

'That's amazing. And I don't necessarily mean that as a compliment,' Bhattacharya remarked.

'Be that as it may, Smelt was content to let his vessel drift till his compass and other instruments indicated that he was near land again. In his diary he notes that he was near the north-eastern coast of the Indian subcontinent. If you look at old maps, Calcutta is the most prominent port in coastal north-eastern India. Smelt probably didn't know that this was no

longer the route to reach Calcutta by water. He was
happy to drift along till he reached the city, where he
was sure he could have his engine repaired. Besides,
Smelt had certain ideas about Indians that I have
occasionally seen other Western people share. They
think that we're all devout Hindus, and therefore
nonviolent and peaceful without exception. Many
of them don't even understand that Hinduism is a
religion; they think "Hindu" means a race of people
who live in India. Ingmar Smelt, unfortunately, had
a similarly idealistic view of us. Which is why he
was shocked when he realized that a group of violent
dacoits had landed on his deck. He had just sat down
to a sparse meal – the one that we saw. He managed
to make it to his hidden room before the dacoits saw
him, and locked himself in. He remained locked in
for twelve hours. While inside, he wrote with shock
and disappointment about being attacked by "Hindu
pirates". That was seven days ago.'

'Then?'

'Then, nothing,' Kakababu said, turning to look
towards the confluence of the river and sea. 'There are
no further entries. Either Smelt left the room on his
own after twelve hours, and ran into the second group
by sheer bad luck; or the second group was cleverer
than the first and discovered the room. Either way, it
was the second group that murdered him. Smelt was
a true pacifist. He didn't believe in carrying weapons,
so he was no match for a gang of murderous dacoits.'

'There are signs of struggle in the hidden room,' Biman chimed in.

Kakababu nodded. 'That could have been with Smelt. Or it could have been amongst the dacoits themselves. We really have no way of knowing unless that man over there wakes up and answers our questions.'

'Let's wake him up, then,' Bhattacharya said, stretching and getting to his feet. 'I'm tired of mysteries.'

'He's awake. I saw him blink a few times,' Shontu reported from his corner.

Bhattacharya squatted beside the man and placed his right hand on the man's chest. 'Hey, you. Are you hungry? Can you keep down plain rice?'

The man didn't respond. He was pretending to be asleep.

'Let's splash a little water on his face,' Biman suggested. 'We can get it from the river below.'

'No need,' Bhattacharya said dismissively. 'I'm going to count to three. If he doesn't start talking by then, I'll pick him up and toss him overboard. He was already as good as dead when we found him. If he doesn't make himself useful to us, why should we bother saving his life? Did you hear that, pal? One. Two. Three.'

'Sir, please!' the man begged in a weak, squeaky voice. 'My head's splitting in pain. Please, sir, a little water.'

'What's your name?'

'Kalu Sheikh.'

'Who's done this to you?'

'Ha-Ha-Haru Daf-fa-dar.'

With that, the man's head lolled to the side, and his eyes closed again.

'He's not acting,' Biman said urgently. 'Please, let's not force him. He's not strong enough to speak.'

'Very well,' said Bhattacharya, getting to his feet. 'Let's keep him alive till we get to Gosaba, then transfer him to the hospital. We can get the story out once he's better. If you have one of a gang, you'll eventually have all of them. That's how these things go.'

'All except Haru Dafadar,' Kakababu said. 'You'll never have him.'

'Why not? Oh! Oh, I see. I was wondering why the name sounded familiar. That man on the Matla river, right? With the knife in his back?'

A vivid image of the dead man flashed across Shontu's mind. He shut his eyes and shuddered. It was one of the most dreadful things he had ever seen, right after that morning's accident. What a horrible way to die!

'He was killed by one of the gang, too, I'll bet,' Bhattacharya said. He didn't seem too perturbed by the idea. 'Infighting kills most of these people. They loot, maim and kill, but can't stay alive long enough to enjoy the spoils of their sins.'

'A launch,' Biman suddenly said. 'Look, it's headed this way.'

'They've finally hunted me down,' Bhattacharya said, raising his hands in mock surrender. 'Well, time to wrap this adventure up, boys. What do you say,

Kakababu? I need a decent cup of tea within the next hour, or I'll have a headache all day. We've done all we could do here. Time to head back, eh?'

Kakababu didn't respond.

Akbar Khan and Prashanta Dutta were sitting inside the sareng's open cabin. Once the launch ranged itself alongside the *Heart of the Wind* and dropped anchor, they made their way to the deck.

'Sir! What happened last night?' Khan burst out as soon as he saw Bhattacharya. 'You didn't return, didn't send word ... we were so anxious we couldn't sleep!'

Bhattacharya smiled broadly at both his subordinates. It was not a friendly smile. 'So anxious that you waited till morning to come look for me? I could have been ambushed by dacoits or mauled by a tiger several times by now.'

'We didn't know what to do, sir. Prashanta and I waited till eleven last night for you to return. After that ...'

'After that it was too dark, and you were too scared of dacoits to come for an enquiry. Akbar, if our own people keep bowing down to criminal elements ...'

'No sir! We wanted to set out immediately. But the sareng of the boat had gone home. His home is several villages away from the police station, on an island. We only found him early this morning, sir. We set out immediately.'

'Well, never mind that now,' Bhattacharya said, waving his hand as if brushing it away. 'Is that launch stocked? Can you get us a cup of proper tea?'

The police launch was indeed stocked. In addition to fresh water for washing themselves and a pot of hot tea, they were served a breakfast of freshly-made toast and omelettes. The crew, meanwhile, set about rescuing the *Honey Bee*. They tied it to the new launch with sturdy ropes and started the engine. After only two or three tugs, Mohidhor sareng's launch jolted free of the sandbar. The crew then unhooked the *Honey Bee*, and used the same ropes to tie Ingmar Smelt's boat to the new launch. The nouko from the previous afternoon's misadventure was loaded onto the boat's deck. Kashem took charge of the speedboat, and the five people who had arrived in it the previous evening retook their seats. In short, everyone was ready to return to civilization. All they needed was an order.

'Kakababu, you haven't said a word since the launch arrived,' Bhattacharya observed. 'Is there something that still remains to be done? Have we forgotten something?'

Kakababu let out a slow breath. 'No, Ranabir. I don't suppose there's really anything left to do. We have done all we could. But there's a discomfort ... a niggle at the back of my mind that I cannot shake off. We didn't find Ingmar Smelt's body. Is he really dead?'

'How could he have survived the destruction we saw? Unless you're suggesting there's another secret room?'

Kakababu shook his head. 'I checked for that. That room was the only hidden space on the boat. Still, it's hard to accept a death without seeing the body.'

'Kakababu, what would make it easier for you?'
Bhattacharya prodded gently.

Kakababu hesitated. 'Well, didn't you say the sea
is very close? Can we do a quick sweep of it? We won't
need to go far, just where the currents may have led
a corpse. You know that old adage: the sea doesn't
merely take, it also returns.'

'The chances of such returns are very slim. This
could have happened up to seven days ago, you know.'

'I understand that,' Kakababu said quickly, a frisson
of agitation colouring his voice. 'But Ranabir, it makes
me physically ill to think that a man like Ingmar Smelt
has become fodder for the sharks after his death. If we
can recover his body, we could bury him with honours.'

'He did want to die at sea, though. Some might say
this is the end he would have wanted.'

Kakababu's lips pursed into a thin, aggrieved scowl.
'You mean *you* don't want to make the effort. Fine, let's
go back then.'

'That's not what I said, Kakababu,' Bhattacharya
sighed. 'All right. Very well. The confluence is indeed
very close. We can spare the time for a quick round.
Perhaps we won't even have to go that far. Perhaps
the body is tangled in the brushwood along the way.
It happens sometimes. But I'm going to bring backup.
Then we can split up the search and make it faster.'

The thick ropes were undone, yet again, from the
police launch. It took off for the left bank, while the
speedboat glided along the right. The jungle was
denser on the right, or so Shontu thought. All four of

them – Bhattacharya, Biman, Shontu, and Kakababu, kept their eyes peeled on the banks and on the trailing underbrush. In some places, the impenetrable thickets of the land had melded seamlessly into a compact colony of water-plants. On Bhattacharya's orders, Kashem slowed the boat down to a crawl in those areas for a closer look. After some time, Bhattacharya pointed to a clump of green bushes covered in yellow markings. His good humour had been restored.

'These are the tigers' hiding spots,' he told the rest. 'They're called hetal. See how they match the tigers' stripes? Excellent camouflage, haha! Am I right, Kashem?'

'Yes, sir,' Kashem replied. He was eyeing the bank carefully.

Bhattacharya laughed again. 'Who knows, maybe a tiger is hiding there right now! If it jumps on this boat, someone will have to scour for *our* corpses. Hahaha!'

Shontu glanced at Kakababu. Kakababu was staring straight ahead, his face pinched. It was clear that he found the joke untoward.

'There's a clump of trees in the middle of the river,' Biman suddenly said, pointing to the left. 'Shouldn't we take a look?'

Everyone turned. Biman was right. A small, densely green island rose from the brown waters to their left, completely detached from every bit of surrounding land. Shontu wouldn't have believed that people could live on something that small, but as they came closer, he saw at least eight or ten huts clustered together.

They had been so engrossed in the bank that they had nearly missed it.

'It's a new island, sir,' Kashem informed them. 'Been above water these six years. Used to be infested with snakes, it was. We called it Mawnosha Island. Mawnosha as in the goddess of snakes, sir. Now it's settled by a handful of fishermen.'

The island was shaped like an upturned clay lamp. The head of it narrowed almost to a point, while the rest was rounded, and each side sloped gently into the river. All of it was green and brown, except the very tip. That part was a tiny sandy beach. A boy of about eight was dragging a large dark object up that beach.

'A deck chair!' Kakababu breathed.

Bhattacharya whistled. 'Imagine that. A fancy deck chair on an impoverished little island. That's what I call a lucky break! Honestly, Kakababu, how do you know these things? Do you have a sixth sense? An extra helping of intuition?'

The boy whipped around in fright when he heard the speedboat change course and come closer. When the boat sped onto the shallows and dropped anchor, he abandoned the deck chair and tried to run away. But he was thin and small, and no match for Biman. Biman launched himself off the boat and landed practically at the boy's feet. In a second, he had put his arms around the boy's thin shoulders. The boy immediately started wailing.

Bhattacharya trudged quickly up to them through the bit of sand. 'Don't cry, don't cry! We aren't kidnappers. We just want to know where you found the chair. Where's your father?'

Two women had come running out of the huts at the child's crying. Seeing four city-men, they stopped short and quickly pulled the loose ends of their sarees over their heads and faces.

'The menfolk are out at sea,' one of them said. 'Who are you?'

'Where did this chair come from?' Bhattacharya asked.

The woman shrugged, half turning back towards the hut. 'Who knows. People dump things at night, like. We don't ask nothing. Noku, come here!'

Noku, the boy, was twisting and turning in Biman's hold. 'Tell us where you found the chair and I'll let you go,' Biman offered.

The boy didn't answer. He kicked and twisted, twisted and kicked.

Bhattacharya began strolling towards the huts. A large mound of hay lay between the first three or four huts. A third woman shot out from one of the huts and planted herself firmly in his way. Her face and head were completely covered by her saree, too. 'The men ain't here,' she said sharply. 'You lot come back in the evening.'

Bhattacharya simply walked around her with that cheerful, affable smile on his face. On his way, he casually picked up a split piece of bamboo and twirled it. Then, without warning, he thrust it inside the mound of hay. There was a loud clang.

'Useful things, hay mounds,' he shouted cheerfully back at the boat. 'You can hide any number of things in it. Now let's see, what do we have here … more chairs, a dynamo … why, Kakababu, this island is a veritable trove of stolen goods!'

Kakababu hadn't left the boat. 'We'll have to search the whole island, then' he called back, watching the women's reaction.

Bhattacharya turned towards the woman who had tried to stop him from coming inland. 'Who gave you these things?'

'We don't know nothing, babu,' the woman said stubbornly. 'Someone must've left them here.'

'And you helpfully picked them up and hid them, eh?'

The woman shrugged. 'We know nothing,' she repeated.

Bhattacharya scanned the left bank. The police launch had travelled much further ahead. There was no hope of calling them back without a wireless set.

'Well, we're in no hurry,' he said. 'We'll wait till that launch comes back, then set up an outpost here.'

Meanwhile, several other women had come out of their huts. They formed a loose circle at a distance, eyeing the men sullenly. Their young children hid behind their legs and peeked, drinking in the sight of four strangely-dressed men. Bhattacharya's mouth twisted in bitterness.

'Looks like such a quaint, peaceful mid-river hamlet, doesn't it,' he bit out. 'But even this place is crawling with murderers and thieves!'

'Or perhaps they really are innocent,' Biman ventured. 'The dacoits may well have dumped their loot here in the middle of the night, not realizing it's inhabited. Their only crime was to probably hide the stuff in the hope of making a little extra money. We should thank this boy, really. Had he not dragged the deck chair to the beach, we would never have found the stash. Shall I let him go?'

'No!' Kakababu shouted from the boat. 'Don't let him go, Biman. Ranabir, could you come here for a second?'

Bhattacharya splashed back to the boat. The two men had a whispered conversation in the shallows, then Bhattacharya nodded his head ostentatiously. 'Of course, Kakababu, of course,' he said loudly. 'One has to do one's duty, painful though it is.'

Then he trudged back to where the women had gathered, and raised his voice. 'My dear ladies, you have been caught hiding stolen goods. That's a fact. On the strength of that alone, I should arrest all of you. But I don't want to do that. I can see that it's just families here, trying to get by. If you just tell me who gave you these things to hide, we'll go away and leave you in peace.'

The women remained silent. They didn't even twitch.

Bhattacharya sighed dramatically. 'Well, then you leave me with no choice. We didn't see anyone else doing it, but this boy was clearly observed moving stolen goods. We have no choice but to take him in. To the boat, Bimanbabu. I'll give you a hand.'

Together, they picked the boy up and began walking towards the boat. The boy screamed in terror, thrashing wildly and trying to kick them both.

The women broke rank. They ran forward as one, trying to get in the men's way and shouting at them. They may well have been answering Bhattacharya's questions, but it was impossible to tell in the din. Bhattacharya acted like he didn't care.

'No no, don't impede the government's work,' he said bossily. 'This boy was caught with stolen goods. He has to be taken to the station.'

The boy suddenly stopped thrashing and screaming. 'Let me go, babu,' he implored. 'It was Haru Dafadar what stoled your stuff, not me!'

Bhattacharya stopped. 'Haru Dafadar again! Are you telling the truth?'

'Yes babu, he is!' one of the women burst out. 'We know nothing about nothing. That Haru, he comes and tips his stash here. Gets us in trouble, he does. He ain't one of us, babu. He ain't from our island. He's an outsider!'

Bhattacharya put the boy down on the sand. 'All right, I believe you. Go back to your mother,' he said genially.

The boy fled.

When Bhattacharya and Biman made their way back to the boat, Kakababu said, 'This Haru Dafadar seems to have been the leader. But I doubt he'd have the initiative to loot a foreign boat. I suspect there's someone above him, directing things from behind the scenes. That's the man we have to find.'

Bhattacharya stretched. 'We have Chhoto Shadhu in custody, don't worry. Did you see how he reacted to Dafadar's corpse? He's going to sing like a bird to protect himself.'

'There's another man you might want to look into. I took a photo of him with my camera. I'll send you a copy when we develop the reel.'

Bhattacharya frowned. 'You photographed a smuggler?'

'Well, I didn't know he was a smuggler then. To be honest I don't really know it now, but given how eager he was to get out of the delta, I'd say it was a fair guess.' He then filled Bhattacharya in on the accident the previous morning. 'I didn't think I'd ever say this, but I'm glad the man was seriously injured. It'll make escaping from the health centre slightly more difficult.'

'We need to act quickly, Kakababu. Let's chase down the police launch. We'll bring it back and set up guard here, then head back to Canning. These people can't escape. They said themselves that their men have taken all the boats out to sea.'

They piled back into the boat. Kashem had started the engine when Biman cried, 'Shontu! Where's Shontu?'

'Stop!' Kakababu shouted at Kashem. 'Stop the boat!'

A second later they heard Shontu's voice from the middle of the island. 'Kakababu! Kakababu! Come see this!'

And then there were two gunshots. Their sound travelled across the vastness of the river, and echoed from the banks.

For the second time that morning, Biman jumped into the shallows and raced across the beach. Bhattacharya turned to Kakababu. 'Stay here,' he warned. 'Let me go first and see. That was a real revolver.' Then he, too, ran inland.

Kakababu didn't hear either of them. His eyes had gone from placid to furious. He was a stern and reticent man, but he truly loved his nephew. The very idea of someone shooting at Shontu made him see red. Had it happened in front of him, he would have shot that person down like a rabid dog, and to hell with his pacifist principles! He used his crutches to vault over the speedboat's railings and made his way inland as fast as he could. The shifting sand tried to swallow his crutches at every step, but he barely noticed. Pure rage propelled him forward.

The women had fled to their huts at the sound of the first shot. But the boy Noku, inexplicably, was still outside, hiding behind the deck chair he had been pulling. When he saw Kakababu stop briefly and look around, he silently jabbed his finger towards one of the huts. Kakababu set off towards it. Biman and Bhattacharya were already there. They had plastered themselves against the wall on either side of the doorway, and were snatching quick glances inside. Shontu was nowhere in sight.

'Shontu!' Kakababu whispered urgently. 'Shontu!!!'

There was no response. Kakababu fished out his revolver and hobbled to Biman. 'Where's Shontu?' he demanded.

'He's fine,' Biman whispered back. 'But take a look inside.'

Kakababu peered into the darkness. He hadn't known what to expect, but he certainly didn't expect what he saw. The room was empty, except for a hole in the ground. A human hand rose cautiously from that hole, tightly grasping a revolver. It darted back and forth, as if feeling around for an invisible enemy. A soot-blackened clay pot lay on one side.

'But where's Shontu?' Kakababu insisted.

'He's fine,' Biman whispered back. 'I saw him deliberately drop to the ground, then roll away towards the water. Even if he's taken a hit, it's superficial.'

The man in the hole was now peering outside. He had a shiny bald head, and absolutely terrified eyes. They now darted all around the room, probably trying to see if he had hit anyone. When he saw that the room was empty, he tried to brace himself on his arms and climb out, but then grunted in pain and fell back in.

'Ranabir, let's not waste time being cautious,' Kakababu called loudly, startling the man. 'There's one of him and three of us. Let's just get him out of that hole. If he so much as looks at his revolver, we'll blow his brains out.'

'Why bother with getting him out?' Bhattacharya growled. 'This scoundrel shot at Shontu. I say we shoot him and leave him to rot in that hole.' As if to prove his intent, he then fired two warning shots into the sky.

The man screamed in terror and tried to dive back inside the hole. By the time he realized he hadn't been shot, three men were standing over him, two of them armed. The fight seemed to physically seep out of the man. Dropping his revolver, he hid his head in his hands and began weeping.

Bhattacharya rolled his eyes. Kicking the revolver aside, he said, 'Take the other hand, Bimanbabu. Let's get this bastard out of his hole.'

Once the man was disarmed, Kakababu lost all interest in him. He hobbled towards the doorway to look for Shontu. This time, he saw his nephew right away. Shontu was only a few yards away from the hut, neck deep in the water and grinning at him. When he saw Kakababu glaring at him, he shook off some of the water and ran back to the hut.

'I don't even have a scratch!' he said, before his uncle could shout at him.

'Why were you here in the first place?' Kakababu growled.

'Well, you were busy talking to the people, so I thought I'd slip away and take a look at the village. There were noises from this hut. When I looked inside, I saw an upturned black pot moving on its own. I was just curious, Kakababu. Honestly! I tiptoed in and lifted the pot, and that man shot at me. He was hiding his head under the pot! But I had been standing behind him, not in front, so he didn't actually hit me. I ran away.'

'You should have called us when you saw the moving pot!' his uncle admonished. 'Why didn't you?'

Shontu didn't answer. He pretended to be contrite, but Kakababu saw his bright, mischievous smile. Shontu knew he had made a big breakthrough in the mystery, and he was proud of it.

In the meanwhile, Biman and Bhattacharya had lifted the man out of his hiding place and laid him down on the ground. Kakababu heard Biman gasp. The man had a deep, dark gash on his abdomen. It hadn't been cleaned or dressed. An oozing ointment of sorts had been applied directly on the matted blood, making it look far ghastlier. Throughout the lifting and laying down, the man hadn't stopped weeping.

'Who did this to you?' Kakababu asked.

'Kill me, babu,' the man begged. 'End this life. I can't take this pain no more. Please babu!'

'Don't be ridiculous. We'll take you to a hospital in a few hours. You'll be fine before you know it.'

The man stared at Kakababu. 'You want to save me? But I'm a sinner. I left Kalu in that hellhole to die alone. I, I ... babu, the gods will never forgive me.'

'So it was you who attacked Kalu Sheikh? Did you attack the saheb, too?'

'No babu. I swear in Ma Kali's name. I didn't touch the saheb.'

'Then who did? Who killed the saheb?'

'Just put a bullet in me, babu. I can't bear this pain.'

'No!' Kakababu snapped. 'Boys, get this man on the boat. He's going to live, and he's going to tell us what happened to Ingmar Smelt.'

'You were in Haru Dafadar's group, weren't you?' Bhattacharya asked shrewdly. 'So who killed Haru?'

The man took a few deep breaths. When he spoke again, his voice was clearer than it had been before. 'Me. I killed that beast. Traitor! Scum! He was my friend since we were lads, babu. We had done so much together. And then he shoots me in the belly! For a handful of *stuff*! But I had my revenge, didn't I? Drove my knife right into his liver. Yes, I did!'

The man began to pant, his face losing colour. Kakababu leaned forward and raised the man's face with a finger under his chin. When their eyes met, he said, 'The truth this time, friend. Who killed the saheb? You? Or Haru Dafadar?'

The man's breath had become laboured. Faintly, he said, 'Neither, sir. I swear by Ma Kali. I swear by Bon Bibi. We were not even near him. Kalu Sheikh had pinned his arms to his side, but before Haru could even take his knife out, the saheb jumped into the river. We never saw him again.'

CHAPTER 7

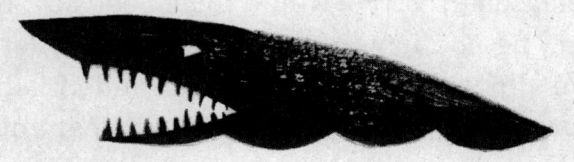

When he later thought about that day, Shontu felt that he had stepped off the island and into a living fairy tale.

After it was established that Ingmar Smelt had not been murdered, but had voluntarily jumped into the river, police boats scoured the banks and water for him for five full hours. Not an inch of the surrounding villages was left unsearched. They travelled so much that the speedboat ran out of fuel and had to borrow some from the police launch's reserves. But no trace of Smelt could be found. Finally, at two in the afternoon, with their own boat idling at the mouth of the sea, Bhattacharya called off the search.

'Jumping into these rivers is just as dangerous as facing the dacoits,' Biman reasoned. 'Have you felt the current here? It's strong! Besides, there are those kamoths. The chance that Professor Smelt has survived in these waters for a week is practically nil. He was getting on in years too, wasn't he, Kakababu?'

Kakababu was watching the distant horizon with tired, defeated eyes. 'He would have been seventy-four this year,' he confirmed quietly. 'All right, let's head back. We did our best, but in the end Smelt's own wishes prevailed. He wanted to die at sea, and die at sea he did.'

Bhattacharya signalled to Kashem to turn around. After their antics yesterday and this morning, Kashem had probably expected them to insist upon being taken out to sea. When Bhattacharya indicated that they were ready to return, he didn't give them an extra second to change their minds. The boat whipped around so fast that everyone except him lost their balance a little. By the time they righted themselves, their little speedboat was zooming through the water at top speed, its engine roaring so loudly that Shontu's head nearly exploded.

'Slower, Kashem, slower!' Bhattacharya called. But though he was sitting right behind the pilot, the roar of the engine swallowed his voice completely. So Bhattacharya leaned forward and patted Kashem on the back. 'Kashem, slow down!'

Kashem was focusing entirely on the route. 'What, sir? What?' he shouted back, without taking his eyes off the wide river.

'Slower!' bellowed Bhattacharya. 'Do you want to kill us? We'll go flying off the boat at this rate!'

Kashem whipped around, alarmed. He had only heard the crucial word. 'Kill? Who's dead, sir?'

And then catastrophe hit. Shontu wasn't sure exactly what happened, but one minute he was sitting on his seat, holding on for dear life ... and the next minute he was in the water.

His first thought was, 'Oh no, kamoth!' But his next thought was about his uncle. Kakababu had said that his leg made swimming impossible. Where was he? After frantically kicking his feet and looking around, Shontu spotted Kakababu's head bobbling in the water a few metres away. He immediately swam over, as fast as he could, and tried to pull his uncle to safety. But Kakababu evaded his desperate grasp. 'Don't! I can manage. It's safer to tread water on our own. Look, the police launch has spotted us.'

The police launch had indeed spotted them. The speedboat had hurtled past them just a few minutes earlier, and had probably upended in full view of the launch's crew. As they approached, the waves sent by their sides propelled Kakababu towards the nearest bank. Shontu was grateful for the time of day. Afternoon was the time of low tide in these islands. The water, unlike morning and evening, was calm and still. That was probably why Kashem had risked piloting at such speed. Had the rotting carcass of a tree not drifted into his path, they would have been perfectly safe. At least they had been thrown towards the bank, and not towards the middle of the river. In less than ten minutes, all five of them had pulled themselves up on the muddy bank.

'It was me, wasn't it?' Bhattacharya asked ruefully, dripping water from head to toe. 'Had I not distracted Kashem he would have taken us past that tree ...'

An unexpected soaking had washed away Kashem's respectful deference towards the big-city officer. 'Yes, I would have!' he retorted angrily. 'You forced me to turn around, sir. We know how to pilot our boats!'

'Well, let's just call it part of the full package,' Bhattacharya said, with familiar cheerfulness. 'We've found corpses, dacoits, secret rooms, and new islands. I have been bashed on the head and Shontu's been shot at. Why leave out a possible drowning? We're still standing, aren't we? That's what matters!'

The police launch, meanwhile, had come within shouting distance. 'We're fine!' Bhattacharya bellowed at them, pointing at the gently drifting speedboat. 'Go after that! We'll wait here for you!'

The crew ran over to the other side of the deck, clutching the now-familiar thick ropes.

'We're lucky this happened between tides,' Kashem said reproachfully, nodding at Kakababu. 'Otherwise, this sir would have been dragged out to sea.'

Bhattacharya looked sheepish. But Kakababu merely hummed. His attention had drifted inland.

'Do you hear that sound?' he asked after a few seconds, frowning heavily.

'What sound?' Bhattacharya asked, trying to follow Kakababu's gaze.

'There, from the jungle. It's like ... it's like music.'

Unconsciously, everyone leaned slightly towards the jungle. After a few seconds Shontu heard it, too. Underneath the rustling of leaves and the whisper of breeze on the river, there was a faint musical note. It sounded like tuneful whistling, but not quite.

'Sir, that's the snakes' whistle,' Kashem said nervously. 'Cobras do it. You can hear them in the deep jungles sometimes.'

'Don't spin me your old wives' tales,' Kakababu said irritably. 'Snakes can't whistle. But my crutches have been washed away. How shall I walk?'

'Walk? Walk where?' Bhattacharya asked. 'We're waiting here for the launch to fetch us.'

'Don't you want to know what that sound is?' Kakababu challenged. 'Someone's playing a musical instrument in the jungle, Ranabir. I'm sure of it. It reminds me of the flutes I saw in Romania. They look like harmonicas, but sound just like our flutes.'

Bhattacharya looked sceptical. 'That's a bit of a stretch, Kakababu. We're not in Europe. Or even in Calcutta. We're on an uninhabited island in the Sundarban. How can one possibly hear a Romanian flute here?'

Kakababu pursed his lips. 'Shontu, Biman – can you two support me? I can rest on your shoulders and move.'

Alarmed, Kashem stepped forward and grasped Kakababu's hands. 'Sir, listen to me. I'm from these parts. Those jungles are not good places, sir. There are tigers, there are snakes ... and then there are other things. Please stay here, sir. In the clear.'

'I'm sorry, Kashem,' Kakababu said, gently shaking his hand off. 'The boys and I are not afraid of the jungles. And I won't leave this island without getting to the bottom of this.'

'Well, then I suppose I'll come along too,' Bhattacharya said, getting to his feet. 'Dacoits, head-wounds, drowning ... why leave snakebites and tigers out? Kashem, you wait here.'

It took them a few minutes to find the source of the music. But when they did, Shontu almost stopped breathing at the beauty of the scene before them. A man was lying underneath a mangrove tree, playing what looked like a mouth organ. He was tall, and had flowing white hair and a long white beard. He looked exactly like the second-coming of Rabindranath Tagore. But unlike Tagore's flowing jobba, he wore blue trousers and a loose tunic. When he heard them break through the bushes, the man stopped playing and calmly looked up. His eyes were quiet pools of unearthly peace.

Shontu felt Kakababu slide slowly to his knees. His hands, which were clasped in front of him, were trembling.

'You must be Ingmar Smelt,' his uncle said, his voice taut with emotion. 'Please accept our respects, professor. You were attacked on our waters by our countrymen. But we are very glad to see that you have survived. Please, come with us. We have come to rescue you.'

The man smiled, but he did not move. In a soothing, gentle voice, he said, 'My dear Indian friends, I thank you for your kindness. I'm touched that you have come this far to look for me. But I'm happy to remain in this jungle. Pardon me for not standing. My spine has been hurt too badly to allow it.'

'We will carry you,' Kakababu said immediately.

'There is no need for that,' Smelt said, in his gentle voice. 'It is enough for me to have known your kindness, but I had promised myself, long ago, not to impose upon others.'

'We offer aid willingly,' Bhattacharya cut in. 'Please, professor, allow us to make amends for your plight. Let us help you. And let me tell you right now: I'm not going to listen if you demur.'

Smelt smiled again, but it was a detached, distant smile. 'Very well. Thank you for your generosity. If you must help, then please help me back to my boat.'

Shontu exchanged a swift look with his uncle. Everything inside Smelt's boat had been destroyed. More importantly, the boat was now attached to the police launch, and on its way back to civilization. Perhaps they could get him help, after all. But would Smelt survive the ride back to Gosaba?

Meanwhile, Biman and Bhattacharya had put Smelt's arms around their shoulders and lifted him off the ground. Sharp pain pinched the old scientist's features for a second, before his face relaxed again in acceptance.

'I can't believe you survived six days in this jungle,' Bhattacharya said, as they began to walk back to the bank. 'This place is full of snakes and tigers. If this doesn't qualify for a miracle, I don't know what does.'

'I heard a roar once,' Smelt said placidly. 'And I may have felt snakes slither by as I lay under the tree. Perhaps they understood my infirmity and showed me mercy. I hope you'll believe me when I tell you that no animal is as cruel as a human can be. I used to be a scientist, and I saw this personally. All the animals of the world couldn't kill as many people as a few chemical weapons can in a few minutes. We boast of our civilization, but our progress is built on bloodshed, my friend.'

He paused for breath. They were almost at the bank now. Ahead of them, the river stretched endlessly into the sea.

'Then again,' Smelt resumed, his voice musical. 'I remind myself that there are still people like you. Kind, compassionate, determined. So I suppose there is hope for the world, after all.'

Then he looked at their wet, tired faces, and smiled.

It was the smile of a man ready to meet his maker after a long, lonely life, but Shontu thought it was the sweetest thing he had seen in a long, long time.

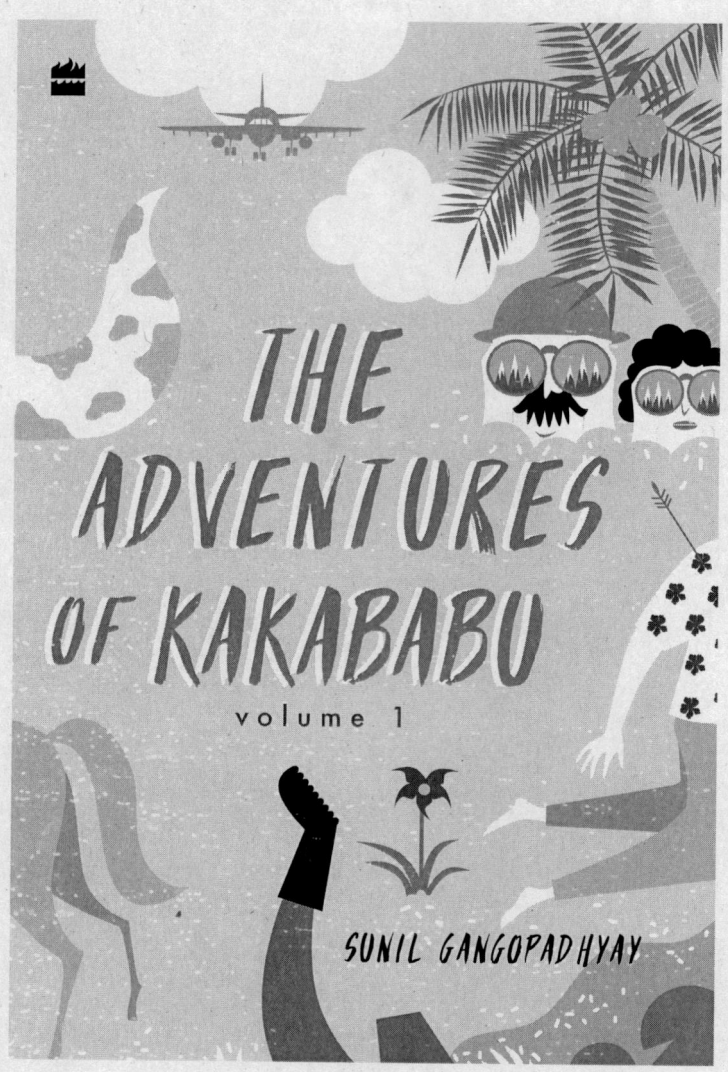

THE ADVENTURES OF KAKABABU

volume 1

SUNIL GANGOPADHYAY

VOLUME 1

THE ADVENTURES OF KAKABABU
VOLUME 1

After a secret mission in Afghanistan ends in a terrible accident, Raja Roychoudhuri, fondly known as Kakababu, resigns as the director of the Archaeological Survey of India and goes home to his secondhand books. But despite an amputated leg, his desire to hunt down old, unsolved mysteries in remote corners of the world refuses to leave him alone. Now that his nephew Shontu has turned thirteen, Kakababu considers him old enough to accompany him on these adventures.

The Adventures of Kakababu, Volume 1, is the first book in the Kakababu series, featuring 'The Emperor's Lost Head' and 'King of the Emerald Isle'.

In 'The Emperor's Lost Head', Kakababu takes Shontu to Kashmir to find a hidden sulphur mine. 'King of the Emerald Isle' finds uncle and nephew on an uncharted island in the Indian Ocean. Stubbornly secretive as always, Kakababu refuses to tell Shontu what has brought him on these trips. Is Shontu ready for the answers he might find?

Originally written by veteran Bengali writer Sunil Gangopadhyay, these Bengali classics have been translated by Rimi.

Sunil Gangopadhyay was an Indian poet and novelist with over 200 books to his name. A prolific and versatile writer, Gangopadhyay was associated with the Ananda Bazar group, a major publishing house in Kolkata. He was also the founder and editor of the popular seminal magazine *Krittibas*.

Rimi is an award-winning translator of literary classics and speculative fiction from Bangla to English. Her works include Sunil Gangopadhyay's *The Adventures of Kakababu* in three volumes, short stories for the National Reading Programme, and Bibhutibhushan Bandopadhyay's *Pather Panchali*. She also takes a keen interest in the goings-on of stray animals, and can often be spotted on the streets of Bombay courting new canine and feline acquaintances.

Kalyani Ganapathy enjoys illustrating fiction and non-fiction picture books. When she's not making picture books she's busy planting in her garden or learning about holistic health. Her books include *A is for Anaar, Hambreelmai's Loom, Janice goes to Chinatown, Amrita Sher-Gil – Rebel with a Paintbrush* and *The Song at the Heart of the River*. You can follow her on Instagram @ganapathy_kalyani and see more of her work at www.kalyani-ganapathy.com.